Unsung Women i~ ~

by Helen F

Cover design by Helen Pugh using images in the public domain.

All photographs and other images belong to Helen Pugh or are in the public domain unless otherwise stated.

"Successa Petronia, [who] lived 3 years, 4 months, 9 days. Vettius Romulus and Victoria Sabina set this up to their dearest daughter."

– Victoria Sabina

"I, Wulfwaru, entreat my dear lord king Æthelred, for his charity, that I may be entitled to make my will." – Wulfwaru

"Pray to God for the soul of Johane Burwasch who was Lady of Mohun." – Johane Mohun

"Life is a short day, but it is a working day." – Hannah More

"The nearer I am approaching to immortality, the more extensive and enlarged I find the principles of amity and good-will in my soul."

– Elizabeth Singer Rowe

Midwifery is "an art so important to the lives and wellbeing of the sex". – Sarah Stone

"'Twas Fielding's talent, with ingenious Art to trace the secret mazes of the heart." – Mary Scott

"I do not regret my situation. I thank God that he has been pleased to make me as I am, nor do I envy the enjoyment of others."

– Sarah Biffin

"That brain of mine is something more than merely mortal; as time will show." – Ada Lovelace

"All arbitrary distinctions based on differences of social rank [are] contrary to the mind of Christ." – Catherine Impey

"It is very nice to have a definite object in life." – Adela Breton

"Don't call me Lady!" – Alice Seeley Harris

"With a thousand women fighters we can free the woman-half of our nation." — Emmeline Pethick Lawrence

"Future generations will need lots of help to deal with environmental problems and world peace." — Kathleen Tacchi-Morris

"I think also that Women should be represented on the Council. At present, there are no Women Councillors." — Doris Hatt

"I was born with courage. I did not allow cruel people to find in me a person they could torture." — Andrée Peel

This is a journey of women and girls,
Who passed through this county before us,
And left traces of their lives
In stone and in parchment,
In books and in bones.
This is a voyage of urban and rural,
Of country lanes and market squares,
Of rugged hills and stony paths,
Of glistening valleys and winding roads,
Of crashing waves and trickling streams,
Of lonely fields and bustling streets,
Of places long forgotten and those better remembered.

Table of Contents

Introduction – p8

A–Z Index of Somerset Place Names – p11

PREHISTORIC TIMES:

Prologue: Ancient Female Footsteps – p20

Ch. 1: The Prince of Pigs and the Goddess (Iron Age) – p28

BRITANNIA:

Ch. 2: Romance in Roman Times (2nd century) – p46

POST-ROMAN YEARS:

Ch. 3: The Heroic Hermitess (5th century) – p74

Ch. 4: Letter to Lady G (6th century) – p87

WESSEX:

Ch. 5: Ethelburg's Exit (7th –8th century) – p102

Ch. 6: Albion's Fate in Athelney's Hands (9th century) – p132

ENGLAND:

Ch. 7: Miraculous Mead (early 10th century) – p160

Ch. 8: The Words of Wulfwaru (late 10th century) – p181

Interlude (11th century) – p202

Ch. 9: Fina the First (12th–13th century) – p209

Ch. 10: The Barefoot Baroness (14th century) – p237

Ch. 11: The Translator That Time Forgot (early 15th century) – p264

Ch. 12: A Year of Leadership in Yatton (late 15th century) – p282

Ch. 13: Death Defier (16th century) – p298

Ch. 14: A Witch in the Woods (17th century) – p314

GREAT BRITAIN:

Ch. 15: Solange, the Asylum Seeker (17th–18th century) – p330

Ch. 16: The Mores in Mendip (late 18th century) – p350

Ch. 17: Destiny and Deceit (early 19th century) – p376

Ch. 18: A Princess of Sea and Studies (mid-19th century) – p397

Ch. 19: Catherine vs Caste (late 19th century) – p425

Ch. 20: Talk of the Town Hall (19th–20th century) – p452

Ch. 21: Women in War (early 20th century, a Quick Tributes Chapter) – p472

Ch. 22: Disarmament and Dance (early to mid-20th century) – p483

Ch. 23: Margery's Memories (early to mid-20th century) – p499

Appendices:

Named After Her – p517

Recommended Reading – p522

Acknowledgements – p524

A Note on Inclusivity – p525

About the Author – p526

Introduction

"For most of history, Anonymous was a woman."

This famous quote, adapted from a line by Virginia Woolf hits the nail on the head when it comes to researching historical women. Actions by women (and other people who were assigned female at birth) are often expressed using the passive voice e.g. "The convent was founded" rather than "[Insert woman's name] founded the convent". Oftentimes, female protagonists are nearly erased from the story when their stories make up the fabric of history, just as their male counterparts made history.

Moreover, countless women have pushed boundaries so that future women could lead better lives- entering male-dominated spheres, demanding women's rights, breaking gender norms, taking on positions of power and so on.

That's why books like this one are so vital.

The history in this book begins before the idea of counties, including Somerset, was first conceived. Indeed, there were times when different parts of Somerset were ruled by different kingdoms (such as Bath being part of Hwicce and then Mercia from 577 to 878) or incorporated into different counties (such as Avon). There are currently 3 counties with the name Somerset in them: Bath and North East Somerset (also called BANES or BathNES), North Somerset and Somerset itself. Together they form the so-called 'ceremonial county of Somerset' and are all included in the book. This reflects the county's motto: "all the people of Somerset" or "Somersaete ealle" in Old English.

Somerset came into being around the 700s and takes its name from Somerton, which in turn means 'summer settlement', suggesting that initially it was only inhabited in warmer months.

When I embarked on this journey, I was determined that I wasn't going to make it only about rich, upper-class, White, heterosexual, non-disabled, Christian women. I wanted to make the book as inclusive as possible. That wasn't easy! If women have been marginalised by historical records, imagine how rare it is to find a woman who faced additional discrimination based on her ethnicity, sexuality, disability etc.

Sadly, when I did discover doubly marginalised women, often the records only briefly mentioned them (e.g. Galatia). So I have to admit that the multiply discriminated women don't feature in this book as much as I'd like but I hope you understand that I made a big effort to include them. I may write a second book or second edition to include more such women, so please do get in touch if you know of any.

As this is a long book that spans several millennia, I'd like you to know that you can dip in and out of the chapters, as each one is more or less a standalone story. You certainly don't have to read it all in one go.

I'll end this section by writing that for those of us who live in Somerset or have ever visited, we are literally walking the same ground that these women stood on throughout the ages. We are breathing the Somerset air that filled their lungs all those years ago. And don't mind me if you ever come across me standing on a pavement looking at a building in utter wonder and with a tear in my eye, while the world buzzes by completely unaware of the incredible story that's touched my heart. Welcome to…

the history of Somerset like never before.

A–Z Index of Somerset Place Names

Abbas Combe: Appendices (Named After Her)

Alford: Appendices (Named After Her)

Aller: Chapter 6

Athelney: Chapter 6

Aveline's Hole: Prologue

Avon River: Appendices (Named After Her)

Axbridge: Chapter 5 (Notes), Chapter 14 (Quick Tribute), Chapter 16

Baltonsborough: Chapter 5 (Quick Tribute), Chapter 7

Banwell: Chapter 16

Barrow Gurney: Chapter 21

Bath: Chapter 1, Chapter 2, Chapter 5 (Quick Tribute), Chapter 7 (Notes), Chapter 8, Interlude, Chapter 15, Chapter 16 (Notes & Quick Tribute), Chapter 17, Chapter 18, Chapter 19 (Quick Tributes), Chapter 23

Batheaston: Chapter 1, Interlude, Chapter 16 (Quick Tributes), Chapter 20 (Quick Tribute), Appendices (Named After Her)

Beckery: Chapter 4, Chapter 5, Appendices (Named After Her)

Beckington: Chapter 9 (Notes)

Binegar: Appendices (Named After Her)

Bishop's Hull: Chapter 19 (Quick Tributes)

Blagdon: Chapter 16

Bleadney: Chapter 5

Bleadon: Chapter 6

Brent Knoll: Chapter 5

Bridgwater: Chapter 14, Chapter 15 (Quick Tributes), Chapter 16 (Quick Tribute), Chapter 17 (Notes), Chapter 19, Chapter 23 (Quick Tributes)

Brompton Regis: Chapter 5 (Notes), Interlude

Bruton: Chapter 5, Chapter 10

Buckland St Mary: Appendices (Named After Her)

Butcombe: Chapter 8, Interlude, Appendices (Named After Her)

Cannington: Chapter 4 (Quick Tribute), Chapter 11

Carhampton: Chapter 10

Castle Cary: Chapter 14 (Quick Tribute)

Chard: Chapter 14 (Quick Tribute), Chapter 20 (Quick Tribute)

Charlcombe: Chapter 16 (Quick Tribute)

Charlton Horethorne: Chapter 8 (Notes)

Cheddar: Prologue, Chapter 6 (Notes), Chapter 8, Chapter 12, Chapter 16

Chedzoy: Chapter 9 (Notes)

Chew Valley: Chapter 3 (Quick Tribute), Appendices (Named After Her)

Chewton Keynsham: Appendices (Named After Her)

Chewton Mendip: Interlude

Chilcompton: Chapter 22 (Quick Tribute)

Chinnock: Chapter 8 (Notes)

Churchill: Chapter 16

Claverham: Interlude, Chapter 12

Claverton: Chapter 8, Interlude

Clevedon: Chapter 11, Chapter 23

Congresbury: Chapter 16

Coxley: Interlude, Appendices (Named After Her)

Creech St Michael: Interlude

Crewkerne: Interlude

Croscombe: Chapter 14 (Notes)

Culbone: Chapter 17 (Quick Tribute)

Curry Mallet: Chapter 11

Cutcombe: Chapter 10

Donyatt: Chapter 10, Appendices (Named After Her)

Doulting: Chapter 5

Dunster: Chapter 10, Chapter 13

Durleigh: Chapter 9 (Quick Tribute)

East Coker: Interlude

East Cranmore: Chapter 21

East Dundry: Chapter 23 (Quick Tribute)

East Lyng: Chapter 6

East Quantoxhead: Chapter 17

Ebbor Gorge: Appendices (Named After Her)

Edington: Appendices (Named After Her)

Edithmead: Appendices (Named After Her)

Egford: Chapter 23 (Quick Tributes)

Enmore: Chapter 11

Evercreech: Chapter 10, Chapter 21

Farleigh Hungerford: Appendices (Recommended Reading)

Freshford: Chapter 8, Interlude

Frome: Chapter 5, Chapter 8 (Notes), Chapter 14 (Quick Tribute), Chapter 16 (Quick Tributes), Chapter 19 (Quick Tributes), Chapter 23 (Quick Tributes)

Glastonbury: Chapter 2 (Notes), Chapter 4, Chapter 5, Chapter 7, Chapter 8, Chapter 9 (Quick Tribute), Chapter 12 (Notes), Chapter 13 (Quick Tributes), Chapter 14 (Quick Tribute) Chapter 16

Goathurst: Chapter 15 (Quick Tributes)

Godney: Prologue (Notes), Chapter 5, Appendices (Named After Her)

Halse: Chapter 12 (Quick Tribute)

Hardington Mandeville: Interlude

Holford: Chapter 17 (Notes)

Holnicote: Chapter 22

Holton: Chapter 8, Interlude

Huish Episcopi: Chapter 5

Huntspill: Chapter 16 (Quick Tribute)

Ilchester: Chapter 9 (Quick Tribute), Chapter 14 (Quick Tribute), Chapter 16 (Quick Tributes)

Ilminster: Chapter 5, Chapter 13 (Quick Tributes)

Ilton: Chapter 13 (Notes and Quick Tributes)

Kenn: Chapter 12

Kewstoke: Chapter 3 (Quick Tribute), Appendices (Named After Her)

Keynsham: Chapter 3, Interlude, Chapter 9 (Quick Tribute), Appendices (Named After Her)

Kilmersdon: Chapter 9 (Notes)

Kilton: Chapter 10, Chapter 17

Kingston St Mary: Appendices (Named After Her)

Langport: Chapter 10, Chapter 14

Leigh-on-Mendip: Chapter 8

Long Ashton: Chapter 21

Lottisham: Chapter 5 (Quick Tribute)

Lower Durston: Chapter 9

Lydford-on-Fosse: Chapter 5 (Quick Tribute)

Marchey: Chapter 5 (Notes)

Martock: Interlude

Meare: Prologue (Notes), Chapter 4, Chapter 5

Middlezoy: Chapter 5

Midsomer Norton: Chapter 15 (Quick Tributes), Chapter 18 (Quick Tribute) Chapter 20 (Quick Tribute)

Milborne Port: Chapter 16 (Quick Tribute)

Minehead: Chapter 10

Muchelney: Chapter 5

Nailsea: Chapter 16

Nettlecombe: Chapter 12 (Quick Tribute)

North Curry: Chapter 22

North Petherton: Chapter 6 (Notes), Chapter 9 (Notes)

North Stoke: Interlude

Nyland: Chapter 5

Oakhill: Chapter 20 (Quick Tribute)

Pennard (unclear whether East or West): Chapter 5 (Notes)

Pill: Chapter 19 (Quick Tributes)

Pilton: Chapter 5

Porlock Weir: Chapter 17 (Quick Tribute)

Priddy: Chapter 5

Queen Camel: Interlude, Chapter 9 (Quick Tribute), Chapter 14 (Notes), Appendices (Named After Her)

Queen Charlton: Chapter 16 (Quick Tributes), Appendices (Named After Her)

Rowberrow: Chapter 16

Sampford Brett: Chapter 13 (Notes)

Sandford: Chapter 16

Seavington St Mary: Appendices (Named After Her)

Shapwick: Prologue (Notes), Chapter 5

Shepton Beauchamp: Chapter 9 (Quick Tribute)

Shepton Mallet: Chapter 11, Chapter 14 (main part & Quick Tribute), Chapter 20 (Notes), Chapter 21

Shipham: Chapter 16

Somerton: Chapter 5 (Quick Tribute), Chapter 9 (Quick Tribute), Chapter 10

South Brewham: Chapter 6 (Notes)

South Cadbury: Chapter 4

South Petherton: Chapter 5 (Notes)

St Catherine: Appendices (Named After Her)

Stanton Drew: Prologue, Interlude

Stogumber: Chapter 20 (Quick Tribute)

Stoke St Mary: Appendices (Named After Her)

Ston Easton: Interlude

Street: Chapter 5 (Quick Tribute), Chapter 19, Chapter 20 (Quick Tribute), Appendices (Named After Her)

Taunton: Chapter 5, Chapter 9 (Notes) Chapter 12 (Notes), Chapter 14 (main part & Quick Tribute), Chapter 15 (Quick Tributes), Chapter 16 (Quick Tribute), Chapter 20 (Quick Tribute), Chapter 22

Temple Cloud: Appendices (Named After Her)

Thorne St Margaret: Appendices (Named After Her)

Timsbury: Chapter 18 (Quick Tribute)

Tintinhull: Chapter 12 (Quick Tribute)

Trull: Chapter 12 (Quick Tribute)

Uphill: Chapter 21

Watchet: Chapter 8, Chapter 13, Chapter 23

Wedmore: Chapter 6, Interlude, Chapter 16

Wellington: Chapter 20 (Quick Tributes)

Wells: Chapter 4, Chapter 5, Chapter 7 (Notes), Interlude, Chapter 12, Chapter 14 (main part & Quick Tribute), Chapter 16, Chapter 21

Welton: Chapter 15 (Quick Tributes)

West Camel: Chapter 14 (Notes)

West Coker: Interlude

West Quantoxhead: Chapter 11, Chapter 17 (Notes), Appendices (Named After Her)

Westbury-sub-Mendip: Prologue

Weston-super-Mare: Chapter 2 (Notes), Chapter 19, Chapter 20 (Quick Tributes), Chapter 21, Chapter 23

Westonzoyland: Chapter 5 (Notes), Chapter 14

Whatley: Chapter 23 (Quick Tributes)

Wincanton: Chapter 21

Winford: Chapter 8, Interlude

Winscombe: Chapter 16, Chapter 19 (Quick Tributes)

Wiveliscombe: Chapter 10, Chapter 14 (Quick Tribute)

Wookey Hole: Chapter 14 (Quick Tribute)

Wrington: Chapter 16

Yatton: Chapter 12, Chapter 16

Yeovil: Chapter 20

PREHISTORIC TIMES

Prologue: Ancient Female Footsteps

What female feet passed this way

And from female mouths, what sounds?

What women lived and breathed and loved

Upon these ancient grounds?

What names were uttered as they laid to rest

Their sisters in age-old burial mounds?

And was Aveline's Hole where you interred your friends,

So their spirits would live on safe and warm?

And did you travel on to Cheddar Gorge

To paint limestone walls with shapes and forms?

Did you crouch in the damp to eat berries and nuts

All huddled by the fire, resting from a storm?

Ancestor of mine, weary traveller,

What led your leather-clad feet to this place?

Was it to worship shadowy deities

At Stanton Drew stones, this mystical space,

And watch open-eyed as the hunters sacrificed beasts

To satisfy the spirits and earn their grace?

What are the names of those who built

The wooden tracks to connect the islands

And platforms among marshes as lake villages?
Your logs unearthed but names time has silenced.

How harsh your short life must've been,
How tiring, hungry, fearful and cold.
The threat of bears and endless toils
Your shivering bones unlikely to grow old.
Childbirth risky, babies weak and frail,
Infancy a trail of tears to behold.

What female feet passed this way
What hands touched these boulders?
Blue-eyed, brown-skinned beauty, did you
Lean against them with your shoulders
And wonder as you gazed into the starry night's glow
What women came before you and who will follow?

Notes

Flints found in Westbury-sub-Mendip are the earliest evidence of humans in Somerset. They date back 480,000 years and would've been used by early species of humans. At that time, England was joined to mainland Europe because the sea levels were lower than they are now.

It seems the whole of Britain was abandoned from around

180,000 to 60,00 years ago because no human bones or tools have been found for this time period. The reasons were probably that it was too cold for a time and then sea levels rose, cutting England off from mainland Europe. Our species, *Homo sapiens*, arrived in England 40,000 years ago but left again 25,000 years ago as the Ice Age swept across the land. About 15,000 years ago, the country's conditions allowed humans to return for visits.

This poem is a sweeping look at prehistoric women across several millennia.

Looking at the poem chronologically, the cave painting in Cheddar Gorge refers to the one of a mammoth found in Cheddar, which dates back to 11,000 BC. Back then, England was inhabited sporadically only, with continuous habitation beginning in 10,000 BC because the Ice Age was coming to an end, which in turn meant better weather and landscape conditions.

Aveline's Hole at Burrington Combe is Britain's earliest scientifically dated cemetery. The bones, representing at least 21 people, date back to around 8,300 BC. The artefacts found there include red deer teeth. Scientists have confirmed that those buried in the cave had lived nearby because of the levels of the element strontium found both in the bones and the local area. The remains also revealed that the individuals were often malnourished.

(Looking down into Aveline's Hole)

The "blue-eyed, brown-skinned beauty" makes reference to the fact that Cheddar Man, the oldest complete skeleton ever discovered in Britain, has been identified with those characteristics. The man died in his twenties around 8000 BC and his features were the standard for those living in our country at that time, who had come from Africa via the Middle East over many generations. Other people with paler skin probably came to these shores (also via the Middle East) in approximately 4000 BC and they started to farm the land. It's currently thought that Cheddar Man and his peers were mainly replaced by the second influx. All the same, DNA tests have shown that the average present-day British person shares about 10% of their genetic ancestry with Cheddar Man and his group of ancient hunter-gatherers.

Wooden trackways were built in prehistoric times when there was a system of islands in salty marshlands in parts of the county. These islands were popular places to live due to the fish and aquatic birds the inhabitants could hunt in the waters. The wet landscape preserved many of these tracks. One example is the Sweet Track, over a mile long, which connected the Meare-Westhay island to the Polden Hills ridge peninsula, i.e. the mainland. The walkway consisted of logs placed in a series of x's along the route with planks of wood laid on top of them and fastened into place with pegs. Tree-ring dating shows that it was constructed in the spring of 3806 BC and was used and repaired for the next 9–12 years. It replaced an even earlier walkway called the Post Track, made in 3838 BC, the oldest known trackway in the UK.

Along the sides of the Sweet Track, many offerings were left, such as combs, yew pins, axes and fine ceramic bowls, and these are thought to have been gifts to the gods and goddesses of the wetlands. One axe is jadeite and was made in the northern Italian Alps. It passed through many hands over 500 years before reaching Somerset, where it was finally laid beside the track, having never been used. Therefore, it was a sacred object and the track is the earliest known structure with a religious function in the UK. This was a time when people were settling and farming the land, clearing the primary forest in order to do so. Fats extracted from those bowls came from cows, making this the earliest known example of dairy farming in the country. Beside another Meare-Westhay island track, the wooden "God dolly" was unearthed, which is the earliest known human figurine in the UK.

(Reconstruction of the Sweet Track at Shapwick Nature Reserve)

Stanton Drew, where 'stanton' means stone enclosure, is the third-largest complex of prehistoric standing stones in England. It was put together around 2500 BC as a religious site. The three stone circles there have never been excavated. As a result, little is known about how or why they were constructed. As for the lake villages, one such settlement in Somerset is the best-preserved Iron Age settlement in the country. That's because on top of the boggy marshes, these villagers created platforms of peat and clay and then constructed houses that rested on the platforms. The buildings' foundations sank into the peat, which preserved them along with the remains of plants and bones. The bones show that the villagers were eating all sorts of animals, for instance eels, trout, frogs, otters, beavers, pelicans, cranes, swans, sheep, pigs and dogs. Also preserved were all kinds of objects– pots, saws, a chopping board, baskets, brooches, spindle whorls, glass beads and so on. Even a ladder was found, the only prehistoric one found in Britain and one of just 3 in all of Europe. Known as Glastonbury Lake Village, the settlement was actually closer to Godney and was inhabited from c.250 to 50 BC. For more on this, I invite you to visit the Avalon Marshes Centre and/or its website.

The Iron Age is the setting for the following pages of this book, its first full-length chapter, where we'll meet a goddess.

Prologue Bibliography

Cheddar Man: Mesolithic Britain's blue-eyed boy by Kerry Lotzof

Palaeolithic and Mesolithic Somerset by Robert Hosfield, Vanessa Straker and Paula Gardiner

www.english-heritage.co.uk

www.bbc.co.uk

The Lost Islands of Somerset by Richard Brunning

Avalon Marshes Archaeology by Richard Brunning

Avalon Marshes website

Chapter 1: The Prince of Pigs and the Goddess (Iron Age)

To look at him, nobody would've thought him a prince. Standing in the king's hall, desperately thin under his dirty rags, he looked like a pauper. But the queen knew this man to be her son who had returned to her at last, thanks to her own cunning.

This unusual sight of a filthy prince was due to a tragic chain of events that had been initiated many years ago when the prince, named Bladud, had lived a life of luxury and ease, a life of golden cups, jewels, feasts, hunts and games. Back when he was handsome and well-groomed.

This story took place many centuries before Christ walked the Earth. At that time, King Lud was one of many kings of the early Britons and when his wife, the queen, gave birth to a little boy, the kingdom was overjoyed. Naming him Bladud, they had feasts aplenty to celebrate his birth.

The baby grew into a boy who could outwit the servants and charm them into submission with his handsome smile. He took long walks with his father in which they conversed at length about trade, diplomacy, governance and battle strategies.

Then, in the blink of an eye, Bladud became a young man. His future looked as bright as the twinkling stars in the night sky. One day, he would sit on his father's throne and rule the kingdom with a powerful queen by his side.

However, fortune handed him a devastating blow. Though he tried to convince himself that his body was healthy, soon he could no longer ignore the white blemishes forming on his hands and feet. It was a sure sign of leprosy.

King Lud knew that a hard decision had to be made. He took his wife aside and whispered in his Celtic tongue, "Undoubtedly, you've noticed Bladud's skin. If we do nothing, it could spread to the slaves, the servants, the nobles of the court, to us, even to our other children."

Holding back tears, the queen answered, "Yes, he is certainly afflicted with that dreaded disease. I prayed to the gracious god Nodens to heal him. But it seems Bladud is fated to suffer this disease."

"I didn't want to worry you, but not only have I prayed I've also had animals sacrificed to try and get the gods' attention. But it has all been futile. There's nothing for it. There's nothing for it. We must ba–"

"Don't say it. Please. At least, give me a day and a night to think of a plan." She bit her lip and fidgeted with the exquisitely engraved gold ring on her left hand that had been made for her upon her marriage to the king. This was a souvenir from the blissful days of her youth, a bliss that was now withering away just as Bladud's body was wasting away.

"Very well," the king replied and left her to her thoughts. He fervently hoped she could come up with some scheme that would mean they didn't have to banish their beloved son.

The following day, he asked his wife if she had reached a solution, yet all she said was, "If you bring Bladud before us, I will explain. Do what you must and then I will soften the blow."

Despite the aching in his soul, the king clapped his hands and servants rushed off to fetch the prince, who arrived limping along with a cane. The hands clutching the cane were withdrawn into his sleeves and his face lay hidden under a large cloak.

Tenderly, the king relayed to his son that he had no other choice but to exile him from court in order to keep everyone safe, explaining how they had prayed and sacrificed to the gods to no avail.

"Father, I- I understand," stammered Bladud. He opened his mouth to say more but the words caught in his throat and being so overcome with emotion, he was unable to utter another word.

"We will not lose hope," the queen announced, staring directly into the eyes of her son, surrounded as they were by white marks. "We will continue to pray for healing, for a miracle. And you will always be a prince of this realm, no matter where you go. If you ever need to prove to anyone whose son you are, you can show them this ring." With that, she eased her opulent wedding ring off her finger.

She gently moved forward, dropped the ring on the floor and stepped back again, her lip trembling at the thought of being unable to touch her own child. Bladud stepped forwards and reached out a hand for the ring. The queen and king flinched to see how gnarled his fingers had already become. They shared with him a look of love that would have to last for years, perhaps a whole lifetime. The queen couldn't help but think how this child that had grown inside her and been nurtured by her from cradle to manhood and was now leaving her with no way of keeping in touch and no way of knowing whether their paths would ever cross again.

His wife's astute provision struck a chord with the king. He wiped a tear from his eye and handed his son a bell to wear around his neck so as to signal his arrival to anyone on the road, that they might hide away from this diseased outcast. It was a symbol of how Bladud would from now on live a life of lonely solitude.

They watched their son amble gingerly away, leaning heavily on his stick as if every step was excruciating.

"What will become of him?" asked the queen in a voice cracking with heartache.

"Who can say?" King Lud whispered back.

*

Bladud winced with the effort of easing himself down gently to sit beneath the oak tree. A groan of relief escaped from his mouth the moment his ulcerated feet got a chance to rest. Trying desperately to push away thoughts of the roasted pheasants and beef he had eaten at the palace washed down with huge goblets of ale, Bladud rummaged in his bag to see what meagre supplies he had left. Just a handful of hazelnuts and blackberries as it turned out. Living in the wilderness was a colossal challenge for someone born with a silver spoon in his mouth. Over the past few weeks, he'd had to learn the hard way which berries and mushrooms would make him double over in pain and which would strengthen him.

He shivered in the midday breeze. He had yet to face a winter outdoors and dreaded it. The autumnal chill was bad enough for him. Pulling his chequered blanket tightly around his aching limbs, he wondered how much longer he could go on before he was forced to sell it for food. It was all he had left after selling his intricate gold brooches and neck ring that resembled two golden ropes entwined together. The ring was a symbol of nobility but what good was a symbol when he had none of the privileges of nobility? Yes, the blanket was all that was left, except for his mother's ring and he would never sell that.

Therefore, another solution had to be reached. With a sigh, he acknowledged to himself for the hundredth time that he simply couldn't go on as he was. He had to do something about his predicament or admit defeat and wait for death. But what could he do? That was the question. He murmured to the air, "Please, gods, help me."

Gazing up at the sky, he began to see what images the clouds would make. It was one of the few pleasures in life still available to him. It wasn't as fun as flirting with young maidens or stalking deer atop his favourite horse but for now, it would have to do. "Face, tree, rabbit, pig," he muttered to himself. "Pig! That's it! I can become a swineherd. The farmer would give me food and let me forage on his land in exchange for caring for his herd."

With a half-smile, he began to pop the nuts one by one into his mouth.

*

Bladud sat down heavily against the elm tree. He pushed away a greedy pink snout. "You pigs never let me eat my lunch in peace," he grumbled. But really, he appreciated the company. It was the only company he could get these days.

It was his first day out with the animals. The owner of the pigs had been loath to go anywhere near Bladud, but the prince showed him his mother's ring and declared, "The gods and goddesses will reward you for helping a prince." This had made the owner sigh and reluctantly agree to the idea, provided that Bladud didn't come anywhere near his house. The owner said he would leave Bladud food on a tree stump each day and scurry away before the prince approached to collect the nourishment.

Bladud's lunch consisted of a large mug of milk, a bowl of berries and some bread. "Don't expect this every day," the owner had said gruffly. "But you're all skin and bones. You won't last a week as you are."

Gratefully, Bladud hadn't tried to contest this. There was no use trying to charm the surly owner into regularly delivering substantial food. Bladud was a nobody now, bottom of the pile. He had to accept whatever morsel of kindness he could get.

He drank the milk greedily, remembering the fine herd of cows his parents owned. The bread was a tad stale and the berries sour, but he barely noticed, given how hungry he was.

This new life was not ideal by any means, but at least he would not starve and at least he had someone to talk to, even if they were just silly old pigs. From absolute rock-bottom, he had picked himself up and created some sort of life for himself and that gave him the tiniest amount of hope.

A few weeks later, however, the exiled prince's hope began to fade. He could no longer deny the fact that two of the pigs were developing dry, cracked skin- tell-tale signs of leprosy. A number of the others had small patches of broken skin, as well. Bladud had infected these innocent animals. He had thought it was impossible for a human to pass the disease onto a pig. The pigs' owner had said the same.

"The owner! By the gods, he will be furious," Bladud whispered to himself.

There was nothing for it. He would have to leave, taking the pigs with him to stop the infection from spreading to anyone else. But Bladud feared telling the owner what had happened and having to face his wrath. Bladud had cost him his livelihood.

So early one morning, under the cover of darkness, they set off, heading west because eastwards lay his parents' kingdom and he couldn't return there.

Days and days went by. It was slow work encouraging ailing animals to keep moving on. But somehow, they managed it and Bladud went back to foraging for food in lonely forests.

More days went by, all the same as the last, with the exception of the one in which they had to find a bridge to cross over the mighty River Avon at a place now aptly named Swineford. That was an extraordinarily arduous day of traipsing around. Bladud's life was harder than ever. The disease was only getting worse in his body and now he had to watch the friendly pigs grow weak as well. Then, one day at the crack of dawn, the pigs came across a muddy thermal spring and that was when the prince's fortunes changed entirely.

The frosty dawn had chilled everyone to the bone, so it was no wonder that the pigs, upon discovering a bubbling brown spring, dragged themselves eagerly over to it. Bladud was equally excited. The creatures eased their aching bodies into the warm murky water, rolled around with snorts of delight and gulped greedily at the water to quench the unsatisfiable thirst that leprosy had given them. They were as happy as… well, pigs in mud. Meanwhile, Bladud sat beneath a hazel tree and slowly began to take his sandals off so that he could dip his crooked feet in the welcoming water.

In the process, he noticed how one of the pigs seemed to have clearer skin than before. He shook his head and muttered to himself, "You're seeing things now, little prince. You're going mad." And yet, even as he said these words, another of the pigs appeared to no longer have cracked and blotchy skin. Bladud froze. "By the gods, could it be?" he murmured. "Are these the waters I heard of during my childhood? The waters that belong to the goddess Sulis and give healing to princes and paupers alike?"

He edged towards the filthy spring water and dipped one foot in. Within moments, the crooked bones on his foot had realigned themselves and all the blemishes had vanished. In went the other foot. The same thing happened.

Amazed, Bladud bowed his head and said, "Goddess Sulis, if these waters are indeed yours, take pity on this poor prince. I have suffered for so long with this infliction. Be kind to me the same way you have to these boars."

Taking a deep breath, he began to strip naked to see if his prayer had been heeded. He walked steadily into the spring and knelt down beside the pigs.

"Sulis! Great Mother!" he exclaimed when he saw his hands transform before his very eyes. Plunged beneath the glimmering surface of the water, the missing fingers grew back, the wrinkles disappeared and soon they looked as smooth as a child's. Bladud was overcome with emotion. Wiping a tear from his eye, he thanked Sulis over and over again for the miracle.

Just before dusk, or dimpsey for Somerset folk, Bladud fell asleep and dreamt a thousand dreams- that he still had leprosy, that he was a child sitting on his mother's lap, that his pigs were sitting around him in a circle clapping their trotters together. And when he awoke, he was afraid to open his eyes in case the wonders of the previous day had been another one of the myriad dreams he'd experienced. He cautiously began to wiggle his fingers and touch his left hand with his right one. Everything seemed intact. Steeling himself, he opened one eye and saw beautifully soft hands. He breathed a huge sigh of relief and sat up with a smile.

"Well, piggies, Sulis has certainly been generous to us. And I don't mean to squander this gift. It's time to get you back to where you belong and me to where I belong."

*

The owner had been livid with Bladud. When he caught sight of the young man running out along the dusty path, he boxed Bladud about the ears for kidnapping (or pignapping!) his animals. Bladud desperately exclaimed that he was a prince and would make sure the owner was rewarded for his kindness, which had stopped the man in his tracks but only so that he could laugh in Bladud's face. That had given the prince enough time to produce the ring his mother had entrusted to him and from then on, it was plain sailing. The pig farmer was stunned and let the young man go. "I might as well believe you. The gods know I could do with a reward!" he shrugged and turned his head to spit out the rest of his anger.

Bladud smiled at this memory during his easy stroll along the path, running his fingers through his shoulder-length hair and braiding some of it in the Celtic style. If he was to reclaim his place, he needed to make a bit of an effort with his hair at least since his clothing wasn't as easily rectified. The pig farmer hadn't believed him enough to lend him any clothes and he had barely a finely woven garment himself anyway.

When his father's palace came into sight, that was the issue gnawing at the back of Bladud's mind: how to actually reach his parents given that no servants would allow a dirty, ragged man into the king and queen's presence and if he showed the ring, there was a chance they would have him killed for a thief. He needed to find a servant who'd been in attendance on the day his mother had gifted it to him.

As if the deities could hear his thoughts, just such a servant was now approaching him. Steadying himself, Bladud called out to the woman, "Excuse me!"

She gave him a pitying look and walked on.

He tried again. "Branwen, it's me, Bladud. The goddess Sulis cured me and I have the ring to prove it!"

At that, she turned back.

"Bl- Bladud? In truth? Let me see the ring."

When he handed it to her, she examined it carefully and studied his face to see if it matched her memory of the young prince before the curse had fallen on him.

"Branwen, you're to take this band and drop it in my mother's cup this night. Once she sees it, she will know. I'll be waiting beside the south gate for when they come to fetch me."

The servant nodded and hurried away to do as her young master had bid her and just as Bladud predicted, in no time at all, a small group of retainers burst out of the palace and dashed over to him at the south gate.

"Bladud! Your mother has seen the ring. She demanded to know how it'd got there," one began excitedly.

"And then Branwen began to explain–" a second continued.

"So we offered to bring you to the king as soon as possible."

He was led along familiar corridors to the monarch's presence chamber. After Bladud had revealed his blemish-free skin and perfectly formed hands, the king laughed with joy and bellowed, "Bathe him at once and give him something decent to eat! And send out a chest of fine clothes to the pig farmer who kept him alive all that time."

And his mother just kept murmuring, "My boy, my boy."

*

The years flew by and Lud himself passed away. Bladud took the throne and Alaron became his queen. Together, they returned to the springs in the west and established a city there in 863 BC so that other people could also be cured of their illnesses. They had a temple erected in honour of Sulis in which eternal fires burned because Sulis was associated with the sun. These fires never burnt out, because whenever the flames dwindled, the ashes turned to rocky lumps. The springs themselves had vast quantities of warm water pouring out for those in need of restoration to drink or bathe in. People felt refreshed by Sulis' generous waters and Bladud felt proud that he had led so many to live beside this extraordinary haven. Pilgrims came too in pursuit of healing. They arrived from far and wide to visit this sacred spring that had once saved a prince of pigs from a life of misery.

Notes

Bladud was the eldest son and heir of King Lud of the ancient Britons who supposedly lived towards the end of the Bronze Age or beginning of the Iron Age. It was around this time that the Celts arrived little by little: c. 1000 to 650 BC. Bladud's wife was Alaron but his mother's name has been lost to time and the servant named Branwen is fictional. Legend has it that Bladud was buried in Twerton Roundhill (al-so called Long Barrow Hill). The hot springs he visited were in Bath, making him the legendary founder of Bath but he would've called it a different name since Bath comes from the Anglo-Saxon 'Badum'.

A number of other places around Bath have links to the story, some of them in terms of etymology. Swainswick (3 miles north of Bath) means either a hamlet where people tended pigs or the hamlet of Swain (or a similar-sounding name). Swineford, mentioned in the story, is in South Gloucestershire and 'ford' means a shallow part of the river that is traversable. And Little Solsbury Hill near modern-day Batheaston might mean 'Sulis' little hillfort'. Centuries after Bladud and Alaron lived, a wooden hill fort was indeed constructed there, at some point between 500 and 100 BC.

(Little Solsbury Hill in the distance)

In terms of the spring water curing Bladud's leprosy, the legend – if it is a Medieval invention – may have been inspired by the story of Naaman in the Bible, whose leprosy is miraculously cured by washing seven times in the River Jordan. The disease is curable nowadays with antibiotics and scientists have demonstrated that certain antibiotics can be found in hot springs, so it's possible that continual bathing might've benefitted him. Certainly, the waters have been found beneficial for arthritis and gout. In the twelfth century, the springs in Bath were said to be particularly good at curing women's ailments (perhaps UTIs since the heat would kill some of the bacteria?).

Leprosy is a horrendous disease that left untreated can lead to blindness, dry patches on limbs that have no sense of heat, cold or touch, loss of eyebrows, contorted fingers, rotting flesh etc. The fact that a goddess (rather than a god) is said to have cured Bladud of this sickness is an example of female power in Celtic society, which got lost when more patriarchal cultures took hold of Britain.

Sulis was a goddess who lived down on Earth, amongst humans, rather than up in the heavens like other deities, such as the sun, another female deity for the Celts. As mentioned in the story, Sulis had a solar association. That was down to the fact that her waters were hot like the sun.

The inextinguishable fires in the temple dedicated to Sulis (or Sul) might have been created using Somerset coal. The goddess was unique to the hot springs of Bath and coins belonging to the Dobunni and Durotriges tribes were found in the mud filling the spring pipe. The Celts had many deities that were associated with a single place. Although Sulis was believed to only work in the hot springs at Bath, people knew about her in places as far-flung as central Germany.

The hazel tree in the story refers to how this tree was a symbol of the goddess. For instance, if it was the middle of summer and you carved a wand out of hazel wood, it was supposed to lead you to buried treasure and a water source.

This connection with hazels carried on into the Roman era when Sulis (which is to the best of my knowledge the earliest female name we have for Somerset, albeit a goddess' name) merged with Minerva to become Sulis Minerva. When British and Roman couples struggled to conceive, the women would throw hazelnuts into the waters, hoping that the goddess would bless them with pregnancy. In the next chapter, we will have a look at how the Romans used the waters of Aquae Sulis, updating the muddy spring to spa waters fit for an empress.

Chapter Bibliography

Avalon- The County of Somerset by Paul Wade-Williams

Belief, Legend and Perceptions of the Sacred in Contemporary Bath by Marion Bowman

Bladud of Bath: The Archaeology of a Legend by John Clark

Bladud: The flying king of Bath by A. T. Fear

Sydney Gardens History and Heritage Trail leaflet

Somerset by G. W. Wade & J. H. Wade

Somerset Folk Tales by Sharon Jacksties

Legends of Somerset by Sally Jones

www.oxfordreference.com

www.nationaltrust.org.uk

BRITANNIA

Chapter 2: Romance in Roman Times (2nd century)

"*Tace,* Trifosa!"

'I don't feel like shutting up,' Trifosa thought.

"And stop looking at the customers in the eye. I'll never sell you at this rate. I called you Trifosa for a reason. Now, act dainty for once!"

Trifosa rolled her eyes at his reference to this Greek nickname he'd given her, following the slave masters' age-old tradition. For a few moments, she looked at the ground. But curiosity soon got the better of her and her gaze began to roam once more.

"I said stop," snarled her slave master through clenched teeth. Her defiant gaze made him raise his hand to slap her hard across the face. She closed her eyes and braced herself for the pain that she knew so well. Except it didn't come.

Gingerly, she opened one eye and saw that the master's hand was being held in a vice-like grip by another man. Opening the other eye, Trifosa saw it was a young and well-dressed member of the Roman elite.

"You will not lay another finger on her." His soft voice had an edge to it. "And to guarantee that you don't, I will purchase her from you this very instant."

Gasping in shock, she watched her enslaver negotiate a price with the stranger. Grudgingly, he unceremoniously unshackled her naked body and gruffly removed the notice around her neck. "There was no harm meant," he snivelled.

"Hmph," the stranger replied. Trifosa felt sudden warmth as he tossed his own cloak around her shoulders and motioned for her to follow him. So far, he had barely looked at her, quite unlike most other men who had leered at her breasts as they'd passed by. Trifosa trotted behind him in a daze.

Within minutes, they had arrived at his medium-sized villa in the centre of Aquae Sulis. Trifosa took in the stone foundations topped with cob walls composed of mud, clay, sand and horse hair. The walls were painted white with vertical and horizontal lines to imitate bricks and housed glass windows and a roof made of red clay tiles. Inside, she was grateful to already know about underfloor heating so she didn't embarrass herself. The first time Trifosa had felt warm mosaic flooring, she'd assumed there was an uncontrolled fire underneath. But the furnaces warming the villas' floors were always tiny and very much under control, with a slave at each villa assigned to keep the fire constantly burning. She'd once been shown how the stacks of tiles in the foundations carried the heat upwards and had always thought this a perfect way to warm houses without the smokiness that open fires created.

Standing in the atrium, Trifosa now had time to look at him properly. She estimated his age to be close to her own- in his mid-30s. His olive skin hinted that he hailed from Rome itself or somewhere nearby and he had kind, hazel eyes framing his clean-shaven face. He hadn't followed the current trend for beards.

"Please sit," he said, indicating a stool at the edge of a large entrance room paved with an exquisite mosaic and enclosed with brightly coloured walls. Part of her was in awe of it all but another part of her scoffed and thought, 'What's the use of all this luxury when you're enslaved as I am?'

"I couldn't bear to see him mistreating you like that. I can be somewhat impulsive, I confess. But here we are. Let me introduce you to me and your new life. My name is Gaius Calpurnius Receptus and I work as a priest at the Sulis Minerva temple here in Aquae Sulis. Have you heard of it?"

"Yes, Sulis our water goddess. But never I go inside, dominus," she replied, struggling to express herself in her second language.

"Well, you soon will, no doubt. My sister, Claudia, does love to bathe there. She lives here with me, as do a few other slaves."

"No wife?"

"No, no wife. My sister is the only domina here."

*

Trifosa didn't have to wait long to see the baths. The very next day, she found herself scurrying along behind Claudia, clutching her mistress' oils and sponge stick. They zigzagged – Claudia gracefully but Trifosa less so – between the traders crowded outside the temple, hawking their wares and services. "Get your lead sheets here!" "Pots and pans!" "A haircut for you, domina?"

Claudia dismissed them all with a toss of her hand. Her sole aim was to get to the baths for a good soak. Like most self-respecting Romans, she would spend nearly all her afternoons at the baths, aside from in the summer when the more clement weather attracted tourists from all over the empire who stood around gawping like lemons, getting in her way. Even then, she would visit every other day and not even the frequent bouts of headlice that she caught there would keep her away. Trifosa was endlessly combing them out of Claudia's long, black hair.

Having never stepped inside the bathing complex before, Trifosa's heart skipped a beat as soon as they had passed through the entrance hall, where the visitors removed their clothing and folded them neatly into chests or had their slaves do it for them. Claudia beckoned her on to begin exploring the labyrinth of rooms. Trifosa stood attentively to one side while Claudia and the other bathers submerged themselves first in the cold bath, then moved to another room for the warm bath, then to the steaming hot bath, into which countless offerings had been flung over the years, and finally the swimming pool, lined with Somerset lead from the nearby Mendip Hills. The enslaved woman suspected that part of her role was to chaperone Claudia and keep her safe from any unwanted attention, as inevitably there were roaming hands and flirtations going on in the pool between other visitors.

If Trifosa were to travel through the length and breadth of Roman Britain, she would know that the swimming pool roof was one of the tallest buildings in the colony, rising 20 metres above the pool and creating an echoing atmosphere that was new to her.

For all their elaborate mosaics and brightly coloured frescoes on lime plaster, none of those rooms could compare with the temple to Sulis Minerva… or so Gaius had told her. Only priests were allowed inside to worship the goddess. In one corner, Trifosa was pleased to hear of the reverence with which the Romans held Sulis' magical waters. The sacred spring was framed with elegant columns while graceful white statues of deities dipped their toes in the shallow water. A gigantic bronze statue of Sulis Minerva stood tall and proud with a serious face, nearly curled hair and a helmet that symbolised Minerva the warrior.

Once Claudia had been oiled and scraped by Trifosa then dried and dressed, they entered the noisy temple courtyard. This paved area contained altars that stank and ran red with the blood of animal sacrifices. They had to step past scribes and sellers of religious trinkets so that Claudia and Trifosa could stand at the entrance to the temple and gaze up at the triangular portico above it. The elaborate design centred around a bearded gorgon head accompanied by all sorts of symbols such as an owl and female Victories. Claudia murmured a private prayer that would never be revealed to anyone, of course. If you told someone what you had wished for, it wouldn't come true.

Trifosa also muttered a quick plea of her own. "Please, Sulis," she began. To her, the goddess would always be Sulis, not Sulis Minerva and never Minerva-Sulis. "Heal me of my loneliness and of my broken heart." Some years past, her parents had succumbed to disease and that was how she had wound up enslaved.

"Ah, I see you approve of Roman workmanship!"

Turning around, she saw that the voice belonged to Gaius, on duty there and dressed in his priestly white toga trimmed with purple.

"Never I see anything like it, dominus," she sighed.

"Hmm, I suppose you haven't. What do you know about Sulis Minerva?"

"I know Sulis well, dominus. She is a goddess of health. She... help women have baby."

"Yes," he smiled. "She is certainly special. That's why we

Romans named this place Aquae Sulis. Our Roman goddess Minerva is associated with health, wisdom, medicine and crafts. Sulis Minerva is a powerful deity indeed with all these things combined. See the owl symbols around us, for example? They represent wisdom. Along with Jupiter and Juno, Minerva is one of the most important of our deities."

"She shows..." Trifosa began and then thought of how to say it in her second language. "She shows women powerful."

He chuckled. "Oh yes. For as well as healer, Sulis Minerva is an avenger of wrongs. You must have seen the lead and pewter tablets that worshippers roll up and throw into the springs?"

She nodded. "Sulis can curse the bad people. The good people... they write prayers for help."

"And I have seen her power. Thieves have been caught, stolen goods recovered and so on. I hope I never have to write one about you." He winked at her.

"I never steal." Her solemn gaze met his eyes squarely.

"Come, Trifosa," Claudia called. Reluctantly, the slave followed but turned to look back at her master. Who was this man, so kind and light-hearted, who had saved her from that vicious slave master?

*

Before long, Trifosa had got into a routine of housework in the mornings and visits to the baths in the afternoon, where she often crossed paths with Gaius and they chatted affably. One day, however, the whole town was in a stir. Trifosa was too busy washing clothes to keep up with the gossip whirring around the streets but when Gaius burst through the door at midday, halfway through his shift at the temple, she knew something was up.

"Claudia? Are you here?" he shouted.

She instantly appeared at his side. "I hope you've come home to tell us whether the rumours are true."

"The ones about the emperor visiting? Oh, they're definitely true. He will be here tomorrow with his wife."

"What a privilege! He is sure to visit the baths and pay his respects to the goddess. I'll take Trifosa and go across at sunrise and stay there all day so we can get a glimpse of him and perhaps even exchange a word or two. Who knows what honours he might bestow on us if he is pleased with us?" she squealed and clutched the folds of her toga.

"Make sure you don't overdo it, sister, or you may end up displeasing him," he replied sternly.

"Yes, yes. I'd better go and find that brooch Mother gave me." And off she skipped to her room, humming tunelessly.

That was how the next day, Trifosa came face to face with Emperor Hadrian and Empress Vibia Sabina, albeit from afar. He was in the temple precinct, nodding his head in satisfaction at the building extensions that had recently been put in place. "However, there will have to be certain adjustments made. I needn't remind you that I have set out a law across the empire that men should bathe separately from women. There will need to be two sets of suites."

"This will protect the women and prevent wandering hands from getting up to mischief in the waters," the empress declared.

Claudia raised her eyebrows at this, thinking it was an excellent idea. She had never felt entirely safe in the waters when certain men were swimming nearby.

Straining her eyes, Trifosa could more or less make out the empress. She stood regally by her husband's side appraising her surroundings. Her coiled hair framed an oval face with green eyeshadow and painted lips. Her brightly coloured toga and headdress were both magnificent. Trifosa sighed and thought of how little choice she had in what she wore- just a plain tunic, wooden shoes and a metal necklace that all slaves had to wear around their necks to indicate their status and with instructions on where to return a runaway slave.

Later, after having failed to get anywhere near the emperor due to the sheer number of people crowding around him, they ambled home to tell Gaius of their day. "Ah yes," he commented. "This is just another example of how much progress we Romans are bringing to your Britain, Trifosa. You must be so thankful for all the architecture, roads, culture and improvements."

Trifosa rolled her eyes. For all his kindness, Gaius was loyal to Rome to a fault. He couldn't see things from a colonised point of view.

"Well," she replied looking straight into his eyes, "there are good things. But also bad things. Taxes, soldiers, gladiators." Not to mention certain strange practices, she thought to herself, such as wiping their behinds with a sea sponge that was dipped in a jar of vinegar to clean it after each use. At least the Celtic idea of using dry moss or leaves meant that you disposed of what you'd used each time. Trifosa had shuddered when she had first seen the sponge and point-blank refused to touch it. Rather, she carried on in her Celtic ways in that regard. But she had already given her master enough to reflect on.

"Hmm, yes, I suppose some gladiators don't enjoy the fighting, but taxes and soldiers keep the empire running." Trifosa couldn't help but feel disappointment. He couldn't quite grasp the depth of pain these issues caused many Britons and lower-class Romans. "Well, we will be busy at the temple implementing these reforms. I'm sure it will please the goddess to have these separate quarters established. And will Hadrian stay long in the town?"

"From what I gathered, no," answered Claudia. "Soon he will journey north to inspect the construction of the wall to keep the barbarians at bay."

"Good, good. We must keep our civilised people safe from those northern savages. If they only knew what good things we Romans bring to our empire, they would be begging us to enter their lands!"

Trifosa rolled her eyes again.

*

More months went by and Trifosa's ability in Latin increased at the same rate as her curiosity about her master. He was equally curious about her.

"Tell me, are you originally from this part of the world? You aren't a native speaker of Latin, to be sure," Gaius commented, then quickly added, "But it's improved mightily these past few months."

"I don't like to talk about the past," she replied squarely.

Her lack of deference never seemed to bother Gaius. If truth be told, he rather liked how upfront and honest she was and how he rarely even addressed him as 'dominus' these days nor Claudia as 'domina'.

"Well then, let us live in the present. My friend Magnus is coming to visit today. In fact, he is due here any moment. The dining room will need mopping to make the mosaics sparkle."

"Then I shall go."

"Yes, I suppose you must. It's a shame we cannot talk more."

"If I weren't your slave, we could," she commented slyly.

He laughed at her cheek. "You aren't suited to the life of a slave, that's for sure. They'd beat you in another house for comments like that!"

"I know!" She beamed and took her leave.

No sooner had she cleaned the floor and stored the mop away in a back room, she heard male voices in the entrance hall. One was in anguish. Unable to help herself, she crept to the doorway but remained concealed in the shadows to hear the conversation.

"Please make yourself comfortable, dear friend." Gaius' voice had a deep tenderness to it.

Magnus shakily made his way to a couch and lay on his side with his left elbow bent. He didn't touch the food laid out on the table in front of him. "She was barely one-and-a-half years old." Magnus was choking on his words.

Gaius reclined on a couch positioned at a right angle to the other one. "The gods can be cruel without reason, at times."

"My wife and I thought that we had found the answer to our prayers. Being unable to have children of our own, there was Mercatilla, such a lively little baby."

"And with goodness in your hearts, you freed the baby from

slavery and cared for her as your foster daughter."

Trifosa wondered grimly what the baby's mother thought of this arrangement where the baby would want for nothing but would grow up never knowing her mother. And in this case, had failed to grow up at all. Had the enslaved mother even been notified of the passing? Or was the mother dead? Best not to make assumptions, she supposed.

But Gaius' voice went on. "I cannot understand why the gods would take her from you, unless it was caprice as I said. The instant she caught that fever, you and your wife were at the baths offering coins and gifts to Sulis Minerva for Mercatilla's health. You gave animals to be sacrificed to Minerva Medica as well... You did everything you could."

"You are kind, Gaius. We must search our souls, for there might be some sin that we are being punished for. Mercatilla should not have paid the price, though. We will raise a gravestone in her honour for all to see, no expense will be spared, and it will detail her short life. 1 year, 6 months, 12 days. That's all the time she got."

"Yes. *Tempus fugit* as they say," commented Gaius and as he did so, the light in the hallway shifted and Trifosa's face emerged from the shadows. He looked her in the eye and added, "We must make the most of every day."

Magnus nodded in agreement. "*Carpe diem.*"

Later that day, Gaius pushed open the kitchen door and found Trifosa standing at a long table cutting up parsnips.

"Listen–" he began but she jumped at the sound of his voice and cut her finger with the knife.

"Sorry. This is a terrible start," he muttered and moved over to bandage the finger gently with a scrap of cloth. Their eyes met and an awkward silence descended.

At last, she said, "What happened to your friend is so sad. It's horrible when bad things happen to good people."

"It is. And I meant what I said about making the most of every day. I should probably just say this before I think about it too much and get nervous." His speech was getting faster and faster. "Well, Trifosa, I... um... well, as we said earlier, slavery doesn't suit you. I think it would be better if I made you a freedwoman and perhaps my wife as well if you want, or just a freedwoman."

Speechless (a very rare thing for Trifosa), she just stared at him while his heart thumped in his chest in anticipation.

"Say something," he mumbled hoarsely.

"You mean to free me just as Magnus freed Mercatilla?"

"I do."

"And you mean to make me part of your family, just as Mercatilla became part of Magnus' family?"

"Yes. If you would like. Otherwise, you are at liberty to start a new life somewhere else a freedwoman."

"Yes," she whispered. "That is, I would like it. To be your wife." With that, she smiled and held out her good hand to hold in his. He fished something out of his leather bag and held it out to her. A large, jangling set of keys to the villa. "These are yours now. You are mistress of the house."

*

According to custom, she took her ex-master's middle name and became Calpurnia Trifosa. (Although she would have preferred to replace both names with her original name, her husband didn't comprehend her desire and dismissed it). With relish, she had removed her slave necklace. Now, she was allowed to wear elegant gold and silver necklaces instead, alongside all manner of other jewellery, expensive perfume, elaborate hairstyles and fashionable makeup. Gone were her wooden shoes and her slave's tunic and in their place were soft sandals and a toga. She was proud of how far she had come despite being a colonised woman at the edge of a mighty empire. Her physical transformation was just one part of this new life she had found for herself.

Claudia was rather disgruntled at first, half suspecting that Trifosa was nothing more than a gold digger, but she shrugged her shoulders and tolerated the unusual matrimony.

Although Trifosa, or rather Calpurnia, was no longer obliged to visit the baths with Claudia, she went several times a week anyway to enjoy the warm waters. She was grateful that she didn't have to worry about unwanted male attention, for Hadrian's command of separate quarters for men and women had been obeyed.

Her first visit following their wedding had a singular purpose- to thank the goddess Sulis for healing her loneliness by bringing Gaius into her life and for answering her prayer for a way out of slavery. She weaved through the maze of rooms until she reached the chamber with the hottest pool in it. She found an empty spot beside the other worshippers who were dangling brooches, jewellery, pewter flagons, cups and all manner of offerings over the pool. Taking out a simple hairpin, she held it reverently in her hands, raised her hands and closed her eyes to whisper a prayer of thanksgiving, then flung it into the depths of the steamy water.

*

Where had all the time gone? Calpurnia was elderly now and Gaius even more so. But they were blessed to reach old age in those ancient days when a person was lucky to reach 25 or 35, let alone their seventies.

She tutted as she gazed through the villa's window out to the street. Gaius had insisted on going to check on the eternal fires, although his health was fading and there were a whole host of younger priests who could do it. But he liked to feel needed. For that reason alone, he had gone to the temple, hobbling along.

Calpurnia turned back to the length of wool she was spinning. Although they had slaves to do that work, she enjoyed it and she needed something to accompany her hands if not her brain. She always worried these days when he decided to pop out to the temple *just to check on things.*

Suddenly, her attention was caught by their slave Marcus charging down towards the front door. He burst through and doubled over with exhaustion.

She leapt up, dropping the wool and spindle, and doing her back a disservice.

"What is it? Is Gaius... has he fallen over?"

"I'm so sorry. I'm not sure dominus will recover. You must come quickly!"

By the time she had managed to stagger and stumble over to the complex, her vision had become blurry with tears and her mind riddled with fear. As always, the whole world and her husband were at the pools. Calpurnia was in no mood to hear exuberance, rather she just wanted to scream at everyone to shut up because her husband was in pain and she needed to find him and how could they be laughing at a time like this?

"This way," said Marcus gently.

They squeezed past the bathers and into a side room. Presumably, he'd been helped over to it (or carried?) to avoid the prying gaze of bystanders. They found him slumped against a wall.

"Gaius, my love. It is I, Calpurnia Trifosa."

He made no response.

"Gaius?"

Marcus moved over to him and laid his hand gently on his master's arm, then cleared his throat. "He's um... he's cold, domina."

"Well now," she whispered, the tears running freely down her cheeks now. "He died in a place he loved, doing what he loved. W- was it his heart?" She looked pleadingly around at the temple assistants.

A young assistant supplied the answer in a sheepish voice: "Yes, domina. It happened suddenly. We tried to help but..."

"Alright, I see. I see. Yes. He did complain of pains in his chest now and then. Oh my Gaius. Not even time to say goodbye. Did he say anything before he passed away?"

"He told us to let you know that he was sorry for insisting on coming here and that you are everything to him."

She nodded gravely. So far, she was surprisingly composed. The stark truth of it hadn't quite sunk in yet.

"He lived a good life," Marcus smiled sadly.

"He must be remembered," she declared. "I will pay for the best tombstone possible."

"You don't have to think of that now."

"No, no. I have to get it right. He always liked oolite stone, which is found in abundance around here. I will use that. In the shape of an altar to represent his profession. I will honour the goddess Sulis and mention that he freed me before marrying me. And that he lived to a great age. That he was a priest, yes." She paused. "And make sure the inscription is of good quality, yes. Praise be to the goddess Sulis for giving him a long and happy life. Seventy-five years. And he loved his job and his family."

"Shall I fetch you some wine?"

Trifosa didn't hear him. "I should never have let him leave the house this morning," she murmured.

"Domina, you weren't to know and besides, he was always so determined about coming here often to make sure everything was in order."

"Because he loved the goddess so much. And me. And I loved him."

With that, she sat down on a nearby stool and succumbed to her grief.

Notes

Although 130 Roman curse tablets have been found in Bath (now listed in the UNESCO Memory of the World UK register), tombstones are rarer. In the whole of Britain, only about 300 have been discovered. Of those, most are headstones for soldiers. Gaius' tombstone is unique in being the only Roman Britain monument to be in a shape that represents the person's occupation. The altar shape shows that Calpurnia Trifosa was proud that her husband was a priest, perhaps partly because it gave her status too. It is also the only evidence to prove that a priest had ever served at Bath. Findings at other sites, however, indicate that the temple would have been served by plenty of priests and their assistants throughout the centuries.

While we have no idea of Calpurnia's age at the time of her husband's death, I decided to keep their ages similar. As the story says, Gaius was fortunate to reach the age of 75. The stone reads:

To the spirits of the departed; Gaius Calpurnius Receptus, priest of the goddess Sulis, lived 75 years; Calpurnia Trifosa, his freedwoman (and) wife, had this set up.

Although Calpurnia was constrained by space on the gravestone and social norms, the stone says what she wanted to tell the world. When we read it, we are repeating the words (albeit in English) that a woman who lived 2000 years ago dictated from her own mouth. We are hearing her speak!

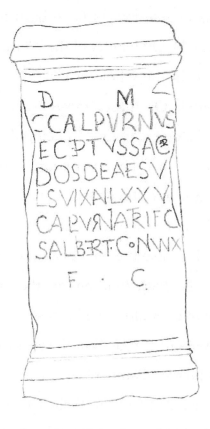

(My attempt at drawing Gaius' tombstone.)

Remarkably, she included her slave name on the stone and the fact that she was a freedwoman. Was she proud of herself for escaping slavery through marriage and elevating her status?

The stone was found when digging and preparing land for the creation of Sydney Gardens in 1793. In Calpurnia's time, this location was just outside the city walls; Roman law forbade burials within towns.

Frustratingly, the stone gives us no indication of when Gaius died. It could have been any time from when the Roman temple at Aquae Sulis (also known as Aquae Calidae) was built in the mid-70s AD to when the Romans abandoned Somerset c.409 AD. Similarly, Mercatilla (whose tombstone was also found near the Romans' north gate) could've died at any point over the course of the Roman occupation. Her stone reads:

To the spirits of the departed; Merc(...), freedwoman and foster-daughter of Magnus, lived 1 year, 6 months, 12 days.

We cannot say if Trifosa and her husband lived at the same time as Mercatilla or if they met but I thought it made a good story to have them as friends of Mercatilla's parents.

I chose the second century because the temple complex was larger and more elaborate by then and I thought incorporating Hadrian's visit to Bath in 122 AD would be interesting. It isn't documented whether the empress, Vibia Sabina, accompanied him; however, she was well-travelled and held in high esteem in Rome and so it isn't outside the realms of possibility. It *is* true that Hadrian prohibited mixed bathing and therefore separate baths for men and women had to be built throughout the empire.

Another important thing to consider is that Gaius didn't *have to* marry the enslaved woman in order to have a relationship with her. Being her master, he could have regular sex with her or even rape her frequently and that would've been socially acceptable. The fact is that he *wanted* to free her and marry her. It paints a picture of a man in love and we hope Calpurnia Trifosa was in love too, or perhaps she simply took the no-brainer option of gaining a better life and social standing for herself. Coincidentally, the name Gaius denotes rejoicing and Calpurnius refers to a chalice of wine. Our heroine would have been jubilant to cross paths with him and eventually become his wife, regardless of whether or not the couple had children (another tantalising mystery).

Claudia is fictional, as are the details of Calpurnia Trifosa's life, for example that her parents died of an illness. We only know what is written on the tombstone. She might have been from the Dobunni tribe since the Celts inhabiting Bath when the Romans arrived belonged to that group, which stretched from Glastonbury in the south to Gloucestershire in the north, and Weston-super-Mare in the west to Wiltshire in the east. (Another interpretation is that the Dobunni territory ended just south of Bath and that Weston-super-Mare, Glastonbury etc. were part of the Belgae tribe. Southwestern Somerset people, on the other hand, were Dumnonii as far as the River Parrett, while southern Somerset people were Durotriges.) The idea that Calpurnia was a Briton comes from the historian Dorothy Watt's excellent hypothesis based on the fact that Calpurnia raised a gravestone for her husband that states he was a priest for the goddess Sulis, rather than calling her the goddess Sulis Minerva or Minerva Sulis in a more Roman manner. Indeed, no inscriptions that mention Minerva alone have been found at Bath, indicating that Sulis took precedence in a society where the Romans were trying to delicately balance allowing the locals to worship their own deities but ensuring that those deities were Romanised to a certain extent. So we have a clue about where Calpurnia Trifosa was from but not about which part of the Roman Empire any of the others came from. Gaius, Magnus and Magnus' wife could have been born in northern Africa, Italy, France, Britain itself...

So, Calpurnia Trifosa may have been born in Britain but if so we can't possibly know where. Neither do we know where she grew up. We know she lived in Bath for a time, but we don't know where she lived after her husband died. Did she stay in Bath or go elsewhere? And what did she do with her life? Did she remarry? Or live with her children if she had any? We'll likely never know.

On a final note, there are very few women or girls mentioned on tombstones in comparison to men. Some more examples from Bath include:

– Rusonia Aventina was a member of the Mediomatrici tribe, meaning she came from north-eastern France, specifically Metz, which is over 400 miles away from Bath as the crow flies.

This shows how many different nationalities were living – or at least spending time – in Bath and some were rich enough to pay for inscribed tombstones, even quite large ones like Rusonia's. This was probably a high-ranking and prominent woman. She certainly had some money and/or possessions to pass on after death as it was her male heir who set the tombstone up after she died at the fairly remarkable age of 58. Her last name is the female version of Aventinus, which is both the Latin name of Aventine, one of the hills Rome was built upon and the name of one of Hercules' sons. Is this another hint that she had high status?

– "Successa Petronia, [who] lived 3 years, 4 months, 9 days. Vettius Romulus and Victoria Sabina set this up to their dearest daughter." As with Mercatilla, the exact age of their toddler has been meticulously documented. Her mother's last name, Sabina, suggests that she was a member of the Sabine people, who lived to the east of the Tiber River in Italy. Her father's name comes from Romulus and Remus, the legendary founders of Rome, and literally means 'of Rome'. It would appear this couple had both been born in the heart of the Roman Empire or at least that their ancestors had.

– One tombstone simply reads: "Vibia Jucunda, aged 30, lies buried here." Jucunda means pleasant or delightful.

I can't get over how fascinating it is to me that we can know the names of people who walked the same pathways as us about 2,000 years ago! We only get brief snippets of their existences but in the case of Mercatilla and Calpurnia, it's enough to get a glimpse into the lives they led so very long ago.

(The Roman Baths in modern times where the columns and statues are Victorian replicas. The warm waters encourage algae.)

Chapter Bibliography

Aquae Sulis: The Roman Baths where two goddesses became one

Bloody British History: Somerset by Andrew May

Curator's Choice: The Roman Baths Museum by Stephen Bird

Early Christianity in South-West Britain: Wessex, Somerset, Devon, Cornwall and the Channel Islands by Elizabeth Rees

Religion and Ritual in the Western Provinces by Louise Revell

Roman Somerset by Peter Leach

romaninscriptionsofbritain.org

Syncretism in the Roman Empire & Sulis Minerva, Bath

www.romanbaths.co.uk

Discover Roman Women (mini documentaries by the Roman Baths)

Sydney Gardens History and Heritage Trail leaflet

The Story of Roman Bath by Patricia Southern

Sulis: Healer and Avenger in The Concept of the Goddess edited by Miranda Green and Sandra Billington

Online Encyclopaedia Britannica

POST-ROMAN YEARS

Chapter 3: The Heroic Hermitess (5th century)

"Move over. Let me have a look!" 10-year-old Brenna said, shoving her older sister out of the way.

"In a moment. Don't be so impatient!" 12-year-old Agnes replied.

They had been on their way to fetch water from the local well when a strange-looking woman had appeared. Dressed very plainly with a long walking staff, she had come along the road singing in an unusual dialect while brushing back her tangled hair.

Being naturally shy, the two Briton girls, their hair neatly plaited, had hidden behind a rock. Now they were taking turns to spy on the woman who was coming ever closer to their house.

"What do you think she wants?" whispered Brenna. "She might be a witch by the looks of her."

"Shhh!"

At length, this woman was at the threshold, calling out in her unique dialect, "Greetings. Is this the home of King Elgin?"

The girls' father appeared at the door. Though her accent was strange, he could understand her perfectly. After all, hers was the same language as his. "Well, yes, that would be me. Do come in."

Brenna and Agnes crept over to sit under a window that they

might hear more.

"My name is Princess Keyne. I have come from yonder way, from Wales, crossing the sea channel on a small boat. My father is King Brychan of Powys and I am the youngest of his many daughters. At my father's court, I had many offers of marriage but I have chosen to never marry and dedicate my life to God. I have travelled this way in search of solitude, that I might live out my life in prayer and devotion as a hermitess."

"My, my. That was a brave journey." He was clearly shocked and the look on his face suggested that he felt that her voyage wasn't a ladylike thing to do, that it was too dangerous for a member of the 'weaker' sex. Yet, Keyne's stoicism in the face of icy sea breezes on board her little raft proved his judgement of women wrong.

Never mind. By the looks of things, Keyne had not heard him for she continued, "Near here, there is a patch of woodland beside a river that would be ideal and I was told you were the owner of that land. So I have come to ask for your permission."

"Woodlands?" Elgin laughed. "The only woodlands in my possession have no humans living in them. They'd make a very quiet place for one seeking solitude if you don't mind the sound of hissing. You see, the area is teeming with all manner of serpents and snakes. The place is dangerous."

"I see. But you do give me your permission?"

"I– Really, the place is uninhabitable!"

"Well, I believe God has led me to those woods. Therefore, with His help, I'll find a way– that is, if you allow me to enter the forest."

"God led you there? Not the gods? You must be one of those Christians. I've heard there are many Christians in Wales. But we do not believe in the God of the Middle East here."

"All I ask is that you let me live in the forest. I won't cause any harm to anyone."

Elgin shrugged. "You're welcome to try but please be careful."

"Thank you," she smiled.

Watching Keyne take her leave, pick up her staff and make her way out of the house and back along the path, Elgin wondered if she were actually mad.

*

"What is she doing?" Brenna giggled.

"Shhh!"

"I hate snakes!"

The sisters had trotted along the road behind Keyne at a distance to see what she might do. Passing boys collecting mud and straw to turn into daub to repair their families' houses and farmers stretching their backs out to rest a while from the back-breaking work of ploughing fields, they followed the woman who seemed oblivious to these worldly goings-on. Instead, she chanted in her unique accent as she strode on, full of purpose.

At the edge of the forest, the princess first looked out and saw the adders and grass snakes slithering about in the undergrowth. Without flinching, she lay face-down on the ground with her arms outstretched and muttered simultaneously. The girls supposed the muttering was some sort of prayer.

"She's so brave. I wouldn't go anywhere near those slimy critters!" Brenna shuddered.

"Me neither!" agreed Agnes.

Not long after the muttering began, something occurred that made the girls' jaws widen in disbelief. One by one, the snakes coiled up into circles and stopped moving. Their stripey bodies turned a sandy colour and from where the girls were crouched down, the serpents looked as hard as stone.

"It must be a miracle," Agnes murmured. "Praise the gods."

"But she prayed to her Christian God. We should thank that one," Brenna decided.

The princess couldn't hear them. She was too busy giving thanks of her own. She raised her head and looked about her with a small smile. "Thank you, Lord, for your provision," she whispered and brought herself up to a kneeling position to continue her prayer of thanksgiving.

The two sisters shot up and sprinted off to spread the word.

The locals all gathered in the woods to see if there was any substance in the girls' claims.

And when they got there, they began to proclaim:

"Upon my word!"

"Who is this foreign woman that she can make such magic?"

"So it's true! It's a miracle."

Keyne herself was nowhere to be seen. She had wasted no time in quietly making her way deeper into the woods to set up her hermitess home. To begin with, she would sleep in a makeshift shelter. In the ensuing months, she could plant wooden posts in the ground and create latticework with hazel branches for the wattle and daub walls. The structure would be thatched with reeds from the surrounding rivers. Nothing like the vast palace of her childhood and a good thing too. Keyne wished for a simple life only, one that reflected the humble life of Christ himself.

And so it was that a village grew up on the fringes of Keyne's forest and it was given the name of Keynsham, meaning Keyne's settlement. The princess never boasted about this honour, however. She was content to live a simple and humble life, telling people about Jesus and helping those in need.

Soon, though, it was time for her to journey further south. She walked for several weeks to reach the place we now call St Michael's Mount in Cornwall. In that mystical place, an island at high tide, a peninsula with a narrow ridgeway at low tide, she was overjoyed to meet up with her nephew Cadoc, son of her sister Gladws.

"Return with me to Powys, Auntie," begged Cadoc. "You have had your adventure. It is dangerous to travel alone for anyone, let alone a woman. You should be with your family, surrounded by our protection."

Keyne bristled. "I have come here on a holy pilgrimage, not an adventure. I am not ready to go back to Wales. God will tell me when it is time to do so."

"Auntie, I'm sure God wants you to return. Perhaps you need to listen more carefully to Him. Please consider your safety."

"I spend almost every hour of every day listening for God's instructions. I have heard nothing of returning to Wales at this time. Besides, the people here are desperate for me to stay. And as for safety, I have been kept safe thus far. You return to Wales with my blessing, Nephew."

Cadoc sighed and made his preparations.

Keyne set to work in Cornwall, founding a church. The well nestled beside it became holy because of her influence and the village attached to the church was named after her, but again she never once boasted of it.

Even when that work was done, she remained in England as an itinerant evangelist, preaching the basic message of Christian redemption whilst travelling around to different villages, staying in each place for only a short period of time.

A number of years later, she felt called to return to her home country, where she set up another hermitage with another holy well that was said to have healing properties.

When Keyne died at her hermitess house, her loving nephew Cadoc buried her. The villagers across Wales and England were distraught and determined to keep the memory of her alive. She was even made into a saint, who was to be remembered every 8th October.

Notes

The characters of Brenna and Agnes are fictional. The local leader's name has been lost to time but Saint Keyne did, so the story goes, ask his permission to live in the woodland as a hermitess- someone who lives in seclusion for religious reasons.

It's worth noting that *somebody* of great wealth and importance lived in Keynsham in Roman times, as a Roman villa with over 30 rooms was constructed there. In fact, it would have been inhabited by a series of important people since archaeological evidence points to occupation from the 1st century AD to the 300s and perhaps beyond. Various coins, including ones of the Emperor Valentinian (364–375), were found there. It's not clear whether the villa was occupied into the 400s as well, but so far this cannot be ruled out. The exquisite mosaics from the villa can be seen in Keynsham's library.

The reference to mud and straw used to make houses is real. A wattle and daub building was made by weaving flexible branches between vertical wooden stakes. This latticework is then daubed with a mixture of clay or mud, hay or straw and sometimes even dung for good measure! In England, this type of housing was used from prehistoric times until around the 1700s and the house would last only about 10 years or so.

All the information about St Keyne (pronounced Cane) is based on legends and her association with Keynsham is up for debate; some believe the name comes from the male name Ceagin, hence Ceagin's ham, meaning settlement. Interestingly, though, there's a primary school in Keynsham called St Keyna and its logo is a colourful ammonite. Keyna is another way of spelling Keyne. She's also known as Keynvake, Keynwen, meaning Keyne the Fair, and Cain Breit, meaning Keyne the Bright One.

The evidence for her actual existence is less shaky. If she did exist, she lived during the so-called Dark Ages and I've maintained this controversial name because it was dark in terms of the fact that there was less documentation in comparison to the Roman era, fewer engraved headstones etc and houses made not of stone but timber, which lasted a lot less time. However, it wasn't dark as in "barbaric" or "backwards". The 5th and 6th centuries were a time when the Celtic Britons in Wales had generally maintained their Christian beliefs from the Roman occupation because most of Wales wasn't conquered by the Angles, Saxons and Jutes, whereas England was invaded by those groups, who were pagan at that time. So, we see Welsh saints sailing over to England and re-Christianising the area little by little. Saints from Ireland also braved the choppy waters with the same goal. Christianity had begun to reach their shores in around 400 AD.

It's not clear when the Saxons arrived in Somerset, but it was certainly by around 650 AD, whereas Keyne lived at the latter end of the 5th century, dying in 490 or 505 AD. Some accounts say that she was born c.461 AD, thus died in her thirties or forties. The point is that she was perhaps Christianising (or re-Christianising) pagan Romano-British people and/or that she was spreading Christianity to very early Saxons.

The saint hailed from the Powys kingdom in eastern Wales. Her father married three times. He had either 17 children according to Welsh records or 24 according to Cornish records, with the latter stating that 11 of his daughters became saints.

The stone snakes in the story are actually Keynsham's local ammonites.

(This ammonite, found by an acquaintance in a Shepton Mallet field, currently lives on my kitchen windowsill!)

As for St Keyne's Welsh dialect, there wouldn't have been a language barrier between her and the inhabitants of Somerset back then. The Celts in Britain all spoke very similar languages at that time so could all understand each other and those in England had maintained their language through the Roman era, even though they became known as Romano-British. There were different accents and dialects but they could understand each other. The Anglo-Saxon conquerors might have found it tricky to understand her, though.

The place in Wales that has a well associated with Keyne could be Kentchurch just over the Welsh Border in Herefordshire or Llangeinor, mid-way between Cardiff and Swansea. According to the historian John Seal, it's more likely to be Llangeinor as it has a holy well nearby and was close to Cadoc's home base of Llancarfan. There is a chapel dedicated to her at Brecon Cathedral.

A prayer to St Keyne, who is credited with bringing Christianity to Keynsham and the village of St Keyne in Cornwall, is as follows:

Having turned serpents to stone, thou didst give thy name to Keynsham, O holy Keyna, and after thy life, resplendent with miracles, our Father Cadoc ministered to thee at thy repose. By thy prayers, may we be granted great mercy.

Chapter Bibliography

A Dictionary of Saintly Women, Volume 1 by Agnes Baillie Cunninghame Dunbar

Folklore of Somerset by Kingsley Palmer

Online Encyclopaedia Britannica

Orthodox saints of the British Isles by Dr John (Ellsworth) Hutchison-Hall

Somerset by GW Wade

The Dark Age Saints of Somerset by John Seal

The Oxford Dictionary of Saints by David Hugh Farmer

historicengland.org.uk

earlybritishkingdoms.com

QUICK TRIBUTE

[These mini sections will be about women who lived at a similar time to the chapter's main protagonist but documents mention them so briefly that I couldn't write a whole chapter on them.]

St Kew

Also known as St Kigwe or St Ciwa, this Welsh saint lived in the 500s or 600s and travelled to Cornwall via Somerset to visit her brother Docco.

She has two specific links to Somerset. The first is that Chew Valley might be named after her. The second is a village near Weston-super-Mare called Kewstoke, which could mean Kew's hamlet because it is said that she founded the church there. The evidence for Kewstoke is particularly compelling– the ancient stone steps leading from the parish church to the woodland on Monk's Hill are generally called Monk's Steps but the alternative name is St Kew's Steps.

After passing through Kewstoke (and perhaps the Chew Valley), she founded a religious centre in the Cornish village now called St Kew. When she arrived, Docco asked her to sort out a human-eating boar. She was up to the job of course and the pig even became her friend (I guess she and Bladud would've got on well).

The village of Llangiwa in southeast Wales is named after her, using the Welsh form of her name– Ciwa.

St Kew's Day falls on 8th February each year.

(Chew Valley Lake was artificially created in the early 1950s but does its name originate with St Kew?)

Sources: Orthodox saints of the British Isles by Dr John (Ellsworth) Hutchison-Hall; The Dark Age Saints of Somerset by John Seal; earlybritishkingdoms.com; www.riverchew.co.uk.

Chapter 4: A Letter to Lady G (6th century)

Dear Guinevere,

This is a letter you will never read but I wanted to write it all the same. The letter is futile, as besides being dead, you wouldn't understand Modern English. So much has changed since your time. Your beautiful language, Southwestern Brittonic, has evolved a lot over the years into various languages: Welsh and Cornish, amongst others. I'm sorry to say that here, we now speak a language not based on yours. Those Saxons you're fighting… basically eradicated England's Celtic languages, except for Cornish. We now speak a language named English, named after the Anglo-Saxons, with only a handful of Celtic words and place names, like coombe and tor. Well, anyway, here are my questions…

Firstly:

Did those feet in ancient time walk upon Cornish soils as a child? Or did your youthful lungs breathe for the first time in Wales? Or in Northumbria even? It is said that you were a princess of Roman ancestry. There are so many conflicting accounts.

There's also the question of when you lived. The Dark Ages is the most common time span. Was it in the 400s, 500s? Later or earlier? Did you live through the terrible bubonic plague of 547?

Were you Queen of Dumnonia, that Cornish kingdom that stretched as far as Wells and Glastonbury in the 6th century? Or Queen of Glastenning, a sub-kingdom of Dumnonia that comprised most of what I know as Somerset? Glastonbury might have been called Avalon in your time, but we'll get to that in a minute.

Also, they say your father sent you to marry Arthur, sending the Round Table and 100 knights along with you, that you were handed over like property from one man to another, that it was a political marriage, not a marriage of hearts. Is it true? And were you crowned at your husband's side by St Dubricius?

Secondly:

Where did you spend your adult life? Did you sweep through magnificent halls at Camelot? Was your capital where South Cadbury now lies? Cadbury means 'the stronghold of a man named Cada'. So, was it named in your time? Did you meet Cada?

The castle's eastern slope shelters Arthur's Well, which seems like another clue or it was named purely due to wishful thinking. Cadbury Castle was certainly refortified and used during the 6th century as a fortress and trading post, possibly as a Dumnonia base. An immense timber hall was erected at that time. Did you dance there?

Archaeologists also found fine red bowls and wine jars from

the Mediterranean, in addition to grey bowls from France. It astounds me to think that even then, there were extensive trading routes stretching past the Alps. Did you eat and drink from those bowls and jars while the servants recited poems?

And I wonder if the oak-lined hill was as prone to mud as it is now and if the grass shone with a bluish-green hue. It's home only to rabbits and badgers, these days. But plenty of inquisitive souls clamber up to see the vast plateau where you too might have once looked out at the panoramic views stretching out for miles and miles– Glastonbury Tor, Ham Hill, even Tintagel on a clear day (which is another candidate for Camelot).

One time, so they say, Arthur went off to fight in mainland Europe, leaving you and his nephew as regents based in Camelot. True or false?! Another of your great deeds was when Arthur's steward wished to leave court. He would not remain for Arthur's sake and so your husband turned to you and asked that you would intercede. For your sake alone, the steward stayed. Was that the case?

Thirdly:

And another thing, did Melwas ensnare you and keep you under lock and key? Was it at the Isle of Avalon, which we now call Glastonbury Tor? Did he throw you in a boat and have a lad pole the boat through the salty marshes to get there?

People have dug the ground at the Tor and found evidence for Dark-Age occupation. Plus, when the Saxons turned up at Glastonbury in 658 AD, there was already a church there. *Somebody* was living in the area at least! By the way, the name Glastonbury is due to the Saxons. Sorry to tell you but those people you're fighting all the time are going to invade this area and subjugate you Britons. Your heyday is coming to an end. Anyway, the Saxons thought of the water around there as resembling glass and so named it the stronghold of glass–Glastingeburh. Would you be sad to know that the Saxons will one day occupy these lands? Although the name Britain will live on to refer to the whole island, a new word will emerge to describe your area: Wessex, land of the West Saxons. And later, England will describe a new country formed on the island, its name derived from the conquering Angles.

But, back to your life. What was it like to be stranded on that tiny island of Avalon in the marshes, connected to the mainland only by a narrow peninsula? Was it as windy as it is nowadays? Did you have to wrap your shawl around you extra tight? Despite the climate, some claim you actually didn't mind being captured by King Melwas of Summerland, because you had more freedom there than when you were at Arthur's court. Yet, you were rescued all the same by Arthur and his knights of the Round Table.

The good news is that Glastonbury Tor has left its mark on the history of England. People have been fascinated by it for century upon century, thanks in part to you. Druids celebrate the summer solstice up there once a year, archaeologists excavate now and again, and scholars study documents related to its history.

You'd be surprised to see that Avalon isn't an island anymore after more of the marshlands were reclaimed little by little. And in fact, you'd be shocked to see Cadbury Castle abandoned with only the foundations still in place... if you existed and ever set foot in any of these places!

Fourthly:

Rumour has it that your husband was extremely unfaithful, that he had 15 children with other women scattered across the nation, while you were unable to have children. You then reached an age at which you knew you would never bear a child. Was it any wonder you couldn't resist Lancelot's love? Is it true that he became your lover? It seems there was a strong love between the two of you, that you inspired the knight to be the best version of himself once he dedicated his every action to serving you. I've even heard that you knighted Lancelot with your own hand after Arthur forgot to.

Also:

Tell me about the Lady of the Lake. Was she real? Did you meet her? There are claims that the lake from which she pulled the sword in the stone, Excalibur itself, was in Meare village, a stone's throw from Glastonbury. And did she tell Lancelot the principles of chivalry and how a knight should behave? Did this female adviser warn him to only give his heart to someone who could better him, not make him lazy? I hope that once Lancelot dedicated his every waking moment to you, it allowed for positive personal growth. Speaking of other people in the narratives, was your sister-in-law Morgaine truly evil? Did she use evil magic to try and do you wrong? Was Merlin real?

Another point:

The story goes that Arthur travelled to St Bridget's settlement at Beckery, a place very close to Glastonbury Tor (Avalon to you, I presume). You must have heard of St Bridget, the 5th-century Irish saint who, according to legends, visited the nunnery at Beckery and left behind a bag, a necklace, a little bell and some weaving tools. Back in Ireland, she was possibly consecrated as a bishop and founded the very first nunnery there. Anyway, they say that Arthur made a pilgrimage to see where the holy saint had once passed by. Inside the Beckery nunnery, Arthur was taken by a nun to the 'Chapel Adventurous', a place dedicated to St Mary Magdalene that was full of mysteries and visions. At night, he heard a voice beckoning him to the chapel so off he went. Did he really have a vision of Mary, the Mother of God, in that chapel?

And how religious were you? Were you literate? Did you write using runes?

Lastly:

They say you travelled to Wiltshire many years later and entered a nunnery at Amesbury. Or was it Caerleon at St Julius the Martyr church? It is written that you fasted, did good deeds, prayed and then became abbess until the end of your days. You probably felt at home in a position of power, like the queen of a world of women.

Did Lancelot become a monk at Glastonbury and, when you lay dying, have a vision that you were on your deathbed? Did he ride out like a knight in shining armour to be with you only to find you already dead and so he died of grief? And was your body was taken to Glastonbury for burial alongside your husband?

In conclusion:

Forgive me for being frustrated. The Medieval "history" books write all sorts about you. And is any of it even true?

Guinevere, dear Guinevere, did you live at all? Did any of these people draw breath?

Yours sincerely,

A curious mind

Notes

I decided to write a letter to the legendary Guinevere rather than a story because when researching her, there were so many different accounts, each varying massively from the others. I didn't end up with a central narrative to work with, just question upon question. So I turned those questions into a letter.

Any information about Guinevere must be taken with a pinch of salt. However, since there are so many accounts of Arthur and Guinevere, there could well be a grain of truth in some of them. And even if they are entirely fictitious, they hold a significant place in British culture. Encyclopedia.com refers to Guinevere as "one of the last of the great figures of the ancient world."

I chose the 6th century because the author duo Rosemary Clinch and Michael Williams believe that if Guinevere lived, it was at that time, and indeed encyclopedia.com lists her as dying in the 5th or 6th century. Moreover, we know that the area was extensively drained by Glastonbury Abbey, which was founded in the 7th century. So if we believe that she lived at a time when the Tor was an island connected with a narrow peninsula, as many sources claim, she must have been alive prior to when the draining began at some point after the abbey's foundation.

As for the Isle of Avalon being Glastonbury Tor, plenty of

Medieval people believed in the legendary king and queen and believed in their connection to Glastonbury. We will see this in the Quick Tribute section of Chapter 9.

In regards to the nearby Beckery, the hill there is known as Bride's Mound after St Bridget of Kildare (also known as Bride, Brigid or Brigit). Variations on the names Beckery and Bride have been used over the years. For example, Queen Elizabeth leased the land there to a nobleman in 1570 and called it Becory alias Bryde. An alternative name for Beckery is Little Ireland, due to the wider Glastonbury area's various links with Irish saints. Bridget (c.450–526) is said to have visited Somerset c.488. The Mound was excavated in the late 1800s and the foundations of a timber Saxon chapel, replaced by a stone Norman chapel, were found. Records say that the chapel was dedicated first to St Mary Magdalene and then to Bridget herself once she had died and been sainted. Hence, there is a road named Magdalene Street in Glastonbury. In the 1960s and 70s, the bones of around 63 people were found at Bride's Mound. 60 were male, 1 female and 2 were children and all were from the Saxon period. This sort of ties in with the story of Arthur visiting there, although he supposedly found a nunnery rather than a monastery, though it may have changed from one to the other over time.

In 2016, a team uncovered 7 skeletons from the 5th or early 6th century. Four of them were adult males (therefore likely to have been monks), two younger males (probably novices) and a female (probably a visiting nun). The most remarkable thing is, as the site director stated, "it's the earliest archaeological evidence we've got for monasticism" in the entire UK.

In terms of Guinevere's character, adultery is a terrible thing, however, in her case, being trapped in a marriage with an unfaithful man, it's hard to condemn her for stepping outside it when she found love but couldn't gain a divorce.

Regarding the location of Camelot, there are candidates across the nation. In Somerset, it was a Tudor man who first put forward the idea that it was Cadbury Castle, which was an Iron-Age hillfort that was refortified in the 400s for use throughout that century and the following one. When we visited, I was staggered at how immense the summit was, much larger than it looked from the bottom. The plateau is 18 acres in total. It was hard to take photos that would give you a sense of it. It's best viewed in person or on Google Earth.

(Previous page: Left: part of the ditch around Cadbury Castle's summit; right: a view from the top.)

Other place names in Somerset bear Arthur's name, for instance Arthur's Bridge, which straddles the River Alham along the road between Shepton Mallet and Castle Cary, and Arthur's Point, a little cliff overlooking the Wookey Hole caves.

As with St Keyne, Guinevere – if she existed and was Christian as the legends tell us – is another example of this new religion that emerged in the Dark Ages in England, a religion called Christianity. St Keyne's Christendom was the Celtic Church with its distinctive set of traditions, while due to Guinevere being a Romano-Briton, as the stories tell us, her Christianity would have been different in certain respects. The Romano-Briton's form of Christianity didn't take hold in England and so over the next few centuries, it would be the Celtic and the Anglo-Saxon religious customs that would shape Somerset.

Chapter Bibliography

A Companion to the Folklore, Myths & Customs of Britain by Marc Alexander

A Guide to Dark Age British Politics (documentary)

Beckery Chapel near Glastonbury 'earliest known UK monastic life' (BBC article)

Bel Mooney's Somerset by Bel Mooney

Britain AD: A Quest for Arthur England and the Anglo Saxons by Francis Pryor

encyclopedia.com

Folklore of Somerset by Kingsley Palmer

Guinevere as Lord by Anne P. Longley

Guinevere: a re-appraisal by Susann Samples

King Arthur in Somerset by Rosemary Clinch & Michael Williams

Somerset Folk Tales by Sharon Jacksties

The Story of English Literature by Anna Buckland

Wessex to 1000 A.D. by Barry Cunliffe

www.christianitytoday.com

www.friendsofbridesmound.com

QUICK TRIBUTE
The Child of Cannington

In the early 1960s, an ancient cemetery was excavated in Cannington, where prehistoric, Roman and post-Roman burials were found. On the northern edge, the grave of a (possibly female) teenager, who is believed to have lived in the 6th or 7th century, was marked by a path leading up to it and by a slab and mound of earth over her body. Although she had no grave goods, two pieces of decorated stone were found there. One, a triangular stone with lines carved into it, might have been a grave marker or headstone. All of this suggests that she was particularly important to others and that the deceased girl was visited and worshipped.

She might have been a pagan princess, but it seems that more evidence points to her being a Christian holy person, perhaps even a martyr and/or saint.

We will probably never know why this person, aged around 13, was buried with such care. The authors of 'Cannington Cemetery' poignantly state: "It is sad that there is no well-known local legend of such a young individual, for which the archaeological evidence would be perfectly complementary. Too often we have the legend without any supporting evidence; here we have the evidence without the legend."

The village priest at the time of the excavations became interested in the girl, deciding that she was the first identifiable Christian to have lived in Cannington. In the late 1960s, her bones were placed in a coffin and ceremoniously reburied inside the parish church (St Mary the Virgin). They placed a limestone slab over her body with the inscription: "The child of Cannington. The name is known to God." Above her grave is a small wooden sculpture of a girl in a simple dress. Each year, a small replica of this statue is awarded to a Cannington resident to celebrate their services to the village.

There is no trace of the cemetery nowadays as a result of

extensive quarrying. Below is a field near Cannington.

Sources: Cannington Cemetery: Excavations 1962–3 of prehistoric, Roman, post-Roman, and later features at Cannington Park Quarry, near Bridgwater, Somerset by Philip Rahtz, Sue Hirst and Susan M Wright, The Somerset Village Book by the Somerset Federation of Women's Institutes, www.cannington.org.uk, www.somersetheritage.org.uk.

WESSEX

Chapter 5: Ethelburg's Exit (7th–8th century)

How had it come to this?

Her name was Ethelburg, meaning noble stronghold or fortress. And yet here she was gazing into the ashes of the ruined fortification of Taunton. A gentle breeze tickled the leaves of the trees on the lonely hill she was standing on with shaky legs. The hill was quiet, her warriors subdued and the roar of the flames far away. The distant smoke danced before her eyes, forming images that retold the story of the whole fifty years of her life so far.

Ethelburg first saw a crown in the smoke, representing how she had married Ine as a teenager and risen to power by his side soon afterwards. She remembered how the start of her long and turbulent tenure as queen had begun.

In the year 685, the pagan Caedwalla had emerged from exile in Sussex to battle his way to the throne. Then, completely out of the blue, King Caedwalla became a Christian. Just three years into his kingship, he felt weighed down with remorse for seizing the throne and for his heathen beliefs. His remorse grew and grew to the point where he decided to abdicate. Caedwalla left Wessex for good to spend the rest of his days as a pilgrim in Rome, where he was baptised by the pope himself. This new life was incredibly short-lived: Caedwalla died a few days later. Caedwalla's sudden departure left Wessex in disarray. A struggle for power ensued. Ethelburg's husband Ine successfully grappled his way to the top and took the throne with Ethelburg at his side.

Straight away, he set to work on a law code. "I feel concerned for the welfare of the Britons in this land, dear wife," he told her. "I may be a Saxon, but I aim to be fair to them. Since many of them are enslaved, I will enact a law stating that not even enslaved people can be made to work on Sundays."

"I agree, husband," Ethelburg replied. "After all, slaves have souls and can be converted to the Christian faith. Sundays should be for confessing, praying and worshipping."

A baby now appeared to materialise out of smoke matter. This was apt as Ine and Ethelburg's piety had led to the creation of a law instructing their citizens to baptise newborn babies within 30 days of birth, lest they die unbaptised and float forever outside of heaven. After all, why else did babes cry during baptism if it were not the Devil himself escaping from their bodies? Indeed, no lytling should suffer for all eternity as a result of their parents' lack of foresight and heel-dragging. Failure to baptise in time incurred a fine of 30 shillings. If avoiding the torment of everlasting Limbo for their baby wasn't enough of an incentive, then a hefty penalty would be. The queen and king were proud of their provision for the innocent ones.

Then Ethelburg thought she saw a palace emerging from the clouds of smoke. It took her back to the time when her husband had constructed a temporary palace in Paredton and they had dwelt there for a time while he strengthened their hold on the River Parrett area with its collection of boggy islands in the marshes. In truth, the whole time she had been Queen of Wessex, there had been endless fighting in order for her husband to retain control of his lands and conquer new territory.

Not long after their stay at Paredton, they moved on to their newly built earthen castle at Taunton. She closed her eyes in pain at the memory. Although it was constructed 22 years ago, it seemed like only yesterday. That castle was presently a smouldering wreckage.

Ethelburg put that difficult recollection to one side and thought instead of the friends they had had.

Aldhelm was the first to spring to mind. Dear, gentle and scholarly Aldhelm, a relative of Ine's. Together the three of them had set up a church to St Andrew in Wells in 705. Besides that, Aldhelm founded a monastery to St John at the side of an ancient spring in the royal forest of Selwood and the settlement of Frome 'sprang up' from there. Further south, Aldhelm dedicated a church to St Peter in Bruton, while the royals established a church to St Mary there.

When they weren't busy founding churches, they had whiled away the hours listening to his tales of things such as his studies at Canterbury. Aldhelm had listened intently any time his respected teacher, Abbot Adrian, had spoken about his native land in North Africa, of the Berber people. Aldhelm himself had memorised these fascinating narratives and enthralled the queen and king with them.

The next smoky form to appear was an altar, reminding her of the story Aldhelm had told of his holy expedition to Rome upon being invited there by the pope himself. How she had gasped to hear that Aldhelm had got a camel to help him carry home a collection of relics and a marble altar. When they reached the Alps, the animal slipped. The heavy altar hit the ground and broke in two, crushing the camel as it fell. In hindsight, Aldhelm realised that was to be expected— after all, camels were not created for snowy peaks. But when it occurred, rather than panic, Aldhelm trusted in God. He made the sign of the cross, which was enough to heal the camel and repair the altar.

"Of course, you will be more likely to gain a place in heaven having been there," remarked Ethelburg. "And it sounds like a treacherous journey, so you have earned your place in sweat and tears!"

"Thank you, my lady," replied Aldhelm gracefully. "May I

present to you the altar itself?"

Before their astonished eyes, Aldhelm brought forward the altar, pointing to the crack down the middle where the miraculous restoration had happened. In awe of this proof, they placed the artefact in their church dedicated to St Mary in Bruton.

The marvels of Aldhelm didn't stop there. Some 17 years back, the king and queen had founded Sherborne Abbey and Aldhelm had become its first-ever bishop, titled the Bishop of Selwoodshire. His role was to oversee religious matters for the whole area to the west of the Forest of Selwood- Somersetshire, Dorset and Devonshire. Ethelburg and Ine trusted him deeply in this position, bestowing gifts to help him in his new role such as 7 hides of land near Priddy. He leapt into the role with energy and excitement. He would go about the ordinary folk, joking around to get their attention and then singing hymns and reading the gospel to them.

Yet how short-lived Aldhelm's time as bishop was! Just five years later, he visited Doulting on tour through the villages of Mendip. There at the well, the old man breathed his last. Yet even in death, he left a gift for his people- many miraculous healings were now associated with the waters there.

The queen went there in person not long after to pay her respects. On the steep verge to the side of the well, she stood beneath the gnarled trees with their roots jutting out and tangling together on the ground. The roots were like tentacles that seemed to be gripping at her heart while tears streamed from her eyes. She and her ladies climbed the grass-lined knoll nearby and looked out at the breathtaking view of the surrounding landscape that stretched to Glastonbury Tor and beyond. They said a prayer for Aldhelm's soul and for themselves, that they might have the strength to bear the loss.

Her heart ached to think that the people of Wessex had lost such a vibrant man and to think of his inkpot going dry, for he would never write another hymn, poem or treatise.

No amount of funerary splendour could take away their pain, but it was fitting that the country be given the chance to say a proper farewell to their friend and shepherd. The funeral cortege set out from Doulting and made a 37-mile journey to Malmsbury, stopping every 7 miles or so to erect a stone cross. The first place to receive a cross was Frome, a settlement he had sparked into life with the monastery he'd set up there. Crowds came out to weep and watch. Little girls picked flowers to place on the coffin. The men who heaved the cross into place never once complained, though their muscles visibly strained with the effort.

Around the same time, Ethelburg and Ine lost two more friends– Dominica and Indract. The sister and her brother, a deacon, were of Irish royalty. Returning from Rome on a pilgrimage with nine companions, Dominica and Indract had stopped off at Glastonbury to worship God and venerate the saints, particularly the grave that the abbey's monks claimed belonged to St Patrick, who was their fellow countryman. When the travellers visited the royal court at Paredton, Ethelburg was enchanted by their tales of Rome, that far-off sacred city.

"How I would love to set foot on that hallowed ground!" exclaimed Ethelburg at the time.

"Rome is wonderful, but Glastonbury is magnificent too," Dominica soothed. "Its alternative name of 'Second Rome' is well-deserved, for a whole multitude of saints are buried here or associated with the town. We have seen our countryman St Patrick's tomb and worshipped at St Bridget's Chapel at Beckery."

"We are blessed indeed to be surrounded by holy people, both dead and alive." These are the words Ethelburg wished she had said at that time but in actual fact, she merely smiled and sighed to think of the capital of the Papal States.

Having paid homage to the queen and king, Dominica and her brother settled in the Polden Hills, believing it to be a safe place. But – and this was the part that filled Ethelburg with shame and distress – a band of servants from the royal court thought that the travelling group were rich merchants whose bags were filled with treasures. The band mistook the pilgrims' brass-tipped walking poles for staffs plated with gold. Ruthlessly, the servants killed all 11 of them in Shapwick or was it Huish Episcopi? The endless tales that stampeded through the county to eventually reach the royals' ears differed on that point. Ethelburg for a time had been obsessed with finding out the location to know where her friends had breathed their last. But she had to give up and try to move on with her life. No matter where Dominica, Indract and the others died, the brutes threw the devout companions into a deep pit nearby, only to find seeds and bedding in the pilgrims' bags.

On the night of the martyrdom, the king and queen were tucked into their comfortable bed at Paredton Palace. Yet neither could sleep. Looking out of their palace window, they saw a column of fire lighting up the sky, just as the fire at Taunton would later illuminate the landscape. It looked most unnatural. At the first break of dawn, they rushed out with servants to see what this wondrous sign might mean. Upon searching the area, they found the pitiful sight. Ine and Ethelburg took it upon themselves to honour the siblings and their companions in death, as they had been unable to prevent their deaths. Lovingly, they took the corpses to the church at Glastonbury, which had been restored and re-founded by the royals, and buried the martyrs there in the Lady Chapel. Like Aldhelm, they became saints, remembered for the miraculous fire, and people would come from far and wide to venerate their shrine. And the pillar of fire would appear every now and then as a terrible omen of impending doom.

How blessed Ethelburg felt to have met such wonderful people in her life and how wretched she felt to know they were gone. Ethelburg shed a tear at the thought.

That episode served to remind her of how fragile Christianity was in the kingdom and of the difficulties of living in a multicultural and multireligious land when neither side showed any sign of wanting to tolerate the other.

Perhaps it was grief for Aldhelm, Dominica and Indract that had made her husband so determined to invade northern Dumnonia and bring the Celtic Christians there into the Saxon Church. He was successful in this, which added greatly to their sense of security.

That security was not to last forever, though. Her mind hurtled forward to the discord that was now raging between alternative claimants to Ine's throne, claimants who would displace her just the same and put another woman in her stead. One of those was Ealdbert, who had shut himself up in Taunton castle, a fort that her husband had built. He would not come out, which was why Ethelburg had besieged the settlement.

And so it was that on that day in 722, Queen Ethelburg of Wessex, her veil blowing in the wind underneath her golden crown, had ordered the destruction of Taunton.

"My lady, my lady." A soldier came jogging up to her.

"Speak," she replied numbly.

"None of us can understand it. We cannot fathom how it happened. But…" He paused.

"Well?"

"Ealdbert has escaped."

Ethelburg almost took the Lord's name in vain in her anger. She had burnt down this whole fortress to be rid of him and yet he had managed to sneak away.

"Has anyone gone looking for him?"

"Yes. They're scouting along the road leading west to Dumnonia."

"Send a troop out in each of the other three directions, then. Quickly."

"Yes, my lady."

The civil war was far from over.

*

Four years had now passed since the obliteration of Taunton, since her husband had ridden to that hilltop and expressed immense pride in her. Despite destroying what he had once built and despite not eradicating the target, she had shown courage and grit. And although Ealdbert was still alive, he had fled and an enemy on the run is always better than an enemy with a fortress under their command. Ine had likened his wife to Seaxburg, who had ruled Wessex some fifty years previously. Seaxburg had first ruled for many decades in the role of consort, supporting her husband the king, then, following his death she had ruled in her own right over the course of a year.

After the debacle at Taunton, nearly four years of battles ensued. It was only recently, a few months ago, that the threat of Ealdbert had been quashed once and for all: the rebel had finally been killed in battle. Years of civil war had taken their toll on the royals' well-being and the months that had passed since the end of it had dulled the strain on their nerves but not removed it. Ever since the Witan had elected Ine as King of Wessex, it had been twenty long years of rule and strife, sweetened now and then by friends and faith.

Ethelburg was exhausted. And she was in her mid-50s, too old for all this fighting. Nodding to herself and gazing out of her bedchamber window, she knew it was time to put her plan into action.

The previous day, the royal couple had sat down with the ladies and lords of the realm for an ostentatious feast in the long hall at the royal house they were currently staying at. The servants had busied themselves for days beforehand displaying the best wall hangings and cleaning the royals' best gold and silver vessels. The finest wild game, fish and fruit were served, washed down with the sweetest wine and ale. Ine and his men had stayed up late in drunken revelry while Ethelburg had sighed at the silliness of it all and retired to bed early.

Groaning at the sound of her husband's loud snores, she slipped out of the room and went to find the steward.

"You, man, come here. As you know, we plan to take our leave of this palace today and travel westwards to another. After you and the other servants have stripped this house bare of all the furnishings, I have additional instructions for you."

She went into detail about her plan, at which the steward replied, "My lady?" His face was a picture of utter astonishment.

"You heard me. See to it that it is done. And not a word to the king!"

"Yes, my lady."

She couldn't help but grin to watch him strolling off, shaking his head in bewilderment, probably cross at how much extra work she had just created for him. Not only did the servants have to carry out their usual task of removing every single footrest, ornately carved chair, chest and any other furniture as well as pack up the silver basins, goblets, spoons and all the other plateware, now they also had to set up Ethelburg's plan *and* clean it away afterwards!

Later that day, they began their procession with their servants and horses carrying their possessions on to their next lodgings. Whilst still on the palace grounds, Ethelburg stopped and looked her husband straight in the eye. "My lord, turn back to the royal house that we have just now departed." His eyes fell on her quizzically. "It will do you great good to see it in its current state."

"Current state, wife? I saw our people remove all the fineries. I know what it shall look like."

"I think what meets your eye there will surprise you."

"Very well. Halt here, everyone, I say. Bring me the keys to the house. My wife and I shall return forthwith."

They hastened back. Ine was impatient to begin their onward expedition and wanted to get his wife's strange request out of the way. The large single-storey timber building looked as it usually did from the outside, its wooden columns spaced a few inches apart with wattle and daub in between each oak post. Yet, before they opened the heavy door, Ine nearly choked on the foul smell that was hanging heavily in the air. His face went bright red and he chortled, "Who has created such a stench?"

"Open the door, husband."

He did so and a terrible scene met his eyes. The floors in the palace's long hall, made of rammed earth, were strewn with vegetable peelings, dirt, cattle dung and all manner of foul things that lay festering everywhere. Even the fire logs in the central pit were covered with filth. *Even* the raised platform where skilfully crafted chairs usually sat ready to receive the royals' bodies!

"What is the meaning of this? It is here that I hold court, entertain honoured guests, host meetings with councillors. These disgusting articles belong in the rubbish piles of the palace's farming quarters, in the kitchens. Who dares to disgrace our hall?"

"The bedroom is worse, husband." Her voice was so calm. What was going on?

Frowning, he entered their chamber. Upon the oak-framed bed, with its intricate carvings of dragons and knots, was a sow suckling her litter.

"Who has done such a thing? Have they no respect for their king?" he thundered.

"I ordered it, husband. And I shall tell you why. Yesterday, this place was bursting with splendour and majesty. Now, it is full of rotten, decaying matter. Here we see how the grandeur of this world is fleeting and passes away in the blink of an eye. Even our palace is temporary. Why, the oak shingles on the roof will last but twenty-five years. Our fine rings and gold chains...

all are meaningless in comparison to what really matters in life. We must leave behind worldly goods and focus our minds on spiritual matters. I have said this to you before. We are getting old and our time left upon this earth is but short. As St Paul wrote to the Colossians, 'Fix your minds on heavenly things, not on earthly things'."

For a moment, he was speechless. Then, he contended with, "That's all very well, wife. But we are the rulers of this land. We cannot spend all day in prayer when there are matters of state to deal with."

"You are right. A sovereign cannot dedicate his life solely to God, but a former sovereign can. My dear, in the same way that Caedwalla and his wife, Cynethrith, abdicated the throne, so now must you and I. We have expanded and strengthened Wessex from the River Tamar in the west to beyond London in the east. It is time to leave the kingdom to a younger man and woman. Having no children of our own, we have nothing to keep us in the kingdom."

He leaned against a doorway and let her words sink in. Merriment was all well and good, but he had had too much of it since they'd defeated Ealdbert and it did not nourish his soul anymore. Besides which, he'd had enough of the difficulties that came hand-in-hand with governing a kingdom.

Smiling indulgently, he commented, "I suppose you have been

praying to St James, patron of pilgrims."

Her smile in return confirmed his supposition. "Where do you suggest we go, wife?"

"Remember how Dominica and Indract exalted the marvels of Rome, husband? And how that was the city Caedwalla chose when he abdicated? I had thought it would do just as well for us, a place where we could serve God."

"To retire to Rome as a pilgrim. How well it sounds. Very well, wife. You have succeeded. We must gradually put our affairs in order so as to journey forth to the holy city, meet with Our Father, Pope Gregory II, and live out the rest of our days in simplicity and humility."

"Yes, husband. And in light of the fact that we have no children to bequeath our lands to, I had thought of giving certain portions of it to the Church at Glastonbury. Lands such as Brent, Pilton, Bleadney, the quarries at Doulting, the fisheries on the Isle of Meare, the islands of Beckery and Godney..."

He chuckled. "My, my, you have been busy plotting and scheming! At our next stopping point, I will fetch a scribe to me that we may begin this loosening of our ties to Wessex. Lands at Ilminster would do nicely for the monastery at Muchelney, say I."

"Now, the matter of who will replace us as rulers–"

"I suppose you have thought of that as well."

"It goes without saying that the Witan council must select the next king. But we might suggest my brother Athelheard to be supported by his wife, Frithugyth."

"In all honesty, I cannot think of a better pair. Wessex would be in good hands with them. We shall call the Witan at once to let them know of our resignation."

On account of their decision, they called the local leaders together for a Witan meeting. Stood before the noblemen of the realm, they officially resigned from their positions. Over the coming days, the Witan council spoke at length together to appoint their next sovereign. As hoped, Athelheard was chosen.

Having put aside their crowns and their jewels, Ethelburg and Ine rode, sailed and trekked for over a thousand miles to a land they had never seen before. With buoyant hearts, the royals left behind the heavy weight of queenship and kingship, and travelled in pursuit of holiness as common people with plain clothing. Ine even had his head shaved like a monk's. King Ine was now simply Ine, and Queen Ethelburg was Ethelburg.

Finally, the longed-for city of Rome came into sight, where they met the pope and were baptised by his hand, still in plain clothes and with no jewels adorning their bodies. They lived as they had travelled– in simplicity and with kindness. Ethelburg and her husband were also anxious for all pilgrims from

England to find shelter and assistance in the city and so were moved to set up an English pilgrimage hospice and accommodation centre in Rome.

Two short years later, in 728, Ine departed this life and was buried in the Papal capital at the church dedicated to St Peter. Ethelburg, noblewoman, queen, pilgrim, then finally commoner, decided to add one more string to her bow- nun. Arriving back on her native shores, she chose to live out the remainder of her life at Barking Abbey in London in Mercia.

When in 740, Ethelburg finally took her leave of this world, she looked back in wonder at all she had seen and done, and all the people she had met. The one detail that stood out in all of it was, she remembered with a smirk, filling the royal house with animal muck, filth and a suckling pig.

Notes

Seaxburg (or Seaxburh), where seax means knife and burg a fortified settlement, was queen consort of Wessex from 643 to 672, by which point Somerset was a part of Wessex. She then ran the country alone as queen regnant for slightly more than a year. Female rulers were incredibly rare in Anglo-Saxon England. She was called a "woman of courage" and of a "subtle and extensive genius". However, misogyny caught up with her soon enough. The noblemen removed her in 674 because they refused to obey the commands of a female head of state and chroniclers snubbed her by not stating her ancestry or outlining what happened to her after she was kicked out of office. I could only find vague links to Somerset through her husband and so decided against giving her a full chapter. She needed a shout-out at least, though!

Ethelburg (or Ethelburh) (died c.740) ruled as consort from 688 to 726, yet we know little of her ancestry. She was certainly part of the nobility and it's been stated that she was distantly related to Caedwalla. Sadly, a lot of old genealogies for the Dark Ages and Anglo-Saxons don't even mention the women, not even queens! Ethelburg's brother Athelheard is the only relative of hers mentioned frequently in historical documents.

Ine was descended from previous kings and had 2 sisters (Cwenburh and Cuthburh, who both took holy orders) and a brother. The laws that Ine put in place in Wessex marked "the end of tribalism and the beginning of the state" according to Barry Cunliffe. I believe Ethelburg might have helped establish some of the laws, which are the earliest surviving laws of Wessex. The laws show concern for those at the longest rungs of the ladder, including slaves, though the scales are still tipped very much towards favouring the Anglo-Saxon rulers over the subjugated Britons.

Ethelburg was certainly associated with some of her husband's acts of devotion, including the establishment of Wells' first-ever church. Other acts that the chroniclers attribute only to Ine, I have attributed to both because they fit in with this image of a pious woman. Women were scarcely mentioned in ancient records and so we have to pencil them back in where it seems appropriate. For instance, we know that she persuaded her husband to retire to Rome, so it makes sense that she helped bury St Dominica and St Indract, who were killed c.710, and that she was friends with St Aldhelm.

As for Aldhelm, he was a relative of King Ine's, possibly his nephew. Aldhelm became the Bishop of Selwoodshire (later called the Diocese of Sherborne) in 705. His English writings, which were hymns and songs, have been lost to time, yet some of his Latin writings have survived including a poem written as a tribute to holy maidens and a treatise on virginity.

The stone church in Doulting dates back to the 1100s but may have replaced an older wooden church. Amazingly enough, it has a gargoyle eating an unbaptised baby, perhaps a nod to King Ine's law codes. The charming well is tucked away on a little parcel of land, just on the edge of the village. The historian Ethelbert Horne dubbed it "one of the most authentic holy wells of Somerset".

St Aldhelm's Well in Doulting is shown on the next page.

It's no surprise that the royals had various links to Somerset since along with Dorset, Wiltshire and Hampshire, it formed the Wessex heartlands. As such, regarding other places mentioned in this chapter, the palace at 'Paredton' is in the village we now call South Petherton and stood somewhere to the south of the church. A house there was given the name of King Ina's Palace (an alternative spelling of the king's name). It dates back to the 1300s but whether it was built on the site of the royal palace is contentious.

Ine granted hundreds of acres of land at Ilminster to the monastery at Muchelney (later called Muchelney Abbey), which was founded by the king himself. The locations referenced in the document whereby Ine granted lands to Glastonbury are Brent Knoll, Middlezoy, Westonzoyland, Pilton, Doulting, Bleadney, Meare, Beckery, Godney, Marchey, Nyland (now part of Axbridge), Pennard (unclear whether East or West) and the Polden Hills, which extend over 10 miles from Street towards the west. In Ethelburg's days, Brent Knoll, Bleadney, Beckery, Nyland, Meare, Marchey and Godney were islands, Westonzoyland and Middlezoy were on Sowy island and the Polden Hills formed a peninsula ridge that reached out to the west. In fact, there were over 100 islands in the Somerset marshes before peat began to reshape the terrain and, piece by piece, land was reclaimed over the centuries. The Romans first started to reclaim Somerset land but they focussed on the Axe Valley rather than the Brue Valley, which was slowly drained after Ethelburg's time.

The land donation gives us an insight into the king's extensive wealth that was then bestowed to Glastonbury, adding to their wealth. It shows what Ine was willing to give up at his wife's request! Ethelburg was present for the drawing up of the manuscript and is referred to as the second witness for it. She is listed only under the king himself and thus shown precedence over anyone named below her.

Ethelburg's contemporaries certainly didn't see her military operation at Taunton as problematic. In fact, she was sainted after her death and, according to some sources, so was her husband. Her feast day is sometimes recorded as 9th July and at others as 6th February, the latter in conjunction with her husband's feast day. This idea of celebrating both wife and husband on the same day shows that they were viewed as a team who had acted together on many matters.

(Marshland near Meare)

Alive towards the latter end of the Age of Saints (c.450–c.750), Ethelburg and her fellow saints were part of an evangelising movement that aimed to convert pagan rulers and society at large. By her time, paganism had been largely pushed out of Somerset to Dumnonia.

It's worth noting that so far, all the saints I've written about in this book were noble-born, even if they chose lives of poverty. Society seemed to be sainting the nobility left, right and centre back then. In fact, it was easier to become a saint before the strict canonisation process was enforced in the twelfth century. Before then, a saint didn't necessarily have to have performed a miracle, for instance.

The historian Agnes Baillie Cunninghame Dunbar describes Ethelburg as "the first English queen to visit Rome". Incidentally, the hospice and accommodation centre for English pilgrims that Ine and Ethelburg set up there flourished for about 300 years. Two hundred years after its demise, it inspired others to set up an English pilgrimage centre in Rome in 1362, which was refounded as a seminary in 1576. Named the English College, it is still going strong.

Ethelburg's successor as Queen of Wessex, her sister-in-law Frithugyth (who reigned 726–740), also journeyed to Rome. Along with the Bishop of Sherborne, Frithugyth went on pilgrimage to Rome in 737. It was a popular destination for the

Wessex royals at that time and they probably took the same arduous route as Aldhelm, i.e. over the Alps. Before this journey, Frithugyth went a step further than Ethelburg, who granted land alongside her husband. Frithugyth granted land in her own right- namely, land at Taunton given to the Church at Winchester, and land at Brompton Regis given to Glastonbury Abbey. Frithugyth and her husband had no known children and were succeeded by another relative.

As a final note, this was not the last time that Taunton would be set fire to! During another civil war, the eastern part of the town was set alight in 1645 by the royalists.

Chapter Bibliography

1911 Encyclopaedia Britannica, Volume 14

A Dictionary of Saintly Women, Volume 1 by Agnes Baillie Cunninghame Dunbar

A History of the County of Somerset: Volume 2, edited by William Page

Authority and Gender in Medieval and Renaissance Chronicles, edited by Juliana Dresvina and Nicholas Sparks

historicengland.org.uk

King Ine of Wessex by Jean Harper

Lives of British Saints by Vladimir Moss

Online catalogue of Anglo-Saxon charters

oxfordreference.com

South Petherton in the Olden Time by Hugh Norris

Tales of Old Somerset by Sally Norris

The Avenel Dictionary of Saints by Donald Attwater

The Place Names of Somerset by James S Hill

The Saxon bishops of Wells, a historical study in the tenth century by J. Armitage Robinson

Wessex to 1000 A.D. by Barry Cunliffe

Women in world history: a biographical encyclopedia, Volume 14 by Anne Commire & Deborah Klezmer

Ine, The First King of Wessex by Ray Gibbs

The Celtic Church in Somerset by HM Porter

www.encyclopedia.com

www.oldenglishtranslator.co.uk

www.pase.ac.uk

QUICK TRIBUTES

Abbess Bertana

In the 7th century, when Bath formed the southern tip of Hwicce (a sub-kingdom of Mercia), we find a charter stating that on 6th November 676, King Osric of Hwicce granted 100 hides of land (i.e. enough land to support 100 peasants) to Abbess Bertana to set up a nunnery there, which was the first-ever religious house in the town. The King of Wessex had to give his stamp of approval for the endowment. It is believed Bertana was of French origin but little else about her can be inferred. We can't know anything about her personality (she might've been horrible!) but she is an example of a woman in leadership who started a new community from scratch, possibly in a foreign land.

Another charter for the nunnery was written around the year 681 and granted lands to the women. By then, the abbess was Bernguidis and the prioress was Folcburga.

Sadly, the convent at Bath lasted only 80 years, if that. It was destroyed before 758 and re-founded exclusively as a house of monks.

Sources: Proceedings of the Society of Antiquaries of London. Second Series, Vol. VII; www.wessexarch.co.uk; Two Chartularies R717 of the Priory of St. Peter at Bath– The Somerset Record Society; www.british-history.ac.uk

Lulla of Baltonsborough

On 10th July 744, during the reign of Athelheard and Frithugyth, a document was written up in which Lulla gave lands at Baltonsborough to Glastonbury Abbey and she placed nearby lands at Lottisham and Lydford-on-Fosse at the King of Mercia's disposal. This is because Mercia had gained substantial influence over Wessex at that time and had even taken some parts of Wessex including Somerton. Lulla is described as a handmaid of Christ, denoting that she took holy orders. Her possession of vast areas of land shows she was most likely noble and, as Elizabeth Rees emphasises, possibly a foremother or great-great-great aunt to Dunstan since how many noble families could come from a place as small as Baltonsborough at that time? That would make her an ancestral relative of Elfleda too, who will we meet in the following chapter.

The same author believes she was possibly the abbess of a double monastery- a religious house of both monks and nuns that was ruled by either an abbot or abbess. That's right- there were Anglo-Saxon monks being ruled by women! This idea began in the 600s, was outlawed in the late 700s and re-emerged again in the 1100s and 1200s.

Sources: Early Christianity in South-West Britain: Wessex, Somerset, Devon, Cornwall and the Channel Islands by Elizabeth Rees; A History of the County of Somerset: Volume 9, Glastonbury and Street edited by R W Dunning; Online catalogue of Anglo-Saxon charters.

St Thecla

An early Celtic name for Street is Lantokay (or Lantocal), where llan means the enclosed area around a church i.e. a settlement.

The second part could be a reference to the male saint St Kea, who was associated with Arthur, or to St Thecla, who lived in the 1st century AD.

The evidence for Thecla being linked to Street is that its parish church is consecrated to the Holy Trinity but some records state that centuries ago, the village had a church dedicated to St Thecla. This church may or may not have been in the same place as the current church and would've been built during the Roman occupation (probably after 380 when the Roman Empire became Christian) or soon afterwards. Interestingly, Roman pottery, parts of a wall and parts of 2 wells have been found in the church graveyard.

A new church was built in the Middle Ages and dedicated to St Gildas, a 6th-century monk who spent time in the Glastonbury area. So it would seem the Thecla church predated Gildas' time, but the name Lantokay was still in use until at least the late 7th century. By 1066, the name Leigh was being used for the village instead.

A pub in Street bears the name Lantokay, which in my opinion should be reintroduced as a more beautiful and less confusing name for the town itself.

On the following page, we have a window inside the parish church in Street that depicts St Gildas and St Dunstan alongside Biblical figures, but sadly St Thecla is absent.

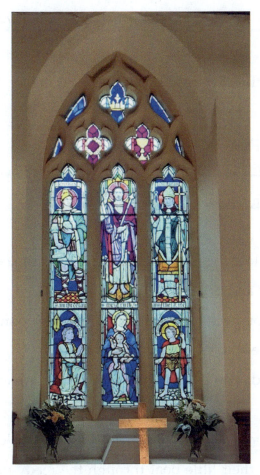

Sources: *Glastonbury: Her Saints* by Lionel Smithett Lewis, *A History of Street* by Roger Burdock, *A Visitor's Guide to Holy Trinity Church*.

Chapter 6: Albion's Fate in Athelney's Hands (9th century)

"It's horrible here, Mother! These boggy marshes stink."

"I know, little Edward, but we have no choice. We must be brave."

"I no want speak Viking."

"Ethelgeofu! It won't come to that. We won't have to succumb to the Danish language or their ways."

"I'm cold."

"If we stay close together, Aethelflaed, we will keep warm."

"I'm hungry and tired too."

"Be quiet. You need to set an example to the younger ones."

"Mother, I need to empty my bladder."

"Oh, Edward. You'll have to go in this pot. We can't afford to stop."

Like a mama bear, Ealswitha kept her head held high as the men punted their little boat through the reedy marshlands of Somerset in the spring of 878. She tried not to think of the indignity of a Wessex prince peeing into a pot in plain sight. Wrapped in thick woollen shawls and huddled next to her were her daughters Aethelflaed, aged 8, Ethelgeofu, aged 3, and Elthrith, just a baby, along with her son, Edward, aged 4.

Carrying and giving birth to those children, in addition to the ones who had died in infancy, had been a huge strain on her body. With gritted teeth, she had pushed them out of her body one by one and had fiercely protected and cared for them afterwards. She had not gone through all of that to give up now. She was a survivor, through and through. After all, her very name Ealswitha meant all-strong. Her Mercian parents had gifted it to her in the hope that it would give her courage in times of trouble, and times couldn't be more troublesome than at that moment.

At the head of the boat, sat on a rustic plank of wood balanced across the boat, was the father of those children– King Alfred of Wessex, son of King Aethelwulf and Osburh, the daughter of Aethelwulf's cupbearer and an extremely devout and honourable woman of noble ancestry. Ealswitha and Alfred had married young, a year before Aethelflaed's birth. Now, they were practically the last royal family left in England thanks to the Vikings.

Despite Alfred's military prowess, they had found themselves on the run from the Vikings. Somerset was the only safe haven left for the royal family and a few soldiers, servants and slaves who had stayed by their side. Ironically, it was the very danger of the marshlands – the bogs, the entangling reeds and the isolation – that made them safe for the time being.

The future of their kingdom rested on their shoulders alone. Ealswitha's daughter, Ethelgeofu, had voiced their greatest fear– that the Danes would overrun the whole island and they would have to speak Danish, convert to the Viking religion and be utterly subordinate to the Danes. That is, those of them whose lives would be spared. Alfred would be put to death without question.

How tired she was from all the worry. They had arrived in these low-lying terrains in January ever since they had been attacked at their royal manor in Chippenham just after celebrating the Twelfth Night of Christmas there. Memories of feasting, lyres, harps, jugglers, dancing turned to enemies arriving in the dead of night. The Vikings, led by Guthrum, with the aim of assassinating them all in her beds. She shuddered at the thought.

The family had fled at once with very few provisions, almost with just the clothes on their backs and few servants, slaves and soldiers. A few days after their hurried departure, Ealswitha was dismayed to discover that her monthly blood had come and she had no sanitary cloths to hand. How she had longed for some linen pads stuffed with sheep's wool. In the bitter cold, she did not think it wise to rip her petticoat to shreds. Instead, she had been forced to make do with dry moss from the Wiltshire countryside and prayed that no infection would follow. Her life had become totally undignified.

And their woes had gone on and on. They had not had a moment's rest ever since that night when they began their rapid, stealthy trek from Wiltshire to Somerset. It was now nearly Easter– nearly 11 weeks, two-and-a-half months, of flooded roads, remote forests, a crying babe, trepidation, icy cold hands, boats getting tangled in the marshland reeds, sleeping in tents or locals' shacks, nightmares of Vikings and eating whatever they could find or receiving hand-outs from loyal villagers. They had even resorted to attacking and raiding not only various groups of Vikings but also local people who had submitted to the invaders. The rulers who had once set out the laws of the land were now the ones breaking them; the raided people had become the raiders!

How humiliating to raid like that, not just because theft was so abhorrent but also because certain people were refusing to help their own king. For they had begged alms from the rural folk and often found nobody willing to give. Ealswitha understood that times were hard and the Vikings had looted and pillaged towns to the point of deep poverty, yet this was their king, their royal family, asking for help in a time of need.

And this was no normal life for princes and princesses. They were used to being pampered and now found themselves living from hand to mouth with humble folk or in tents, constantly on the move. They would awake screaming in the night from their nightmares and patiently Ealswitha had comforted them back to sleep.

Twenty-nine-year-old Alfred's nerves had never been good, but they were more frayed than ever out here in the swamps. One day, they had found shelter from the pouring rain at a cow herder's modest dwelling. Ealswitha and the children had fallen asleep in exhaustion and Alfred had been left to watch over some bread in the oven, lest it burn. The herder and his wife had had to step out. Well, his mind must have wandered off to strategising battle plans against the Danes, for the bread burnt to a crisp and was not fit to be eaten even by dogs. The cow herder's wife had berated him, wailing that rich folk had no idea what amount of effort goes into creating food. She was exasperated that she had wasted all those hours and energy cultivating and harvesting wheat, grinding the flour on a quern stone, kneading the dough and forming bread rolls for it to be burnt beyond use. King or not, he had left them all without any supper on an evening when hunting for game would be quite impossible.

Such was the life for these royal refugees. And to think that she had endured all of this and was not even given her due privilege of being called a queen! Indeed, the West Saxons did not permit a king's wife to sit beside him and dubbed each royal woman simply "the king's wife", all because of one Queen of Wessex in the late 700s who had been labelled stubborn and evil. It was hardly Ealswitha's fault (I will give her back the honour she deserves and refer to her as queen here).

Not that titles counted for much in these watery moorlands. She put those thoughts to one side. They had to stay alert in the present moment to ensure their future safety.

On they punted, battling through the thick reeds of the River Tone to their destination– Athelney, the isle of princes as it was named by their predecessors because a prince of Wessex had lived there as a hermit in the mid-600s. And that prince had chosen a good place to live as a recluse. Remote and inaccessible, it could only be reached by river or via a causeway from East Lyng. They were heading towards the middle of nowhere, a place that felt like a borderland between Wessex and where the sea began in earnest.

The queen was looking forward to resting there after weeks on foot, horses and boats. On Athelney, they could plant their feet, build a fort and keep watch for their enemies.

Alfred was already giving orders to the servants. "A large ditch around the outside. The fort'll have to be hastily erected, no frills. Somewhere to pray. A few huts. Fences. A wooden bridge over the ditch for access." His intense eyes darted around to make sure they were all listening.

Ealswitha closed her eyes. A few months ago, she had enjoyed merry feasts, brightly coloured frescoes, magnificent halls and exquisite food. She would have shuddered at the prospect of living in an emergency fort with no comforts to speak of and only otters and egrets as neighbours. But now, it felt like a huge relief, a blessing even.

The mound came into sight. Soon they would be settled atop the hill and could get a roaring fire going to warm little hands up. She hoped the men would be able to fell nearby trees easily and prepare the wood quickly. She hoped that in a few days, they would have one or two wooden rooms to lodge in. She hoped for many things. But she just had to take one moment at a time. And today, keeping up the lytlings' morale was her top priority.

That evening's fire rallied the little ones' spirits so much that they began to gossip about the past while Ealswitha brushed and plaited her long hair. "Mummy, is it true Uncle Aethelbald married Grandmother?" Aethelflaed piped up.

The queen's eyebrows rose up in her forehead. "Who told you that?"

"Just a servant. Is it true then?"

She sighed, pulling her headscarf more tightly around her icy-cold face. "You might as well know the truth now that King Aethelbald is no longer with us. When your grandfather Aethelwulf died, his second wife Judith outlived him. Aethelbald married Judith of Flanders, his stepmother."

"Yuck!" Ethelgeofu exclaimed.

"I'd never do that," Edward vowed.

They all giggled, even baby Elthrith.

"And she was a bad queen. That is why I am not allowed to be called queen. But come, enough of this. Let us instead enjoy some poetry. Alfred, come hither. I know how fond you are of verses. I will start with Caedmon's Hymn." Ealswitha cleared her throat and took a sip of wine from her leather vessel.

"Now we ought to praise the Guardian of the heavenly kingdom,
The might of the Architect and his conception,
The work of the glorious Father,
As he, Eternal Lord, established the beginning of wonders..."

Alfred clapped when she reached the end and smiled sadly at his wife.

"Praise God indeed," he murmured. "We will be out of harm's way here. I know a great deal of the local villagers–"

"Like the cow woman!" Edward interrupted.

Alfred grinned despite himself. "Yes, like the cow herder's wife. That's why she forgave me in the end. My point is, I know this area. I have hunted around these fens countless times. We will have food and friends nearby, people who trust and love us. And more permanent shelter very soon."

Later, nestled down in their tent, the queen knew that she would sleep soundly, despite the discomfort of another night spent sleeping on hard ground. She was convinced that better days were on their way. And they were sorely needed. If they didn't find a way to drive the Danes back, then the whole of England would be at the Viking's mercy. This small band of servants, slaves, friends and the royals were England's last chance.

*

Ealswitha and the others soon settled into new patterns of living that revolved around establishing the fort, caring for the little ones, entertaining themselves around the fire in the evenings, gathering food and drink by fishing, hunting or foraging and going on scouting expeditions through the surrounding water-logged terrain to gather information about enemy forces. The last two activities often went hand in hand. Food supplies got so short that they had to continue to beg, steal or borrow for their daily existence. Arriving with hardly anything, they had need of everything– blankets, firewood, pots, cups, *everything*.

Little by little, the fort sprang up around them. Everyone had to help assemble it, even the princes and princesses. There would be time later for pampering but at that moment, they needed every pair of hands on the task.

It was good to keep busy, anyway. It kept their minds from thinking terrible thoughts about what might befall them. There was also the guilt of fleeing that troubled Alfred's mind.

"I should have stayed and fought in Chippenham," he would say.

"For the hundredth time, my love, you couldn't have stayed and won."

"Yes, but–"

"You would have died in vain. Nobody could stay, that's why everyone who could flee *did* flee. What use is another martyr to England? They need a king, a living king. Besides, other Saxon kings and local leaders fled abroad when the Vikings struck their lands. You have remained in the country, living as a peasant. Here we will regroup and begin a counterattack that we *can* win."

"You're right," he would sigh. He didn't correct her that some kings and leaders had been killed by the Vikings. Not all had fled. And the survivor's guilt was hard to shake off.

Soon (and yet it felt like an era of waiting), they moved out of their tents and into the relative cosiness of the fort in time to celebrate Easter on 27th March. Their exhausted bodies weren't up to much dancing but there was plenty of singing and they lit a huge bonfire.

They were wise to conserve their energies, for even when the Athelney site was up and running, they couldn't rest on their laurels. Next, it was time to erect another defence at East Lyng with a ditch and embankment complete with a fighting platform running over 100m with posts, fences and 100 men to defend it. Anyone wishing to reach their safe haven by land would have to pass through all those defences first.

After that was all put in place, Alfred had to arm his men. They set about making the weapons – knives, swords and axes – right there on the isle.

This was not how Ealswitha had imagined her life. It was not what her parents had hoped for. They were down on their luck without a doubt. The kingdom of Wessex had once stretched for hundreds of miles, far more than the eye could see. Now it was reduced to this one little island with its twin peaks, if you could even call them peaks. The raised areas were no more than 10 metres higher than the surrounding boggy lands and measured little more than 35 acres in area. That was all their kingdom measured now.

Nonetheless, their kingdom *had* been nowhere at all for 11 weeks. At least now they had a base at which they could receive visitors to plot with. The local people finally knew where they could find the royal family at any given moment. Planning their counterattack on the Vikings would be much easier now.

Yes, this rustic and inelegant military base was a steppingstone towards greater things. Tucked away in the Somerset lowlands, it was a beacon of hope to them and to all those in Wessex who still cared about independence. They were literally rebuilding their kingdom from scratch. Athelney's hill fort was a symbol of what could be achieved against all odds and out of nothing.

*

March turned to April. The royal household received visitors from Somerset, Wiltshire and Hampshire, allies who plotted and planned to oust the invaders.

One such visitor had news from the coast.

"My lord, my lady, greetings to you all. My master tells me you haven't yet heard the news from Bleadon?"

"Where is Bleadon?" Aethelflaed, ever confident, piped up.

"Near Weston, near the coast to the west of us." Ealswitha's voice was hurried. "We've heard no such news. Continue, please."

"The people are saying such a tale, your lordship, your ladyship! The Vikings, they say, were out plundering the winter just gone. They sailed from the sea, you see, up the River Axe to a spot just south of Bleadon. On the banks of that there river, they did tie up their nasty boats."

"Is this good news or bad?" Alfred interjected.

"Fairly good, m' lord. What happened was that them Vikings left their boats alone and went off to start raiding. But there was this old woman, see, disabled and all she was. And she wasn't having any of it! She hobbled over to their boats and with great effort, she cut the ropes of many of them boats. She weren't afraid or nothing, she just thought, 'If I die, I die.' Well, she managed to cut them ropes clean off and them boats went drifting off downstream right out to sea. The Vikings were stranded but didn't know it."

"And so?"

"Well, the Vikings got wind of it and sprinted back to the river to save the rest of their fleet, like. That was when the villagers attacked them and were successful, like. They did slaughter those horrid Vikings and saved themselves."

"How many did they kill?"

"81, m' lord."

"Not bad. We have very little to offer here but you can bunk with the soldiers in Lyng and eat good food before you have to journey on."

"Thanking ye, m' lord."

Back in their tents that evening, Ealswitha removed her veil and rolled her aching shoulders that were complaining from all the rough sleeping they'd had previously. Turning to Alfred, she reflected, "The people here have great courage. See how even a disabled elderly woman took such a risk to protect the lands. They are hungry for victory."

"I know, my dear. It is a sign that our fortune is turning a corner. With the warmer weather coming in and alliances strengthened, it will soon be time, it will be time to give the people that victory they're hankering for."

*

April turned to May. A meeting was called at Egburh's Stones in Selwood Forest. Leaders from the three counties were due to meet there to pledge their loyalty to their king and prepare for battle.

Ealswitha stayed in Athelney with the children, bouncing baby Elthrith on her knee, commanding the servants and praying for a good turn-out for her husband, that he'd be able to rally enough troops to engage the Danes in battle and win. They needed a turning point in this war. It was a make-or-break moment. If the Scandinavians slew most of the local leaders or – God forbid – Alfred himself, Wessex would fall.

"I am Queen of Wessex in all but name," she murmured to the wind. "And I will help rule these lands once more."

The days and weeks of waiting were hard to bear. With her team of servants, she had done her best to care for the lytlings, distracting them with stories and games, saying prayers with them, finding food, keeping them warm, giving them tonics when they coughed, disciplining them and helping the girls learn to weave. Together, they assembled crude furniture from the willow growing in the marshlands. As head of her young family, she had been brave and never let her voice falter in their presence when they asked after their father. She had been resolute and stoic.

Then, one morning in June, a messenger arrived to tell them to meet Alfred at the Isle of Aller, just a few hours to the east by boat. She extended her thanks to the Almighty and called her children to her to share the good news. Their father was still alive, if nothing else, and it was clearly safe enough for them to leave their hideaway and gather together at Aller, home to the nearest church to Athelney.

Aller, the Isle of Alder trees, was the furthest she had travelled from Athelney since arriving there. It felt strange after so many weeks spent stranded on that island with a handful of trips to East Lyng and other nearby hamlets.

When they arrived, Alfred was already there. Much changed too from when she had last seen him, he was heartily swigging from a pitcher of ale and chortling with his friends.

"Wife!" he bellowed. "Come! Come!"

Collecting herself, she swept into the hall of Aller's manor house with her children behind, the younger ones clutching at her cloak. They hadn't been in a raucous environment for so long, they were overcome with shyness.

Alfred hugged each child by turn and gave them his blessing, all the while trying to hide the pains that were gripping his stomach as they so often did.

Turning to Ealswitha, he boasted, "It was a great victory! We-

Well, let me start at the beginning. I rallied our allies at Egburh's Stones. We could not be certain if anyone at all would arrive, but we numbered 5,000 in the end. Then we met our opponents in a ferocious engagement just outside Edington. We slaughtered them in great numbers, even those who fled, for we chased after them and brought them down to boot! We stole their cattle and horses. They retreated to their fortress at Chippenham with us hot on their heels. For fourteen days and nights, we were camped outside, cutting off their supply routes. How they cried out with the hunger and fear. Finally, they could stand it no longer and gave their word that they would make peace with the kingdom of Wessex. In Chippenham! Where this nasty episode all began! Negotiations got underway. Guthrum, their leader, vowed that he would convert to the Christian faith and receive the sacrament of baptism in exchange for his life. So, here we are with Guthrum and thirty of his men, all ready to bow their heads before the holy font. That will satisfy The Lord, to be sure."

Although Ealswitha's stomach turned to hear of the bloodshed, she was relieved that they had the upper hand. Their entire world had shifted and turned on its head. The victorious Danes were now the vanquished Danes. Instead of the West Saxons having to convert to the Viking religion, the Vikings were converting to the West Saxon's religion of Christianity! They had long feared that these warriors were divine punishment and now they could show God just how faithful they were to Him by having the men converted and later by strengthening the Church throughout the land.

"You have shown great mercy, husband. Had he won the battle, he would not have shown the same kindness to you, I fear."

"I'm sure you're right, wife. But, we want peace in the land. We need it. And for there to be peace, someone has to take the first step. We have to show the forgiveness that Christ taught us."

She nodded at his wisdom and hoped Guthrum would not betray his generosity.

It was soon time for the ceremony to take place there at Aller. Guthrum and 3 scores of men entered the church clad in white baptismal robes and holding lighted tapers. An incense burner swung low from left to right at the head of the church. Heads down, they shuffled to the front of the church for the robed priest to anoint their brows with water and a special oil called chrism. Around their foreheads, chrismal linens were bound to remain in place for 8 days.

The Queen of Wessex was glad she hadn't been called upon to make a speech of any kind. She was at a loss for words by the tableau playing out before her.

Her children, on the other hand, were garrulous once the

ceremony was over.

"Are Viking boys good now, mummy? Are they?" The question came from Ethelgeofu.

"These ones are," Aethelflaed replied for her.

"Hurrah!"

"And they'd better stay good because our daddy's a super king and our mummy's a super queen!"

Ealswitha ruffled her hair as the two continued to chatter away. From Aller, they slowly navigated northwards through the marshes, passing around the Polden Hills ridge and up to Wedmore, the largest island. All the while, Guthrum was dressed in white and attended mass with Alfred each day. At Wedmore, an additional ceremony- the unbinding of the chrism- took place. On the 8th day, in accordance with tradition, the chrismal linen cloths were formally untied from the Vikings' foreheads and with that, Alfred was publicly accepted as Guthrum's godfather. This conversation paved the way for the Treaty of Wedmore, drawn up and agreed upon.

For 12 days, the royal estate at Wedmore was a hive of activities, in which the surrendering Vikings were honoured with feasts and gifts. Easter that year had been a fairly dismal affair and even though the previous Christmas had been joyful, their memories of it were marred by the surprise attack that had followed it. It was time to make up for it with these 12 days of festivities.

Later that year, Guthrum left Wessex for good and settled peaceably as King of East Anglia. Further reassurance of safety was gained when the Treaty of Wedmore, previously agreed upon, was officially written up and signed in 890. It stated that East Anglia, the Midlands and the northern lands were under Danish control, while Wessex and Mercia were Anglo-Saxon lands. The royal family showed their gratitude to God by establishing an abbey monastery on the Isle of Athelney in 893. Guthrum and his friends would bother Ealswitha and her family no more.

Notes

Let's have a look at the later lives of Ealswitha and her family. Below is a genealogical chart.

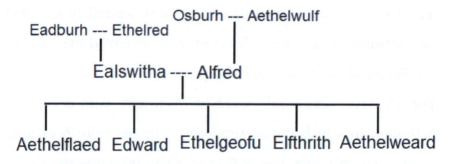

Born c.850, Ealswitha (also spelt Aelswith or Ealhswith) had links to the Mercian royal family through her mother, Eadburh (or Eadburg). Ealswitha married Alfred in the late 860s when she was just a teenager. Ealswitha became queen two years later. Behind every great man is a great (or greater) woman and this case is no exception. She championed her husband's rule of Wessex from 23rd April 871 to c.886 through many upheavals, the lowest point being their wandering through the Somerset Levels in her mid- to late twenties. It is now believed that Alfred had Crohn's Disease so she would have been supporting him in very rough conditions alongside all her little ones long before modern medicine.

When Alfred died aged around 50, in 899, he left many lands to his wife, including Edington in Wiltshire. (As a side note, the date for Somerset Day was chosen as 11th May because that battle was fought in early May.) Could this gift be a clue that she had been a great support to him during their time of refuge-seeking at Athelney and beyond, when they incorporated Bath into Wessex, reoccupied London and added Kent to the Kingdom of Wessex? It certainly shows respect and love, as does his bequeathing of Wantage to her, which is where he was born.

Following her tenure as queen, Ealswitha became an abbess, founding St Mary's Convent in Winchester, the city her husband had selected as Wessex's capital. This role would probably have suited her well according to Barbara Yorke: "It can be argued that life as an abbess would be congenial to a woman who had previously been queen and would provide her with a position of power, wealth and independence of action." She died on 5th December 902, was buried next to her husband in Winchester, and was later sainted with 20th July as her feast day. On top of that, Ealswitha was acclaimed by two tenth-century calendars as the "true and dear lady of the English".

Regarding her children (5 in total, 1 most likely born after their time in Athelney), all of them were well-educated at the school set up at the royal court. Alfred was the first literate King of Wessex and was keen for his children to follow suit. I tried in vain to discover if Ealswitha could read and write.

Aethelflaed, born c.870, married the King of Mercia in 889, creating a powerful alliance between Wessex and Mercia that lasted beyond her death. With the impressive alias of Lady of the Mercians, she led various successful military operations against the Vikings, having started her military training at the age of 8 in Somerset (!). Then when her husband died in 911, she ruled alone for 7 years and was highly regarded. At nearly 50 years of age, she died in 918.

Edward, born c.874, became King of Wessex (and was later called Edward the Elder). Edward's first wife (or woman he had a liaison with), Ecgwynn, died or was put aside at a similar time to her mother-in-law. Edward married twice more:

Aelfflaed of Wessex, then Eadgifu of Kent. He had at least 13 children with the three wives before he died in 924.

Ethelgeofu (also spelt Aethelgifu), born c.875, became the abbess of Shaftesbury Abbey, just over the border in Dorset, which was founded by Alfred. She died young in 896 and became a saint, commemorated on 9th December.

Elthrith (or Aelthryth) was born c. 878. She was a diligent student and learnt the Psalms and many Saxon books, especially those of poetry. She went on to marry a count of Flanders at some stage after 893 and lived there until her death on 7th June 929.

Aethelweard, born c.880, was educated in literature and learnt to read in Latin and Old English. He died on 16th October, probably in 920.

Caedmon, whose hymn Ealswitha recited, was the earliest English poet to be named. He lived at Whitby Abbey in Wiltshire, where his patron was Abbess Hilda, making her the first-ever patron of a named poet in the English language.

As for the places mentioned, Albion is an archaic word for Great Britain, the earliest name for the island, in fact, going back to at least 300 BC. Athelney Abbey was an incredibly unhappy one in its early years due to its location in such a desolate place and being ruled by an extremely austere and unpopular abbot. This further highlights the plight of Ealswitha and her family, who suffered all the more for living there in temporary housing and in wartime. These days, the Isle of Athelney has no abbey, having been destroyed in the Dissolution, and isn't an island anymore, the water having been drained away, yet the land gets boggy and flooding can occur. (You can get a sense of the reedy marshlands by looking at the photo in Chapter 5's Notes section, taken at a nature reserve.) In 1801, a small monument was erected on the spot where Athelney Abbey used to be, on one of the island's twin "peaks" (if you can call that them since they're very gentle inclines). The royal family's fortress was located on the other "peak".

(Athelney with its monument)

An ornate jewel found in North Petherton, just a few miles from Athelney bears the inscription: AELFRED MEC HEHT GEWYRCAN – 'Alfred ordered me to be made'. It represents another link between Alfred, Ealswitha and the Somerset Levels, as do the ruins of Cheddar Palace, built under Alfred's order. Likewise, the 9th-century Cheddar Brooch, found on a farm near Cheddar in 2020, may have been buried when this royal family stayed there. Its design includes wyverns, dragon-like creatures that came to be the symbol of Wessex.

Moving north, the area around the River Axe certainly suffered several Viking attacks according to the contemporary Anglo-Saxon Chronicle. Twenty-three ships sailed out there in 878 and 81 Vikings were killed. The elderly woman who cut the Viking boat ropes is more of a legend. It was first written down in the 1600s. Even if it didn't take place, it could be that the rumour spread even in Ealswitha's time, so I decided to include the gossip.

Egburh's (or Ecgbert's or Egbert's) Stones in Selwood Forest was where Alfred rallied his troops and the stones are named after King Egburh, Alfred's grandfather. Some believe these are the sarsen stones on Court Hill in Kingston Deverill, Wiltshire. Its name does suggest a link with the monarchy, but the Wiltshire government's website states that this link only goes back to the Norman Conquest. It's also worth noting that the adjacent village Monkton Deverill has a deconsecrated church dedicated to St Alfred the Great, whose tower dates back to the 1300s. Another contender for the location is 8 miles to the west.

One of the 18th-century owners of the Stourhead estate decided that the place (rather conveniently) was a hill on his lands. And so, close to South Brewham village, the folly Alfred's Tower was built and the hill came to be known as Kingsettle Hill since the king supposedly settled his standard there. At one point, each of the three points was in a different county- Somerset, Wiltshire and Dorset. The Dorset border moved but it still straddles Somerset and Wiltshire.

(King Alfred's Tower and surrounding forest)

It isn't certain that Ealswitha accompanied Alfred and Guthrum on their progress through Somerset, but I can't see why she wouldn't have. It was her triumph as well. Besides, the peace had only just been brokered, making it tenuous and so Alfred would have wanted to keep his family near him to keep them safe and benefit from their support.

In 1901, Wedmore church commemorated the thousand-year anniversary of Alfred's death with a plaque. (It was believed Alfred had died in 901 but this has been revised to 899.) It's ironic to think that the Saxon invaders, who the native Britons once fought against in previous centuries, had now become patriotic heroes in the fight against the Vikings, the new invading foreigners.

Chapter Bibliography

Aethelflaed, Lady of the Mercians by Tim Clarkson

Antiochian Orthodox Christian Archdiocese of North America (online)

Asser's Life of King Alfred by Albert S. Cook

Basileos Anglorum: a study of the life and reign of King Athelstan of England, 924–939 by Philip Nathaniel Cronenwett

Bel Mooney's Somerset by Bel Mooney

historicengland.org.uk

In search of the Dark Ages with Michael Wood (documentary)

Orthodox Saints British Isles by John (Ellsworth) Hutchison-Hall

oxforddnb.com

'Sisters Under the Skin'? Anglo-Saxon Nuns and Nunneries in Southern England by Barbara Yorke

Somerset Folk Tales by Sharon Jacksties

Somerset Stories by Robin Bush

Somersetshire Archaeological Natural History Society's Proceedings, 1884

Time Team: The Guerrilla Base of the King & Back to Our Roots (documentary)

Unquiet Women: From the Dusk of the Roman Empire to the Dawn of the Enlightenment by Max Adams

Alfred the Great by Marshall Foster

British Library website

www.celticsaints.org

www.oldenglishtranslator.co.uk

www.thewestonmercury.co.uk

apps.wiltshire.gov.uk/communityhistory/

The Lost Islands of Somerset by Richard Brunning

ENGLAND

Chapter 7: Miraculous Mead (early 10th century)

Elfleda had never wanted to marry. She had felt called by God to give her life to Him in service to the community. However, her royal blood forced her to put aside those wishes when one day, the royal court was out riding. King Edward the Elder, son of Ealswitha and Alfred the Great, pulled his stallion alongside hers.

"Elfleda, kinswoman of mine, it is high time you were wed." There was no preamble. He cut straight to it with an easy smile spreading across his red face.

Devastated, she clutched the horse's mane for support and mumbled, "Yes, my lord."

"It will be a great marital alliance, a great honour for you. This is how you can serve God and the kingdom at the same time, do you see?" He was attempting to sell the idea to her now as he wished for her to be satisfied with the prospect, not just obedient.

"Yes, my lord." She let the mane go.

That short dialogue crushed her dreams. A lifetime of marital subordination flashed before her teenage eyes. But the king was the king and marry she must.

And so the young Elfleda continued to live at court in Winchester with her husband, Baldwin, as well as travelling from one royal manor to another in the footsteps of the monarch. She served the queen as first lady of the bedchamber and governess to the royal children, while trying her best to steer clear of the court's insipid gossip and underhand duplicities. Educating the princes and princesses certainly helped her stay out of the court intrigues and she relished visits from the eldest prince, Athelstan, who was a similar age to her and lived up north with his father's sister, Queen Aethelflaed in Mercia since his own mother, Ecgwynn, King Edward's first wife, was dead, having died close to the time when Queen Ealswitha did. Moreover, the plan was to merge Wessex and Mercia, so the heir to both needed to have an understanding of both kingdoms.

Aethelflaed willingly took in her nephew Athelstan. A warrior queen, great strategist and the first to rule in her own right in Mercia once her husband passed away, Aethelflaed taught her nephew the art of war to protect one's kingdom and reconquer land from the Danes. Not something Elfleda's sensitive ears wished to hear. What is more, as Athelstan got older, she detected aggression and ambition in him that went beyond the desire to protect and became a desire to conquer other Saxons, not just Danish land. He dreamt of uniting all the Saxon lands under one king, a Wessex king, preferably himself, whether or not the current kings wished to submit to Wessex. Elfleda and Athelstan shared a keen sense of piety and desire to be generous to the country's churches and abbeys yet differed in their ideas about kingly ways. Elfleda sighed herself to sleep each night. These worldly ways were not her own. Her girlhood dream had been to completely dedicate her life to God.

She shuddered any time Baldwin approached her at nightfall. The act felt wrong and painful, and she couldn't envisage herself in the role of mother. It simply wasn't what she wanted out of life. How she prayed for the strength to bear it all.

However, God's will was God's will. Not long after the nuptials, Baldwin died. Guiltily, instead of feeling heartache, Elfleda could only feel relief. Being a widow, she had her own money and freedom for the first time in her life.

Steeling herself, she approached King Edward one evening while a raucous feast was underway. Her hope was that his tipsiness would put him in a better mood for what she was about to ask. Currently, he appeared merry but not too drunk so as not to comprehend her words.

"My lord–" She doubted he could hear her over the music and cheering. Raising her voice, she restarted, "My lord." This time he turned around. "I have come before you with a humble request. You know that it has long been my wish to lead a life of poverty, prayer and service."

"Yes, yes, what of it, my dear?"

"Well, I would like to establish myself as a recluse so as to focus my time on godly matters. Now that I'm a widow, I have the means to do so. St Paula, patron saint of widows as you know, has offered me guidance. She suggested I travel to Glastonbury."

"Semi-solitude in Glastonbury you say? You mean a vowess?"

"Yes, my lord, I wish to be a vowess. For if you could be so kind as to consent, I would take a vow of celibacy and live in semi-solitude but still live in my own house. I would be associated with the monastery at Glastonbury Abbey."

"I see, I see. Well, God saw fit to cut your marriage short. Perhaps it is a sign. And Lord knows we could benefit from a virtuous woman who would pray for us all. You would keep the royal family in your prayers each day, correct?"

"Of course, my lord."

"In that case, far be it from me to get in the way of God's plan."

Her heart skipped a beat. The biggest obstacle to her goal of a prayer-orientated life had just been overcome. All that was left was to plan the logistics of it all. Praise God, what a relief! She would be safe from the perils of the outside world (forced marriage, rape, harassment on the streets, infections and so on), not to mention the distractions of the world. All her time could now be focused on godly matters.

Precisely as she had outlined to the king, she scurried off to Glastonbury, purchased a house close to the abbey and lived there in seclusion with just a handful of loyal female servants. Living simply, she spent a great deal of time in prayer and the rest caring for the sick and destitute in Glastonbury. Whatever money she saved by her frugal lifestyle, she used to support those in need.

It was there that she crossed paths with a bright little boy by the name of Dunstan, to whom she was distantly related. Born into a noble family in the nearby village of Baltonsborough, he was studying each day with the Celtic Irish monks at Glastonbury, learning botany, gardening and crafts alongside monkish knowledge of prayers, plainchant and the Bible. His mother, Kynedritha, and his father, Heorstan, had made this decision after little Dunstan had started seeing visions and had shown his academic potential.

Feeling inquisitive, Elfleda had one day taken the rare decision to leave her house and travel by foot to Baltonsborough to meet with his mother, who told her an incredible story.

"We knew our baby was going to be special ever since I was pregnant with him," Kynedritha said. "I can tell you the story if you have the time."

"Please do."

"A bitterly cold February morning it was. Dressed in our finest cloaks, we had gone to St Mary's church in Glastonbury for Candlemas to celebrate the moment when Jesus was presented to the temple. Well, my baby wanted to be part of the festivities. There we all were, warming our hands with our lighted candles when all of a sudden, every single candle in the church went out. But the instant my own candle went out, it rekindled. We were in complete darkness on that wintry morning, all except for the light from my little candle. We felt the presence of God in that chamber. Everyone came to me one by one in stunned silence to relight their candles from mine. The priest came over to me. I'll never forget his words. He declared, 'What we have seen here is a symbol. It shows that your lytling will shine as a great light of inspiration in the Church.'"

"How incredible." Elfleda's voice was barely audible and she clutched the large wooden cross hanging from a chain around her neck.

"Then there was the time that Dunstan's father took him on pilgrimage to Glastonbury Abbey. They settled down for the night in their rooms when Dunstan had a great vision. An old man clad in shining white clothes appeared and took him through all the abbey chambers. The man pointed to empty grassland. Out of nowhere, monastic buildings sprang up from the ground. Dunstan was told that one day he would be abbot of this place and would oversee the construction of those buildings."

"Two miracles already in one so young," marvelled Elfleda.

"Yes, and so when we realised that on top of being anointed by God, he was also quick-witted, we knew what we would have to do. We decided to have him spend time at Glastonbury Abbey for his education and we hear that he is thriving. When he turns 12, we will send him to live with them. One day he is sure to take holy orders. And our other son, Wulfric, can follow Dunstan to learn at the abbey. He is a rather capable lad himself."

*

A thunder of hooves brought up a dust cloud under the scorching summer sun.

Many years on from her visit to Baltonsborough, Elfleda found her courtyard being invaded by two blurry riders who sprang from their horses and approached her house with all haste. They bowed and one gabbled, "My lady, our lord King Athelstan has been hunting in the forests nearby this day and will be staying with you tonight with all his men, who are in need of food and rest. We have been sent ahead to ensure that there are adequate provisions for everyone." The man was in quite a flap. He was well aware of Athelstan's warlike ways and knew not how such a small household could adequately feed and entertain such a man.

Elfleda took a moment to take in the news. Although it was some time since Edward the Elder had passed away and his son

Athelstan had gained the throne, this was Athelstan's first visit to her in Glastonbury. His kingship was not welcome by all: Athelstan had been declared illegitimate by those who claimed his parents had never been married.

And now, here was the king's servant on her doorstep. Although her life as a recluse meant that she was not used to such commotion, there was not so much as a flutter of panic in her heart. This was her relative, after all, and all life events were in God's hands.

"I am glad that my kinsman wishes to honour me with a visit. We have sheep, chickens and pigs that can easily be slaughtered and we have trout and eel preserved in the pantry. Then, there are the apples in the orchard being grown for cider that can be harvested and eaten instead. And we have flour for making bread aplenty," she replied serenely.

"And ale? Do you have ale or mead? Show us your stock."

She did so and they were shocked to find only enough mead to fill one drinking horn. Although the well in her garden had a good supply of water in it, that liquid was far too dangerous for human consumption. It was for washing, cooking with and making alcohol, which was far safer to drink. In essence, Elfleda had no beverages to offer the thirsty pack of men who would be arriving very soon.

"Do not fear. St Mary will provide unto me an abundance of

mead and any other necessities for the king's visit." She smiled. The man crossed himself and said earnestly, "You had better hope for some divine help in this matter, for the king is fast approaching and you don't have time to brew anything."

"Return to your master and tell him that everything will be in order," she replied firmly.

Once the sound of pounding hooves had quietened down and the dust left behind by the horsemen had begun to settle in the courtyard, Elfleda took herself off to her small private chapel. She knelt down before an exquisite illustration of Mary the Mother of God and with deep faith, she began to pray.

"Oh Mary, patron of enlightenment, my protector, Mary who carried Jesus into the world, hear the words of your daughter Elfleda. Exactly as your son turned water into wine at Cana and you allowed your Irish servant St Bridget to turn water into ale on several occasions, so now provide unto your sovereign king a miracle. Queen of heaven, come to our aid!"

Many an hour she spent in her chapel, speaking to the Mother of God, when slower hooves were heard outside, announcing King Athelstan's arrival.

This was a great warrior of a king. The first king of all England, who had inherited the kingdoms of Wessex, Mercia and East Anglia from his father, King Edward. In the wake of his ascension to power, he had conquered Northumbria, then

Danelaw by attacking its capital York. Thus, he had united the English nations. Despite that and despite arriving at Elfleda's house with a huge entourage while she still had only one drinking horn's worth of mead, Elfleda was not afraid. In fact, her first thought was rather trivial. The multitude of men descending on her home was a rather smelly one. There was one practice alone that she wished they had learnt from the Danes– frequent baths! It was well-known that the Scandinavian men had better hygiene practices than their Anglo-Saxon counterparts and Elfleda's nostrils were protesting at the rising stench in her hallway.

After greeting each other, the recluse and the king heard mass together. Unchanged in his strong spirituality and generosity to the churches, Athelstan reverently pulled out his pocket-sized book of psalms with its intricate patterns, colourful illustrations and meticulously neat calligraphy. He kissed the book and held it at his heart for the duration and thought how happy he was that his kinswoman had devoted her life to Christ in this way. He was proud of the service she rendered to the local community.

Following mass, they sat down to eat. It was the moment of truth. Fearfully, Elfleda's servants presented Athelstan with a goblet. Just as fearfully, they poured the mead from the drinking horn into it, knowing that the horn would be left empty and then no one else could be served anything to drink. Calmly, Elfleda watched these proceedings.

To the servants' utter astonishment, the horn began to fill up again as soon as the last drop of mead had left it. They looked to their mistress in stunned silence. Elfleda was smiling confidently.

"Never in m' life," whispered a soldier. "Praise be to God and his servant Elfleda."

"Praise indeed," murmured another.

On and on they poured from the drinking horn into each cup and the mead kept returning to the horn. For the whole day, this continued until the king became aware of the miracle.

He stood up hurriedly and with his usual charisma, he announced, "We have committed a great sin by imposing on this handmaiden of God with our huge number of people. May God and the saints forgive us!" He frantically crossed himself. "We must journey on and let her enjoy some peace."

Elfleda opened her mouth to protest and let King Athelstan know that they were most welcome there. But his men had already begun to obey- they had risen from their seats, fastened their cloaks to their shoulders with gold brooches and were filing out of the room.

*

As his mother had predicted, Dunstan did indeed become a

monk at Glastonbury when he reached adulthood. He regularly visited his kinswoman and friend over the years. It was a great joy to Elfleda to have him living so close to her. Given that Elfleda and Dunstan were both deeply religious, they found kindred spirits in each other and often spoke together about spiritual matters. Truthfully, Elfleda loved Dunstan more than anyone else. With no children of her own, she poured out maternal love on him.

They didn't always agree on things and she felt that his mistrust of Wessex queens was uncalled for and that he could be arrogant from time to time. She counselled him whenever she felt that he was stepping outside the lines of Christian charity.

The years passed by with Athelstan using his army to strengthen the fledgling nation. Meanwhile, in Glastonbury, Elfleda's peaceful and regular walks in her garden were becoming less frequent as her health became more and more fragile. Although far from being elderly, she was suffering from some strange aches and pains these days. Still, she enjoyed talking with her monastic friend. One evening, their discussion had gone on so long that he had lost track of time and was now late for Vespers.

Excusing himself, he dashed back to Glastonbury Abbey and in doing so, he passed some villagers huddled together in a doorway.

One of them was repeating an old flight-of-fancy tale that Dunstan had heard many a time. "And so it was that Joseph of Arimathea took Christ's body and laid it to rest in his own tomb, his own tomb I tell you, after which Joseph did travel over from the Holy Lands, bringing with him the sacred chalice used at the Last Supper. Our own dear town was his destination, of course, and it was here that he planted the holy thorn–"

'Codswallop,' Dunstan thought. 'But it keeps the peasants' imaginations alive.'

Gasping for air, he kept on hastening through the town. Once the abbey's timber buildings came into view, he slowed his pace down so as not to arrive flustered. At last, he strode into the church to join his brothers for the dusk service, avoiding their accusatory stares.

Later on, whilst they were chanting psalms in the fresh air outside the church, he saw a snow-white dove flying from the abbey over to Elfleda's home. The twilight sun made the bird's white wings come to life and dazzle, turning the white into a bright golden colour that almost hurt his eyes to look at.

It reminded the monk of Noah and his ark when a dove had carried back a twig to signify that the floods were abating and the land was drying up. A symbol of hope and tranquillity, the dove could also represent the Holy Spirit. He felt in his gut that something remarkable was about to occur.

Once Vespers was over, Dunstan had to satisfy his curiosity by going back to his friend's house. There was no answer to his knocking. So, tentatively, he opened the door to her home once more and entered her bedroom, where he knew she would be. He found her in her four-poster bed with the curtains drawn around her. She was talking to someone and so he turned to the servants who were attending to her. "With whom is my kinswoman conversing?"

"My lord, we know not," one replied.

"It must be angels," he whispered in awe.

The nurse nodded. "Before you entered, I saw a luminous red light shining out from behind the bed curtains. It's gone now but she's still in there, talking away to someone." Her eyes were bright with wonder.

After a time, Elfleda's conversation came to an abrupt end. Dunstan approached to ask her directly who she had been speaking with.

"Why are you asking that?" Her voice was playful. "Do you not know? It was with the one you saw flying this way from the abbey."

She was claiming it was the dove. Tongue-tied and wondering whether it was a secret discussion that he should not pry into, Dunstan didn't ask any more questions.

"But I'm glad you returned tonight," Elfleda commented. "I need to give you instructions about how my body must be washed and laid out once I am dead."

He jerked his head sharply towards her at those words. Why was she thinking of death when her room had just been filled with so much life and vitality?

Scared of what might come, he listened to her outline all the details to him– that he ought to get a funeral vestment ready for her, that he must give away all her possessions to the poor and sell her house and land for the Church's benefit, and that no one was to mourn for her, for she would be with her Lord and Saviour.

After all of this transpired, he made his way home with a heavy heart and a very long to-do list.

The next day, Elfleda's male servant knocked on the monastery door. "Brother Dunstan."

Dunstan recognised the voice. "Come in."

As soon as the servant entered, Dunstan read the news all across his face. "She is truly gone, then?" asked the monk.

"Y- Yes. Lady Elfleda, erm, did call for him this morning, a priest that is. She received the last sacraments and then she were gone. Off to be with Our Lord."

"Then heaven is a better place for it."

"She left you money, did you know, Brother Dunstan? A great

sum of it."

Dunstan cleared his throat. "Then Glastonbury will do its best to honour her memory and spend it wisely. Here's a penny for the trouble you took in coming to tell me and have the kitchen give you a plateful to eat. I must prepare for sext. We will miss her."

Notes

St Elfleda's feast day is given as either 23rd October or 14th April. In terms of figuring out when she lived, we don't know the names of her parents, which king married her off or the name of her husband. (I used the name Baldwin to make the story easier to read.) On the other hand, we do know she was a widow by the time King Athelstan (c.894–939) came to visit and his reign ran from 924 to 939. Accounts also state that she was a widow when Dunstan (909–988) was a boy, therefore let's say she was around 20 by around 915 since she was widowed at a young age and teenage marriages were common among the nobility. So I suggest she was born c.895 (at the latter end of Alfred the Great's reign) and married in the early 910s, by which point Edward the Elder was king. He had 3 wives over the course of his reign and more than a dozen children, but I felt there wasn't space in a short story to go into the details of the royal family. We do know roughly when Elfleda died: c.936, a few years prior to Athelstan's death and by my calculations, she would've been in her early 40s. The great Battle of Brunanburh happened around or just after her death, in which the unity of England was maintained (until Athelstan died but that's another story altogether).

St Elfleda is not to be confused with St Elfleda of Whitney who lived from 654–714 and was abbess of Strensall-Whitby in Wiltshire or with Elfleda, the lover of Edwy with whom St Dunstan also had dealings. Other variations on the name Elfleda, as seen in historical documents, are: Alfgina, Algina, Algisa, Elfgiva, Elgina, Elgiva, Aelgisa, Elgisa, Ethelfleda, Ielgisa, Ithelgeofu and Aethelflaed. If she wanted to moonlight as a spy, she was well-equipped with some aliases!

Sadly, we don't know precisely how she fitted into the royal family, but it is evident from Athelstan's visit that she was "part of court networks" (Els Schröder). Some sources say she was Athelstan's niece but even then, the documents don't state the identity of her parents. As we believe Elfleda was around 20 in 915, she was about the same age as Athelstan, who was Edward the Elder's first-born child. *If* she was a niece, the only possibility is that her mother or father was born from a liaison Edward had prior to being with Ecgwynn (a relationship that was either a marriage or a liaison itself). Here's a family tree to make it clearer. 'A' is the possible relationship I'm talking about.

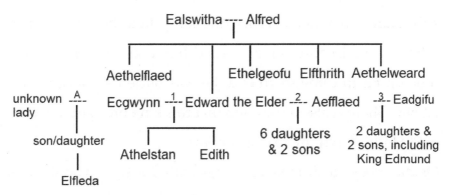

I have a theory about who Elfleda was named after. Athelstan was brought up "with great care" (so the chronicles say) by his aunt Aethelflaed, the Lady of the Mercians, whom we saw earlier taking refuge at Athelney with her parents. Aethelflaed is one way of spelling and pronouncing our protagonist's name.

King Alfred had made Winchester the capital city of Wessex and it remained the capital of Wessex then England until 1066. Yet the kings liked to travel about as well, including to the holy town of Glastonbury. Whether Athelstan took his little book of psalms (called a psalter) with him to Glastonbury is not known but he is known to have carried it around with him. The book begins with the psalms written out in Latin (as religious texts tended to be before the Reformation) and ends with the litany written in Greek. It's currently housed at the British Library. You can view it here: https://www.bl.uk/collection-items/athelstan-psalter.

The royal family's links with Glastonbury didn't end with Athelstan and Elfleda. When the king died, his half-brother Edmund the Deed-Doer succeeded him and when Edmund's time on Earth came to an end, he was buried at Glastonbury Abbey. There is also a tradition that this king brought the relics of St Hilda of Whitby to Glastonbury.

On the subject of Elfleda's dealings with Dunstan, who she was distantly related to, the money she left him in her will was put towards Glastonbury Abbey and to the monastic reforms he put in place, such as insisting that all brothers in monasteries had to be celibate. Before, there were "secular clergy" living in the larger monasteries who had wives and children.

Dunstan was appointed abbot of Glastonbury in 943 and he selected his brother, Wulfric, to be his steward, meaning that Wulfric was in charge of administrating all of the abbey's estates. When Wulfric, whose name means 'wolf power', passed away in the 950s, he was taken to Glastonbury Abbey for burial. That means at least one of Elfleda's relatives was buried at the abbey. And he died a rich man, bequeathing a great deal of money to the abbey in his will. Dunstan outlived his younger brother by many decades, dying in 988, but before that, in 960, he was appointed Archbishop of Canterbury. More on this in the next chapter!

It's also interesting to note that two more of their kinsmen were pious– one of Dunstan's uncles was Bishop of Winchester and another was the first Bishop of Wells then Archbishop of Canterbury. Els Schröder states that friendships between men and women were rarely described in Anglo-Saxon documents but Dunstan and Elfleda were able to be friends without any unwanted gossip because they had both taken vows and were family members.

The only point I have elaborated on is Elfleda walking out to Baltonsborough to meet Kynedritha, which isn't out of the question since they were related by blood or marriage. The church of St Mary's seems to be the Old Church of St Mary in Glastonbury, as the church in Baltonsborough and those in the surrounding villages were built in later centuries. Little is known about Kynedritha (also spelt Cynethryth) and her

husband, Heorstan, besides the fact that they were nobles living in Baltonsborough. The afore-mentioned church in Baltonsborough was dedicated to Dunstan, who was sainted after his death. On the left is a wall hanging in St Dunstan's Church, Baltonsborough.

Chapter Bibliography

A Century of English Sanctity by Vladimir Moss

A Dictionary of Saintly Women, Volume 1 by Agnes Baillie Cunninghame Dunbar

Basileos Anglorum: a study of the life and reign of King Athelstan of England, 924–939 by Philip Nathaniel Cronenwett

Encyclopaedia Britannica

Friendship and Favour in Late Anglo-Saxon Elite Culture by Els Schröder

In search of the Dark Ages with Michael Wood (documentary)

Orthodox Outlet for Dogmatic Enquiries (online)

Orthodox Saints British Isles by John (Ellsworth) Hutchison-Hall

The Lives of the Saints: Volume 12, October, Pt. 2 by Sabine Baring-Gould

The Saints: A Concise Biographical Dictionary by John Coulson

www.encyclopedia.com

www.heritage-history.com

www.catholicity.com

Chapter 8: The Words of Wulfwaru (late 10th century)

[See the notes section for a list of characters as they have quite similar names!]

The day had arrived. The mistress had called her two sons and two daughters to the great hall to discuss something important. Mildrith, an enslaved woman under the mistress' control, was from Leigh village but worked at Wulfwaru's Claverton manor house.

"As you know, I'm getting on in years, which is why I have given thought as to what will happen once I'm gone. In short, I plan soon to dictate my will."

Mildrith's ears pricked up. Her mistress, or rather slave owner, was writing her will! Sometimes, just sometimes, that meant a handful of slaves would be granted freedom once the will-maker died. Mildrith could only hope.

Not daring to breathe, she listened on, whilst attending to the room. Today, Mildrith would build up and light the fire a bit more slowly and linger each time she poured her mistress more wine so she could hang on Mistress Wulfwaru's every word. This will could change everything.

"Mother, really, you do not need to talk of this. You have many more years left, surely," the younger daughter, Aelfwaru, said. "Don't patronise her. Let Mother continue," the eldest son, Wulfmaer, cut in. He was eager to hear what his inheritance would be.

The elderly lady continued: "I'll have to start the will with a salutation to the king to get the formalities out of the way."

The sisters, Gode and Aelfwaru, shared a look. Their mother did like to itemise, ramble and specify. On she went: "It is hard to truly respect a king when he is so incompetent. Ethelred. My, my. Ascended the throne of England, the richest country in Europe, at just 10 years of age. A huge amount of responsibility was thrust into hands so young. Besides, those rumours that told of his involvement with his brother King Edward the Martyr's assassination never did go away. That event still chills me to the bone, especially since it took place in nearby Dorset. One doesn't know what to think, especially when those omens appeared in 979, a year after he took the crown- the blood-red streak of light speeding across the night sky and the famine we all endured.

"I do hope some peace agreement is reached with the Danes or that we Anglo-Saxons overcome them once and for all; otherwise, I am organising this will in vain. The Danes could very well take all my lands or they could burn our properties to the ground in their raids, even slaughter us all. When they sacked Watchet in 988, that was too close for comfort!"

Her children nodded gravely, trying to be patient.

Mildrith felt her heart skip a beat at the mention of invaders.

Everyone was fearful of what the Danish might do next. During Alfred and Ealswitha's time, there were wars, but the Danes did have an interest in settling and making treaties. Now, with such an ineffectual king on the throne, they wanted nothing more than to pillage and plunder. Dubbed Ethelred (or Æthelred) Unraed, Ethelred the Badly Advised, the monarch was known for listening to poor advice, issuing bad guidelines and making terrible U-turns.

"Of course, I must give offerings to the Church on behalf of my soul and the souls of my ancestors." And Wulfwaru began to detail gifts for St Peter's minster in Bath– an armlet, two gold crucifixes, a set of mass vestments, large quantities of gold, a set of bedding and a tapestry, amongst other costly items. But she soon became distracted again. "Ah, Bath. You know, I attended King Edgar's coronation there on Whitsunday in 973?"

The sons and daughters smiled. So did Mildrith. Everyone had been told this story about Ethelred's father countless times.

"Now, he was a king! Edgar the Peaceful. I first laid eyes on him in um... 968 I believe it was, when he was on his way to a Witan council meeting at Cheddar with scores of noblemen and archbishops and half a dozen bishops... Edgar spent so long making England strong and unifying it that his coronation had to happen decades after he began his rule. It was a beautiful ceremony. Dunstan of Glastonbury, our great friend, crowned him of course, then crowned his wife Aelfthryth of Devon. She was the first queen consort to be referred to as Queen since Judith of Flanders, more than a hundred years before, and that was of Wessex, not England. Aelfthryth was the first woman to actually be crowned as Queen of England and it happened here, in our Somersetshire and by a Somerset-born archbishop! Ah, Edgar and Aelfthryth. They both put so much effort into encouraging trade and improving administration. The queen was appointed defender and guardian of the nuns, and she advocated on behalf of many female litigants." She sighed happily.

Her children nodded indulgently. Nobody wanted to remind Wulfwaru how the king and queen hadn't had a fairy-tale romance. Edgar had heard rumours of a beautiful Wessex woman and had sent out a nobleman to discover more. The nobleman met her and was so dazzled by her beauty that he risked it all by marrying her himself. The king was furious when he heard and insisted on meeting the woman himself. There were reports that her husband's sudden death during a hunting expedition with the king shortly afterwards was not an accident. And whilst Aelfthryth had been an outstanding queen consort, she was an atrocious queen dowager. Some say that it was not only Ethelred who had Edward the Martyr murdered;

they pointed the finger at blame at her door as well as stepmother of the martyred king.

"Now, where was I? Bath. I must leave a portion of my Somersetshire lands to the abbot there. Freshford with its produce, people and all its profits should do."

Wulfwaru took a sip of wine, while Mildrith muttered under her breath, 'That doesn't affect me. Keep going.'

"Let's move on to you, my dear children. I'm well aware of how blessed I am to have four of my offspring reach adulthood." The lady sighed and thought of those less fortunate, who had only one or two adult children, or none at all. Likewise, Wulfwaru knew how lucky she was to have survived childbirth four times when others had not.

"Wulfmaer." He sat up straighter upon hearing his name. "You shall have Claverton, Compton and Butcombe with their produce and people."

Aelfwaru's face fell and she began to nervously fiddle with her long hair.

"Now, I know what you're thinking, dear." Wulfwaru turned to face her. "I'm well aware that you love the house at Butcombe just as much as Wulfmaer and in view of the fact that you're not yet married, you need a man to watch over you. Don't roll your eyes at me! These are dangerous times with the Danish threat ever upon us. So, I've thought of that. And I believe you will be able to share Butcombe tolerably. The other half of Butcombe with its produce and people will go to you, Aelfwaru, and the two of you will share the main house."

"Share?" Wulfmaer muttered.

"Yes. Share," Wulfwaru repeated sternly. "There is plenty of space."

"Very well, Mother." He sighed.

But Wulfwaru's mind had wondered. She was now reminiscing about her daughter as a little child. Aelfwaru. Elf guardian. It had turned out to be an apt name, for she had often had elflock hair- the strands got so tangled as though mischievous little elves had wrapped them around their fingers and pulled them this way and that. Aelfwaru wouldn't appreciate being reminded of such things now! 'Besides, back to the task at hand,' thought Wulfwaru.

'Yes, please,' thought Mildrith desperately.

"Now, on to Aelfwine." Her younger son held his breath. "Northern lands have gone to Wulfmaer, so I shall place you more to the south. Leigh. With its produce and people. That shall go to you. As will Holton and Hogston. Plus thirty mancuses of gold."

'A mention of Leigh,' thought Mildrith. 'So, we will be under Aelfwine's thumb in the future. Unless the mistress thinks to free any of us in her will. So far, there's been no mention of freeing any slaves! No matter how many times I smile at her, the old lady isn't taking the hint. Or she's choosing to ignore it.' Mildrith briefly turned her mind to wondering how Aelfwine would invest that gold and hoped he wouldn't squander it. Each mancus of gold was worth what a craftsman would earn in a month. Thirty of them equalled two-and-a-half years of a craftsman's wages.

"Right. Gode." Wulfwaru's words brought Mildrith back to the present as she addressed her eldest daughter. "I'll put you up north close to Wulfmaer and Aelfwaru. Winford is but an hour's walk from Butcombe and will do nicely for you, especially given that it is my largest estate. You boys with 3 estates each should be satisfied and Aelfwaru you love Butcombe, so I believe it is just."

She looked sternly at each of them in turn, almost daring them to complain. They remained silent, even Wulfmaer, though he wanted to point out that he had been granted 2 and a half estates rather than 3.

"Good. Then there will be some personal items and gold for you daughters. Things for you to remember me by. And all of my clothes will go to you girls."

Wulfwaru was well aware that the young Aelfwaru would enjoy those clothes. She loved to dress up and she could attract a handsome man with fine clothes. Wulfwaru sighed. It wasn't particularly godly to think of attracting a man with rich attire rather than with an honourable personality and kind ways, but she hoped that Aelfwaru would use the latter too in addition to the clothing when meeting young gentlemen at gatherings. Again, it was the Danish threat that made her wish to secure her daughter's future with everything she had at her disposal.

She then went on to outline other little trinkets to her children, making sure that her second son received two tapestries for Leigh village was on a hill and tended to get chilly. 'No tapestries for us slaves, though,' Mildrith thought.

"Well now, my faithful servants must not be forgotten. I believe Aelfmaer is listening outside the door."

The guilty servant stepped into the room with a bow. "M- my lady, I can only apologise m- most profusely and–"

"Be at peace, Aelfmaer. It is only natural. I was about to mention servants, as it happens."

By this point, Mildrith had stopped poking the fire and sat deadly still. She was getting to the good part!

Wulfwaru giggled suddenly. Why not have some fun? She stifled a pretend yawn and looked at the gathering dusk outside. "Goodness, it must be getting late. Mayhap we should recommence this upon the morrow."

"Ah, if your good self so desires," snivelled Aelfmaer.

"Mother, do continue," urged Wulfmaer. "That way, tomorrow

you may have more time for pleasant activities, such as a long walk through the herb garden."

"If I have time! I have an island of clothes that must be sewn and wool that must be spun, not to mention accounts that must be looked over. Nevertheless, your counsel is wise, son. One must not waste time when there is always ever so much work to do to keep the farms running. Methinks I shall finish this topic now."

Everyone's shoulders visibly relaxed.

Wulfwaru only smiled. It was so easy to jest with Aelfmaer!

"Very well. To my four retainers, Aelfmaer and Aelfweard and Wulfric and Wulfstan, I plan to leave a band consisting of twenty mancuses of gold. And I grant to all my household women, in common, a good chest well-decorated."

She paused to see Aelfmaer's reaction. A smile tugged at the corners of his mouth. He was pleased, then, to know he would receive a generous gift upon her death and his wife would be granted one of those ornate chests for her clothes.

As she took another sip of wine from her opulent silver goblet, Wulfwaru looked at Aelfmaer intently and spotted that his expression changed. No doubt now he was considering whether she would follow the custom of freeing some of her slaves upon her death. He had one or two friends among the enslaved class, after all. She briefly glanced at Mildrith too. But she was reluctant to name which slaves to free. It was never easy to decide such matters and she preferred for her children to choose. By the time she died, certain slaves might have proved themselves more worthy of freedom than at present. And in contrast, those who were working hard now might become lazy if they knew freedom was around the corner. Yes, better to let her children decide.

She hoped she had not been too hard a slave mistress in comparison to others. Yes, she had had one castrated but he had raped a fellow slave and so it was just punishment in Wulfwaru's eyes. But she had never had any male slave stoned to death or a female slave burnt to death as others were wont to do.

"Now, as for the manumission of slaves," Wulfwaru said, which made Mildrith freeze in anticipation. "I shall leave the choice to you, my children. You will free twenty slaves– ten in the east and ten in the west. And you shall supply a food-rent to Bath, the very best you can afford."

'That was all she'll say of slaves?' thought Mildrith. 'In that case, I will have to work hard to impress her children, especially Aelfwine.'

"The food-rent will prove your loyalty to King Ethelred. It is he who can keep them safe in times of war... in theory anyway."

She exhaled. She didn't have very high hopes of the current

king protecting the country from the Danes, who were ever ready to invade. But some protection was better than none and they had no choice but to supply taxes according to the law of the land. At least she was asking something fair of her children- they could select how much to send based on what was affordable and on what would be a generous gift, and they could choose what season would be most appropriate for sending it. The king's agent in the 'royal village' of Bath would be satisfied, she believed. Across her lands, there were plenty of herds of livestock, endless barrels of ale and mead, as well as field upon field of barley and rye, the land ploughed by her men and the seeds sown by her women.

She was getting tired now and the light was fading. It was time to finish with a customary blessing that also served as a warning to show her loyalty to the crown and to God. "Well, that is all. Fast comes the twilight. God bless you, my children."

Mildrith had to keep her face firmly looking into the flames, still reeling in disappointment. No slaves would be freed by Wulfwaru's hand. And they would have to learn to serve a new master in Aelfwine. As she had nothing more to do in the room, she made her exit.

Aelfmaer followed suit, bowing before he left. Then the children filed out, one by one.

Wulfwaru sat by the crackling fire, allowing her mind to take flight and reflect on her life. It had been such a struggle when her husband had died and left her with four little ones. But she had gritted her teeth with courage and determination to raise them the best she could and administer her lands well to feed her family and all those in her charge. She had safeguarded the lands for her children to inherit, making sure that her daughters had something to call their own as well.

Wulfwaru wondered if anyone would remember her in years to come, if her life would matter in the grand scheme of things or whether all trace of her would disappear.

Shaking her hand, she laughed and scolded herself. What a silly thought on a midsummer's night. She called her maid in to help her get ready for the night and turned her thoughts instead to God and what she would pray for that night. She would begin with gratitude for her children's health and for her position in the world, then ask that He bless them when she was no longer than to watch over them and keep them safe from temptation and any harm.

A deep slumber awaited Wulfwaru as she removed her fur-lined cloak and climbed into her sumptuous bed and blew out the candle.

Notes

Sadly, none of the enslaved people are mentioned in

Wulfwaru's will nor are any of her female servants, so Mildrith's name is invented. But let's take a look at the meanings of some of the names that are mentioned in Wulfwaru's will:

Wulfwaru – wolf guardian, which reminds me a little of the wolf mother in the Romulus and Remus tale

Wulfmaer (her eldest son) – wolf praise

Gode (her eldest daughter) – could mean 'I improve' or be related to the word good or God

Aelfwaru (her youngest daughter) – elf guardian

Aelfwine (her youngest son) – elf friend. The modern name Alvin is based on this name.

Aelfmaer (her retainer) – elf praise.

Some sources believe Wulfwaru lived at the end of the 800s or early 900s but most point to the tenth century and there are more surviving wills from the 10th century. Therefore, I have opted for the Ethelred in question to be not Alfred's brother and predecessor Ethelred I of Wessex (who ruled from c.865–871) but Ethelred Unraed of England. This king ruled from 978–1013 and then 1014–1016. The break in his reign was when Sweyn of Denmark conquered the land, ruled it for five weeks, then promptly died.

The family tree below outlines Ethelred Unraed's ancestry. Underlined people are the kings and queens of Wessex and then England (although not all queens were recognised as such at the time). Several kings never married.

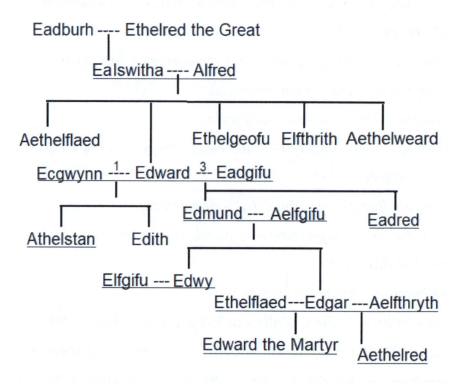

We don't know how old she was when she wrote the will, how much longer she lived after she had written it or the age at which she died. I got the impression that her children were already grown and that Wulfwaru was beyond childbearing age as there is no clause for any other children she might have. Hence, I believe she was no younger than in her late 30s at the very least.

Indeed, she needn't have been particularly old despite being a widow. Max Adam highlights how Anglo-Saxon men often died young in battles, leaving wealthy widows with power over vast estates. This class of women could "exercise moral, intellectual and creative influence in an otherwise testosterone-driven world of martial glory and court intrigue."

There is no evidence that she attended Edgar's coronation or that she was friends with St Dunstan, yet since she was a rich noblewoman with lands near Bath and Glastonbury, both ideas are possible, as is the idea that a young Wulfwaru knew Elfleda. Wulfwaru may have also met King Edmund when he came to Cheddar to hunt and nearly fell off the cliff. Having treated Dunstan unfairly, he promised God to make amends if the Lord would save him. Edmund's life was spared and so he hurried off to Glastonbury straight afterwards to make peace with Dunstan. Edmund's brother King Eadred may have had contact with Wulfwaru too as he visited and died in Frome. Dunstan, when he heard the news, rushed over to ease the king's passing only to find that the monarch was already dead.

What I love about Wulfwaru, who was probably a widow when she wrote her will, is that her daughters inherited alongside her sons. The historian Marie-Françoise Alamichel points out that her estates were of moderate size and that although the sons were favoured with 3 estates each, Winford was by far the largest of all and it went to her elder daughter, Gode. "The daughter was not cheated," the historian remarks. To think,

Winford and part of the Butcombe estate were owned by at least two generations of women!

When reading the will, a few questions arose in my mind about her younger daughter, Aelfwaru. Was she unmarried and so needed a man to keep her safe hence she was mandated to live with her brother at Butcombe? And did her mother want her to have more clothes so she could attract a man? For the purposes of the story, I decided that both were true.

I also wonder what images adorned the huge tapestries that she decided to bequeath. In the days before modern heating, fires were the radiators of the Middle Ages and tapestries the wall insulation.

As regards places mentioned in this chapter, we can start with Cheddar. At least three times over the course of the tenth century, kings met their witan (council) at Cheddar: King Edmund I in 941, King Eadwig in 956 and King Edgar in April 968 when they might have stayed for Easter, which was 19th April that year. Among the king's entourage on this last occasion were the Archbishops Dunstan and Oscytel together with seven bishops, nine abbots and eight earls.

Of the villages named in the will, most are easily established but two are slightly trickier. Leage (which Old English experts translate to Modern English as Leigh) is deemed by the historian W. Hunt to be Leigh-on-Mendip and I hunted for other possibilities in Somerset without finding anything. Meanwhile, Hocgestune (which translates to Hogston) has me foxed. I can't find any similar-sounding place name in Somerset, Wiltshire or Dorset. Perhaps it's a settlement that was later abandoned or completely renamed.

(Leigh-on-Mendip in early spring)

Wulfwaru was not the only Anglo-Saxon widow to make out a will. Wynflaed dictated hers in the mid-10th century, a few decades before Wulfwaru. Wynflaed's is the "earliest surviving woman's will in British history" according to Michael Wood. Far wealthier than our protagonist, she might have been King Edgar's grandmother, who was called Wynflaed. Either way, this lady had land in 5 counties: Dorset, Somerset, Wiltshire, Hampshire and Oxfordshire. Accordingly, her will is nearly twice the length of Wulfwaru's and mentions a wide range of gifts, for example herds of tamed and untamed horses, buffalo horns (used as drinking vessels) and even people, for instance a female weaver and a seamstress. Wynflaed's "bequests offer us a rare insight into a close-knit female network, in which female servants were also included", as Els Schröder points out. Wynflaed and Wulfwaru may have known each other, both being wealthy widows with land in Somerset. Moreover, when Wynflaed had a land dispute in 990 in Berkshire, she was supported by a number of people, including an Aelfwaru and an Aelfwine, who were probably Wulfwaru's children.

Wynflaed's will mentions the freeing of enslaved people in Somerset: two male slaves and one female slave at Charlton Horethorne, near Wincanton. The men are named but the woman is just described as the wife of a man whose name isn't clear enough to make out on the parchment. Another group of enslaved people at Chinnock, near Yeovil, were not as lucky – they would remain in slavery after her death and would be owned by her son. In contrast, the actual land at Chinnock was given to Shaftesbury Abbey. Wynflaed was a pious, well-read woman who bequeathed all her books to a female relative, books that would've been painstakingly handwritten in the days before the printing press. Her daughter is her principal heiress. Wynflaed made sure that her daughter could own the land she would inherit irrespective of any future marriage. It is apparent, then, that devout, intellectual women were not opposed to slavery in Anglo-Saxon England, where at least 10% of the population were slaves and Bristol was regularly shipping out English slaves to Ireland. It was a cultural norm. There are documents that mention abbots owning slaves. Yet life was generally unbearable for the slaves: rape, filth, brandings, castrations and being treated as animals were all commonplace. Punishment could be mutilation or a gruesome death.

I hope that Wulfwaru wasn't a particularly cruel slave mistress but there is no evidence to suggest either to be the case. Being a slave mistress means that I cannot fully admire her, this woman of her time, distributing people around as if they were objects, which I why I chose to centre an enslaved woman and her servant in the story.

The Anglo-Saxons did not introduce slavery to Britain (both the Celts and the Romans kept slaves) but they certainly maintained it. Surprisingly, the decline in slavery on our shores is thanks to the Norman Conquest (which is not to say the invasion and subjugation were not extremely brutal in other ways). William the Conqueror and his pals were part of a culture that had recently left enslavement behind. Little by little, this was introduced and enforced in England. Sadly, we know that slavery would later rear its ugly head again in an even more horrific way and in chapter 19, we will meet an intrepid woman determined to see an end to the slave trade and slavery itself.

Finally, Wulfwaru's will in its entirety can be read here: https://esawyer.lib.cam.ac.uk/charter/1538.html.

(Holton village, near Wincanton)

Chapter Bibliography

Anglo-Saxon Wills, edited by Dorothy Whitelock

British Library website

Encyclopaedia Britannica

Friendship and Favour in Late Anglo-Saxon Elite Culture by Els Schröder

historic-uk.com

In search of the Dark Ages with Michael Wood (documentary)

Kinship in Anglo-Saxon Society: II by Lorraine Lancaster

Normans and Slavery: Breaking the Bonds by Marc Morris

Often lost behind stories of kings, queens, bishops and saints, what was life like for an Anglo-Saxon woman below the upper ranks of society? by Michael Wood

Online catalogue of Anglo-Saxon charters

Slavery in Anglo-Saxon England by Octavia Randolph

Unquiet Women: From the Dusk of the Roman Empire to the Dawn of the Enlightenment by Max Adams

Wealthy Wynflaed's wonderful will by Kate H Thomas

Widows in Anglo-Saxon and Medieval Britain by Marie-Françoise Alamichel

Women of the Middle Ages by Frances Gies

Somerset Historical Essays by Joseph Armitage Robinson

www.oldenglishtranslator.co.uk

The Glories of Glastonbury, her legends, history and saints by Armine le S. Campbell

Interlude (11th century)

The late 11th century spelt the end of Anglo-Saxon rule and any Viking influence. It was the beginning of the Norman regime, with William the Conqueror's invasion in 1066. I searched high and low for a well-documented and noteworthy woman living in Somerset to no avail.

Someone briefly mentioned in the records is an enslaved woman whose freedom was purchased from the Abbot of Bath. The abbots and monks at Bath were actually all Anglo-Saxon for the first few decades after the Conquest and we find Abbot Aelfsige mentioned as a slave owner in a manuscript written between 1075 and 1087.

The document states that one enslaved woman under his control was Leofgifu and her role was working as a dairymaid and her name means 'beloved gift'. Leofgifu's freedom and that of her offspring were bought by Godwig the Buck in the village of North Stoke, about 5 miles northwest of the centre of Bath. The price was half a pound of silver and was witnessed by the community at Bath.

Was Godwig her husband? The father of her child(ren)? A relative? We'll probably never know for sure.

As regards women and land ownership, the Normans created their huge, famous database called the Domesday Book in 1086, twenty years after their takeover. It documents England like never before and demonstrates how the Anglo-Saxon landowners, regardless of gender, had been almost completely replaced by Normans. The Online Open Domesday database shows us that by 1086, Wulfwaru's lands in Holton, Winford, Butcombe, Freshford and Claverton had passed into the hands of Anglo-Saxon or Viking men and subsequently Norman men. A woman who is mentioned in the Domesday Book is Countess Gytha, a Danish woman who married Godwin, Earl of Wessex, and became the mother of several children, including Queen Edith of Wessex (c.1023–1075), the penultimate Anglo-Saxon queen (as wife of Edward the Confessor), and King Harold Godwinson, who lost his throne and his life at the Battle of Hastings. Gytha instigated an anti-Norman rebellion in Exeter after her son's death before fleeing abroad. All of her lands across several counties were snatched by King William I, including the Somerset villages of Queen Camel (originally called East Camel), Brompton Regis, West Coker and East Coker. She died some time after 1069.

Queen Edith's lands in Somerset included Chewton Mendip, Keynsham, Martock, Stanton Drew, Batheaston and Bath. She also persuaded her husband to grant Wedmore to the Bishop of Wells.

Another of Gytha's daughters, Gunhild (d. 1087), had Hardington Mandeville, Creech St Michael and Claverham in

Somerset along with one holding in Sussex. Her lands were all seized by the new king and she fled abroad with her mother.

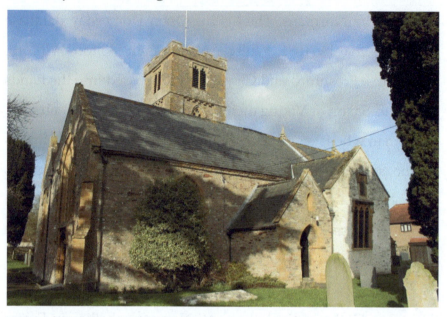

(Creech St Michael's parish church)

Edith Swanneck, Harold's common-law wife before he became king, held Crewkerne in Somerset and many other lands outside Somerset.

Sadly, I was unable to find out how much time any of these women spent in Somerset. Gytha owned lands in 10 counties so perhaps didn't visit Somerset that often. Gytha, Edith and Gunhild certainly lived their latter days and died elsewhere. The new owner of their Somerset lands was King William. His wife, Matilda of Flanders, and niece, Countess Judith, held lands in England. Indeed, Judith, with over 190 properties in total but none in Somerset, was the country's wealthiest landlady.

In Somerset, there were a handful of Norman women who gained small parcels of land, for example the wife of Manasseh (also spelt Manasses). Her husband was the royal household's cook. She – we have no idea what her name was – gained a manor at Ston Easton that included tenants and 6 acres of pastureland, in addition to land in Wells. In fact, the village of Coxley (right next to Wells) means 'wood or clearing belonging to the cook', which could be a reference to Manasseh's wife. What she did she do to earn land in such a military-oriented society remains a mystery.

The name Manasseh is a Hebrew name that appears twice in the Old Testament– firstly to Joseph's eldest son and secondly to an evil king who repented and changed. As Biblical names in general were unpopular at that time amongst Anglo-Saxons and Normans (aside from certain New Testament names such as Thomas, John and its female version Joan), this suggests he was Jewish. Jews first settled in England in the 1070s, having been invited over by William the Conqueror to act as moneylenders, administrators and sometimes cooks apparently! There was certainly a Jewish population in Bristol during the latter end of the 1000s. It seems likely that Manasseh was part of this first wave of Jewish newcomers. Considering that inter-marriage between Jews and Christians was outlawed, we can tentatively say that if Manasseh was a Jew, then so was his wife.

(A footpath leading to Ston Easton. Did Manasseh's wife walk along it?)

Nevertheless, the cook's wife is an exception to the rule; there were plenty of Anglo-Saxon women whose vast lands were confiscated and handed to Norman men. Female landowners became scarce. The Normans generally distributed land to men who could form and lead a troop of fighting men if needed. Another reason for this uprooting of women was that the invaders were highly patriarchal.

Women's position in society nose-dived. There are plenty of other 11th-century records that include women but, in general, merely to state each woman's name along with whose wife she was and/or whose mother. The records generally don't mention any actions the women took. The iconic Bayeux Tapestry's main narrative has a decidedly male skew: Queen Edith is one of only 3 women to appear in it.

Another consequence of the Conquest was that priests had been able to marry in Anglo-Saxon times, although many chose not to. The Normans insisted on celibate priests and so women could no longer become the wife of a priest and whisper advice into his ear each night. Many scholars thought that women could only become pregnant if they'd orgasmed. Thus, it was believed that a pregnant woman who was raped must have consented to the act. This meant rape victims were stigmatised instead of being offered assistance. Overall, the Normans viewed women as defective males, as children who needed to be looked after by a man, especially if they were married, in which case the husband was given control.

Despite this, we find a few examples of 12th- and 13th-century women fighting back against the system. Let's get to know them.

Sources: opendomesday.org, pase.ac.uk, A Brief History of Life in the Middle Ages by Martyn Whittock, A Dictionary of British Place-Names by A. D. Mills, british-history.ac.uk, Slavery in Anglo-Saxon England by Octavia Randolph.

Chapter 9: Fina the First (12th–13th century)

When Christina de Hogshaw awoke the day after it had happened, she felt as though it must have been a dream, a crushingly realistic dream. The woman who had walked by her side for six decades simply could not have perished; the lady who she had admired all this time could not have left her. Prioress Fina had come close to death's door many a time but had always pulled through due to sheer willpower, her inexhaustible strength of character and of course her piousness. Many a time she had been brought relics to clutch and holy water to drink.

Yet, how difficult it was to deny Fina's passing when Christina herself had entered the nuns' dormitory and held the prioress' frail hand while it grew colder and colder. Thankfully, Fina had died well, having received the last rites that guaranteed the soul a smooth passage from this world to the next. Christina had witnessed all the steps. Fina first confessed her sins to the priest in a thin whisper and was accordingly absolved so that her soul would be free from transgression. Next, the priest had cleared the prioress' body of all transgression by anointing her with oil. Christina's hands shook with emotion as she watched the process: eyes, nose, mouth, ears, hands... Finally, Fina prised her jaw open to receive holy communion for the last time and the priest commended her spirit unto the Lord. Christina had sighed with relief, knowing that her friend and mentor was now fully equipped to meet her Maker.

When Fina's chest had eventually ceased to expand up and down in shallow, laboured breaths, Christina herself had closed her sister's eyes for the very last time. Then, Christina had been one of the first to participate in the vigil for Prioress Fina's soul. She had stood in the shadowy room with the body laid out on sackcloth and surrounded by flickering candles. There, with a trembling voice, she had said Mass for her departed friend alongside her sisters.

The nuns of Minchin Buckland Priory had lost a leader, a mother and a dear friend. Her absence was felt keenly in the dormitory, where one bed now stood empty and cold with no trace of the terrible event that had just occurred there. The sisters were even quieter than normal at daybreak.

Sitting on the edge of the straw-stuffed mattress on her narrow bed, Christina slipped on her black habit and ran her fingers across the white eight-pointed cross sewn onto its front. Each point represented one of the Beatitudes from scripture: humility, sorrow for sin, meekness, thirst for righteousness, mercy, purity, peace and suffering under persecution. This was the symbol of the Order Christina and Fina had joined as young women– St John of Jerusalem. For six decades, they had stood side by side dressed in identical habits topped with wimples.

Her clothes were a symbol of the friendship she had shared with Fina, a symbol too of Fina's leadership in the nunnery. Christina gave herself up to reminiscing about happier times. Fina, along with Christina de Hogshaw, from a village of the same name in Buckinghamshire, had been pioneers in their time. So too had seven other sisters from across the country–Milesene and Johanna from Hertfordshire, Basilia from Norfolk, Amabilia and Amicia de Malketon from Cambridgeshire, and Petronella and Agnes from Oxfordshire. Once King Henry II had granted lands just outside of Taunton to the Order of St John of Jerusalem, it was declared that a nunnery belonging to the Order would be set up there. As a result, the sisters left behind the mixed male-female communities where they had been serving and made long cross-country journeys to join Fina at Minchin Buckland Priory in Somerset. This was the very first all-female community of the Order in the country and they had been proud to be a part of it. Christina was now the only one of those original nine still alive and she was very much living through the winter days of her life.

A gentle tap at her door.

Christina smiled to herself. She knew who it was: young Agnes, whose very name harked back to the original Agnes from Oxfordshire who represented the early days of the priory but had long since passed away. The Agnes before her now was the daughter of the Earl of Arundel. She had joined the community a few years ago, well 8 years ago but to someone as old as Christina it seemed like only a few. Agnes was a sensitive soul. Prioress Fina's death had gnawed at the girl's soul.

"Come through," Christina called.

A sniffle and sigh announced Agnes' entrance.

"How are you, my child?" Christina made her voice as soothing as possible.

"God bless you for asking, sister. It is a sad time. I have just this moment come from my turn at the vigil for Prioress Fina." Agnes was fidgeting with her hands as her mind drifted back to that candlelit chamber where everyone else had been so composed while tears had trickled endlessly down Agnes' cheeks to fall on her ebony-coloured habit.

"Come, sit." Agnes did so. "Is it purgatory you're thinking of? We know that Prioress Fina will not spend too long there. She was compassionate to a fault and we will continue to pray for her soul for many a year in order to shorten her time there. There will also be a secular priest saying masses for her soul and the souls of the house's founders and benefactors. Soon they will rest with the Lord in eternal peace and joy."

"Amen. How she will be missed, however." Another sigh. "Her soothing voice in the chapter house whenever she read her sermons to us. Her laughter. Her warm hands. Her chiding included! And I never… I never got the chance to hear all her stories."

"Well, if you like, I could tell you more about her."

"Please, sister. It would mean so much to me."

Christina couldn't help but smile. "Very well. In truth, it would be pleasant to narrate her story to you and we should have a few moments before prayer time. This community was set up long before you were born, in the year of our Lord 1186. Myself and seven other sisters – all dead now of course – came from all across England to serve here in Durston village under Prioress Fina, and a community of brothers belonging to the Order was established at the same time. Their house has been adjacent to ours ever since with just a few members to help us out."

"Fina was unique when she started, wasn't she? The first-ever prioress for our Order in England, I heard."

"Just so. Minchin Buckland Priory is a special place that we are privileged to be a part of, serving our community, caring for the sick, sheltering pilgrims, ministering to the poor and raising money for the Holy Wars in the east."

"And Fina oversaw it all, didn't she? The Muslims conquered Jerusalem just before the priory opened, I believe."

"Actually, it was the following year. Imagine, a young woman newly made prioress and the Christian world fell into chaos soon after! The hospital in Jerusalem, built in 1080 by monks who were later recognised as an order in 1113, the hospital that was the catalyst for the entire Order of St John of Jerusalem, had to be closed down. But the Muslims had such respect for our Order that they gave the monks there a whole year to transfer the patients and then shut the hospital doors for the very last time. So that would have been in the year 1188."

"It must've been a shock for you all."

"Yes. We fasted and prayed for the safety of the monks and patients. And I confess that my heart skipped a beat any time a messenger arrived at our gate. Well, God in His great wisdom allowed the Muslims to overrun the holy city of Jerusalem. The closure in 1188 was the end of the hospital in Jerusalem but the Christians managed to reconquer nearby Acre in 1191 and so we regained our hospital in that city."

"Ah, so that's why Acre is the headquarters of the Order."

"Exactly."

"And to think that you lived through all of that!"

Christina nodded. "Now, what else can I tell you? Oh, did you know that right from the start, it was announced that the Order of St John of Jerusalem would have no other sisterhood in England other than our own, here in Buckland?"

"No, I did not, though I knew that ours happens to be the only one in the country."

"Just so. It is the only one *now*. But did you ever hear of Aconbury in Herefordshire?"

Agnes shook her head.

"Well, it was a little later on from when our priory was brought into being in 1186. From what I've heard, during King John's reign, by which we're talking about the early 1200s, Margaret de Lacy had set up a nunnery. By 1233, she had entrusted the house to St John of Jerusalem despite the former king, Henry II, insisting that our convent was to be the only one in the country."

"Goodness!"

"Yes, well, the funny thing is that after defying the royal command, Margaret herself, a married woman nonetheless, petitioned the pope. Her request was that the nunnery would be disconnected from the order!"

"Extraordinary. Why was that?"

"She discovered that she and her nuns could not act completely independently, that they had to be obedient to the Order."

"The lady got her wish, didn't she?"

"Yes, the pope agreed to it three years ago, in 1237, and they are Augustinian nuns now. So they only spent four years being attached to our Order. Let us hope that nobody else tries to found a St John of Jerusalem nunnery in England. I rather like being unique!"

"I wouldn't mind. But I suppose I don't carry around the whole history of this place in my heart, like you do. Because you have been at this priory all these decades, haven't you?"

Christina chuckled. "Yes, I am a wrinkly old nun, to be sure! And Fina was my constant companion until yesterday."

"Because she served as prioress for all these years ever since the priory opened?"

"She did. For 54 years. I have known her longer than you have been alive. She trained me in so many things that are useful to our Order- how to care for the sick and poor both in our local community and how to treat foreign ailments should we ever be called abroad. She taught me how to keep the accounts, tend the plants, make up herbal ointments for the Knights to use out in the Holy Lands… But hark." A dull bell was sounding in the background. "It is time for Lauds. We must make haste to the chapel to join our sisters."

They rose, smoothed out their habits and strolled behind their sisters to the chapel. Christina reflected on an interesting fact about the chapel. Ever since 1227, some thirteen years back, a daily mass to St Mary, the Mother of God, was recited at the nun's chapel, which was in fact dedicated to St Mary as well as St Nicholas. The Countess of Leicester herself had been given permission to choose the chaplain whose sole occupation was to recite this mass each day. In exchange for this permission, the countess had given extensive lands to the priory. She made a mental note to relate this to young Agnes at some point.

Distractions aside, she settled in for the morning's session of prayers in Latin, as were all their services, where she especially held Fina in her heart during the moments of silence.

As was the custom among nuns, the burial took place swiftly and without any great pageantry, not even for this woman who had been the very cornerstone of their priory. Following their prayer time, the sisters stepped outside and formed a circle around a pit that had been dug by the priory's male labourers. When the men emerged from the building reverently carrying a shrouded body, a squeak escaped Agnes' mouth. A stern middle-aged nun glared at her. Agnes ducked her head in embarrassment and watched silently as the men lowered the body into the ground beside Fina's favourite pear tree to the tune of bleating lambs in nearby farms and the sound of trickling water from the nearby stream. The labourers lowered their dirt-covered faces and scratched their heads, for they too would grieve the loss of Fina. To the side of them, Agnes, though free of tears, was pale and wide-eyed through the prayers recited by the older members of the community.

As the black serpentine procession of nuns ambled back to the house in silence, Christina felt Agnes' eyes on her back. Turning, she met Agnes' searching gaze. The girl's pained expression indicated that she was seeking more comfort from the older nun.

Yet, chores were awaiting Christina and Agnes. Life had to go on. The younger woman had to go to the priory's well to fetch water while it was the senior nun's turn to sit down and have a look at the priory's incomes and outgoings for the month. She was pleased to see the mill was still functioning well after last week's repairs and that wheat had been delivered to the granary the day before. She wrote down how much grain they would sell that week and how much they would use for their own consumption– in baking bread, brewing beer and making gruel.

With regard to wool, the prioress was the one who controlled its sale. Thankfully, the sheep had only just been sheered and the wool sold on so nothing was needed that day except to ensure that the coins received matched the figures in the accounts.

She moved on to revenue and ran her finger down the list of tithes from the villagers: calves, lambs, wool, piglets, geese, cheese, garlic, leeks, cider, herbs, milk and honey. It would just about do. Lord knew the sisters had always suffered financially while the brothers next door lived in relative comfort seeing as how a lot more produce went to the men. It was not the fault of the villagers; they did as they were told.

The rents from their lands did not quite add up. Christina realised that it was the prioress who had last checked them. Fina's failing body had likely made her tired and prone to mistakes. No matter. It was only a slight error and easily rectified. How strange to think that Fina, who had written accounts for 54 years, would never again dip her quill in the ink pot and mark the paper with her own hand. It would be other women now who would pick up the quill and write where Fina had left off.

Brushing aside those sentiments, Christina pressed onwards to any unresolved maintenance or repair issues. The labourers had been regularly carting up firewood from the adjacent forest to the priory. Good. The barn roof still had a hole in it, so she composed a note for one of the brothers to find a builder that afternoon. She sighed in frustration. It was a nuisance that the sisters could not go out and about in the village to run errands by themselves.

Following her time with the finances, the sisters had a mid-morning mass to attend. Just had she had done so many times with her prioress, a dear friend and counsellor, Christina slowly succeeded in getting down on her knees and prayed the Hail Mary in unison with the others:

Ave Maria, gratia plena,
Dominus tecum.

Benedicta tu in mulieribus,

et benedictus fructus ventris tui, Jesus.

This was followed by a meagre lunch in the refectory of bread, parsnips and turnips washed down with water. Although there were sheep, pigs, orchard fruits and even pike in the priory's fishponds, the nuns had vowed to a life of poverty, chastity and obedience. It was far holier to live humbly and abstain from luxuries such as meat and fruit. Fish was permitted, but only on Fridays.

Oh, the orchards! Christina smiled to remember how cross Fina had got with the local peasants for wanting to go wassailing through their orchard at Twelfth Night. It was an awful pagan tradition of processing amid the fruit trees while making a raucous din in order that the spirits would ensure a good cider harvest. Formidable Fina soon put paid to that upon her arrival in Durston village.

As Christina delicately placed the last morsel of parsnip into her mouth, she gazed along the table to see Agnes only halfway through her meal, her eyes fixed on the empty chair where Fina would have sat.

That was why the elderly nun sought Agnes out during their afternoon gardening session. Christina's knees complained any time she stooped down and so she had to limit kneeling to worship time only. Thus, she sat on a stool and cut sage and coriander, which would be ground into medicine for the Knights out in the Holy Lands. Meanwhile, Agnes laboured with the garlic plants, another plant vital for wounded Knights. Clipping the plant sent Christina automatically into a state of deep peacefulness, yet before long Agnes interrupted her dream-like state with a sudden question.

"Do you recall, sister, when the house partially burnt down some 6 years ago?"

Christina knew where this was going but simply replied, "Of course. Praise God that we were able to achieve its reconstruction."

"Yes. It was a daunting undertaking when we lost so much and had to start again, brick by brick. Thank goodness Prioress Fina was there to steer us. She was instrumental in supervising the rebuilding once King Henry III had granted us those thirty oak trees from his own parkland."

"She was a great leader, the greatest. And at least Henry III and his granddad before him, Henry II, are men who have championed our cause. I wish the same could be said for the brothers who live beside us and belong to our very Order. Betwixt we women and the brothers, there have always been..." Agnes puzzled over how to express herself respectfully.

"Struggles over money?" Christina was too old for politeness where it wasn't warranted.

"Yes."

"Fina was never silent about the fact that we sisters did not always get our fair share of the profits from the tithes and lands. And how the brothers still complain to this day about having to look after us as if we are such troublesome creatures!"

Agnes giggled.

"Honestly! On the whole, we operate as separate entities. It is not too much for them to say mass for us and go out into the villages to collect our rents, and occasionally represent us legally given that we are not allowed to as women. Women are no less rational than men, whatever the scholars may write. For the Good Book tells us that we were both made in the image of God, Our Lord."

Agnes mulled this over, having never thought of it that way before.

Christina ploughed on. "Those monks next door expect us to be quiet and obliging while they hog the money that is rightfully ours. But our late prioress was a great advocate for us and her successor will need to be equally bold. We have a sisterhood that keeps getting larger and larger - praise God - but with incomes that do not increase accordingly. And we have other outgoings- helping the sick and needy. I don't need to remind you that being fairly close to Poole as we are, we receive many ailing pilgrims who are in need of care. Some contribute and some cannot."

Agnes nodded. Poole was known for being a port frequently used by those journeying out to the Hold Land.

Two middle-aged sisters, who were toiling with the onion plants nearby, overheard these words and began to murmur to each other, shaking their heads. All of the sisters were disgruntled about the way they were discriminated against.

Agnes piped up, "I am always grateful to my father for providing for me here. When I entered the sisterhood, I knew I would not be a burden on the priory. I am grateful, in addition, to the king for ensuring the payments continued after my father's death."

For a moment, Christina looked out at the surrounding patchwork of gentle fields stretching out across the flat terrain, then asked, "Was it a great change for you coming from Arundel Castle in the east to this remote little priory?"

"It was like… coming across another world. But I would do it again gladly. I have no regrets. I feel called to this life and to this landscape."

The girl's earnestness warmed Christina's heart. Though the latter's days at the priory and in this world were numbered as her body dwindled, at least there would be fresh, enthusiastic youths to carry on their work.

"I was about to say something else before," Agnes continued. "Something you said made me think... Oh, that's it. You mentioned her successor. Who *will* replace her?"

"Well, you know the procedure. We sisters will all vote upon a replacement and we are fortunate to have a say in who shall preside over us. Lay women do not enjoy the same privilege- they must obey their fathers and then their husbands."

Agnes nodded. She didn't envy married women their lot in life. "At the same time," continued Christina, "It is a great responsibility that each and every one of us has. We should not take it lightly but rather pray continually for God's guidance over this matter of great importance. So then, we vote and the prior of our province has to then approve it."

"But who do you think will be chosen?"

"Only time will tell, dear Agnes, time will tell and God will speak unto us."

Notes

The Minchin Buckland or Buckland Sororum Priory was established in Lower Durston. Both names refer to its purpose as a nunnery. Minchin (or Mynchin) comes from the Old English word 'mynecen', meaning nun, and 'sororum' is from the Latin for sister. These additions were possibly used to distinguish it from the monks who had lived there before. You see, the priory, set up in 1186, wasn't the first religious house there. In c.1166, a house for Augustinian men was set up but they committed one crime too many and behaved badly in public, so King Henry II made them give up the house as well as other properties given to the monks, including the churches at North Petherton, Chedzoy, Kilmersdon and Beckington. Henry's queen, Eleanor of Aquitaine, was a tremendously powerful and pious woman but was imprisoned for rebelling against her husband from 1173–1189; otherwise, she might have assisted in the foundation.

As concerns Henry, certain historians believe his participation in establishing Buckland Priory was partly due to the guilt he felt for causing the murder of the Archbishop of Canterbury, St Thomas a Becket. Creating a female-only nunnery for St John of Jerusalem sisters might have been an act of penance and a way to ingratiate himself with the pope.

The nuns' names suggest they were not Anglo-Saxons but Normans or foreigners. Wherever they were born, they travelled to Durston from other centres across England (Carbrooke, Norfolk; Clanfield, Hampshire; Gosford, Oxfordshire; Hogshaw, Buckinghamshire; Shingay, Cambridgeshire; and Standon, Hertfordshire) to form a female-only community. The thinking was that having celibate men and women in close proximity might not be such a good idea after all. However, the women had a community of brothers next door to take care of them although the men often took more than their fair share of the income.

The Order of St John of Jerusalem (also called the Knights Hospitaller) was founded in Jerusalem c.1092. In 1100, the first English house for brothers opened in London, which became its headquarters for the country. It differed from its rival, The Knights Templar, in that it committed to accepting women into the order. The Templars temporarily accepted women but in 1129 decided that they no longer would.

These military orders were involved in the Crusades and some of the St John of Jerusalem monks sadly engaged in warfare in the Middle East. The English had been indoctrinated to believe that fighting the "infidels" was necessary for the "defence of the catholic faith", a statement added to the Order's mission in 1187, by which point they had already been involved in warfare for some time. For them, Jerusalem had to be saved and protected from the Muslims. Myra Struckmeyer affirms that "the Hospitallers saw no contradiction in combining care to the sick and poor with warfare against the Muslims: both were acts of charity." The latter was seen as military service for God, an act of devotion because the Muslims were viewed as the enemies of God.

Therefore, part of the money that the Buckland nuns raised for their Order would fund warfare, therefore Fina and the other sisters can never be held up as perfect examples to follow but as women of their time. My admiration for them stems only from how they were able to exercise a certain amount of control over their own lives in a male-dominated country and to serve the local poor people in Somerset. They also provided employment. In fact, the Church in Somerset – and other parts of the country – was the largest employer for most of the Medieval Era.

Regarding the prioress, Fina is short for Serafina or Josefina in Romance languages. I wonder if she was born in southern Europe or had ancestors from there. She is reported to have ruled there for the first 54 or so years of the priory's life (1186–c.1240), spanning the reigns of 4 sets of English kings and queens, and outliving seven different leaders (masters) of the Order of St John of Jerusalem, whose headquarters were in London.

We don't know anything about Fina's personality (or any of the other nuns) but the concrete fact that she ruled for approximately 54 years suggests that she was vibrant and strong as an ox. Since Fina must have begun her rule while still a young woman, even in her youth she must have been mature, wise and adept at management and leadership. The backdrop for her life began with the 1066 Norman Conquest, which brought about great change to England: ending Anglo-Saxon slavery but at the same time introducing increased patriarchy and the removal of almost all Anglo-Saxon landowners.

Christina de Hogshaw was one of the original sisters. Whether she outlived Fina is unknown, but I thought it would be a nice way to tell Fina's story.

Young Agnes was the Earl of Arundel's daughter. In 1232, he granted 40 shillings a year for her upkeep there and after his death, Henry III instructed that these payments continue for the rest of Agnes' life. Presumably, Agnes witnessed the passing of Fina.

The Countess of Leicester, who chose the chaplain for the masses to St Mary in a charter dated 16th July 1227, was named Loretta de Briouze (or Lauretta de Braose). A widow, she took a vow of chastity in 1221 and set herself up as a recluse near Canterbury. Becoming a chaste recluse allowed her to help the poor and have a measure of control over her own affairs and money. She died around the year 1266.

Margaret de Lacy (née de Briouze/Braose) was Loretta's sister. She was the patron and founder of a house in Herefordshire, set up in 1216. It was the only rival to Buckland's claim as the only female Knights Hospitaller house in England.

The dispute between the nuns, monks and priests at Buckland is documented. For instance, the pope himself responded to the sisters' complaint in 1229 that the vicar of Petherton was taking too much of the church's income and not giving enough to the nunnery. It appears that the women were ultimately unsuccessful but shows that they were keen to stand up for themselves.

Fina's dispute against wassailing is my imagination but it was certainly frowned upon by pious people. To this day, people in Somerset go wassailing in early January but it has largely been replaced by carol-singing in December.

The nuns would have prayed in Latin, hence the Hail Mary appearing in the text as "Ave Maria…" The final lines of the prayer weren't commonly in use until the 1300s, so I have omitted them.

Fina's successor is unknown, but she would have had to deal with a fire in 1264, which highlights the nuns' lack of funds. Afterwards, it was noted that there were fire-damaged buildings in need of mending but also some buildings not affected by the fire needed repair. The nuns at that time complained about their steward and after some negotiation, they were allowed to suspend him but not kick him out forever. The successor might have been Eleanor (or Alienor) of Actune. She was definitely the prioress by around 1280. Eleanor was probably from the village of Acton Bridge in Cheshire since it was formerly known as Actune. Eleanor's tenure ended in either 1292 or 1301.

By 1500, the brothers' house existed only as land. Only one brother remained as the sisters' chaplain. The sisters' time was by then numbered. On 10th February 1539, during the Dissolution of the Monasteries, Prioress Katherine Bourchier and her sisters had to surrender the house to Henry VIII's commissioners in exchange for pensions from the crown. This marked the closing of the only house of St John of Jerusalem sisters ever to be established in England after 359 years of existence.

None of the priory buildings has survived to this day, except for the walls, the current farm's barn and the triangular-shaped fishponds. In fact, we only have a rough idea of how the structures were laid out. Another lasting remnant of the nuns is Eleanor of Actune's grave slab, currently housed at the Museum of Somerset in Taunton. A large, heavy rectangular block of stone, it is simple and humble in style. It has faded somewhat over the years, but you can make out the cross of St John of Jerusalem.

The first image on the next page is my reproduction of the unsymmetrical cross on Eleanor of Actune's grave slab. Below it is the Order's symbol, which is still in use today. This is rather less decorative than the one used for Eleanor's final resting place.

Chapter Bibliography:

A Brief History of Life in the Middle Ages by Martyn Whittock

A History of the County of Somerset: Volume 2, edited by William Page

A monastic funeral by Ruth Johnson

Female Hospitallers in the Twelfth and Thirteenth Centuries by Myra Struckmeyer

http://pastscape.english-heritage.org.uk

Knights Hospitaller by Mark Cartwright

Margaret de Lacy and the Hospital of St John at Aconbury, Herefordshire by Helen Jane Nicholson

'Merely Nuns'? Exploring Female Agency in Hospitaller Houses in the Middle Ages by Nancy Mavroudi

Monastic sites and monastic estates in Somerset and Wiltshire in the Middle Ages: a regional approach by Jenni Butterworth

Mynchin Buckland Priory by Jimmy Graham

The History of Mynchin Buckland Priory and Preceptory by Thomas Hugo

The Sisters of the Order of Saint John at Mynchin Buckland by Myra Struckmeyer

Women with the healing touch by Duncan McAra

The Commandery and Priory of the Order of St John in Somerset by Desmond Bastick

A Short History of the Order of St John and in particular the City of Wells Division by Paul Fry

www.encyclopedia.com

www.oxforddnb.com

QUICK TRIBUTE

Queens of Queen Camel

The first royal woman to own land in the village of East Camel was Countess Gytha, who we met in the Interlude. Although William the Conqueror confiscated the land, it would later be owned by more female royals and so would come to be known as Queen Camel, so we'll call it that from now on.

The next woman lived in the twelfth century. Isabella of Gloucester (1173-1217) was married to King John before he gained the throne. But Isabella and John couldn't have children together. Plus John wanted to snap up a better-connected wife. So, he had the marriage annulled on the grounds that they were distant cousins. Poor Isabella of Gloucester was married to a prince but not a king and as such, she did not become queen. At least Isabella didn't have to give up Queen Camel! If Isabella visited the Somerset village, she may have stopped off at the Buckland Priory as well and become friendly with the nuns there, but this is pure speculation. We do know that Isabella died at Keynsham Abbey, founded by her father, on 14th October 1217, by which point Henry III was the king.

Henry III took possession of the property upon Isabella's death and gave it to his wife, Queen Eleanor of Provence (1223-1291), who established a deer park there.

Then, in October 1275, her son, Edward I, gave the royal land to his wife Eleanor of Castile (1241-1290), whose other properties in Somerset included Somerton (granted in 1265). Remarkably, this Eleanor was appointed the Sheriff of Somerset and Dorset on 28th July 1285, the first woman to hold the office. John St Loe was her deputy and some documents state that he exercised the duties of the role and that he carried out duties until 1289, so perhaps Eleanor retained her position until then, the year before her death. It could be that Eleanor was overseeing it all from a distance. We certainly know that she was a prolific letter writer due to her constant travelling with Edward and her keen interest in managing her various properties. If she did attend any of the county court meetings, they were held in the county town, which was Somerton between 1276 and 1376 (before the meetings and county town moved back to Ilchester). Eleanor's adept linguistic skills in French, Latin, Castilian and possibly English and her flair for business would have been very helpful for this role. There would not be another female Sheriff of Somerset until more than 700 years had passed and Elizabeth Gass was invested in 1994, by which point it had become merely a ceremonial office. Eleanor of Castile stayed in Queen Camel with her husband at least twice. One visit was in late 1285, during her time as sheriff. An earlier stopover was from 9th to 12th April 1278, before they headed on to Glastonbury, where they celebrated Easter on 17th April. The purpose of this trip was to see the reburial of bodies alleged to be those of Guinevere and Arthur, found at Glastonbury Abbey nearly a hundred years previously. Cynical people will note that the 1191 "discovery" led to more pilgrims heading to Glastonbury and therefore more income for the abbey, just what the monks needed after the buildings were devastated by fire in 1184. When previous fundraising – including laying out the relics of saints such as Patrick, Dunstan, Indract and possibly Dominica for the general public to touch – proved insufficient, the monks just so happened to find a king and queen buried on their land! The (probably fake) royal skeletons of Arthur and Guinevere were wrapped in silk and ceremoniously laid to rest in a marble tomb in front of the abbey church's altar, which was later destroyed on Henry VIII's orders.

Speaking of that king, he himself came to own Queen Camel, inheriting it from his formidable grandmother Margaret Beaufort, who styled herself as My Lady the King's Mother. Also, as a side note, Henry VIII's wife Jane Seymour has two tenuous links to Somerset: she may have been born at West Bower Manor in Durleigh (though Wolfhall in Wiltshire is more probable) and when her father was Sheriff of Somerset from 1515 to 1516, he lived in Shepton Beauchamp and may have brought his young daughter to live with him.

But, back to Queen Camel. Between Eleanor of Provence and Margaret Beaufort, a succession of queen consorts had owned the village. However, when our first queen regnant, Mary I, took possession of it, she chose to swap it with the chancellor for another village in Northamptonshire.

(Keynsham Abbey, where Isabella of Gloucester died. The abbey was not spared demolition during the Dissolution, even though Henry VIII's own great-uncle, Jasper Tudor, was buried there.)

Sources: King Arthur in Somerset by Rosemary Clinch & Michael Williams, The Place-Names of Somerset by James S. Hill, Royal Interest in Glastonbury and Cadbury: Two Arthurian Itineraries by Caroline Shenton, A History of Somerset by Robert Dunning, The Sheriffs of Somerset from the eleventh to the twentieth century by Sophia W Rawlins, Somerset Villages by Robin Bush, www.queen-camel.co.uk, www.keynshamabbey.com, historicengland.org.uk, sheptonbeauchamp.org.uk, Eleanor of Castile: The Shadow Queen by Sara Cockerill.

Chapter 10: The Barefoot Baroness (14th century)

It was 1341 and the eleven-year-old Johane Burwasch was about to marry.

Particularly unfortunate was that her husband-to-be lived in a far-off county and his family was known for their ruthlessness. Ever since William de Mohun, otherwise known as 'The Scourge of the West', had arrived in England over three hundred years ago with the Conqueror himself in 1066, the Mohuns had followed in the footsteps of this villain. William had pillaged and slaughtered to stake his claim on the Somerset coast, establishing his formidable castle at Dunster village and the Mohuns had used the fortress as their base ever since.

Johane's Uncle Henry announced it one evening to her father, Bartholomew, once they had finished the evening meal.

"This wine is divine as always, Bartholomew, but let me get down to business now. My ward, John de Mohun, descended from the great William de Mohun himself, has come of age now."

"Ah yes, the fellow whose father died when John was but a boy. Remind me of him."

"Indeed. The father was therefore outlived by both John and John's paternal grandfather. That made little John the heir to his paternal grandfather's fortune. Then, aged 10, the grandfather in turn breathed his last."

"Hmm, so John inherited everything?"

"He did. His paternal grandmother, Sibyl de Mohun, was granted custody of the castle while I became John's ward."

"And he's 21 years of age now?"

"Exactly. He has taken possession of his inheritance. And a baron to boot! He's now looking to sire an heir of his own. Your Johane would be ideal."

"So, this John de Mohun has Dunster Castle. What of other properties?"

"He has good lands in Kilton, Minehead, Carhampton and so on… all in Somersetshire."

"Then it's settled. When shall the marriage take place?"

"As soon as possible. She'll have a son in no time and I vow you won't regret this, brother."

The men's tones indicated that Johane would have no say in the matter, that they barely registered her presence in the room.

Johane would leave behind her family homes in Sussex and carve out a new life for herself in far-off Somerset, or at least try to survive out there. Because how much autonomy would an 11-year-old be given? And what kind of a life could it be? She had heard stories about John, gossip that reached her ears through keyholes when the servants thought no one was listening.

"…soon be living beyond his means, I reckon."

"'Tis never good when a bloke comes into 'is inheritance so young. He's liable to squander it, mark m' words."

"He's certainly squandering it at the moment. I 'eard that baron be already starting to borrow money here and there."

"Blimey. If I had as much coinage as 'e, I'd never need to borrow from others. Fancy the master agreeing to marry her off to the likes of 'im, a young'un with no thought for how 'e will keep her comfortable. We better pray this John sees sense, for the young mistress' sake."

"Sense? 'Im? No, too much money and not enough sense, if thou ask me!"

Johane's eyes had filled with tears. She had clutched her rag doll tight to her chest and bolted off to find fresh air, to fill her body with something wholesome to replace these ugly thoughts that were creeping in.

Ugly thoughts but true thoughts. Johane was under no pretence that this extravagant, selfish man would be an easy one to live with. She couldn't imagine he could be patient with her, a serious child who was being raised to manage a household discerningly and behave with dignity.

*

She'd had no choice in the matter, of course. Hence, Johane Burwasch became Johane de Mohun and she swapped Sussex for Somerset. The de Mohuns held land in Somerset alone; she would be in that county constantly from now on unless they visited court.

She found that she had nothing against the sceneries. The beauty of Dunster Castle went some way towards cheering her up, at least to begin with. Her eleven-year-old eyes saw it as a fairy-tale palace perched on top of a hill lined with luscious green trees and views of Dunster village below, the wide, murky sea and the picturesque Exmoor Forest landscape.

Yet, the enchantment soon wore off and Johane took the chateau's luxuries for granted. They didn't make up for John de Mohun's temperament. The feudal baron was almost as bad as Johane had expected. He walked around with a scowl on his face most of the time, frequently shouted at the peasants, and the thought of how he behaved in the bedchamber was enough to make Johane shudder.

The first two years in the cold, lonely castle passed very slowly for Johane. The maids tried to cheer her up with little Somerset ditties:

> *St Dunstan as the story goes,*
> *Once pulled the devil by the nose,*
> *With red-hot tongs, which made him roar,*
> *That he was heard three miles or more.*

The arrival of children made life more pleasant. Her first came when she had seen just 13 summers.

"Her name shall be Elizabeth. For my mother." Johane's eyes gleamed with pride.

"Call her what you will. She is only a girl, after all." John barely glanced at the newborn babe before returning to his own bedchamber. "Hand her to the wet nurse and get yourself bleeding again so you can give me a boy next time." She blanched at his crude words.

The second was another girl.

"This one will be Maud, for both of my grandmothers had that name."

"I care not in the least. All you are good for is girls. Your mother produced three healthy boys and yet you give me girl after girl. Your humours are out of balance, no doubt. Perhaps the leeches need to be employed again."

She hugged her daughter tight to protect her from his dismissive words and hoped he would be called to fight for the king against foreign enemies before the dreaded leeches could make a reappearance. He had already been summoned a few times since the marriage began and this always brought Johane much-needed relief from him.

During one such absence, disaster struck the country.

1348 had seen John honoured along with other noblemen in becoming one of the founding members of the king's Order of the Garter before riding off to war in France. However, the summer of that year was particularly wet, devastating the harvests across England. People went hungry and immunity was low.

That provided the perfect circumstances for a plague outbreak. The Bishop of Bath and Wells was fully aware of the risk. On 17th August, two days after the Feast of the Assumption of the Virgin Mary, he composed a letter from Evercreech, urging congregations to pray against plague by stating, amongst other things:

"You should arrange for processions and stations to be performed at least every Friday in every collegiate, conventual and parish church, so that, abasing themselves humbly before the eyes of divine mercy, they should be contrite and penitent for their sins, and should not omit to expiate them with devout prayers, so that the mercies of God may speedily prevent us and that he will, for his kindness' sake, turn away from his people this pestilence and the other harsh blows."

St George's Church in Dunster was no exception and the de Mohuns regularly attended, alongside praying in their private chapel dedicated to St Stephen within the castle grounds. Johane's fervent prayers continued into the colder months at the latter end of the year when her hands stung with the bitter cold that blew into the draughty chapel.

'But 'twas in vain,' thought Johane in December, by which point the bubonic plague was spreading like wildfire through the towns and villages of Somerset. What had they all done to deserve this?

Aged just 17, Johane found herself in charge of a household during a pandemic outbreak. She had no choice but to be brave and firm in the face of a terrible situation.

"Bolt the castle gate and admit no one."

"Not even for the celebrations of the Feast of St Nicholas?" a maid asked meekly.

"No, nor even for Christmas. If outside purchases need to be made, vendors can approach the gate alone; they shall not pass it," she ordered the men. For once, she felt grateful to live on a hill in such a rural village. Grateful too was she for their extensive fields with livestock and an accompanying dairy house, and for their two corn mills at the foot of the hill, powered by the River Avill, from which flour could be taken to the bakehouse. They were unlikely to starve, at least.

January saw no improvement. Walled up in his manor at Wiveliscombe, the bishop wrote another letter, lamenting how many parish churches had been left without a priest to care for them. A practical man, he went on to advise that due to this shortage of clergymen, a dying person could now confess their sins to a layman, and even a laywoman if there was nobody else about, rather than die unconfessed. Many in Somersetshire thought this a scandalous idea, but Johane could see the reasoning behind it.

The months wore on and the plague took its victims. The clergy in the Dunster parish were dropping dead like flies, leaving the churches vacant. Cutcombe, for instance, just seven miles from Dunster, was left without a priest. It was a terrifying time for all, not least because nobody knew how to cure an inflicted patient. They could only isolate the person and pray to God for recovery. Some survived and some did not. Nor could anyone be sure how the disease was spreading and how to stop it. The astrologists blamed the alignment of the stars, others saw it as divine punishment and whipped themselves daily to try and atone for their sins.

One servant had a theory that the huge flocks of sheep in the Dunster area were to blame for their having higher rates of death than other regions without sheep.

"It could be so, it could be so," Johane mused. "We will purchase no sheep products from now on," she determined.

On and on the pandemic struck. Worryingly, healthy, young people were succumbing to it in vast numbers. The workforce was dying off, creating food shortages for those fortunate enough to still be alive.

Then, it was too close for comfort. The very servant who had blamed the sheep complained of a tingling sensation. Johane bade him retire to his room at once. And so, he took to his bed with painful boils on his armpits that soon spread to his arms and legs. He thrashed around feverishly on top of his blanket and clutched at his head in agony.

Steeling herself, she ordered the servants to leave food outside his room as well as herbs so that he could rub the boils with them but under no circumstances was anybody to enter the room. Her daughters were not allowed to even step onto the corridor that led to the room.

Prayers were said, candles were lit but within a week, the servant lay dead.

The next to die was a maid who had taken food to the first servant. Mercifully, she didn't suffer long, dying on the very day she caught it. Yet that itself was frightening- that somebody could be fighting fit one day and dead the next.

Crossing herself, Johane swept up her children, Elizabeth and Maud, entered a suite of rooms within the castle and locked the door behind them. A healthy maid was to bring food and remove waste each day.

How the little girls howled with the boredom and lack of fresh air. But Johane stayed firm. With prayers and planning, this hideous disease was not going to claim her children.

Slowly and steadily, the dying became less frequent. That's what the maid told her. Johane dared to open the door to her prison just an inch and peek along the corridor. The next day, she strolled up and down the corridor, just to make certain that the servants hadn't stolen all her belongings in the time she had been shut away.

Within a week, she was wandering freely around the castle, assessing the damage caused by the storm of plague.

Months went by before real normality returned, though. It wasn't until December 1349 that the country could say that the Great Pestilence had left its shores, having taken lives from practically every single household.

Johane had just got over the shock and was feeling endlessly grateful that she and her daughters had survived the pandemic when little Elizabeth was plucked from her life. Late that year saw the celebration of a marriage arranged by John, who was by then back in the country. The bride was none other than Johane's eldest daughter, the 6-year-old Elizabeth who married an aristocrat named William Montacute, Earl of Salisbury, who had been born in Donyatt, Somerset, 21 years previously.

Without a second glance, John was happy to dismiss his eldest daughter from the castle, sending her out to Berkshire to live with her husband's family. Of course, the marriage would not be consummated until she reached the age of 12, but she would now be raised far away, trained to be William's perfect wife. Johane was powerless to stop this transaction from taking place. Instead of a cause for merriment, for her it was another hardship to bear after more than a year of nothing but hardships.

Little Elizabeth was tearful as she hugged her mother tightly. Promises of visits were made. Vows to pray for each other were sworn. 'At least she did not perish in the Great Pestilence, as did so many other children,' thought Johane. 'And at least I still have my darling Maud to keep me company.'

Unfortunately, John let her down yet again just months later.

Johane was never privy to her husband's actions or whereabouts; he saw it as beneath himself to discuss them with her. Thus, she heard about it first by overhearing two servants gossiping in the courtyard.

"Well see, this man, a tenant and all, 'e took our master to court over lands. 'E was called to give evidence in a town called Somerton or such like–"

"Yeah, o' course I knows Somerton, you dunce! They made it the county town not long ago."

"Alright, alright. Dost thou want to hear the story, or no?"

"Yeah, get on wi' it!"

"Well, the king's judges were sat to hear cases and the like in our *glorious* county town. The point is, that tenant got to Somerton alright but never bloomin' got to the courthouse. On 'is way, 'e were set upon."

"And you reckon it was our master what ordered the attack?"

"Worse! Down in the village, they be sayin' that the master hisself assaulted the fellow right in the middle of town."

"No!"

"Yeah! Whereupon the fellow scarpered. So, John chased after 'im as far as the churchyard where 'e grabbed the tenant and pulled 'im up onto the horse behind 'im. Carried the poor fella all the way to Langport, I swear to you."

"That's a good 4 or 5 miles!"

"Blimey."

"What a disgrace. So, what happened in Langport?"

"The Sheriff of Somerset rallied the local villagers in Somerton and off they all went and rescued the fellow."

"Just as well! What'll 'appen now?"

"Prison most likely for our master for the assault. 'Tis what 'e deserves."

"Quite right. Our mistress don't deserve all this. With their money, they should be livin' easy. But 'e goes about throwing 'is money away, borrowing all over the place, mortgaging the castle and now comporting himself like a regular thug and–"

"Hark, I reckon as someone's nearby. Best get back to it, Rich."

Johane's head began to ache with this new knowledge. She didn't know what to hope for. On one hand, a prison sentence would be humiliating for all; on the other hand, it would be another pleasant break from John.

It was not her choice to make, of course, and sadly, the outcome was a jail sentence not long enough for Johane to enjoy properly. Whilst he was incarcerated, Johane had one day been struck with a mad idea to sweep up her daughters, hitch her skirt up, steal a boat from the harbour and sail away on the horizon to... where? That was the problem. As a married woman, she was financially dependent on John and had nowhere to escape to. What is more, she hadn't the foggiest idea how to sail.

Besides, before she knew it, he returned, brazen and rude, as if nothing at all had transpired. He'd been given a royal pardon, public enough to bring more shame on the family.

"One rule for us, another for them," a maid muttered to herself, not realising Johane was standing nearby.

That comment was part of the driving force behind Johane's act of boldness several months later. The inhabitants of Dunster had got together and approached the lord of the castle in his audience chamber.

"Humbly, we beseech you to allow us access to your lands on the outskirts of the village for us to put our cattle to grass, m' lord," the bravest member of the gathering said.

"I will not," John cut in no sooner had the man finished. His face was stony.

"Respectfully, m' lord, those lands are not in use and if the plague should visit us once more, God forbid, 'twould be good to have well-fed cows to put to slaughter. Then, we wouldn't need to buy from outside, see, and risk more plague."

"My answer is no."

'What a cretin,' thought Johane. But her words were more tactful. "Husband, this man speaks wise words. It is in all of our interests to have healthy cows in the parish to provide food for ourselves as a community, rather than buy from elsewhere."

"What dost thou care for these peasants?" John scoffed. Recently, he always used the familiar 'thou' with her whilst she was forced to address him with the more formal 'you'.

"It is a mutually beneficial agreement." It was hard to keep her voice level.

"If thou carest so much for this scruffy, barefoot rabble, here's a proposal for thee. I shall grant them as much land as thou canst walk around on. In one day. Barefoot, that is," he sneered.

She swallowed. It would be mortifying for a lady of her rank to go unshod through the fields. Then again, the villagers needed her help and she had already pledged it.

"Very well, husband." She raised her chin and stared him dead in the eyes.

His left eye twitched. "Thou wouldst degrade thyself for *them*?"

"If you think it necessary, husband, yes."

Never one to back down, John nodded gruffly. "So be it.

Tomorrow at seven in the morning."

The next day, grateful that it was summer rather than winter with its harsh frosts, Johane kissed Maud and swept out of the castle in a magnificent, pleated dress. 'I might as well do this with style,' she thought.

The servants grinned as she passed them by, whereas John tutted when he caught sight of her but he grasped her hand and marched her down to the village at the same.

The fields were packed with locals. The men knelt down as she drew near and the women shouted out blessings.

Her cheeks reddened in gratitude for their encouragement. John folded his arms and glared at her, silently willing her to give up. Instead, she met his gaze and slowly crouched down to remove her slippers. With a smile, she held them up to him, at which a cheer went up through the crowds.

After a quick prayer, she lifted her skirts up ever so slightly so as not to trip on them and began to tread through the dew-laced grass, trying not to look at the mud smearing the hems of her dress.

It seemed like an eternity. With every step, she wondered how John would punish her for this act of defiance. But each step got her one step closer to success on behalf of the Dunster inhabitants.

At last, it was over.

"God bless you, m' lady. A finer mistress has never been seen."

"We will pray for you and yours every night from now on."

"We shall forever be grateful; I promise you that."

These were the generous words given to her as soon as her feet had touched the point at which they'd begun.

Through gritted teeth, John consented to his end of the bargain. From that point on, Johane grinned to herself any time she heard the contented moos of cows echoing around the village and up to her ears in the castle.

*

John's irresponsible attitude towards money did not improve as he aged. In fact, by the time Johane's father had died in August 1355, John had laid out forty-three title deeds relating to their Dunster manors and other holdings and put them in his wife's name to save the family from utter bankruptcy.

'The Lord gives and the Lord takes away,' thought Johane when a few years after her father passed away, she brought another daughter into the world.

"I married thee to produce *sons*. To give me *heirs*. And here we have yet another member of the weaker sex."

Johane wouldn't rise to his vitriol. She cleared her throat. "I would like to call her Philippa, after the queen."

"Ha! That dark-skinned half-Moor? If thou dost wish. It might curry favour with the royals, after all."

Even Queen Philippa becoming the girl's godmother did little to improve John's dismissive attitude towards the daughters. Instead, he continued accruing debts left, right and centre. There were times when Johane wished she could shove him into the oubliette- the castle's dungeon beside the gateway where victims were thrown into a chamber and left alone until starvation claimed their lives.

And yet, John lived on, while Johane's dear mother breathed her last in 1360 and her second eldest daughter, Maud, married in 1369, leaving Johane and Philippa alone in Dunster with John.

Johane could not deny how gloomy those years were for her, until finally in 1375, the Lord took away the one she most wanted Him to- the immature 55-year-old John. At his burial at Bruton Priory on a blustery, autumnal day, Johane and Philippa, now a young lady, barely shed a tear.

Indeed, Johane wasted no time in radically taking the reins of her life. Mired in debt by her husband's carelessness, she sold the reversion of the castle, the manors of Minehead and Kilton, and the Hundred of Carhampton to a lady named Elizabeth Luttrell. This reversion meant that the properties would continue to belong to Johane until her death, but her daughters would not inherit them, rather Elizabeth and her heirs would once Johane died. The deal was finalised in November 1376.

The thick wooden castle gates were firmly shut and Johane set out to live at court with her daughter Philippa, thus exchanging the isolated castle for the vivacious royal palaces.

Her years of widowhood were just as eventful as her marital years. It all began with the death of the current king in the following year, bringing a new king to the throne – Richard II, who had seen but 10 years of life.

With the need for an heir, he married at the age of 15 in the same year that Philippa de Mohun married for the first time (1382). Anne of Bohemia became Richard II's wife and Johane became a firm court favourite, exemplified in 1384 when she and her daughter Elizabeth were given livery of the Order of the Garter along with other widows and daughters of the founding Knights of the Garter. Though separated when Elizabeth was young, mother and daughter had a close bond.

She fell from triumph to downfall in 1387. Rebel lords forced Richard to execute some of his favourite councillors and temporarily stripped him of almost all his authority. Johane was spared death but along with three other favoured ladies, she was banished from court.

Ever the survivor, her fortune changed once more when Richard gained his kingly authority a few years later. By the early 1390s, the baroness was back at court.

Understandably, by 1395, the 65-year-old Johane was growing

tired of the lively court and she had lost her dear friend Queen Anne the previous year. She made the decision to retire to Leeds Castle in Kent, which had been granted to her by Anne. Her last visit to Somerset was in 1398 when she took up residence at her property in Minehead for a short while. When asked if she desired to see Dunster Castle, she answered, "No. I have no interest in seeing the castle at all. I'll never forgive it for all the difficulties we experienced there so long ago."

Also in the late 1390s, she began to make plans for her death. Johane did not want to be buried at the little priory in Bruton where her no-good husband was, a priory that had been founded by John's ancestor, William de Mohun, the 'Scourge of the West'. Rather, she opted for the splendid Canterbury Cathedral.

She entered into a formal agreement with the Prior and Convent of Christ Church in Canterbury. As she told her eldest daughter and confidant, "Elizabeth, I have certain standards that must be met once I have died. The monks know of this, but I wish for you to know also to ensure that my instructions are carried out to the letter. For instance, I insist that my body be buried in the tomb that I have prepared and never be removed thereupon. I cannot have it reburied next to John." She shuddered at the thought.

"I understand, Mama."

"The agreement also states that every poor person attending my funeral will receive a shilling and twelve poor men clothed in black at my expense will hold torches. There will also be four candles weighing 20 pounds each that must be lit for the ceremony."

"And masses?"

"One of the monks will be assigned to say mass daily for myself and other people dear to me at the altar of St Mary or, or certain holy days, at the altar of St John the Baptist, near the tomb of St Thomas a Beckett."

"Who are the other people, Mama?"

"King Richard, of course, plus you, my niece Elizabeth, Queen Philippa, Queen Anne of Bohemia and two other royals. I have included John as well, out of duty. Nine of us in total."

"Not your other daughters, Mother?"

"No, not for Maud or Philippa."

Elizabeth didn't want to push her on the subject. Something had happened during the adult lives of Maud and Philippa that put a strain on their relationship with their mother, but Elizabeth had never discovered what exactly.

And so, the elderly lady continued her life at the nearby Leeds Castle, which remained in Johane's possession until Henry IV, who had forced Richard II off the throne, married Joan of Navarre in 1403 and it was granted to the new queen.

Thankfully, Johane was honoured by the cathedral despite her eviction; she was given lodgings at their lavish guest house.

On 4th October 1404, the great baroness lay dead, having outlived her husband, her grandson William, Elizabeth's husband, Maud's first husband and two of Philippa's husbands. On top of that, she lived longer than Elizabeth Luttrell and so it was Lady Luttrell's son who took possession of Dunster Castle instead of her.

At the extraordinary age of 74 (an achievement in itself), Johane had survived marriage at a young age, an irresponsible husband, childbirth, plague and court intrigues. According to Johane's wishes, her body has never been moved from its place in Canterbury Cathedral.

Notes

Most books refer to our protagonist as Joan de Mohun and her maiden name as Burghesh; however, I opted for Johane Burwasch because that is what's written on her stone monument in the crypt of Canterbury Cathedral. I like to think I'm honouring her wishes in this way, although it may not have been her decision to choose that spelling. The monument reads: 'Por dieu priez por l'ame Johane Burwaschs que fut Dame de Mohun', meaning 'Pray to God for the soul of Johane Burwasch who was Lady of Mohun'. Though her tomb remains, it has been damaged over the years by careless builders, including the dog lying at her feet (which suggests she was a besotted pet owner).

A manuscript entitled 'The Mohun Chronicle' was written between 1341 and 1348 by monks in Devon. Probably commissioned by Joan on behalf of her daughters, it outlines, amongst other things, the arrival of the de Mohuns with William the Conqueror. It also describes the myth of the founding of Britain by a Greek king called Brut. Unusually, the chronicle centres around a female character, Albina, Brut's daughter, who travels to the Dunster area with her sister.

Noblewomen didn't breastfeed so that their periods would start up again and they'd be fertile more quickly, hence the reference to periods. As for the plague, the information about the bishop is factual as are the statistics about Somerset and Dunster parish and the fact that John was abroad. However, we don't know how Johane's household was affected by the bubonic plague, later dubbed the Black Death, but no doubt some of her servants died. We only know that she and her daughters survived it and we can imagine the lengths Johane would have gone to in order to keep them safe. For instance, I imagine she bolted the huge castle door in the castle gateway, which is the only part of the castle from Johane's time that still exists today, having been built in the 1200s.

(Dunster Castle gateway, photobombed by my family!)

Thinking now about the three daughters, sources don't state outright that their father was disinterested but we can imagine that his irresponsible approach to money made him an unreliable father. Moreover, I think it's significant that two of the daughters were named after Johane's family members and not his (John's female ancestors were named Christian and Sybil) unless there were other children who didn't survive infancy. And there's the fact that he was his grandfather's sole heir. He was probably pretty keen to have a son who could become the next baron and rule Dunster Castle.

Whether or not Johane and John got on well is also unclear. But there is some evidence that Johane wasn't fond of him- he was terrible with money, she steered clear of Dunster when she visited Somerset in 1398, she didn't wish to be buried with him and (if the legend is true) he humiliated her by making her walk barefoot.

We don't have dates of birth for Maud (aka Matilda) or Philippa. Regarding Maud, I put her close in age to Elizabeth, but she might have been born after the Great Plague. As for Philippa, some sources claim she was the second child, but more reliable sources state she was the youngest for three reasons: she died after the other two, her first marriage took place more than 10 years after Maud's and her third husband was born c.1373. She had to have been born before 1367, given that Queen Philippa, her godmother, became seriously ill with dropsy in that year. It claimed her life in 1369. Therefore, I estimated her birth date at around 1357, making her 15 or 16 years older than her husband. She might have been 20 years older but any more than that would be highly unusual, as Rosemary Horrox wisely asserts. The age gap leads historians to believe it was a love match, one that elevated Philippa to the status of duchess.

I also wonder if these two fell out with their mother because she sold Dunster Castle and the other lands to Elizabeth Luttrell, rather than leaving them for the daughters to inherit.

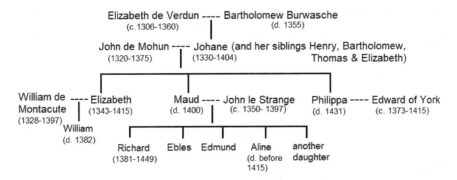

It is known that Elizabeth de Mohun eventually lived in Berkshire with her husband. Although records don't state whether she went to live with her husband's family at the age of 6 or stayed with her own, we can take the case of Richard II's second wife as an example of what happened at the time. In that case, the wife, Isabella de Valois, travelled over from her native France to live in England, visited by but living separately to Richard until she hit puberty.

The notion that Johane walked around the land barefoot on behalf of the villagers has been dismissed as a myth by some historians. I decided to include it because there's no smoke without fire as they say and it could be an allegory that shows her compassionate nature, cleverness and ability to negotiate with her husband. The legend has no date assigned to it, but I mused that if it did occur, it could have been after John attacked his tenant in order to humiliate his wife and distract from his disgraceful action and I theorised that the plague might have motivated the villagers to want pastureland.

Below is St Mary's Church in the background and the surviving boundary wall of Bruton Priory, where John was buried but Johane was categorically not interred!

(Bruton Priory)

Chapter Bibliography

A History of Bubonic Plague in the British Isles by J. F. D. Shrewsbury

A History of Dunster and the Families of Mohun and Luttrell by Sir H C Maxwell Lyte

Bloody British History: Somerset by Andrew May

Dictionary of National Biography, 1885-1900 by Edmund

Venables

Dunster Castle and Gardens Guidebook by the National Trust

Folklore of Somerset by Kingsley Palmer

historicengland.org.uk

History of Somerset by Robert Dunning

History of the Hundred of Carhampton: In the County of Somerset by James Savage

Ladies of Dunster Castle by Jim Lee

Memorials of the Order of the Garter from its Foundation to the Present Time by George Frederick Beltz

Mother or Stepmother to History? Joan de Mohun and her Chronicle by Jocelyn Wogan-Browne

Tombscape: the tomb of Lady Joan de Mohun in the crypt of Canterbury Cathedral by Diane Heath

Plantagenet Ancestry – A Study in Colonial and Medieval Families by Douglas Richardson

The Black Death, translated and edited by Rosemary Horrox

www.encyclopedia.com

www.oxforddnb.com

www.victoriacountyhistory.ac.uk

Encyclopedia of the Medieval Chronicle

Chapter 11: The Translator That Time Forgot (early 15th century)

Eleanor had always loved language. Even before she knew any words, her chubby little mouth would be full of baby babble from dusk to dawn as she plodded about on all fours around her home- St Audries Manor at West Quantoxhead at the northern edge of the vivid Quantocks Hills. She would "comment" on the dramatic cliffs that the area boasted, the soft sand, the tall tower of the village church dedicated to St Etheldreda.

When Eleanor started to learn words, 'mama' was very much a part of her vocabulary but not 'dada' because her father died before she was even a year old.

As such, she didn't grow up hearing Sir John Malet recount tales of his time serving John of Gaunt. Rather, she heard of it second-hand from her mother, Joan, who also instilled in her a sense of her heritage as part of the noble family of the Malets who had great landowning kin for whom towns such as Shepton Mallet and Curry Mallet had been named. Joan also taught Eleanor about her maternal Devonshire ancestry.

Education, not just concerning ancestry but a variety of subjects, was vital to Joan. She took great care to ensure that this, her only child, learnt to read and write in English, French and Latin. In fact, learning these languages would be essential to Eleanor later in life. Unbeknown to Eleanor, King Henry IV's marriage to Joan of Navarre, which happened when Eleanor was 7, would one day hold great significance for our Somerset maiden and her linguistic abilities.

Eleanor Malet's religious education was also central to her life. She would attend her local village church and when visiting her grandparents inland at Enmore Castle, where Eleanor was born, she knelt down in St Michael's Church and recited psalm after psalm with her relatives.

Of course, education was all very well and good but as a noblewoman, the only path for her (besides taking holy orders) was to marry, which she did in her teenage years. The gentleman chosen for her was John Hull, a much older man who, as a faithful Lancastrian, had once been a loyal servant to Prince John of Gaunt. With him, Eleanor began to spend more time outside of Somerset, including a lot of time in Hertfordshire.

A son, Edward, was soon born to the couple and by 1417, he had grown into a bouncing little boy. It was during that year that Eleanor, John and Edward were admitted to the confraternity of St Albans in Hertfordshire, meaning that they were joining a group of lay people whose aim was to promote special acts of Christian charity or devotion. The family showed their affection for the abbey community by making regular gifts.

As well as linking herself to a high-status religious house, her marriage to John meant that she began to spend more and more time with people from court. Her husband went on diplomatic missions for Henry IV, while Eleanor began to serve Queen Joan of Navarre from that same year, 1417, onwards. This French-speaking queen gave Eleanor the chance to improve her French and improve her income with an annual salary. A far cry from rural Somerset, Eleanor spent most of her time at the king's favourite palace, Eltham, in London. The king and queen had married for love against others' opinions and one of King Henry's gifts to her was to build two-storey lodgings for Joan at the palace.

Things were on the up for Mistress Hull, yet her fortunes were about to change, as were those of Queen Joan, whose love story was to have an unhappy ending.

The end of the 1419s and beginning of the 1420s dealt two heavy blows to Eleanor. The first was that her mistress, Joan of Navarre, was accused of witchcraft. Her husband had died a few years back, paving the way for her stepson to become King Henry V. The young man trumped up charges against his stepmother in order to take possession of her dower lands, her income and even her personal belongings. Poor Joan was obliged to dismiss all her household servants. And so she was confined – in comfortable conditions and with people to serve her – under house arrest for three tedious years, mainly at Leeds Castle, the very property gifted to her by her deceased husband. Her release only came just before Henry V's death in 1422. He also restored her lands and properties. Basically, or so Eleanor thought, as soon as he realised that he was about to depart this world and would no longer benefit from the wealth he had stolen from her, he was kind enough to drop all charges. The second blow was more permanent: Eleanor's husband died. This marked the beginning of a new era for her. But she did not take a traditional path for widows– either remarrying or becoming a nun. Although deeply pious, she chose not to take holy orders but to remain as a laywoman, using her status as a widow to maintain some autonomy.

Continuing in the footsteps of her family, who were generous patrons of St Michael's Church in Enmore, and continuing her role as a member of the St Alban's confraternity, Eleanor frequently bestowed the abbey with gifts.

And it was through the abbey that 1427 was the year in which she became remarkable. By this point, yet another Henry sat on the throne: little Henry VI. Eleanor began to occasionally live as a laywoman at Sopwell Priory, a dependent of the nearby St Alban's abbey. She took on the task to translate from Old French a piece entitled Meditations upon the Seven Days of the

Week as well as a series of meditations based on Biblical psalms that focussed on the repenting of sins after having been forgiven by God.

Competently and diligently, she laboured away for hour after hour in the draughty Benedictine nunnery with the deep theological works handwritten not in her native tongue and transformed them without the help of modern luxuries such as dictionaries, phrasebooks and thesauruses.

In the cold scriptorium, Eleanor was huddled over in front of the manuscript with quill at the ready when Prioress Letitia moved over to her.

"Good day to you, Lady Hull."

There was no response. Our protagonist was engrossed in her work.

"Lady Hull."

"Ah, forgive me, prioress. I am working on a piece about St Mary and wondering what phrases of my own to include so that the reader can understand more fully the significance of her name. I think I shall add: 'How rightfully she is called Maria' to hark back at the opening of the meditation where the writer dwells on the fact that Mary means 'star of the sea'."

"How charming to see you hard at work with the reader's benefit at the forefront of your mind!"

"I undertake the task seriously indeed. From time to time, it can be challenging to render the French into our own language and the usual questions of the translator impose themselves on me: Should I use a cognate or a more English word? When should I insert additional words to aid understanding? How do I use gendered French words in English, a language that has many gender-neutral terms?"

"From what I have read of your work so far, you are a most skilled linguist, one who is thoughtful and capable."

"I thank you. My daily prayers to St Katherine, blessed patron of scholars and learning, have certainly helped."

"And to St Jerome, I imagine."

"Oh yes, I could never omit to pray to our patron of translators. And I am grateful to be here, engaging in important spiritual matters and not at court."

The prioress sighed. "It has been hard these five years since your mistress' stepson, Henry V, died. Henry VI now, so many Henrys and yet this one a mere babe in arms when he was declared king. All the infighting between the nobles to see who would become Lord Protector… it is not to my taste either."

"I am almost finished with these works now and cannot hide away forever. I will visit my mistress soon and see how she fares."

Eleanor duly finished her translations, the years wore on and it was the mid-1440s. Henry VI was now a young adult and ready for marriage. Eleanor's language skills paved the way for her to be involved in a much more worldly matter than her religious translations. She had made her mark in the spiritual community, now she had just returned from a political event. Her friend and confessor, Roger Huswyf, was speechless when Eleanor told him upon returning to England.

"Tell me again where you have been."

"To Tours in central France for the proxy wedding of our king to Margaret of Anjou."

"Yes, I know *why*. I simply couldn't recall the name of the city. Newly made the capital of France, if I'm not mistaken."

"Correct. You must do better at keeping up with courtly news, Roger."

"Haha, I am but a simple man. I would rather talk to God and read my books. I'm not an adventurer like you. What a journey indeed! I shouldn't like to undertake such a thing. My lady, you ought to take care of yourself at your age."

Eleanor smiled indulgently. She might have been close to 50 but this she had leapt at the chance to visit the country whose language she had studied for so long, that had become a part of her life journey.

"My son Edward joined me," she explained. "There was a whole entourage of people. Besides, here you see me safely home, praise God."

"That is true enough. Well now, do tell me about it all."

"The sea crossing was unpleasant; I don't care to dwell on that. But our stay was agreeable and we enjoyed the May-time sun. Then, the ceremony itself… goodness, it was stunning. First, the queen-to-be processed through the streets with her parents and the King and Queen of France themselves."

"And were all godly observances adhered to?"

"Oh yes. The proxy marriage took place in the church of St Martin with all the splendour you might imagine for a lady whose aunt is the Queen of France. Of course, there was an immense turnout– French lords and ladies all dressed in their finest clothes alongside all of we English nobles. Lord Suffolk stood as proxy for the king and when the service had ended, Queen Margaret was placed in the care of his wife, who was to look after her throughout the proceedings. Then, blessings and greetings came pouring in from all those attending for the new queen as we headed towards a great hall for a feast, where no expenses were spared by the French– even the commoners were given food and drink. Four days later, we began our long homecoming voyage to England while Margaret returned to Anjou. I believe that in less than 12 months, a second expedition will set out to bring her over. How strange it must be to be wed to someone for months and months before you even set eyes on them."

"I hope you will not be among those who fetch the bride!" Roger warned sternly, for which Eleanor stifled a smile. "Well now, the most important factor to remember is that this marriage has brought about a truce to the interminable war between our nation and theirs."

"That is true. May it please God to maintain the truce forever. I will await the king's commands as to whether or not I go again. The sad truth is I may never have another opportunity to go to France in my lifetime but my son might."

Sadly, she was right. And both were wrong about the truce, which lasted just five years. The proxy marriage occurred in 1444, Margaret of Anjou reached English shores in April 1445 (accompanied by Lady Suffolk, several baronesses and countesses but not by Eleanor) and by 1449, the Treaty of Tours was in tatters.

After 4 years of resumed fighting, the Battle of Castillon transpired in southern France, altering Eleanor's life forever…

*

Dear Roger,

It has been a while since my last letter. I have been unable to write to anybody. Perhaps you have heard the news but I wish to tell you myself, seeing that you are a treasured friend of mine. It concerns my son, Edward.

She put her quill down. Even though several weeks had passed, she still struggled to accept the tragic truth that Edward had given his life in battle during the unrelenting Hundred Years' War that had ended soon after that very battle. He had nearly survived the war.

Breathe in. Breathe out.

Again.

Breathe in. Breathe out.

Better. She could write again.

My dear friend, the worst tragedy has befallen me. Edward is dead. The only child I ever had gone forever, leaving behind no grandchild to soften the blow. Though he was in his early forties, he left no grandchildren to console me and there never will be any now. I may be a linguist, adept in three languages, but words fail me in any of those tongues. There are no words for the depth of pain I feel.

I know you would tell me to take heart in the knowledge that he is with our Heavenly Father. All the indulgences I bought and masses that have been said will surely have allowed him to move out of purgatory by now.

You'd be right to tell me so! And I do take comfort in that, while still praying for his soul just in case. I am happy that he is in a better place and at the same time my heart aches that he is no longer with me. Both are true.

My beloved mistress, Queen Joan, went to dwell with Our Lord some twenty years ago, as you of course know. I feel the loss of her ever more keenly now that my son has passed on too.

Edward lived well. I'm sure I have told you too many times of how he was Sheriff of Somerset and Dorset three times, Justice of the Peace for Somerset from 1440 to his death and a Member of Parliament for my county in 1447. I like to think I supported him well in those roles. He went on numerous expeditions to France in service to the king. Alas, his last act of duty robbed him of his life.

Somerset feels quiet without him. Only memories come to me. His marriage in 1431 was to Margery Lovell, who is of Clevedon if I did not tell you before. A childless marriage but a good match, being the two of them of a similar age.

Arriving to live at Cannington Priory, I was able to visit them often whenever they were in Somerset. The priory is close to Enmore Castle, which Edward inherited. It has just occurred to me that the castle is mine now. I would exchange a thousand castles for his life to be restored.

'Take more deep breaths, Eleanor. You can do this,' she told herself.

She dipped her quill in the inkpot and continued.

Cannington is still a wonderful place to live. I know you were concerned when I first moved there given that it is small and somewhat impoverished. Not to mention the scandals of the previous century. But the scandals are behind us and a poor nunnery suits me as I have no need of fineries. And as a Benedictine house, it is similar to Sopwell, to what I am accustomed to. Prioress Johanna Gofyse leads the community well, the nuns are pleasant, the atmosphere is positive...

I am glad, above all, to be away from politics. I know not how you manage living closer to London. England finally stopped fighting with France only to begin engaging in domestic battles, cousins again cousins. The Duke of York has begun causing havoc and I for one am too old for it all, for prideful battles that please not God. Hoping that you are well and that my news does not cause you undue distress, for I know how fond you were of Edward,

Your dear friend,

Eleanor

Notes

The historians Liz Herbert McAvoy and Diane Watt believe that Eleanor Hull (also spelt Alyanor Hulle) was born c.1394, which would fit in with when her son was described as a small child in 1417. Although it's not known when exactly she married John Hull (died c. 1420), who was probably a distant cousin, it was at some point between 1407 and 1413 because of the aforementioned description of her son in 1417. Likewise, I couldn't discover where Edward was born or where John and Eleanor lived when they married. John was from Exeter so perhaps it was there with visits to family in Somerset and of course to court and St Albans.

As a translator myself, I take my hat off to Eleanor. I can only imagine the difficulties of working with texts handwritten without modern pens that may be tricky to decipher at times. She probably had no access to a dictionary as the first French dictionary that we know of today was compiled in 1464, four years after her death and decades before she completed her translations.

The historian Alexandra Barratt has called her "a conscious craftsperson" who "was aware that she had choices, and she made measured and considered decisions. Many if not all of them seem designed to help the reader." Barratt praises her ability, noting that there are very few definite mistranslations and most of those could be errors committed by the scribe who copied her work into the book that has survived today. Barratt points out that Eleanor is the only medieval woman who translated from French or Latin into English whose name we know. The full texts that she translated from have not been found, but Barratt notes that the parts that are available show that Eleanor was a highly skilled translator. As well as translating the texts, Eleanor also inserted extra parts where she felt those words would add something to the reader's experience. For instance, at one point she adds 'how rightfully she is called Maria' to remind the reader of the link between Mary and stars since the name means 'star of the sea'.

To other sections, she adds more words to enhance clarity or provide more details. At another point, she reassures the reader that they can stop and start the meditative readings whenever they like and that the prayers can be read in any order. Eleanor shows herself to be a thoughtful writer.

I chose not to dwell too long on Joan of Navarre's imprisonment as I was unable to discern whether Eleanor was with Joan when she was informed of the accusation and taken from the home in which she was living to her first place of house arrest. Neither could I ascertain whether Eleanor ever visited Joan in any of the three locations in which she was confined, though she might well have done as Joan was permitted visitors without restrictions. It seems highly unlikely that Eleanor would have lived with Joan during her incarceration, though, as Joan's household staff were all chosen for her at that time.

When Eleanor retired to Cannington Priory is unknown, only that it was by 1458, which is when she wrote her will there. This was 4 years after her son died. I chose to have her move to Somerset at some point before his death. She received the last rites and died at the priory in 1460, probably in December because her will was proved on 2nd January of the following year. This will was written in her own hand and copied into the register of the Bishop of Bath and Wells. In it, she requested to be buried at Cannington Priory and bequeathed four books to her dear friend Roger.

Eleanor would be sad to learn the fate of the buildings she was associated with. Experts can only give a rough approximation of where the buildings lay for Cannington Priory. Nothing remains anymore, only historical accounts such as the nuns fornicating in the cloisters in the 1300s! The priory was dissolved in 1536 by yet another Henry: the eighth one of course. The last prioress, Cecilia de Verney, willingly submitted after leading the community for 32 years. So the priory has vanished, but the village church dedicated to St Mary has kept its 14th-century tower and a slit in the north wall is thought to have been a viewing window that was used by the nuns at the priory.

St Albans and Sopwell Priory were dissolved in 1539. The lands at Sopwell Priory were given to a nobleman. He knocked the priory down and built a house in its place; the ruins of the latter can be seen today. As a side note, Prioress Letitia is not fictitious; she was in charge of Sopwell Priory from 1418 to 1435.

All the buildings belonging to St Albans Abbey were demolished except the Great Gateway, which continued to be used as a jail. The church survived and although it suffered centuries of neglect, it became a cathedral in the 1800s. Forgive me for including an image from outside of

Somerset, but I feel this is the best option for Eleanor Hull since these religious places meant so much to her.

(Gateway to the former St Albans)

Focussing now on Somerset, although Enmore's parish church remains, the Enmore Castle that can be seen today was built in the 1750s, while St Audries Manor and West Quantoxhead's church were rebuilt in the 1800s. At least Eleanor's educating spirit lived on in Enmore– in 1810, the Enmore National School opened as the first free elementary school in England.

Chapter Bibliography

A review by David Lyle Jeffrey of The Seven Psalms: A Commentary on the Penitential Psalms Translated from

French into English by Dame Eleanor Hull

british-history.ac.uk

Chapter 13: Dame Eleanor Hull in Women's writing in Middle English edited by Alexandra Barratt

Dame Eleanor Hull: The Translator at Work by Alexandra Barratt

Encyclopaedia Britannica

English Queenship 1445-1503 by Joanna L Chamberlayne

henrysixth.com

Medieval English Nunneries c. 1275 to 1535 by Eileen Edna Power

Religion, society and godly women: the nature of female piety in a late medieval urban community by Stephanie Jane Adams

stalbansmuseums.org.uk

The History of British Women's Writing, 700-1500: Volume One edited by Liz Herbert McAvoy and Diane Watt

The penitential psalms as a focus point for lay piety in late medieval England by Rosemary Ruth Hordern Collerson

The Somerset Coast by Charles G. Harper

The Somerset Village Book by the Somerset Federation of Women's Institutes

Thomas of Erceldoune's prophecy, Eleanor Hull's Commentary on the penitential Psalms, and Thomas

Norton's Ordinal of alchemy by Heather Blatt

Translators and their Prologues in Medieval England by Elizabeth Dearnley

www.cannington.org.uk

www.oxforddnb.com

History Of Parliament (1439-1509) by Josiah C Wedgwood

Chapter 12: A Year of Leadership in Yatton (late 15th century)

"A woman? Really?"

"Lady Newton is a gentlewoman of excellent standing who is a great benefactor to the church. Along with her parents-in-law and late husband, she has contributed towards rebuilding and improving the church for the fifty-odd years she has lived in Yatton. Ever since she came here as a young bride, she has worked hard for our church. I am sure she will continue to do likewise."

The priest sighed. "I can't deny she is of high standing. Her husband was a member of parliament just before he died. But there is the matter of her sex. If only *he* were still alive, he would have been an ideal churchwarden."

"Without a doubt. And yet here we have a widow whose advanced age can only add to her wisdom and moral standing. She has no young children to demand her time."

"Ah, yes. Three grown sons, is it?"

John Bulbeke tried not to roll his eyes. The priest was getting forgetful in his dotage. "Four sons and a daughter. All grown. There were others, yet they were taken to Heaven as babes. Back to the matter at hand. It would not be seen as scandalous for her to engage in lengthy conversations with men at her age. Therefore, her gender should be no barrier."

"And you would act as the other churchwarden alongside

her?"

John nodded.

The priest continued, "And yet the scriptures warn against a woman having authority over a man. People could think it unholy. A female churchwarden… it's unheard of in the history of the whole country, to the best of my knowledge at least."

"And yet, why not?" John smiled. "Leave aside St Paul's writings for a moment. Think upon Our Lord Jesus, instead. He had female followers– Mary Magdalene as well as Mary and Martha of Bethany. The early Church had its female leaders, Priscilla and Phoebe among them."

"Hmm, well, if we can justify it biblically and there are no better-suited men coming forward – and they haven't so far – I suppose it is a possibility."

"Indeed," John replied in a whisper. "Few men wish to at such a time when the Pretender could rise up and snatch the throne from King Henry. Nobody knows whether to support Perkin Warbeck, possibly a York prince, or our Lancastrian king."

"Precisely. The Cousin's War could ignite all over again. Well, we could proceed with her nomination and see if the congregation elects her."

"God bless you, Father. You will see how it benefits our community."

*

Nearby, at her Court de Wyck manor in Claverham, Lady Isabel Newton awaited the news. The words of Mass, said daily for the souls of her husband and other deceased family members at her private chapel, were still fresh in her ears and her rosary beads were still clinking together in her hands. She was convinced the priest would soon see sense. After all, she was the cream of the crop, a member of the most important family in Yatton. Lady Newton was the daughter-in-law of the late Chief Justice of the Common Pleas and widow of a Member of Parliament for Somerset. And she had not just married into nobility, her own family was not to be sniffed at either. The fine Court de Wyck manor was her inheritance from her father– a wealthy merchant and knight who had held the manor at Cheddar, a village famous for making its own distinctive cheese since the 1100s. Upon Isabel's marriage to John Newton many years ago, her father paid for a window to be made in St Andrew's church in Cheddar showing St John with the de Cheddar coat of arms impaled by the Newton arms, symbolising the union of the two families. The de Cheddars and Newtons were known throughout the county. And was not her own sister, Joan, buried at Wells Cathedral itself?

Not to mention how her family had survived the civil war that had raged between Yorkists and Lancastrians; they had survived the transition from Plantagenet kings to a Tudor king.

It had served them well in the end when the Yorkist Richard III had removed John Newton from his position as knight of the shire, only for the Lancastrian Henry VII to restore him. In fact, soon after Henry's victory at Bosworth, her eldest son had married a woman related to the king himself.

Then there was what her family had done for Yatton's parish church. Her late husband, John, had erected a magnificent tomb for the bodies of her father- and mother-in-law there, thus adding splendour to the church and respect from anyone visiting from another parish. Furthermore, he had had a south porch built, through which visitors and worshippers would pass, the most ornate porch for miles around. Whenever business deals were sealed at the church door, they would marvel at their surroundings. John made sure that shields in honour of himself and Isabel adorned that porch so that all would know who had paid for the bulk of it.

Over the last five or so years, Isabel herself had paid for and supervised the building of a chantry chapel to St John the Evangelist around the beautifully carved tombs of her parents-in-law. She had followed all the typical customs for a chantry chapel, purchasing high-quality furnishings and employing a priest to sing Latin masses for the dead buried there, in this case focussing on her parents-in-law and husband. With her help, their souls would spend very little time in purgatory. Already people were referring to it as the Chapel of my Lady Newton.

As soon as the messenger appeared, Isabel smiled smugly. And she was right- the vicar had not stood in her way.

Likewise, she was right that the congregation would elect her. In March 1496, she took her place beside John Bulbeke as churchwarden of St Mary's church in Yatton. In over 200 years of the church's existence, she was the first female churchwarden as far as anyone could tell.

If people grumbled about a woman taking a leadership role in the church, they did so amongst themselves. Nobody dared to confront Isabel directly about the matter.

*

How quickly the year had sped by. February 1497 had come around. Isabel's year of leadership was nearly at an end.

Patting her beautiful bay horse through gloved fingers, she rode side-saddle towards the familiar church and reflected on the busy year it had been for her with the festivities of Easter and Christmas to organise and many others besides.

As she rode on along the stony path, her mind drifted to the ale fairs they had held, as per tradition, to raise funds for the church. They had gathered at the Church House, built in 1445, for Whitsuntide (Pentecost), Hocktide the week afterwards and St James' Day in the summer. Those were merry occasions indeed with feasting, drinking, sports, minstrels, Morris dancers and maypoles.

The church soon appeared in the distance, lightly covered in frost.

"Ah, Lady Newton. Impeccable timing as usual."

"And you," she replied to Bulbeke, adjusting her headdress slightly.

"Are you ready for our last big event as wardens?"

She smiled regally as he helped her dismount from her horse by the churchyard. "I'm sure the Candlemas service will go as smoothly as always. All the linens are washed and ready; the new candles we purchased arrived in time. Why, are you worried?" she asked, gathering her fur cloak around her as a wintry chill blustered by.

"No, no, I want to ensure things go to plan, that's all. We shall be remembered poorly otherwise."

"Nobody would dare to remember us as poor churchwardens!" Her reply was jovial but there was a hint of sincerity too.

Well aware that she was the first lady to carry out the role, Isabel was determined to leave no room for criticism. She had indeed carried out her duties as well as any other churchwarden, despite the political upheaval the country suffered. In September 1496, Scotland had attempted to invade England on behalf of the Pretender, Perkin Warbeck. Thank God it was unsuccessful and quickly dealt with. All the same, the uncertainty was hard for all to bear and England's future still hung in the balance as 1497 progressed.

Worse than that was the personal tragedy that had struck her during her period of service. A mother who must bury her own child is a gut-wrenching situation and it was her second son, Thomas, whom she had to lay to rest in her chantry chapel.

All gathered round: her daughter, son-in-law, grandson, three remaining sons, daughter-in-law, granddaughters and of course Thomas' newly widowed wife, Lucy. Isabel had clutched Lucy's hand, which was icy cold and white as snow. Isabel held on to comfort poor Lucy but also to steady herself. Thomas' sons sniffed back tears.

What had she done to deserve that? Even when giving birth to Thomas, she had followed all the correct procedures. She had prayed to St Margaret, patron of pregnant women, she had clutched the family's relics and had a prayer roll wrapped around her stomach. He had been baptised as soon as possible and brought up in the faith. The family had been loyal to the king, whichever one was on the throne at any one time. And yet God had punished her, along with taking other sons, taken so young.

Still, during her time of need, the Lord had provided her with comfort too in the form of her daughter, Elizabeth, who had stayed local when she married, settling at Kenn Court in the village of the same name, just two miles from Yatton. What a pillar of support they had been for each other during those weeks of sobbing and despair.

In some ways, it was a blessing to have her leadership role to keep her busy and not dwell too much on her loss. She had propelled herself even more into the work as a distraction, ensuring the congregation paid their tithes, overseeing the keeping of the law and encouraging generous donations. Unlike other churches, St Mary's had no lands of its own to make money from so the parishioners had to provide all the money needed to keep the church going.

Isabel had worked herself to the bone, worked too hard perhaps. She could feel old age setting in, not helped by outliving so many sons.

"Well, my lady, shall we go in?"

Pushing her thoughts aside and staring up at the magnificent south porch, she nodded. "Yes, let's."

Notes

A timeline of Isabel's life:

1429: Isabel is born.

1443: Her father, Thomas, dies on 3rd June.

1449: Her father-in-law, Richard, dies.

Late 1440s/early 1450s: Isabel marries John Newton.

1453: Her sister's husband dies at the Battle of Castillon, the same battle that Eleanor Hull's son died at.

1453–4: Her husband, John, is MP for Somerset.

1455–7: Her husband, John, oversees and pays for most of the south porch.

1458: Her eldest son, Richard, is born.

1460s and 70s: Isabel has 4 more children.

1464: Isabel's sister, Joan, dies.

1470: Isabel's nephew, Thomas, dies aged 21 on 20th March during a battle about a land dispute between two lords.

1471: Her husband, John, is knighted.

1474: Her mother, Isabel, dies.

1475: Her mother-in-law, Emmota, dies.

1487: Her granddaughter Isabel is born.

1488: John dies aged around 63.

1491–5: Isabel has the chantry chapel built.

1495: Her granddaughter Jane is born.

1496: She is elected churchwarden of Yatton in February and serves from March 1496–February 1497. / Scotland attempts to invade England. / Her second son, Thomas Newton, dies.

1497: In autumn, Perkin Warbeck deserts his army at Glastonbury before the king can attack. Perkin is imprisoned in Taunton, then London and then executed.

1498: Isabel dies on 14th May aged about 69.

1500: The tomb of John and Isabel Newton is made.

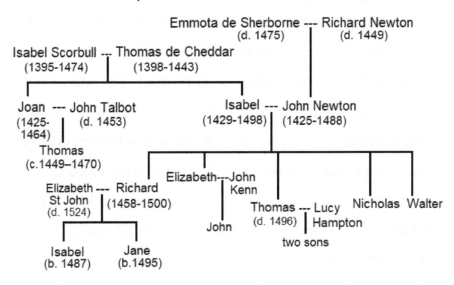

Churchwardens were first established in the 1100s. They appear in parish records from the 1200s onwards and by the mid-1300s, they were elected by and from among the congregation.

It is not known how Isabel Newton née de Cheddar (also spelt Cheddre or Chedder) came to be the first ever recorded female churchwarden in England. It's been suggested that her gender was overlooked due to her high status and great involvement with the church. She wasn't the last woman to become a churchwarden (more on this below). Most female churchwardens were widows and therefore were financially and domestically independent.

Isabel lived through the Wars of the Roses (1455–85) and although Margaret of Anjou did send a decoy into Selwood

Forest to try and fool Edward IV in 1471, the Wars didn't have a huge impact on Somerset. That's because none of the big players had power bases in Somerset. The Newton family seems to have steered their way through the wars deftly. Isabel's father-in-law's effigy in Yatton church has a Lancaster collar but also a white rose of York. He seems to have changed sides when needed. Isabel's son Richard also managed to serve both York (Richard III) and then Lancaster (Henry VII). Isabel's husband, John, seems to have fallen out with Richard III, who, as mentioned before, removed him from his position but Henry VII restored him, so perhaps his enmity with King Richard turned out well for him.

Let's continue to look at her children. Isabel was around 29 when her first son Richard was born, which was old for a first-time mother in those days; however, the babies she lost may have been born previously. The evidence that they lost young children is that they bought two funeral torches in 1454, 1465 and 1469. Richard's first wife Eleanor was the daughter of King Henry's chief counsellor and the second was Elizabeth St John. Meanwhile, her son Thomas married Lucy Hampton and died before his mother. Nicholas became a lawyer, while Walter studied at Oxford and became a priest.

The idea of founding chantry chapels began in the 1200s in Western Europe. They were mainly abolished during

England's Reformation but not destroyed. So much money was poured into Isabel's chantry chapel only for prayers for the dead to be outlawed in the mid-1500s (although briefly restored for the 5 years of Mary I's rule). Hence, the Latin prayers have gone but Isabel's chapel stands to this day, having been restored for worship in 1906. Interestingly, this building is part of a wider shift happening in England in the 15th century. People began to give less money to monasteries and nunneries as donations or for masses to be said etc. and were now spending money on parish churches. Some felt monastic houses had enough money, perhaps too much.

Her chapel in the church remains but Court de Wyck Manor has vanished. It was ruined in a fire in 1815 and demolished soon afterwards. However, a late 2023 excavation uncovered foundation walls and ceramics from the 13th–14th century that probably belonged to Isabel's ancestors or were heirlooms that she herself used.

What is more, Isabel's line lives on. Not surprisingly, her descendants were also among the cream of the crop. An example is Frances Newton, lady of the bedchamber to Elizabeth I. In modern times, her descendants include Princess Diana and Elizabeth II.

Some say Isabel herself still likes to keep watch over her church. Her friendly ghost is said to haunt St Mary's churchyard.

(Above left: Isabel de Cheddar's parents' tomb in Cheddar with brass images of them. Above right: Isabel de Cheddar and her husband's tomb tucked into the corner behind the crucifix with her parents-in-law's tomb in the foreground, Wyke Chapel, Yatton parish church. This is the best picture I could get as access was restricted! Below: Yatton church, showing the south porch built by Isabel and her husband.)

Chapter Bibliography

oxforddnb.com

Let the Stones Talk: Glimpses of English History Through the People of the Moor by Christopher Steed

Biographies of the Members of the Commons House by Josiah C. Wedgwood and Anne D. Holt

The People of the Parish: Community Life in a Late Medieval English Diocese by Katherine L. French

The parochial and family history of the deanery of Trigg Minor, in the county of Cornwall by Sir John Maclean

British Library website

Early churchwardens by Don Redman

Historic England website

Tale of Two Families – John Brown and Abbe Lavina Colaw by Diana J. Muir

Church-wardens' accounts of Croscombe, Pilton, Patton, Tintinhull, Morebath, and St. Michael's, Bath, ranging from A.D. 1349 to 1560 by Edmund Hobhouse

The Somerset Coast by Charles G. Harper

Christianity in Somerset edited by Robert Dunning

www.findagrave.com

Polluting the Sacred: Violence, Faith, and the 'civilizing' of Parishioners in Late Medieval England by Daniel Thiery

heritagedaily.com

QUICK TRIBUTE

Other Female Churchwardens

In the Middle Ages, female churchwardens were rare but not unheard of in the West Country.

Aside from St Mary's in Yatton, whose churchwarden accounts are among the most detailed ones in England, at least 4 other parishes in Somerset appointed women, but later on in the Tudor period than Isabel de Cheddar's stint; they were as follows.

Nettlecombe- Eleanor Mychell in 1523, Alison Fermer in 1540, Alice Thorn in 1541, Anne Goher in 1542 and Alice Harper in 1544

Trull- Agnes Shorter in 1542 and Christine Voyse in 1544

Halse- Joanne Wassher in 1543, Jane Raxworthyin 1548 and Joan Lawrence in 1550

Tintinhull- Sibyl Smith in 1547

It's been suggested that the reason why the majority of these female churchwardens were appointed in the 1540s is due to the religious turmoil resulting from the Reformation, which made it harder to recruit men as churchwardens. That the women were willing to step into these roles during so much upheaval is a testament to their courage and determination to hold leadership positions.

(The Church of St Margaret, Tintinhull, near Yeovil)

Sources: Patterns of Piety: Women, Gender and Religion in Late Medieval and Reformation England by Christine Peters, The Good Women of the Parish: Gender and Religion After the Black Death by Katherine L. French, The People of the Parish: Community Life in a Late Medieval English Diocese by Katherine L. French.

Chapter 13: Death Defier (16th century)

"For goodness' sake, man, close those shutters! Why is that wall bare? Bring in another tapestry and–"

"My lord, she is gone. I believe she has been gone for quite some hours now. There is nothing more we can do for her." The doctor shook his head sadly at John Wyndham.

"Surely you can try leeches again?"

"No, my lord. We have tried several times to revive her. I'm sorry for your loss."

"Well, well." John reached under his ruff to rub his stiff neck. Tears pricked his eyes.

"We must take her body unto St Decuman's."

"Yes, yes. Robert, find a stretcher and three other men." With that, he walked briskly to his bedchamber and tried to ignore the comments of his loudest servant, Betty.

"God have mercy on 'im! Not even a year married. Last year, we was celebratin' a new queen, Good Queen Bess as is, and Lady Florence being our new mistress. Now we'm burying Mistress Florence with a babe inside 'er and she's all but 21 years of age!"

"Keep your voice down," Robert hissed back at her.

Within the hour, a solemn procession was making its way uphill across Kentsford Manor's acres of land, two hundred in total with plenty of crops grown. Crops that the lady would never again taste. No, the procession was taking her to St Decuman's church on the outskirts of Watchet. Into the family vault in St Peter's chapel, Florence Wyndham's heavily pregnant body was laid in an exquisitely carved coffin.

John took the priest aside and laid out his plans for a lavish funeral the following day using Queen Elizabeth's newly authorised book of common prayers. The ceremony alone was a headache for John. For instance, purgatory was no longer part of the official religion and so prayers for the dead were not to be said. Everyone had been through five years of a return to Catholic worship and now Protestant ways were being restored. It was difficult to keep up-to-date with it all and avoid angering the queen.

"What is more, have two candles placed on either side of her body. Set the sexton up to hold vigil over her through the night."

"Yes, my lord." The priest bowed.

"I shall make my way home and have the seamstress come to discuss having a…" John cleared his throat. "Having a shroud made for Florence. Everything must be just so, just so." He patted the priest on the shoulder and drifted off in an otherworldly state of his own.

That night, instead of keeping watch and praying as he was meant to do, the sexton had other ideas. How brightly the rings on Florence's fingers shone in the candlelight! Why not pinch one? Who even knew which jewellery she had on when she entered the vault? He could merely claim that he had never seen it, that it must have fallen off somewhere along the way. It would bring in a pretty penny when he sold it on the sly later on. And as for respecting the dead, well, Florence had no need of rings wherever she was now!

He took Florence's cold, blotchy finger in his and pulled. The ring didn't budge. He turned it this way and that to loosen it up and still it wouldn't move. He licked his finger and rubbed the saliva over hers to loosen it all up, but it still wouldn't pass the knuckle. Swearing to himself, he decided there was only one thing for it: he'd have to saw her finger clean off. 'But everyone in Watchet will know what I've done. I can't stay. No matter. I'll just have to flee once I've got this stupid ring,' he thought.

After retrieving his pocketknife from his belt, he crossed himself, then remembered that was a Catholic thing, and started to cut the finger... which started to bleed.

Dead bodies don't bleed.

Dead bodies don't stir either.

Swearing once more, he abandoned his theft. He didn't fancy hanging around to see what Florence would do next. Instead, he dropped his lantern and flung himself out of the church and into the dark night, never to be seen again.

The fully revived Florence stared in horror at her finger and then, as her vision became clearer and clearer, at her cold surroundings. Slowly, she grasped what had taken place. Her husband had for some bizarre reason thought she was dead. They'd brought her to the church ready for a funeral the next day. But why her finger was bleeding was a mystery for a few moments until she remembered seeing the sexton with a knife. At least the sexton had left her a lantern to light her way home. A less courageous person would have stayed in the church overnight, but Florence was determined to return home to prevent her husband and servants from mourning her unnecessarily. Besides, a cold church was less appealing to her than a warm bed.

Shakily, she hauled herself to her feet that were swollen with pregnancy, passed through the open doors of the church and gasped as a wall of cold air hit her.

Praise God that home was only half a mile away!

An owl hooted. She waddled between the graveyards, clutching her heavy belly and trying to find her bearings, though everything looked the same in the dark.

Somehow, Florence stumbled back to Kentsford Manor's front door. She had to pound on it several times before anyone awoke and decided the noise was worth investigating.

It was Betty who answered the door, though Florence only saw a blur of her face because she slammed it almost immediately afterwards.

"Erm, Lady Florence, we was always nice to you. Please don't haunt us. There's a good ghost," Betty's trembling voice came from the other side of the door.

"Goodness me, I am not a ghost. That is a Catholic idea, anyway. I am your mistress and you shall open the door this instant!"

"The doctor-man did say my mistress was dead. Good an' dead, 'e said. We put your body in the chapel with all respect. Please leave us be!"

"The doctor was mistaken. I have just walked back from St Decumen's. Fetch my husband!"

Betty was happy to do so as she wasn't keen on spending half the night chatting with a ghost.

John moved the fluttering Betty out of the way, found his way to the door and gingerly opened it.

"By St Decumen," he breathed.

*

Long ago, around the time of Ine and Ethelburg, Decuman had taken the traditional method of transport that holy people preferred– get on a raft and drift to wherever God sends it. That would surely be an act of obediently and humbly going to the place God was calling him to.

He shoved his favourite cow onto the roughly made raft and set off from the Welsh shores. Across what we now call the Bristol Channel, the two of them bobbed along, arriving close to where Dunster Castle would later be built.

In Watchet, he set himself up in a hermit's cell with his trusty cow tied up outside. His day-to-day life included working miracles, providing advice and milking his cow.

A minor setback was when a non-Christian decided to chop Decumen's head off with a spade while he was praying. Never mind. Decumen shrugged, picked it off the ground, washed it in the local well (because who wants a gravelly throat?!), tucked it under his arm, grabbed his cow and headed back to Wales, supposing that the locals in Somerset were a bit rough, really.

His stay in northern Somerset was remembered by more welcoming folk. He became the patron of Watchet with the well named in his honour. A church dedicated to him was also built on the site where his cell was.

*

"By St Decumen!"

"That's rather Catholic of you to invoke a saint, isn't it?"

"Please begone. You have no reason to haunt me. I was a good husband to you."

"Yes, yes, I'm not a ghost. Touch me."

She reached out her hand, unfortunately the bloody one, to him. He recoiled in horror, then slammed and bolted the door. "Not a ghost but a witch, perchance," she heard him mutter.

Despite her pleading and trying to open other doors, Florence got nowhere. She even attempted to heave her huge belly through an open window, but it was no good.

By dawn, she was still outside and buckled over with pain. Labour had started.

Slumped down on the dew-covered grass, she screamed out in agony for help. Eventually, Betty came flying down to see what was the matter.

"Good Lord! I ain't never seen a ghost having a baby afore!"

"I'm... not.... a ghost," Florence panted.

"I'll fetch the master."

"Yes. Quickly. Arrghhh!"

Apologising over and over, her husband arrived and helped her inside with Robert's help.

"Fetch. The. Midwife," she told Betty through gritted teeth.

Transferred to her four-poster bed with a rope to pull on, she prayed fervently as she pushed and panted, her female servants hurrying around with fresh linen and logs for the fire. All the while, she grumbled about the worst night of her life, a terrible start to giving birth, that vile sexton who ironically had actually saved her life by reviving her with his wretched knife, how stupid everyone was to think she was a ghost, how she would come back and haunt them if she died in labour and how much pain she was in. Finally, the midwife arrived and a son was born to Florence.

"Well done, my lady, nicely done. Just the afterbirth now." The midwife mopped her brow.

"The what?" Florence whispered.

"The afterbirth, my lady. The placenta needs to come out now."

"Nobody told me of this."

Not wanting to let on that this was the most dangerous part of childbirth since it sometimes came out only partially or not at all, the midwife patted her arm. "Nothing to worry about. 'Twill come soon enough."

Thankfully, the midwife was right.

"There now, mistress. From the worst night ever to the best morning ever, eh?" Betty suggested nervously.

Florence said nothing, though a smile twitched at her face as she gazed down at the tiny creature bawling in her arms.

"The wet nurse was fetched, wasn't she?"

"Of course, my lady. Shall I pass him to her?"

"Yes. I must rest now."

She closed her eyes, ignoring the worried look on Betty's face that she would fall into another deep slumber and not wake up this time.

But wake up she did and live a further 37 years, as it happens, and even outlived her much-older husband by 24 years.

Notes

Florence Wyndham née Wadham (1538–1596) came from a large family. She was among the youngest of her mother's children, which may have totalled 20. Her mother, Joan, first married John Kellaway of Cullompton, Devon, and records show 7 children but her memorial stone states they had 14 children, so it would seem that half of these died in infancy. When Kellaway died, Joan married John Wadham (1505–1578) and lived together at Merrifield in Ilton village near Ilminster. They had six children together, all born at Merrifield, except Joan Junior.

Nicholas (1531/2–1609)

Joanna (1533–?)

Joan (1536–?)

Florence (1538–1596)

and two others.

Amazingly, Joan Senior lived to the age of 88, dying in 1583.

Florence married John Wyndham (born sometime after 1528 and died in 1572). As for her brush with death, which occurred around 1559, it could have been a coma. She wasn't pregnant in every version of the story but how could I resist the extra drama it created?! (Though the tale is of course dramatic enough without it: not many people can claim they got two burials in their life.) Plus, it could have been a difficult pregnancy that contributed to the coma in such a young woman. Some narratives state that she was pregnant with twins or that she had twins later on at the Bell Inn in Watchet since she was out and about and couldn't get home in time. If so, only her son, another John (c.1559-1645), survived infancy. Though Florence didn't follow her mother in having 20 children, her son, John, had a large family– 9 sons and 6 daughters with his wife, Joan Portman.

There is also a discrepancy in when she nearly died: if it wasn't 1558, another option is 1562 with her marriage having occurred in 1560.

Two other variations on the story paint the sexton in a better light. In one narrative, he isn't involved at all, rather the coffin bearers heard noises coming from the coffin during the funeral and so the lid was removed and she was rescued. In another, the sexton was closing the vault when he heard sounds coming from her coffin and went to investigate. Since he saved Florence, the Wyndhams offered him a generous monetary reward, but he never claimed it.

The Wyndham chapel dedicated to St Peter within St Decuman's Church has several detailed brass monuments to the family: Florence's husband, John Wyndham (d. 1572), is there, plus his parents and Florence herself.

Three miles away at St George's Church in Sampford Brett, which used to be on the Wyndhams' lands, there is an intricate wooden 16th-century bench-end. It represents a woman surrounded by fruit and flowers with two little cupids blowing trumpets. This could be Florence with her twins.

The Wyndhams never wanted a repeat of Florence's terrible tale. Perhaps they suspected that her coma-like condition could run in the family. To this day, anyone belonging to the Wyndham family must not be buried until three days after their death, just in case.

A woman who had such a near-death experience, was attacked while in a coma and got mistaken for a ghost would have to have a ghost story associated with her! Known as the White Lady, Florence is said to haunt St Decumen's Church and its surroundings.

(a sketch of the bench-end in Sampford Brett)

Chapter Bibliography

A family history, 1410–1688; the Wyndhams of Norfolk and Somerset by HA Wyndham

Deepest Somerset by Fanny Charles and Gay Pirrie-Weir

Legends and Folklore of Watchet by WH Norman

www.quantockonline.co.uk

wadham.oc.ac.uk

The Somerset Coast by Charles G. Harper

Wyndham Family Memorials in St Decuman's Church Watchet

A Century of Sanctity by Vladimir Moss

Tales of Old Somerset by Sally Norris

The Oxford Dictionary of Saints by David Hugh Farmer

Somerset Stories of the Supernatural by Roger Evans

QUICK TRIBUTES

Dorothy Wadham (1534/5 –1618)

As mentioned above, Florence Wyndham's name before marriage was Wadham. Her sister-in-law was Dorothy Wadham née Petre, the wife of Nicholas Wadham (1531/2– 20th October 1609).

Born and raised in Essex, Dorothy married in London on 3rd September 1555 and moved to Merryfield, Ilton, Somerset when she married Nicholas but had no children.

It appears the couple were Catholics but not Papists. So they believed in the Catholic way of worship but rejected the pope as head of the Church and instead accepted the monarch of England as the head.

They would have had to contend with the Great Flood of 1607. Its effects were felt more keenly in the Glastonbury area and western Somerset but still may have impacted the Wadhams' lives in terms of local harvests devastated and friends lost amongst the few hundred people who died.

Two years later, her husband died at Merrifield as one of the richest men in the country. That was when Dorothy made her mark on the country, as she wanted to follow the plan laid down in his will to found a college at Oxford University. It has been suggested that it was in fact her idea since her father had basically refounded Exeter College, but that she had to claim she was acting on her husband's behalf. Nicholas left a huge sum of money (£19,2000) to pay for the project to which she added a substantial amount of her own (£7270).

Despite being around 75 years old, she set to it with energy and determination, fighting off Nicholas' family members' claims to the money set aside for the college and rejecting her brother's offer to do it all for her. She also had to iron out the issues that arose from Nicholas' will being somewhat unclear, petition court, negotiate the purchase of land and compose documents.

In 1610, Wadham College received its royal patent. Dorothy then drafted and approved statues, alongside appointing the first warden, fellows, scholar and cook. 3 years later, the college opened its doors to students in April 1613.

Until her death aged 84 on 16th May 1618, she continued to administer the college from faraway Devon, where she had retired to after Nicholas' death. Surprisingly, she never actually set foot in Oxford, instead dictating letters to "my college" from her manor. This may have been due to frailty.

Like her husband, Dorothy had an Anglican funeral. The couple were buried at the Wadham family chapel in St Mary's Church, Ilminster, and commemorated with detailed brasses. Dorothy's brass has similarities with Florence's brass in St Decumen's church in terms of style and clothing. There are also monuments to the couple in the Church of St Peter, Ilton.

Of course, colleges then were very elitist institutions for upper-class men only. Wadham College only began to accept female students in 1974. Currently, the College now around 250 graduate students and 450 undergraduates. A new building there has been named after the foundress: Dorothy Wadham Annexe.

(Previous page: the face of Dorothy Wadham engraved in brass at St Mary's Church, Ilminster)

Sources: www.wadham.ox.ac.uk, The Letters of Dorothy Wadham 1609-1618 by Dorothy Petre Wadham and Robert Barlow Gardiner, oxforddnb.com.

Galatia (died spring 1605)

England's involvement in the transatlantic trade in enslaved Africans began in 1551 but the unimaginably atrocious trade increased quite suddenly and by a lot in the 1620s, bringing with it widespread racism. Before the 1620s, there were Black people living free in Tudor and early Stuart Britain. One of them was a lady named Galatia. Her name could be a reference to the ancient region of Turkey. Tantalisingly, the only facts we know about her are her name and that she was buried in Stowell, right in the southern tip of Somerset, on 12th May 1605. She is mentioned in one document only- the parish register for the village, which states: "1605, May 12. Galatia the black nigra, buried". The article 'the' suggests she was the only Black woman in the village at that time, which is unsurprising since the village was presumably tiny because Galatia was the only burial registered for the entire year.

Although the village was small, Somerset was actually the 4th most densely populated county in England at the time, with only Devon, Yorkshire and London surpassing it. Perhaps Galatia felt that Somerset was quite a vibrant place to be. But that is pure speculation.

What a life she must have led, having been born (I presume) in Africa and having travelled all the way to this island. What brought her here? At what age? Did she have to endlessly field awkward questions in Stowell about her skin colour and culture? Did she work there, marry there, have children there? We will probably never know the answers to those questions, but thanks to Miranda Kaufmann's meticulous research, we at least know her name and place of burial.

Source: Black Tudors: The Untold Story by Miranda Kaufmann, Notes & Queries for Somerset and Dorset volume 3 edited by Frederic William Weaver and Charles Herbert Mayo, A History of Somerset by Robert Dunning, www.slavevoyages.org/assessment/estimateses.org.

Chapter 14: A Witch in the Woods (17th century)

A witch you say?

Ah, that was the rumour.

Old Nancy was well aware of the stories flying around about her. But if you asked her yourself, this is what she'd say...

"I was poor. I was a wise woman. But a witch? Ye must be joking. I ain't pledged allegiance with no devil. I ain't been to no witches' coven. I ain't cursed no one nor harmed a soul for that matter.

"It all started when I was getting on a bit. Didn't have no family to look out for me but I got by alright. My main occupation were knitting. The very name of our town, Shepton Mallet, means sheep farm or settlement, then they tacked the name Mallet on 'cos of a rich family what came over in the Norman Invasion. See, I ain't as thick as I look! Anyway, in my time, there were lots of us as did earn a living in the wool industry. The fields were dotted with sheep and their baas were the background to our days.

"I got given wool and I worked me fingers to the bone making up stockings and socks and I were paid according to how many I done. They didn't pay me well, mind you. So I had to knit even on Sundays, which the Shepton Mallet folk saw as sinful. Does the Lord want I to starve? I think not. Besides, all them shepherds were out working on the sabbath, same as I, and nobody did call them devil worshippers. So in me old age, if I were knitting on a Sunday to keep me fire going, that were my business.

"I had to find other ways to keep food on me plate for I were all skin and bones as it was. I mentioned afore, I was a wise woman too. My day-to-day life was spent knitting, cooking, sweeping me floors and collecting and crushing up herbs. The women of the town would come to me for help with things like headaches, tummy problems and monthly cramps. The latter treatment had to be kept hushed up. You couldn't even write down the recipes for fear of the men getting cross about it. Like childbirthing, the pain was seen as a woman's punishment for what Eve done in the Garden of Eden. We wasn't meant to stop the pain, like.

"We had it hard in our younger days with that bloomin' Civil War going on. Afore it were Protestants keeping the Catholics down, making 'em pretend to be Protestant and keep quiet. That were bad enough. With the war, it were Protestants fighting betwixt themselves as well– Protestants who supported parliament versus Protestants and Catholics what loved the king. Well, that's how I understood it.

"Folk died in battles, two 'ere in Somerset: Lansdown Hill and Langport. Couple of skirmishes too. And sieges at Bridgwater and Taunton. All the while, widows was getting left behind.

We all suffered hunger with fewer folk out ploughing the crop fields that hadn't been burnt to a crisp and fewer folk to care for the animals what hadn't been killed or thieved. That Cromwell bloke versus the royals did damage the wool trade a great deal too as my old ma did tell me, God rest 'er soul. Desperate times indeed.

"Then Puritan years. Fourteen years of no Christmases! No dances. Nothing, not 'til the new King Charles, what's called the merry monarch, got power. So we thought with Merry King Charles on the throne, things would be good and they was for a time. But then in the 1680s, 'twere abundantly clear that 'is wife couldn't have babbies. So there were no prince for the throne. When Charles died, 'is younger brother James got the throne. But one of Charles' bastard boys, the Duke of Monmouth, thought 'e should be king instead, seeing as how he were Protestant and James were a Catholic.

"Most o' Somerset wanted that duke on the throne, bastard or no. The point is there was a rebellion, during the which Sheptonians had to put up some of the duke's soldiers, not me though, as no one wanted to bunk with an ol' hag. P'rhaps I should think meself lucky for some were scoundrels. One did try rape Mary Bridge's ma over in Westonzoyland, but Mary – 12 years old, mind you – ran a sword through 'im to finish 'im off, like. That's where in all ended, o' course– at the Battle o'

Sedgemoor in Westonzoyland where the duke lost and then lost his head in London. James II stayed as king.

"The courts were full o' Somersetonians being prosecuted for followin' that duke. Hundreds were sentenced to death. Twelve of the duke's followers were hung, drawn and quartered right outside me cottage on Market Square.

"I only be telling ye this 'cos that was the atmosphere at the time when I were turning old. People was resentful and spiteful then. They had to put up with a Catholic king. The countryside folk hadn't been able to control London politics. They couldn't stop the executions here in Somerset but they could try and control other stuff.

"It were round that time that the rumours about me started. I was jeered at the streets for not being pretty no longer, as if a woman ageing be a crime! The whispers started too: *Witch. Mumbling to 'erself. Broomstick. Potions. Evil eye as will bring the plague back to our doors. Possessed by the devil hisself.*

"Ha! What twaddle. But folks who believe stupid stuff are dangerous folks. They began to spit at me 'cos they was afeared of I. Some of them threatened me, saying God do punish folk who don't kill off a witch. I didn't feel safe no more in me home, not with no one around to stand up for me, not with that church casting shadows over me little house. All me wool customers stayed silent at that time. Can't blame 'em, really. Once silly folks get it in their heads that someone's a witch, if anyone tries to defend the woman, they get accused of conversing with the devil an' all.

"Listen, I weren't gonna hang around and wait for them to chuck me in jail, put on a show trial, then tie me to the stake. No, thanks. I began to see the woods surrounding the town as a better option. Little by little, I took what I could from me house out to a cave in the forest and early one morning, I took meself off to that cave. Yeah, I done a runner alright. Not as daft as ye may think.

"It weren't cosy and it weren't pretty but it was quiet and safe. I were free. I got used to it after a spell (no pun intended). I even grew accustomed to having to hitch up me skirts and squat behind trees to do me business, though that took its toll upon me creaky knees. Day in and day out, I'd go out collecting blackberries and water and checkin' me animal trap. Or if I had money, I'd wrap meself in a cloak, clamber down the rocky hill and go to the market. That were a risk. I had to be careful that my cloak didn't slip and that I stayed in the shadows.

"See, I could carry on makin' a bit of money. I told the nice customers where I was to so they could buy their ointments and lotions off of I. I sold 'em firewood too when me back weren't playing up. And they'd even buy the odd pair of socks or stockings when me fingers weren't too cold to knit 'em up. It were cold out there, I can tell you, 'specially in winter. The fires I'd get going outside me cave weren't the same as a fire in your bedroom, o' course. That's why I did pop out from time to time to the pub for a drop o' something to warm up me ol' bones. But I weren't no drunkard. Not with the money I had! The pub took away me loneliness for an hour or two. Even if I sat by meself, I could hear other people and that were a gert comfort.

"The fog and the rain was a difficulty too. The latter not only soaked me through if I were far from me cave but it created big puddles and turned them steep hills into mud slides covered in slippery leaves.

"I heard titbits of news from town. In 1688 I think 'twas, three years after I entered the forest, we got ourselves yet another king: William of Pears or William of Orange, something like that. My mind ain't sharp these days, don't see many people to talk to, see. So we were back to a Protestant king wiv 'is wife Mary II. A lot of change have I seen in my life, a lot of change. And didn't matter which man or woman we had ruling us, life was hard for us poorer townsfolk. And even harder for us women. And harder still for an old woman accused of being a witch. Those accusations never fade. No use trying to clear your name. Nobody'd ever listen.

"And that be me sorry tale. The townsfolk drove me out of me own home and I lived in the forest many a year. And nobody felt guilty 'bout it. They still muttered and moaned about me summoning demons and the like. After a time, more and more people discovered which woodland I were in. P'rhaps they followed my kind customers when they came to buy from I. I started to feel afeared even out there. The witch-hunters were still out for me. But as for what happened in the storm… I'll not be telling. Ye can decide for yourselves."

Oh. That's a shame that Nancy won't narrate the rest of the story. It seems I will have to.

Late in 1703, lightning ripped across the skies, thunder rumbled deep and loud. The Great Storm, which was tearing across the country, had come to the Mendips. It claimed thousands of lives including the Bishop of Bath and Wells and his wife, whose chimney fell through the roof at their palace in Wells and crushed them in their bed, just before Christmas.

On and on it rained, flooding the Somerset Levels, washing people and animals away, and bringing in ships as far as 15 miles inland. Cider orchards were ruined, with apple trees soaked through and uprooted by the howling wind.

The night on which it hit Shepton Mallet the hardest, the townspeople bolted their doors and closed their shutters against the gale-force wind and torrential downpour. The mean-spirited ones blamed Nancy for the storm, believing she was seeking revenge for the way she had been shunned by most of them.

Was it just the whistling tempest or were those the shrieks of the old hag?

They shuddered at the thought.

At daybreak, the sky was calm and quiet as if nothing at all had taken place the night before. A group of men grabbed their pitchforks and squelched through the mud to spy on Nancy. If she were to blame for the deaths and loss of their cider income, she'd be for it now!

Scrambling up the hill, they yelled at her to exit her cave. No reply came. So they tore through the woods, checking behind every tree in the area. But nobody was there.

Nancy had disappeared without a trace from her forest dwelling place.

And yet, what was that? The men swore that those deep grooves in the flat stone slab outside her cave were not natural markings. Oh no. The only explanation was that they'd been caused by Satan's own chariot as he whisked Nancy away to his devilish lair.

The more sceptical inhabitants continued to look for old Nancy over the coming weeks, including among the dead bodies that the storm had produced.

But no sign of Nancy was ever found.

Notes

Nancy Camel (or Nan Scamel) is a legend. There are no traces of her in documents or records so there is no telling when she lived or if she ever lived. Various accounts refer to the Great Storm of 1703 so I stuck with that for when she supposedly caused a storm and was whisked off to an evil den! The political situation in the late 1600s also tied in with her story and it was a time when witch hunts were taking place in earnest.

In terms of her origins, it could be that she came from either Queen Camel or West Camel since her surname was first seen in Somerset in reference to people from those villages. It was the tradition to name foundlings after the place where someone found them so perhaps she was abandoned as a baby in one of those communities.

No version of the legend mentions her treating menstrual cramps but I thought that was a possibility, given the terrible superstition around it.

As regards which forest she hid in, I deliberately didn't name it in the story. There are two candidates: Ham Woods or Darshill Woods, both to the northwest of Shepton Mallet in the parish of Croscombe and both of which have caves named after Nancy Camel.

On the next page, we have- Left: Darshill Woods in winter; Right: Ham Woods in the springtime.

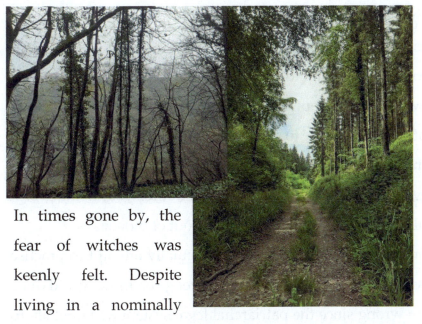

In times gone by, the fear of witches was keenly felt. Despite living in a nominally Christian country, English people have blended pagan beliefs and Christianity for centuries. The fighting between Protestants and Catholics across Europe in the 1500s and 1600s exacerbated the paranoia as people tried to sniff out those who weren't conforming to their ideas. Whereas female "miracle workers" had been sainted in post-Roman Britain (e.g. St Keyne), now any kind of knowledge women had was seen as dangerous. With the printing press up and running across Europe by the late 1400s, hysteric misinformation about "witches" could be spread more quickly than ever before.

Women were seen as naturally weak and easily corruptible by Satan, who would seduce them and turn them to his side. Female sexuality was suppressed and so the idea that certain women were secretly having intercourse with the devil was a terrifying thought.

It could be tempting to pretend to be a witch. Women had little power or career options in such a male-dominated society; professing to be able to summon the devil could cause others to want to kill you *or* it could make them fear you so much that they left you in peace or sought you out for your abilities *or* it could be a viable way to con people out of money.

Women could also feel enticed to actually attempt to practise witchcraft in order to secretly get revenge on those who'd done them wrong since the patriarchal legal system was unlikely to be of much help.

Chapter Bibliography

A brief history of life in the Middle Ages by Martyn Whittock

Sheptonians by C M Ryall

Spooky Shepton Revisited by Mabs Holland

Shepton Mallet, Notes on its history, ancient, descriptive and narrative by John Farbrother

The A–Z of Curious Somerset by Geoffrey Body

Episode 4 of Gods and Monsters with Tony Robinson (documentary)

Somerset: A Troubled Century, 1600 to 1699 by Allan Bunyon

www.houseofnames.com

QUICK TRIBUTE

Other "Sorceresses" in Somerset

Tales of witches have long plagued Somerset. One famous and ancient accusation was launched at a woman about 1,000 years ago. A woman living in Wookey Hole caves was repeatedly blamed for crops failing, cows dying, people disappearing and anything bad happening. Glastonbury Abbey sent a monk to investigate. He approached the caves laden down with holy objects. After a fierce argument, she fled further into the caves. He followed her, sprinkling holy water as he did so. Some of it legendarily landed on her, turning her to stone. Centuries later, bones were found in the caves and purported to belong to the witch, but modern analyses proved the bones were much more than 1,000 years old and belonged to a male skeleton. It's on display at the Wells and Mendip Museum.

Things really kicked off in England in the 15th to 16th century when witch trials took place, with 90% of those killed being women. There are countless tales of women unfortunate enough to have been accused of witchcraft in Somerset. Here are just four more examples.

In Chard, Jane Brooks and her sister Alice Coward were accused of bewitching a boy into being unable to speak and writhing in agony after he gave them bread. (This seems a daft accusation to me because they had no reason to ill-wish him.)

The accusation came in November 1657, when the Puritans were running the country. The women were flung into Shepton Mallet prison. Jane's trial took place at Castle Cary on 8th December, during which she glared at the boy to silence him when he was giving "evidence" (probably because it was all codswallop). The glare worked but others just trumped up more charges against her. As such, she was tried again in Chard in March 1658 and hanged on the 26th day of that month. Meanwhile, her sister died in prison before she could be tried.

The last time a "witch" was subjected to drowning torture in Somerset was in 1730. An old and disabled woman was dragged from her house in Frome, shoved on a horse and taken to a pond two miles away. There, she was stripped naked to the waist and tortured by drowning, an event "enjoyed" by 200 spectators who were convinced that witches had a contract with the devil that made their baptism void; therefore a witch would float in water instead of sinking. When they saw that she wasn't floating and was only clinging to life by a thread, they fished out her and threw her into a stable where she died shortly afterwards. A weak attempt at justice was made. There were 40 people directly involved in her murder, but the coroner couldn't discover who the ringleader was so in the end, just 3 people were charged but not with murder... only manslaughter.

Several years later saw the last burning of a "witch" in Somerset. At the age of 18, a woman from Cardiff named Mary was persuaded by a 45-year-old Axbridge man named Joseph Norwood to marry him. Fast-forward 15 years and she found herself in love with a shoemaker. Unable to divorce her elderly husband, she put poison in his milk until he eventually died. On 8th May 1765, she was brought out barefoot from Ilchester prison (notorious for being the grottiest, most disease-ridden one in Somerset) in front of an audience of 8,000 people. After having time to pray and sing a hymn, she was strangled to death then her body was burnt to cinders. This method was a way of getting rid of her body more thoroughly in order that she wouldn't come back as a ghost to haunt anyone. It also meant she couldn't be brought back to life by God on the Day of Judgement; essentially, she couldn't enter the afterlife.

As time wore on, accusations grew less and less frequent, but they didn't disappear altogether. As late as 1823, there was a case in Wiveliscombe where Elizabeth Bryant accused her elderly neighbour Ann Burges of bewitching two of her daughters. A local wise man advised Elizabeth to draw Ann's blood so that her witchy powers would likewise drain out of her body and any spells she'd cast would be broken. The mother and daughters attacked Ann's arms one night with large iron nails. But this was a new era. After that night, Ann didn't have to hide away or be executed on these trumped-up charges. Instead, even she, a humble rag collector, could seek justice and she got it too. On 26th November, the court case in Taunton resulted in four-month jail sentences for Elizabeth and her daughters.

(Until it closed in 2013, Shepton Mallet Prison was the oldest serving prison in England, receiving its first inmates in 1625.)
Sources: Tales of Old Somerset, Somerset Stories of the Supernatural by Roger Evans, Folklore of Somerset by Kinsley Palmer, Weston Flying Post printed on 13 May 1765, www.bristolhistory.co.uk, The Mammoth Book of Superstition: From Rabbits' Feet to Friday the 13th by Roy Bainton, A History of Witchcraft in England from 1558 to 1718 by Wallace Notestein, wookey.co.uk.

GREAT BRITAIN

Chapter 15: Solange, the Asylum Seeker (17th to 18th century)

Running. Running. Always running.

Time to stop now. Time to find work and put down roots.

This town is as good as anywhere, bigger than most I have seen since stepping off the ship. It has a clean-sounding name, as well: Bath.

Despite the city's name, Solange Luron saw that its roads were just as filthy as anywhere else. Of course they were strewn with rubbish and human waste. All city roads were. With little more than the clothes on her back, she was hoping for a new beginning in this country. She was hoping for a life free from persecution.

"Excuse me." An irritated female voice came from behind her. Turning, Solange realised she was standing in the middle of the street transfixed by the sight of the abbey: a huge place of worship for people like her – for Protestants! – standing proudly in the heart of the town.

"Je suis... ah... sorry."

"Yes, well, some of us are in a rush to get to the bakers afore all the best bread is gone!"

Solange looked blank.

The woman sighed and her eyes softened. "Oh petal, you ain't from round 'ere, is you? I'm saying: I. Go. To. Bakers. Yeah? You know. For. Bread."

"Ah, oui. Yes." Tiredness had made her English even worse

than usual but at least she could pick out some words: baker, bread. A thought struck her: perhaps she could earn a wage in a bakery. Her mother *(gulp, best not dwell on memories of her)* had trained her well in breadmaking.

"I go to bakers also," she declared and off the two of them went. Down the narrow Lilliput Alley they went. Upon arrival at the bakery, the woman busied herself inspecting bread rolls while Solange inspected the baker. Did he look kind enough to offer her employment? Well, there was only one way to find out.

She politely waited her turn in the queue while smoothing out her gown and adjusting her bonnet, then spoke, "Monsieur, excuse me, I would like a work."

He looked her up and down while wiping his floury hands on his apron. As a woman, he didn't think she had the muscles for kneading and her poor English would let her down when serving customers. "You could help us sell buns. Yeah. A walking vendor. Come tomorrow and we'll see how you do. Crack o' dawn you come round, mind."

"You repeat, please?"

He did so, at a snail's pace. Solange shook away the ridiculous sense of disappointment that she wouldn't be baking bread and replied, "Thank you. Thank you. I come tomorrow."

"Where are you staying to, by the way?" he asked slowly.

She was getting used to his accent now and was able to reply without needing repetition. "Ah, I not know. I come today."

"Gosh. You're a long way from home. 'Ere, you ain't one of those Huguenots?"

"Yes. I leave France because not good for... how you say... Protestants."

"Well, listen, a friend of mine runs a guest house. He might just have space for you. Wait here."

Eyes wet with tears, Solange nodded her thanks. It seemed as though she had landed on her feet for once.

The following day, she walked bleary-eyed from the guest house to the bakery. Equipped with a large basket of buns covered with a white cloth, she went out into the streets around the abbey to start selling to the locals and visitors, who had come to drink the spa waters. It was hard work standing or walking slowly about while shouting for many hours and trying to entice buyers with her shaky English. Yet, by late morning, the basket was empty. Back to the baker she went and found him busy drawing water from the bakery's well.

"Good, good." He smiled. "Have a roll and jam for your lunch. Then take a break. Back here at evening-time for more selling."

And so it was that twice a day, she went out with the basket and nearly always returned with an empty one.

On her first Sunday, Solange accompanied the family to the abbey for worship. Tears welled in her eyes as it truly sank in that here she could worship freely without any fear of punishment, even if she could barely understand what was being said.

Little by little, her English improved as her fellow bakery workers and regular customers got to know her. They in turn struggled with her French name and so she became Sally Lunn. As time wore on, Sally took on more hours of work and moved into a room above the bakery with unusually curved walls and uneven floors. She became more and more curious about the breadmaking procedures going on around her and the baker's wife patiently explained everything.

The baker's wife and Sally would position themselves in the doorway to the kitchen, for the women were not allowed in during baking hours, only when it was time to cook for the family using the hearth that was at right-angles to the cavernous hole in the wall that made up the oven. Over the sound of creaking floorboards, shouts of instructions and street noises, Sally commented, "The smells of the bread. They are… delightful!"

"I couldn't live without it," replied the baker's wife. "See the oven, built outside the kitchen with its mouth poking into the building? That there oven is the same design as what they used in Roman times, back when the Romans built their bathhouses in the town centre. 'Tis a faggot oven. This particular one weren't built in Roman times but it's been 'ere 'undreds o' years. Good ol' oven, 'tis. Nice petal shape inside. 'Twas built in the 12th century, I think. Back when a building stood on this spot that 'twas part of the abbey."

"What's a faggot?" Sally asked.

"You see them bundles of thin hazel branches the boys are pushing into the oven? Those be the faggots. You gotta tie 'em ever so tight. And o' course you set them ablaze once you push 'em in, then close the oven door."

"The door… is not cover the oven so good."

"On purpose, as it happens. You gotta make sure the door is at an angle so as to let a bit of air in. That makes the wood burn good and lets smoke out."

"Then the faggots go to ash and the boys sweep ash out?"

"Exactly right. It takes about four hours for that, though. Then you sticks your arm in to see if it's hot enough. The heat that stays in the oven is then used to bake the bread. They use that scuffle to sweep out the ashes." She pointed to a long pole with a rag on the end.

"Much buns go in each time?"

"Sixty buns, my girl. Buns what's been proved, that means left to rise. Now, we better scarper 'fore we get accused of gettin' in the way and neglectin' our duties."

When Christmas came about, she offered to bake some special

French buns for the family, surprising them all with her skill. Sally brought a large plate of large, very light and springy buns to the table. "Maman always said: eat them warm with butter and jam. Sometimes cream too."

"You've kept such a secret from us, you impish girl!" the baker said after just one bite.

Sally looked alarmed. "I... but my English was bad and then I didn't knew if you like this and..."

"Not to worry," the wife smoothed things over while slapping her youngest son's hand away before he could grab a second one before finishing his first. "Thank you for this festive gift, Sally. They taste cosy and gluten-y and, well... delicious."

"Yes, I were only jesting!" laughed the baker.

"It's half the size of my head, mummy."

Smiling indulgently, the adults pulled their buns in half politely and buttered them thickly, while the children ripped chunks of their buns off and wolfed them down. The parents were so busy enjoying their portions that they didn't even scold the boys.

"Want more, mummy. They good. They soft!" the youngest son sulked.

"Hmm... French bread... We could make something of this," the baker mused. "French bread could make us more competitive. It could attract new customers."

"I would be happy to bake," Sally readily agreed.

"Mummy, what's a hugga-not?" the youngest piped up again. Everyone tittered.

"People call me a Huguenot," Sally explained slowly, "because I am Protestant from France. For many years, the Catholics make life difficult for Protestants in France."

"Why?" asked the older boy.

"I think because they not like that we are different. They try to make us Catholic like they are. But we not want to change."

"So you came here instead?"

"Yes."

"What about your family?"

"I... never speak about them."

"Come, show me how to make these buns, Sally. It seems a complex, laborious method but worth it. We must all learn to be as clever and patient as you. I can't get over how light they are!" The baker's wife wisely wanted to change the subject.

Before long, Sally was regularly beating dough in a huge bowl and greasing trays to make her buns, which had become highly sought after. Given that their bakery was central, that they had a chic French treat on offer and that Bath was so popular with the royals and elite society, they were guaranteed success. James II's wife, Mary of Modena, visited Bath in 1687, 7 years after Sally arrived. Poor Mary had experienced 5 stillbirths and

5 more of her children died as infants. She had no living children. Upon drinking the spa waters, Mary fell pregnant and gave birth to a son who went on to live a long life. "It would ne'er have happened had Her Majesty not consumed the waters here," the bakery's customers swore.

Mary's success inspired her stepdaughter, Princess Anne, to turn to Bath for help with fertility. Anne holidayed there in 1688 after facing 2 stillbirths, 2 infant deaths and 2 miscarriages. Sally's heart went out to Anne. For all her money, she could not have this one desire for her own happiness and the good of the nation, while Sally had chosen to remain single, not feeling the pull of motherhood herself to want to risk a life of domestic slavery. Besides, you can't be chastised for being a bad wife if you aren't a wife at all! And how husbands, mothers-in-law, neighbours and the whole world could dig away at a woman, stealing pieces of her self-worth each day over trivialities.

But Bath's waters had the desired effect. Anne gave birth to a healthy son in 1689. Buoyed up, she returned in 1692 and then again as Queen of England in 1702 to once more drink the waters and try to improve her ill health. Although she never had another healthy baby and her son died aged 11 in 1700, she kept trying. All her visits did wonders for enhancing Bath's popularity.

Little by little, the bakery became a firm favourite for wealthy tourists and locals, who were willing to pay a handsome shilling for tea and cake there once word had spread about Sally's buns. The rich cared not that a shilling was the equivalent of a day's wages for a farm labourer.

Sally and the bakery family bought themselves fine clothes and good food on the profits. And the eating house was often alive with the hubbub of conversations, laughter and gossip over newspapers, tea and buns.

In Sally's old age, two distinguished gentlemen in particular became regulars. The Master of Ceremonies for Bath, Beau Nash, came to talk of fashion, merriment and street cleaning, the latter of which pleased Sally greatly. The hygiene in public areas was disgraceful. What didn't please her and her colleagues was the carousel of women he brought in with him, each purported to be his mistress. For the sake of the business, they said not a word about it and swallowed their disapproval. A more salubrious figure was Ralph Allen, who came through her doors to drink his morning coffee there. "Barely 19 and already a postmaster," the baker's wife whispered in wonder. When he built his townhouse a few doors down from them, she commented, "I reckon as he moved close just because of your baking, Sally!"

"We're a team," Sally smiled back. "It's funny, though. Funny to think that I fled my homeland in search of survival with not a penny to my name and little English. Nowadays, I chatter to the aristocracy and they even move house simply to be close to our bakery!" she added with a wink.

"That's the spirit, love. Now, give me a hand getting this batch into the oven."

Notes

Another working woman like Nancy Camel for whom there are no records, grand monuments or archaeological evidence; all we have is a legend. The legend goes that our heroine first set foot in Bath in 1680. Solange Luyon, whose first name means solemn, dignified or religious and so is rather apt for a Huguenot, was lucky to leave France before things got even worse for the Huguenots. In 1685, an edict was revoked, stripping the Huguenots of any precarious rights they had previously had. 400,000 French Protestants left the country as a result. Things were unstable in England that year also; if she lived and arrived in 1680, Sally would've faced the Monmouth Rebellion. As a Protestant, her allegiance would've been firmly with the duke.

I have included Sally in the "Great Britain" section as the GB was created in 1707 and so I believe Sally, if she existed, probably lived to see the creation. In 1801, the United Kingdom of Great Britain and Ireland (later Northern Ireland only) was formed but I didn't want to separate out my chapters too much. The stories about Sally don't mention any member of Sally's family or a baker's wife and children or making buns at Christmas. The latter two are my inventions but the name Lilliput Alley isn't, rather the lane's name changed to North Parade Passage. The abbey complex once stretched to where Sally Lunn's Historic Eating House and Museum is but this section of the abbey was destroyed in a fire in 1137, leaving behind only a few foundations in the cellar and the faggot oven, which had originally been used to bake for the monks at the abbey. The oven had therefore been used to bake bread for centuries upon centuries. The current building was constructed in 1482 or that date could refer just to some rebuilding of fireplaces and chimneys, meaning the edifice is even older.

The street level was raised in the mid-1700s, meaning that the bakery was once on the ground floor and is now in the basement. Sally may have still been alive then, assuming she lived at all! It's possible that she took over the bakery from the original baker as time wore on, becoming a tenant in the building.

Anyone who worked in the bakery must have met some interesting people. Beau Nash (1674-1761) and Ralph Allen (1693-1764) both went regularly in the early 1700s. I believe Sally was young and thus fit enough to flee France in 1680, so so we can surmise that she was still alive when Ralph was made postmaster in 1712.

Bath was also becoming a multicultural place. For example, The Jews of Bath by Malcolm Brown and Judith Samuel mentions that in 1731, the widowed Catherine da Costa (1710–1747) and her children became the first "identifiable" Jewish visitors to the city, arriving so she could recover her strength.

The first mention of a Sally Lunn bun was in a 1780 guidebook to Bath. The first mention of Sally as an actual person was in 1827. William Hone wrote in his Every-day Book: "The bun...called the Sally Lunn originated with a young woman of that name in Bath, about 30 years ago." If this was Sally Lunn, she would've arrived in Bath decades after 1680, more like a French Revolution refugee than a Huguenot. Now, the guidebook mentioning the bun was written 47 years previously so Hone could be right but got his timing a bit wrong.

By 1798, a baker named William Dalmer had bought exclusive rights to Sally Lunn's recipe and started advertising the buns the following year with a ditty: "Buy my nice Sally Lunn, the very best of Bunn, I think her the sweetest of any..." He put away her recipe for these brioche-style bread rolls with the deeds to the house and so the official technique was lost for centuries but similar recipes spread across the world.

An alternative explanation for the term Sally Lunn is that the buns were known as soleil et lune, meaning sun and moon in French in reference to the buns' golden crusts and white interiors. Female bakers were very unusual in the 1600s; for one thing, bakers often belonged to guilds, reserved for men only, but that isn't to say an exception couldn't have been made when a French woman could produce a unique and profitable bun. Either way, Sally Lunn buns are so famous that they have entered the dictionary.

The original recipe was rediscovered when the artist Marie Byng-Johnson took over the house in 1937, writing: "I'd always been fascinated by the ancient house... so, although it seemed mad, I bought it." Her fascination became a published booklet, in which she claimed to know that Sally had married because Marie had spoken to the last descendant of Sally's family. I tried to verify this with research but didn't get anywhere. Nonetheless, it's a good job Marie took on the house so enthusiastically because during restoration work, she found Sally's recipes in a secret cupboard in wooden panelling above a fireplace in a back room. Also at that time, a plaque was put up on the house, which reads: "The oldest house in Bath 1482 Sally Lunn lived here 1680". Sally's secret recipe has been passed on to the Eating House's current owners along with the deeds to the house and the original kitchen in the building's basement has been restored.

Nobody has ever quite managed to replicate Sally's original recipe, even though people have been trying since the early 1700s. Here are some knock-off mini Sally Lunn buns that we made. Although we couldn't use an official recipe, we did our best. It took us a loooong time and was a tricky technique. That shows how super-awesome Sally was. She had to make them without a modern oven, an electric mixer, electric scales etc. Below our buns is an official Sally Lunn bun.

Chapter Bibliography

Bath: A Very Peculiar History by David Arscott

Online Encyclopaedia Britannica

Curious Somerset by Derrick Warren

nationalhuguenotsociety.org

Oxforddnb.com

sallylunns.co.uk and staff at the museum

The Story of Sally Lunn's House by Marie Byng-Johnson

What's Her Name Podcast: The Baker Sally Lunn

janeausten.co.uk

www.thebathmagazine.co.uk

QUICK TRIBUTES

Anne Elizabeth Bourisquot (8th February 1666–29th January 1721)

A Huguenot woman who definitely lived in Somerset, though only for about 6 years, was Anne Elizabeth Bourisquot. Born in Saintonge, western France, she narrowly escaped the country with her fiancé, Jacques "James" Fontaine, a Protestant minister from the same province. Arriving almost penniless, they married on her 20th birthday in Barnstaple, Devon. James Fontaine Jr was born 8 months after their marriage (a shotgun wedding, perhaps, though it appears they did deeply love each other).

They then moved to Bridgwater, where Jacques worked for the town's MP, Halswell Tynte, who was based in Goathurst and also owned Tyntesfield. But soon, they relocated to Taunton, where Anne gave birth to and raised Aaron in 1688, Mary in 1690, Peter in 1691, John in 1693 and Moses in 1694. Jacques, meanwhile, worked as a minister and ran a general store and woollen goods manufacturing business. This became so successful that he angered local tradesmen, who harassed him and took him to court only for Jacques to charm the magistrate into taking his side. The family also had a narrow escape when William of Orange's soldiers arrived in Taunton. Their captain, also a Huguenot, was told Jacques was a French Jesuit, ergo a Catholic. The captain ordered his death and so stormed the house with soldiers only to discover Jacques was a Protestant minister and so hugged him instead!

Perhaps these issues, but definitely his wish to preach to a French congregation, caused the family to move to Ireland in 1694, where there were plenty of French refugees. In that country, they had 2 more children for a total of 8.

Overall, they lived a rollercoaster life of exile, xenophobic threats, a failed fishing venture and pirate attacks, all outlined in her husband's engaging memoir, which he wrote for his children and descendants to know their heritage, but it mainly focuses on his business ventures rather than his wife and children.

After suffering for some time from rheumatism and oedema, Anne died in Dublin and was buried there, as was Jacques 8 years later.

Sources: A Tale of the Huguenots: Or, Memoirs of a French Refugee Family by James Fontaine, ancestors.familysearch.org, www.fontaine maurysociety.com, A Somerset Miscellany by Robert Dunning, findagrave.com.

Bette Gascoin (born c.1658)

Like Sally, Bette was born abroad. Unlike Sally, we have documented evidence of her, albeit not very much information. Bette (possibly short for Elizabeth) was one of several Black people to be baptised in Bath Abbey during the 1600s. On 9th September 1677, the records state that "Bette Gascoin of Bridge Town in Barbados, of about the age of 18 or 19, a black, was baptised Frances Gascoin."

These few words are sadly the only glimpse we get into her specific life, but we can guess a little more from what was going on in Barbados and England at that time.

Bridgetown was founded by the British in 1628, taking its name from a bridge believed to have been built by the Indigenous Arawaks. The colonisers set up sugar plantations and began to tap into the Dutch and Portuguese Transatlantic Slave Trade.

The population exploded. Around the time of Bette's birth, the island's population was about 43,000, of which around 20,000 were people of African descent. Yet Africans forcibly taken to Barbadian sugar plantations had a horrifying life expectancy once they arrived: it was seven years.

Bette may have had a better existence once she stepped foot in England as a freedwoman or she was still an enslaved woman. (There were numerous newspaper adverts for the sale of Black servants as well as wills in which the servants were "passed on" to a relative.) Bette could have come to Bath via Bristol, as it was one of the three main slavery ports.

Black people arriving in England in the 1600s were much rarer than in subsequent centuries and so we can imagine that she was a servant to an aristocratic family, probably called Gascoin, often spelt Gascoigne and of French origin, which highlights the family's elite status as descendants of the Normans. The family probably saw her as a way of showing off their fabulous wealth, of being "fashionable". Whether she was treated well or not is something we will likely never know.

Being baptised a Christian would make her a "civilised" person according to the standards of the time and so might have been a practical action on her behalf or something she was forced to do. Those she worked for probably wanted to further highlight their status by arranging her baptism in the grand abbey. It could have also been symbolic of the end of her enslavement; many enslaved people sought out baptism as they felt becoming a Christian meant they could no longer be held in slavery. There are accounts of enslavers, albeit in the Caribbean, violently preventing the baptism of enslaved people precisely for that reason.

Source: Britain's Forgotten Slave Traders (documentary with David Olusoga), Black servants in Britain by Dr Emma Poulter, The registers of the Abbey church of SS. Peter and Paul, Bath.

Ann Harris (c.1697– 27th May 1719)

A very pious young lady, Ann Harris, lived in a thatched cottage in Welton. Probably in the knowledge that she would die soon at the tender age of 22, she wrote her will in 1719. With no husband or children and having inherited plenty of wealth and land from her father, she decided to leave a generous amount of money for the building of a Charity School for 40 poor children to be taught reading, writing and arithmetic.

Two years after her death, Midsomer Norton Charity School was built on a plot of land at the Island in Midsomer Norton, consisting of a thatched schoolhouse with an outside toilet. As Midsomer Norton's population grew, the school was enlarged. It remained the town's only school until 1830, when a new school for 74 pupils was set up on Rackvernal Road with money donated by Sophia Kelston. In 1841, another piece of Ann Harris' donated land was used to build another school. This was on Redfield Road and is now St John's Primary School.

The original Charity School and Ann's cottage are no longer standing but her legacy lives on, in that she was the first to ensure education in the area. The Ann Harris Academy Trust, which oversaw St John's Primary School, was dissolved only very recently: in 2019. Ann was a pioneer. In the late 18th century, more philanthropists began to look at providing education for poor children, as we will see in the next chapter.

(The Ann Harris Memorial in St John's Church, Midsomer Norton)

Sources: The Ann Harris Memorial leaflet, Midsomer Life magazine, www.stjohnsmsn.co.uk.

Chapter 16: The Mores in Mendip (late 18th century)

It had been Patty's suggestion and now she was regretting it. The day began with a visit to Cheddar Gorge and it began well. Even though she had been many times before, the gorge never failed to amaze her. The fresh, clean air would hit her lungs, as her eyes would be greeted with the magnificent, sheer cliffs on either side that towered over her like craggy giants. The only sound to be heard would be an eagle calling out in the distance. Naturally, she had thought it would be an ideal outing to send Mr Wilberforce out on while he was staying with them. However, by now it was getting harder for Hannah and her sister Patty to not worry. Upon returning from the gorge, their guest had gone straight to his room and had not left it since.

At dinnertime, he had emerged but looked agitated. As soon as the servants had left the room after serving the three of them, an act that took place in excruciating silence, William made an announcement that caused Patty to drop her spoon in alarm:

"Miss Hannah More, something must be done for Cheddar! The poverty I witnessed there today was... indescribable. As I marvelled at God's creation in the gorge, a feeble voice broke my reverie with the words: 'Sir, won't you buy some stalactites?' Looking around, I saw a dirty child in rags sitting at the entrance to a cave with a table of glittering stalactites. I knelt down beside the child to ask if she'd had any breakfast that morning. The child turned red and shook her head. No, she hadn't. A quick glance into the cave – with its blankets, pots and pans – made me realise that the child had not travelled from a cottage to sell the wares. Rather, a whole family was living in the cave. Of course, coins exchanged hands and their gratitude was humbling. Miss More, I met this very same sight several times along the way."

William's face grew ever more creased.

"Cheddar has no resident minister, no manufacturing… The residents have nothing to feed their souls nor their stomachs."

"You're quite right," replied Hannah. "It is not for nothing that the village has come to be known as 'Little Hell'. The vicar lives at the University of Oxford and visits but once a year, though he is very happy to receive the salary for the parish. As you know, it is not uncommon to find absent scholarly priests, yet I still consider it scandalous. The curate lives in Wells and rides over once a week for a few hours for a service then leaves again. The villagers must wait for Sunday for marriages, burials, baptisms…"

"Something must be done. Something that requires financial contributions. If you will condescend to be my alms distributor, you will enable me to employ some of the superfluity it has pleased God to give me, to good purpose. Indeed, if you will be at the trouble, I will be at the expense."

*

In the month of August 1789, Providence directed Mr Wilberforce and his sister to spend a few days at Cowslip Green.

These were the first words Patty wrote in her new journal as she reflected back on that cataclysmic moment with Mr Wilberforce that altered her life forever.

Various ideas had been thrown around until it was decided that a Sunday school must be started up in Cheddar. Patty felt strongly that this was God's work, a project that she would water with watchfulness, even when faced with opposition. Which they did face. Almost immediately.

"Religion will be the ruin of agriculture!" The gentleman farmer banged his fist on the dinner family, making Patty jump. "It has produced much mischief and laziness ever since it was introduced by the monks down at Glastonbury."

Patty didn't tell him that the abbey had been founded in the late 7th century and so that statement seemed hardly fair since the abbey hadn't caused the collapse of agriculture yet and Christianity predated the abbey.

She and Hannah were visiting a total of eleven rich, local farmers to gain their approval for the school. Thankfully, some of the other farmers were more receptive:

"Forgive us, we are all aghast at strangers coming to do good in our area, but you are very welcome."

"A Sunday school you say? That'd keep the nippers from stealing our apples for at least one day a week!"

"As long as they don't get ideas above their station, it could work I suppose."

"Yes, the poor inhabitants around here could benefit, I'm sure, from leading principles and industriousness."

Also necessary was to convince the parents.

"If ye be paying the young'uns to come, then 'course. Hahaha. They gotta be out earning money so as we can fill their bellies."

"I need my girls at home. You rich folk have no idea what's involved to keep a family going. We got clothes to wash, put through the mangle and hang up, fires to stoke, food to cook, a baby to care for, rooms to sweep…"

"What you want wi' our babbies? Why should we trust you?"

"I've heard the rumour, alright. After seven years, you'll be thinking you can have power over 'em and send 'em beyond sea."

"Nonsense!" Patty exclaimed at this last accusation.

Despite all this, the sisters were determined to carry out their plan. Once a house had been rented, they got to work employing teachers and promoting the school.

Finally, on 25th October, the Sunday school opened its doors to reveal a whitewashed classroom with rows of wooden benches and a blackboard. The children, who Patty felt were woefully ignorant and rather "savage", bravely emerged from their cramped and filthy homes to access the only form of education available to them. Patty hoped the newly appointed Mrs Baber and her daughter, Betsy, would be able to "Christianise" the waifs satisfactorily, and that they would sing psalms and learn to read so that they could recite prayers, the catechism and Bible passages. The principal aim was to save their souls, as well as to improve their health and skills but not to encourage them to think or express themselves. "I allow of no writing for the poor," Hannah had previously declared. "My object is to train up the lower classes in the habits of industry and piety."

Fighting off the beginning of one of her migraines, Patty followed Hannah out of the door to leave Mrs and Miss Baber to their work. The elder was heard to say sternly, "Children, you must learn virtues in your time here. Cleanliness is one of them. Tidy hair and no dirt under your nails. You will wash your faces at the entrance each Sunday. Punctuality is also necessary. You must arrive on time. And honesty is golden also. There will be no telling lies or cheating."

After the first day's success, they had to find ways to keep the little ones coming. The Mores coaxed and scolded the mothers and put pressure on local employers to give the children days off. Hannah and Patty also provided the teachers with money so that they could give a penny to every child who came on time for four Sundays in a row.

These tactics bore fruit. The Cheddar children's school was doing so well that six months later, they started a programme to teach parents to sing psalms and read prayers of an evening. They hoped to combat the illiteracy and alcoholism that were so rife in Cheddar. It began with four attendees but soon grew to 60.

Some of the women who turned up in the evenings were asked to go and visit the sick with the aim of evangelising to them. The Mores gave the women medicine and some money to gain the trust of those they visited. The women were essentially doing the work that the vicar was being paid for and should have been doing. The women did the man's job for free. (But then, the world has always relied on the unpaid labour of women. Let that sink in.)

*

With their spirits lifted by the success of Cheddar, the More sisters decided to turn their hands to other villages. The next two villages chosen were Shipham and Rowberrow, located between Cheddar and Wrington. Amazingly, a young and fairly well-educated dairy worker, Patience Seward, had already set up a Sunday school there by herself for 30 children. Despite her own poverty, she herself had bought books for this school. Meanwhile, the actual vicar was shamelessly collecting tithe money but hadn't preached a sermon there for 40 years.

"Patience is a good Christian who knows her scriptures and her letters," Hannah commented to Patty. "The education she has received is far superior to that of most of the people around here. With some guidance on our part, I am sure she will be able to teach according to our methods."

"In that case, it's settled," Patty replied. "She will teach here with her half-sister, Flower Waite."

In collaboration with the other duo of sisters, the Mores opened a Sunday and day school in September 1790 for the two villages. The student total was now 140.

The student population was growing right across the schools. By Christmas 1791, Hannah and Patty were overseeing the education of nearly a thousand children across 10 parishes: Cheddar, Shipham and Rowberrow, Sandford and Winscombe, Banwell, Congresbury, Yatton, Axbridge, Nailsea, Wrington and Churchill. Their influence spanned north to south from Cheddar to Nailsea, 14 miles from each other, and east to west from Banwell to Wrington, a more modest 6 miles distance. Each place had a distinct feel about it too– from Cheddar's rural cave-homes with folk living in abject poverty to Nailsea's glassworks factory and well-fed workers to Axbridge's constantly drunk vicar who got black eyes from fights. The sisters had lifted many Cheddar residents out of destitution, given education to the hardened factory workers and improved morals in Axbridge. Each place had a story to tell.

All of that was certainly something to celebrate and so they shared the joy as per their annual tradition to celebrate the Birth of the Lord. This sharing took the form of handing out meat and money to those who attended the children's schools and adult sessions.

The Mendip schools' star shone brighter and brighter as time wore on: by 1795, Wedmore had been added to the list and in the same year, the curate of Blagdon, Mr Thomas Bere, requested that they open a school there. Yet, the sisters were unsure.

"We simply cannot," Patty lamented to her sister. "We have neither the time nor the money nor the strength or health to take on anything more."

"I quite agree," sighed Hannah. "We have stretched ourselves across numerous parishes. We cannot extend our reach anymore. I will pen a letter to politely decline."

Nevertheless, the villagers were determined. The churchwardens and parish overseers sent a second request, begging the sisters to come.

Patty and Hannah prayed and contemplated the idea. In the end, they couldn't help but accept the proposition.

To begin with, it was a beautiful sight. Coming from troubled backgrounds, the villagers were very keen: 170 turned up when they opened in October 1795, mainly aged 11 to 20. Three of the children had a mother who had been sentenced to death by hanging and several of the adult students had been recently tried for crimes. The parish's vicar, also the local magistrate, was a hard man but was reduced to tears to see these young people aiming for something better in life.

As time went by, improvements were evident such as far less theft and the children becoming capable readers.

But 5 years later, the situation had become so disastrous that the women started to regret their decision to open a school in Blagdon.

Mr Bere wrote a strongly worded letter, in which he accused the Blagdon school teacher, Mr Young, of holding Methodist meetings in the evenings, as the teacher was a known Methodist. This was against the established Church and was not acceptable to the curate, who brandished the schools as "seminaries of fanaticism, vice and sedition". It was also possible that his anger stemmed from the fact that the sisters were doing the work that the Church should have been carrying out in the first place. The Mores made clergymen look lazy and greedy. But nobody could admit that and so trumped-up charges were necessary.

Hannah More stopped Mr Young's evening meetings at once.

Hannah and Patty were both staunchly anti-Methodist, labelling it a "stupid and ruinous idea".

Not long afterwards, Mr Bere again complained with violently explosive words. Using a young lad to give false testimony, he demanded that Mr Young be dismissed right away.

Initially shocked and dismayed, Hannah and Patty soon began to fight back.

"We must take advantage of our being in London at this time," Hannah said, watching her sister groan in pain as yet another migraine attacked her.

"How? Surely it would be better to make at once for Somerset to talk to Mr Bere and other Blagdon inhabitants face-to-face?"

"But would they listen? They see us as belonging to a 'weaker sex' and further conversations might spark more fury and unreasonableness. If only our brother had lived to support us, then perhaps returning to Somerset would make sense. But we do not. Therefore, I believe we can use our contacts in London to our advantage, male contacts who will be taken more seriously by the Blagdon population. For instance, the Londoners I have met through my writing career could help. We can request advice from MPs and bishops."

"Hannah, how right you are! I had not thought of it like that. As soon as this headache abates, we should go at once to visit as many people as possible and write letters to those who are out of town. The children of Blagdon should not suffer because of one man's campaign of hatred against us.

The sisters set to work. All the men they contacted were outraged that the lies of Mr Bere and one Somerset lad were being listened to.

After gaining support from members of the 'stronger sex', things quietened down again. Hannah and Patty returned home and resumed their yearly pattern of work, visiting all the other schools.

After that ceasefire, unrest began to erupt again. After that ceasefire, unrest began to erupt again. On and on the problem grew. Pamphlets began to be published, some for but many against the Mores. Hannah was brandished a "she-bishop" in one of them. (Imagine their shock to know women can become bishops nowadays!) The sisters, once back in Somerset, spent most of their time hiding at home, away from the gossip. The relentless attacks left them with bleary eyes and nerves torn to shreds.

When they could stand it no longer, Hannah asked for a local magistrate to launch an investigation with the participation of Blagdon's rector. The magistrate found Mr Young not guilty of heresy. This did nothing to please the attackers and so the storm brewed on. In the end, Mr Young moved to Ireland and the Mores took the drastic decision to close the Blagdon school in November 1800 to save the reputation of the other schools. Speaking of which, by then, the Sandford and Winscombe, Congresbury, Banwell, Axbridge and Yatton schools had also been closed due to various difficulties.

Perhaps because of the Blagdon school closure but definitely because of his terrible behaviour, the rector asked Bere to resign. This allowed the More sisters to reopen their school in January of the following year. But Bere refused to stand down, so Hannah and Patty closed the school for a second time in September 1801.

"This is a sorrowful time, but the children of Blagdon and the other lost congregations have at least gained some knowledge from the years we worked there. And we still have Shipham and Rowberrow, Nailsea, Wedmore and dear Cheddar," Patty reassured herself and Hannah.

"All the same, we will never forget this atrocious affair, this Blagdon Controversy," Hannah sighed.

Patty echoed Hannah's sigh. A creeping tiredness lay in her bones, the legacy of so much illness and stress. Around that time, she felt so depressed about it all that she gave up writing her journal. She ended it abruptly but on a positive note:

In the afternoon we gave rewards [in Cheddar] of Bibles, etc., to upwards of three hundred children, and in the evening read a sermon to three hundred more. God be praised, it was a prosperous day!

Notes

Martha "Patty" More (1747-1819) was born in Bristol where she grew up, having a very close bond with her four older sisters, all of whom remained unmarried. They were Mary (1738-1813), Elizabeth "Betty" (1740-1816), Sarah (Sally; 1743-1819) and Hannah (2nd February 1745-7th September 1833). A brother named Jacob was born in 1746 but died as a baby.

From their base in Wrington (at Cowslip Green then from 1801 onwards at Barley Wood), Hannah and Patty set up Women's Friendly Societies across some of the villages, such as Rowberrow, Shipham and Wrington. The women paid a small amount each week and in return, they would be given larger sums of money in times of need, such as for illness, marriage, poverty, a new baby and as a pension. These societies continued for over a hundred years, only disbanding around 1948 when the NHS was founded.

That was alongside at least 12 Sunday schools in Somerset, but Cheddar was the first and most successful. For instance, when Mrs Baber passed away in September 1794, almost the whole parish attended her funeral, including her 200 students who walked behind the coffin. Even after Mrs Baber's death, the school community flourished. In fact, the schools at Shipham and Rowberrow, Cheddar and Nailsea were still going strong in 1825. As for Wrington itself, the village already had a good vicar and a school so there was no need to set one up but the sisters supported the education there.

(The school building in Cheddar now belongs to the council and can be hired for events.)

Nowadays, we would see their schools as being a top-down dictatorial type of charity and see the sisters as well-meaning but often patronising, narrowminded, condescending and a bit over-controlling. We would shudder at their idea that poor people should learn to read but not to write and that the lower classes should reconcile themselves to their station in life.

However, at the time, many didn't want the poor to have any access to education. For one thing, if the masses became educated, it would be harder for the rich to see them as "less-than" and so harder to justify oppression and educated people could argue against the morality of such oppression. The Mores were seen as radicals bringing dangerous ideas to the poor. That shows what society the sisters had been born into and that their way of thinking was more generous and modern *for that time!* For that reason, I have included them in this book. They were ahead of their time but not as ahead as we would wish. In the words of Mike Rendell, Hannah "is now largely out of fashion – as if she is in some way to blame for 'not having gone far enough'. Perhaps the answer is that in a relay race, only the runner on the final leg crosses the finishing line – Hannah merely carried the baton on one of the earlier legs." A lot has been written about Hannah, who was also a poet and playwright and led the schooling project, yet not so much about Patty, so I focussed on the younger sister and her journal. Some of the words spoken by Wilberforce and the farmers are taken from Patty's book.

But for a little more on Hannah, she had a successful career as a writer and was also involved in the abolition movement, canvassing MPs by letter and in person, helping to run the Abolition Society and writing the influential 'Slavery, a poem' in January 1788 in support of Wilberforce and his bill to end slavery.

She sat on the Female Anti-Slavery Society at Clifton in Bristol in the 1820s, by which point, poor Hannah had suffered the loss of all four sisters within 6 years of each other. She outlived them all by several decades, dying in 1833 aged 88 and supposedly crying out with her last breath, "Patty! Joy!" Hannah's death came 6 weeks after the announcement of the abolition of slavery in the British Empire; Wilberforce famously died 3 weeks after it. Hannah was one of the most influential abolitionists. After her death, the Christian Observer wrote: "What William Wilberforce was among men, Hannah More was among women."

All 5 sisters were buried in All Saints' Church graveyard in Wrington (see photo on the left). There is a cul-de-sac named after Hannah in Cheddar, a school in Bristol, an infant school and road in Nailsea and a plaque to her outside 76 Great Pulteney Street in Bath where the sisters lived during the colder months from 1792 to 1802.

Chapter Bibliography

Mendip Annals: or a narrative of the charitable labours of Hannah and Martha More in their neighbourhood, being the journal of Martha More edited, with additional matter by Arthur Roberts

Hannah More and her circle by Mary Alden Hopkins

Chapter 15: Hannah More – bluestocking, educationalist and pamphleteer in Trailblazing Women of the Georgian Era by Mike Rendell

Hannah More (Eminent Women Series) by John H Ingram

Hannah More (feature-length film)

Great Western Woman: Hannah More (documentary)

Dictionary of National Biography, 1885–1900

The Life and Correspondence of Mrs Hannah More by William Roberts

www.oxforddnb.com

A Brief Life of Hannah More by Echo Irving

Women Worth Knowing podcast: Hannah More (parts 1 and 2)

QUICK TRIBUTES

Elizabeth Singer Rowe (11th September 1674–20th February 1737)

Elizabeth came from a dissenting family. Her father was jailed in Ilchester for being a nonconformist minister during Charles II's reign. It was then that he met Elizabeth's mother. They settled in Ilchester and had three daughters, Elizabeth being their firstborn.

When Elizabeth's mother died, the family moved to Frome in 1690. From 1691, at age 17, she contributed poems to John Dunton's periodical The Athenian Mercury using the pseudonym "Philomela". Her poems were collected and published as 'Poems on Several Occasions. Written by Philomela' in 1696. Overall, Elizabeth wrote poetry and pieces on morality and religion, becoming one of the most widely read authors of the 1700s.

In 1710 she married Thomas Rowe (1687–1715), also a writer, and moved to London. Once widowed, she returned to her father's house in Frome, Rock Lane House, and wrote 'Friendship in Death: in Twenty Letters from the Dead to the Living' (1728), a series of short visions of the hereafter.

At her father's death in 1719, Elizabeth was the only surviving daughter so inherited large properties in Frome and Ilchester. She gave away half the annual income to charity. Her charity extended to domestic life, too. Elizabeth was known to be very kind to her servants, almost treating them as friends. For instance, if a servant fell ill she would sit by their bedside and read religious books to them.

She stayed in Frome until her death aged 62 of a stroke. Elizabeth was buried at Rock Lane Chapel for nonconformists, which was deconsecrated in 1968.

(the former Rock Lane Chapel)

Sources: www.oxforddnb.com, Secret Frome by Andrew Pickering & Gary Kearley, www.eighteenthcenturypoetry.org, "The Life of Mrs Elizabeth Rowe" in Poems on Several Occasions by Mrs Elizabeth Rowe.

Sarah Stone (née Holmes) (c.1680 sometime after 1737)

Dubbed a "dedicated, knowledgeable, brave, caring, hard-working and ambitious woman" by Anna Bosanquet, Sarah was a midwife like her mother before her and daughter after her. By 1736, she had been practicing for "five and thirty years", as she wrote in her book A Complete Practice of Midwifery, published in 1737. Nearly everything we know about Sarah comes from the pages of her book, which seems to have been written when she was approaching retirement.

Sarah began her career in Somerset. She married Samuel on 24th November 1700 at St Mary's Church in Bridgwater and began working there as a midwife around 1701. The church was also the location for the baptism of her daughter, also Sarah, born on 17th November 1702.

Sadly, the birth was soon followed by the death of Sarah Senior's renowned mother, Mrs Holmes, a very competent midwife who trained Sarah for six years. Though a young adult, Sarah now found herself working alone. As such, and perhaps because Sarah was now married, the family moved to Taunton, where she worked over a wide range of Somerset for about 17 years. Sarah found many local midwives to be poorly trained and Sarah was often called to attend a birth once their efforts were failing. Our heroine also found that expectant mothers' difficult work in the wool industry, such as weaving, caused many problems during pregnancies. All the same, our skilled midwife was bringing around 300 children into the world every year towards the end of her time in Taunton, which came c.1720 when the family moved to Bristol. In

Somerset, Sarah had endured long journeys to other destinations on foot or horseback along bad roads, through flooded fields and rivers, come rain or shine, day or night. The effect this had had on her health was the driving force for her move to Bristol along with the better pay she got there. In the city, Sarah Junior joined her mother in midwifery around 1726. 1726. Sarah was appalled to see many forceps injuries in Bristol, often caused by male midwives who had little training in childbirth and arrogantly thought themselves superior to all female practitioners.

In 1736, Sarah moved to London with Samuel, believed to be an apothecary. His profession, as Janette Allotey suggests, probably gave Sarah access to more medical literature than other midwives, allowing her to gain greater knowledge.

Her 1737 book was written for "all female practitioners in an art so important to the lives and wellbeing of the sex". It uses 43 case studies to demonstrate her strategies for dealing with complex birthing issues. Most of the case studies are from Taunton but three are from Bristol and four from the Bridgwater area, including a mother at a farm in Huntspill (just outside Burnham-on-Sea).

Tragically, we know nothing of Sarah's life after 1737 nor that of her husband and daughter.

(St Mary's Church, Bridgwater)

Sources: Sarah Stone, the "Complete Midwife" by Sharon L. Jansen, Sarah Stone: Enlightenment Midwife by Isobel Grundy, A Complete Practice of Midwifery by Sarah Stone, Inspiration from the Past: Sarah Stone, the Enlightenment midwife by Anna Bosanquet, English midwives' responses to the medicalisation of childbirth (1671–1795) by Janette C. Allotey, The Gossips' Choice: Extending the Possibilities for Biofiction with Creative Uses of Sources by Sara Read, oxforddnb.com, bridgwater-tc.gov.uk.

Sarah Fielding (8th November 1710–9th April 1768) & Friends

The 'mother of children's literature', Sarah was born in the northernmost part of Dorset, close to the Somerset border, in a house bought for the family by her mother's parents. Sarah's parents had 7 children (but one died in infancy). Sarah was particularly close to her oldest brother Henry, who was born at Sharpham Park, near Glastonbury, which belonged to their maternal grandparents. Sarah's mother died around 1717 and so Sarah was then raised by an aunt and her maternal grandmother, Lady Gould. Sarah's father, Edmund, remarried almost immediately, which Lady Gould disapproved of, partly as the new wife was Catholic. Edmund moved to London without Sarah and her siblings. Henry was sent to Eton while the girls lived with their grandmother in Salisbury. Edmund had 6 sons with the new wife but only one survived to adulthood. The grandmother was unhappy with how the income from the house in Dorset wasn't being spent solely on her grandchildren. She took Edmund to court and gained custody of the children and control of the Dorset house.

In 1734, Henry eloped with Charlotte Craddock and married her at St Mary's Church in Charlcombe, just to the north of Bath. Within 10 years, Henry lost both his wife and three of his four daughters, while his only son from the marriage would die in 1750. In the same year (1743), with Henry's encouragement, Sarah published her first novel for adults anonymously: 'The Adventures of David Simple'. This was a courageous act at a time when female writers were seen almost as scandalous. Due to its popularity, a second edition was quickly printed.

On 2nd January 1749, her novel 'The Governess' was published. This book is believed to be the very first novel in the English language aimed specifically at children and written at a time when the novel itself was a new idea. 'The Governess' was incredibly successful and so Sarah kept writing and seeing her work published. Having lived in London for some time, she moved to Widcombe Lodge in southern Bath around 1751, following a series of deaths in London: her three sisters, all in 1750 and 1751, and her friend and co-writer Jane Collier. In Bath, she eked out a living from her writing, a humble inheritance and the generosity of friends such as Ralph Allen who lived nearby. In 1754, Henry died in Portugal, having remarried and had five more children, three of whom died as babies or children. Death was a constant thread in Sarah's life.

The following year, the poet Mary Scott, born and raised in Milborne Port, wrote 'The Female Advocate', a 522-line poem celebrating women's literary achievements and advocating women's right to express themselves in literature. Among the female writers mentioned are Queen Catherine Parr, who owned the manor in Queen Charlton village, and none other than Sarah Fielding.

And this praise was well-deserved. In 1762, Sarah translated a text from Ancient Greek, showcasing her scholarship.

Sarah also possibly wrote a book to raise money for rescued teenage sex workers. The book was published anonymously but her peers and historians have noted that it is very similar to Sarah's style. Sarah's friend Barbara Montagu (c.1722-1765) was definitely involved with the book as its financial sponsor. From 1754-1756, Barbara and another friend, Sarah Scott (21st September 1723-30th November 1795), who had separated from her husband, ran a community in Batheaston where single women could live and teach poor children who'd otherwise not get an education. Sarah Scott was also a writer whose most famous novel, A Description of Millenium Hall (1762), focuses on a utopian female community. The Batheaston community came to an end in 1756 but Sarah's two friends continued living together in the Bath area until Barbara's death.

When Ralph died in 1764, Sarah moved to an old cottage in the village of Wick (now Bathwick Street in Bath). Like Jane Austen, who spent some time in Bath, Sarah supported herself through her writing and never married. This single status was common amongst women who wanted to pursue scholarship because they feared being under the control of a man who would kill their ambitions. Sarah died aged 57 in Walcot, northern Bath. Sarah and Barbara were both buried in St Mary's Church in Charlcombe. Sarah's body lies under the church itself at the entrance of the chancel. There are three monuments to Sarah in Bath– one in this church, one in the abbey and a plaque on Widcombe Lodge.

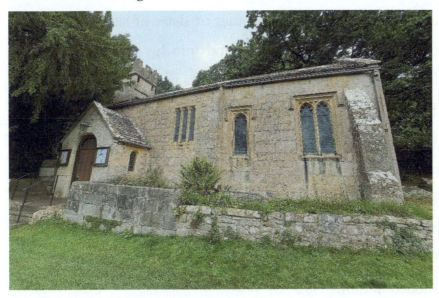

(St Mary's Church, Charlcombe)

Sources: The Governess or Little Female Academy by Sarah Fielding with an introduction and bibliography by Jill E Grey, The First Novel for Children Taught Girls the Power of Reading by Lorraine Boissoneault, Online Encyclopaedia Britannica, The Cambridge Companion to Fairy Tales, hersalisburystory.com, The Bath Magazine August 2015, www.oxforddnb.com, Literary Somerset by James Crowden, The Essay. Shakespeare's Sisters: Sarah Fielding (BBC radio 3 episode), www.nonconformistwomenwriters1650-1850.com, queencharlton.com, oxforddnb.com, batharchives.co.uk.

Chapter 17: Destiny and Deceit (early 19th century)

The thatched cottage in East Quantoxhead was alive with an ear-splitting commotion. Six-year-old Richard was hopping about in excitement. "A brother or sister at last!" he hollered, charging through the house and into his father's workshop, knocking over some half-made shoes in the process.

Sarah Biffin's sisters mopped her brow, kept a supply of clean linen coming and encouraged her as she sweated and panted on the bed.

Richard burst into the room. "I can see the head! Is it a girl or a boy?"

"Get out!" Auntie Mary and Auntie Anne yelled back and shooed him out.

"You're doing wonderfully, sis," Anne pronounced. They turned back to Sarah. "The shoulders are out now. Hmm, that's funny."

"What?!" demanded the woman whose offspring they were commenting on.

"Nothing," Mary reassured and glared at Anne. Now was not the time for that sort of thing. Their sister would see soon enough.

With one final push, the body slithered out.

In silence, the sisters cut the cord, then took the mewing little baby off to wash and dry her.

"Why you so quiet? Does she look weak? I can't–" Sarah broke off. Although it was 10 years since baby John had died, the pain would never leave her. She couldn't go through all that again. "She... We'll bring her to you."

Sarah's left eye twitched and her heart skipped a beat. They placed the baby in Sarah's arms with the wrappings deliberately loose so she could see the issue clearly.

"Oh. Blimey. She's a one-in-a-million baby. My daughter and my child. A sister for Richard. We'll name 'er Sarah after me." She stroked the little one's face.

Mary and Anne sighed with relief. The child would be accepted by the mother at least. Others would have immediately asked for the baby to be removed and left to die. It was partly because 12 years of marriage had only produced one other living child but mainly just out of sheer maternal joy that Sarah overlooked what others would consider to be an unacceptable burden.

Once the placenta had come and the room had been cleaned of all signs of the reality of childbirth, Henry was ushered to the doorway with a warning that his child was rather unique.

"Afternoon, petal. You done good, your sisters say."

"Oh, Henry. Come and meet little Sarah. I'm naming her after me."

She held her breath as her husband entered their small, cluttered bedroom, followed by her son, hopping and waving his arms about.

Gazing down, Henry gasped. "Well, I'll be! Still, she's our little girl, ain't she? Welcome to the Biffin family, little Sarah."

"I got a sister! I got a sister!" yelled Richard.

Afraid that she may not live too long, the baby was baptised as soon as possible. Arriving into the world on Monday 25th October 1784, she was baptised on Sunday 31st October, no matter that it was All Hallows' Eve.

As they filed out of the village church with the fresh sea breeze doing its best to whisk her bonnet up into the air, Mrs Biffin tried her best to enjoy the day. She tried to not get disgruntled when the information on the baptismal register stated that her precious baby was 'born without arms or legs'. That was true. Although Baby Sarah had some kind of feet and toes attached to her hip area, she had no legs or arms or hands, for that matter. But was it necessary to mention her physical body in the register? Why not mention her lovely eyes as well? Or how much she loved being swaddled?

As time flew by, the family's anxiety that Sarah would soon depart this life turned into anxiety that Sarah would harm herself and her surroundings due to being overambitious. Aged 8, she announced at dinnertime, "I want to learn to sew." Her parents exchanged glances over their bowls of mutton and vegetables.

"With what?" six-year-old Johanna asked.

"My mouth, of course," Sarah replied. Then, as if to prove her dexterity, she positioned her spoon into her bowl, then she put her head near the bowl and used her shoulder to press down on the spoon and guide it to her mouth.

"Out of the question!" her father snapped, bouncing his 3-year-old daughter, Betty, on his lap. "You'd be pokin' your eye out, droppin' needles all over the place... It's hard enough as it is with... three kids stampeding about the house."

His words caught in his throat. It should've been five kids. Poor John, their firstborn who had died as a baby. Then Richard who'd passed away in 1793 aged 14.

Her mother sighed and clutched her handkerchief as her mind flooded her with memories of Richard. "I'm too knackered for this. Look, you don't need to sew, Sarah. I can mend things for you. Put it out of your mind."

But she didn't. Anytime her father was busy in his workshop and her mother and siblings had gone out to run errands or walked down the path through the cliffs to stroll along the stoney beach, Sarah used her shoulders, chin and mouth to practise her sewing skills. She threaded needles, tied knots then held the fabric between her chin and shoulder and guided the needle through it with her mouth.

After a few months of doing this in secret, she proudly showed them what she could do. Her mother had tears in her eyes when she whispered, "Glory be, I should be losing my rage with you for disobedience, but you are a little wonder, ain't you?"

With perseverance, Sarah began to make her own dresses with the neatest of stitches. Emboldened, she moved on to painting. To do this, she gripped the brush with her lips and tongue and used her right shoulder muscles to move the brush around. She soon learnt that to wash her brush, it was helpful to bite down on the brush to shake the paint off.

The next challenge she set herself was, at the age of 12, to learn to write. Before long, she was penning letters to friends and family with great capability with the pen in her mouth and her shoulder stump holding the paper still.

People started to take notice of Sarah's paintings. A year or so later, a showman called Emmanuel Dukes became one of her admirers.

"But this work is magnificent! She is simply wasted here. You must let her accompany me and my wife to perform at fairs around the country. The entire nation should see what she can do! And with that endless smile of hers, they'll love her! Of course, we will treat her like our very own daughter and compensate you for parting ways with her."

"Hang about! We ain't sellin' our daughter!" Her mother's eyes blazed indignantly.

"No, sir, no. Of course not. I was not suggesting anything of the sort. Look at it more of an advance on her earnings, as a gesture of goodwill."

"Hmm, that makes more sense." The next part she whispered to keep her daughter from hearing: "And she may never marry. P'rhaps this is the best way for her to earn her way in the world."

Sarah's father nodded but replied, "It'll be tough going, though. All that travelling. And fairs can be noisy, crowded, even dangerous when you think of the pickpockets and–"

"Well, Mama? Papa?" young Sarah interrupted. "Please can I go? Earning a living by doing what I love is all I've ever wanted. And how I long to see the world!" Sarah's face shone with youthful hope.

*

"Roll up! Roll up! Come and see the limbless wonder, the eighth wonder of the world. Before your very eyes, ladies and gentlemen, you shall see her skills in the use of the needle, scissors, pen, pencil and paintbrush. You will marvel at her adroit skills! Watch her make any item of clothing, watch her sew extremely neatly, feast your eyes on her handwriting skills and gape in awe at her drawing and painting, all of which she performs principally with her mouth. Come on over. A mere sixpence to watch her and only 3 guineas for a miniature on ivory."

With her small paintbrush pinned to her puffed sleeve, she leant forwards with her right shoulder nearly touching the table and carefully swept the brush across canvases big and small (from 6cm to 91cm, nearly as tall as she was).

Sarah lost count of the places she visited with the Dukes family– Bath, London, Hull and everywhere in between. She lost count of the comments that came: "What an extraordinary talent, young girl!" "Freak!" "You want a *hand* with that, little one?" "I can't tell you how much I admire your brush control." Sarah tried to hold on to the positive remarks and let the negative ones wash over her.

As she grew older, she became aware that she wasn't earning a fair wage: only £5 a year, which would be about £500 in today's money. *Fourteen years of my life thus passed away without any substantial benefits to me,* she later wrote in her autobiography. Yes, the Dukes treated her well, but the kindness did not extend to financial equality.

It just so happened that in 1812 she found herself at St Bartholomew's Fair in London, where a chance encounter changed her destiny. A kind-looking gentleman in his fifties requested that she paint his portrait.

"Good Lord!" exclaimed the Earl of Morton, as he turned out to be. "I must show this portrait to King George, such is your talent. I'm Queen Charlotte's chamberlain, you see."

Sarah returned his smile and thought not much more of it.

However, the earl was as good as his word. George III was so amazed by her skills when presented with the painting that he arranged for Sarah to be taught miniature painting by the court's miniaturist. This was an honour that her humble family could never have dreamt of for her. Doors were beginning to open for Sarah.

Yet, this invitation to court was met with mixed emotions by Sarah, who at the age of 28 had spent over half her life living with the Dukes family. Although she resented the financial side of things, they knew how to meet her needs and were warm-hearted. Aware of being vulnerable to abuse due to her disability, she was reluctant to change things.

But the earl persuaded her and so she set off to begin a new chapter in her life. She studied hard with the palace's miniaturist and eventually became an independent painter of miniatures under the patronage of Queen Charlotte. Sarah was commissioned to create miniature paintings of the royal family and felt her star rising and rising.

Even the queen's death in 1818, though it was a personal sorrow, did not dampen her success. Sarah was no longer a travelling show-woman; she was now an artist to be taken seriously, supported by the royals, such as King George who she painted in miniature in 1820. Her usual delicate, precise brushstrokes perfectly captured his bicorn hat, shiny uniform and white powdered wig.

Her year of glory came in 1821. To list the wonderful things that happened made her head dizzy in retrospect: she won a large silver medal at the Royal Society of Arts, she began to regularly exhibit her work at the Royal Academy of Arts, she opened a studio in the Strand and she accompanied the earl to Brussels, where for a few months she painted for the future king of the Netherlands before returning to England in 1822.

Back at her studio, Sarah took on female artists as students, women who, like herself, had missed out on formal education. Artists living further afield posted their work to her to receive her feedback on their techniques. Sarah felt respected and cherished. Each self-portrait she now created always included a nod to her profession, such as a paintbrush pinned to her sleeve.

But drama was just around the corner. Sarah's year of mishap was 1824, though she stubbornly refused to think of it in those terms.

Aged 40, she had rather given up on the hope of marriage until William Stephen Wright swanned into her life. What a gentleman! What sweetness! What a handsome face that she would gladly paint over and over again!

A Londoner, William was an ex-navy officer who temporarily moved to Kilve in Somerset in the summer of 1824. But his origins and former occupation weren't what Sarah was attracted to. It was the look of love in William's eyes. He professed, "I care not a jot about your disability. I see your heart and it is beautiful. And I love you with all of my own heart."

When he proposed, she readily accepted. Of course, she had to return to Somerset for the wedding so that all her family might attend, including her cousins Mary Ann and Simon Blackmore. On 6th September 1824, Sarah Biffin gladly became Sarah Wright while seated upon a handsome chair next to the groom at St Nicholas church in Kilton. Her parents had only had to travel 3 miles from their village of East Quantoxhead to witness a ceremony they had never imagined possible. Ignoring the sniggers in the church from those who had come merely to ogle at her, her veil was lifted for the kiss and she was carried outside for the rose petal throwing at the church porch.

Her father wiped a tear from his eye and confessed to his daughter, "I never thought I'd see you merrily wed, my love. But you look at you. And more than that, I'm proud of what you've done with your painting. *My* daughter painting the king's portrait! And in favour with the late queen, God rest 'er soul. You've come a long way, love. A working-class girl from rural Somerset. The neighbours still don't believe a word we say about your achievements!"

Sarah could only blush in response. The whole day was a scene she would paint across her heart forever.

Yet, Mr Wright was not Mr Right. The marriage was an absolute catastrophe for Sarah. William seized hold of all her money then scarpered, leaving his wife abandoned. Before the Married Women's Property Act in 1870, any money made by a woman instantly became her husband's property once she married except for her dowry. Legally, the money was his to do with as he pleased. She was supposed to be grateful for the meagre £40 a year he sent her each year (just £5,500 in our money).

This betrayal was too much for Sarah to take in; instead, she staunchly denied that he'd taken her money until her last breath and exhibited her paintings using the name Mrs Wright for many a year.

Her finances were in tatters. She'd even had to make the switch from painting on ivory to using paper and card. Then, the core of her support network slipped away one by one. The Earl of Morton's death came first in 1827, followed by her father in 1835 and mother in 1839. Though she felt blessed that her parents had lived to incredible ages (87 and 93), she still mourned them keenly. Then in 1840 Princess Augusta died, the second daughter of George III, who had appointed Sarah as her official miniature painter since 1830.

Sarah began to move around a lot- London, Brighton, Bath and Cheltenham. Her eagerness to re-establish herself in the art world was the main cause of this. She was always looking for new clients. Besides, she had grown accustomed to a wandering, rootless lifestyle that gave her the opportunity to meet new and interesting people. People came to know her as a good storyteller who was fun to be around.

With fewer commissions coming in, Sarah had more time on her hands and thus time to reflect on the unusual life she'd led- a disabled girl wholly accepted by a loving family, who somehow found time in their busy working lives to care for her. Yet they assumed she'd never achieve much. She proved them wrong by diligently working and finding creative ways to do all sorts of things by herself- sewing, writing and painting. Then she began to travel and perform as a teenager. She was later discovered by royalty and elevated to high status. Sarah had a sense of pride to have survived with a disability in humble conditions and even thrived for a time in a world that preferred male, non-disabled artists. But her fairytale ended when she fell into poverty (but it couldn't have been her husband's fault!).

As she aged, Sarah found that she couldn't work such long hours as before. The painter felt the sharp sting of society's ruthless neglect of those who can no longer perform. A woman but on top of that a disabled woman competing in a man's world and in a male profession, she was quite the anomaly and as time wore on, she was no longer a novelty.

Her husband wasn't interested either, though she didn't like to think about that. People told her he never had been interested in her. In 1841, she began to use her original name again – Miss Biffin – for her paintings, perhaps out of grief for her parents' passing and/or because she realised her husband truly was a scoundrel. Whatever the case, Sarah would never voice her reasonings out loud, yet she would admit that they had never lived together and soon after the marriage, he had stopped visiting her. She continued to defend her husband, negating his abuse. Perhaps she feared that if she publicly admitted to having been taken advantage of, then others would see fit to do likewise and she loathed being viewed as a victim. Or perhaps he threatened her with removing her miserly annual allowance if she spoke the truth. Her disability meant she was more open to abuse from him and it wasn't as if she could physically defend herself or run away from him.

Sarah was certainly astute enough to know that reverting back to Miss Biffin would help her floundering career as people would remember the Sarah Biffin who was patronised by the queen, whereas Mrs Wright was a comparatively unknown artist. Out of justified pride and to remind her customers of who she was, she would often sign her work as "Painted by Miss Biffin Without Hands".

It seemed that in her mind she was finally free of her husband, in that she no longer thought of him so often. She was regaining her independence. And she was still talented and strong-minded. Yes, our heroine rose from the ashes of a failed marriage like a phoenix taking flight. Her inner strength pulled her out of despair and kept her going, kept her painting, kept her trying, no matter what life threw at her.

Notes

Sarah Biffin (1784–1850) was also spelt as Beffin or Biffen, but she always signed her paintings as Biffin. She had congenital phocomelia, meaning she was born without arms and either without legs or very short legs (the historical records are unclear on that). Below are details about her family.

Her parents married on 11th June 1772 at East Quantoxhead. They were:

– Henry John Biffin. Baptised 11th November 1748 at Stogursey. Buried 12th April 1835 aged 87 at East Quantoxhead.

– Sarah Biffin née Perkins. Born 1746/7. Baptised 30th May 1748. Buried 20th April 1839 aged 93 at East Quantoxhead.

Siblings:

– John. Baptised 6th July 1774 at West Quantoxhead. Buried 4th September 1774 at East Quantoxhead.

– Richard. Baptised 13th September 1778 at East Quantoxhead. Buried 20th January 1793 at St Mary's, Bridgwater at the age of about 14.

– Johanna. Baptised 10th December 1786 at East Quantoxhead. Appears in the 1851 census as 65 years of age and visiting a family in Bridgwater. Her occupation is "independent" and her birthplace is listed as Holford, 3 miles from East Quantoxhead.

– Betty. Baptised 3rd May 1789 at East Quantoxhead. I couldn't find anything more about her.

(a view of the Quantocks Hills)

We don't know if Mrs Biffin's sisters helped her to give birth to our heroine, but they were alive at the time, having married in

East Quantoxhead and so were probably still living in the area. Emmanuel Dukes' words to drum up business are based on posters advertising Sarah's talents. It has been suggested that she began touring with him aged 20 in 1805 and that the royal patronage began in 1819, yet to me this seems impossible because Queen Charlotte died in 1818 and she was named as the first royal patron.

Sarah Biffin wrote an autobiography called 'An Interesting Narrative', published in 1821, but I couldn't find it anywhere online, only a few quotes from it in certain articles.

Little is known about her husband, not helped by his having a very common name. We don't know when he died but he must've been born at some point before 1803 as he was described as a "bachelor of 21+ years" when he applied for a marriage licence in 1824. I made up the idea of Sarah being on a chair for her wedding, but it is known that she disliked walking in public as she felt she was rather ungainly.

As for her later life, she retired aged 59 in 1843, having worked ever since she was a teenager and finding it harder to paint as she got older. Based in the busy port of Liverpool, she dreamed of travelling to America, but her poor health prevented her from crossing the "pond". She did, however, meet American artists on British soil who had a similar disability to her. They were Sarah Rogers and Martha Ann Honeywell and our Sarah inspired them in their art.

Sarah's financial woes continued. Although she got 12 pounds a year from the Crown, this didn't go very far as it was worth less than £2,000 in today's money. An appeal was launched in 1847 to get a pension for her. Many people signed up to donate money to her, including the singer Jenny Lind, who featured in *The Greatest Showman*. The real Jenny was never romantically linked to someone else's husband; rather here we see her kindness towards another talented performer.

Though retired, Sarah did paint Queen Victoria in 1848, having painted 3 other monarchs in turn: George III, George IV and William IV. It is even possible that she once painted the incredible mathematician Ava Lovelace.

Sarah only had three years to enjoy her pension money, as she died in 1850 after a long illness.

Her paintings lay largely forgotten for many years, not helped by the fact that from 1824 to 1841 she signed them as Mrs Wright, hence those works weren't initially attributed to her. But recently, Sarah Biffin is being brought to the forefront once more. As MFPA (Mouth and Foot Painting Artists) affirms, she was "the first recorded British mouth-painter". She continues to inspire people of all diverse body types. For instance, one of her self-portrait miniatures fetched £137,500 at auction in 2019, which was far higher than expected, indicating her influence as a creative, talented and determined woman, and the Holburne Museum in Bath held a Biffin exhibition from autumn-winter 2023/4.

Her gravestone, which hasn't survived, read:

> Reader pause. Deposited beneath are the remains of
>
> S B,
>
> who was born without arms or hands, at Quantox Head, County of Somerset, 25th of October 1784, died at Liverpool, 2nd October 1850.
>
> Few have passed through the vale of life so much the child of hapless fortune as the deceased: and yet possessor of mental endowments of no ordinary kind. Gifted with singular talents as an Artist, thousands have been gratified with the able productions of her pencil! whilst versatile conversation and agreeable manners elicited the admiration of all. This tribute to one so universally admired is paid by those who were best acquainted with the character it so briefly portrays. Do any inquire otherwise—the answer is supplied in the solemn admonition of the Apostle:
>
> —
>
> *Now no longer the subject of tears,*
>
> *Her conflict and trials are o'er,*
>
> *In the presence of God she appears.*

Chapter Bibliography

Somerset's Forgotten Heroes by Roger Evans

https://www.oxforddnb.com/

Was the thalidomide tragedy preventable? by Edmund M R Critchley

Tales of Old Somerset by Sally Norris

philipmould.com

Sarah Biffin: the celebrated nineteenth-century artist born without arms or legs by Essaka Joshua

Curious Epitaphs by William Andrews

First show in 100 years of disabled Victorian artist Sarah Biffin opens in London by Harriet Sherwood

swheritage.org.uk

Front Row: Alison Lapper on Sarah Biffin (BBC Sounds podcast)

Online West Somerset Parish Register Transcriptions

Sarah Biffin (Holburne Museum Exhibition)

freecen.org.uk

freereg.org.uk

QUICK TRIBUTE

Ada Lovelace (10th December–27th November 1852)

This famous mathematician, the world's first computer programmer, had a home in Exmoor, Somerset, and may have sat for a portrait by Sarah Biffin.

In 1835, Augusta Ada Byron married William King (later the first Earl of Lovelace). She was then known as Ada Lovelace. They went on honeymoon to William's mansion, Ashley Combe, on the edge of Yearnor Wood, near Porlock Weir. He'd had it especially renovated for this holiday.

Over the years, William had more work carried out at Ashley Combe and it became their summer retreat. Using Ada's wealth, he planted thousands of trees, designed a system of tunnels for secret deliveries to the house and created landscaped gardens and outhouses. Ada was fascinated by his inventiveness, writing, "Your drawings of Ashley Combe excite my curiosity about the bastions and battlements."

One of the footpaths, leading to the village of Culbone, was known as Philosopher's Walk because that was where Ada would stroll along talking to fellow mathematician Charles Babbage about the Analytical Engine, a distant ancestor of the computer. Proposed but never built by Charles, Ada wrote extensive notes about the engine to explain it to the world and wrote the first-ever algorithm to be processed by a machine. She was programming before computers had even been invented! What's more, she conceptualised a flying machine aged just 12 and was the first person to realise that a machine could do more than just calculations, that it could create art and compose music, for instance. She was a visionary.

Ashley Combe fell into ruin and was demolished in the 1970s but a few of William's shorter tunnels remain. Ada's contribution to science also fell into ruin until 100 years after her death when her notes on the engine were republished. In the 1970s, a computer language was named after her and nowadays International Ada Lovelace Day is celebrated on the 2nd Tuesday of every October.

(Image of Porlock Weir, c.1901)

Sources: Will Stone's article at polockholidays.co.uk, www.exmoor-nationalpark.gov.uk, www.momentousbritain.co.uk/go/ada_lovelace, history.com.

Chapter 18: A Princess of Seas and Studies (mid-19th century)

In 1807, Britain abolished its trade in enslaved Africans, then in the 1830s slavery itself was outlawed in the British Empire. The end. Ah but no. Emancipation was a gradual process and other forms of exploitation flourished in slavery's stead.

Our story begins in 1846, by which point Britain had persuaded more than a dozen countries to sign treaties for the suppression of the slave trade, with some of those nations outlawing their trade in enslaved people altogether. However, the trade carried on illegally and it was one poor girl's misfortune to be captured by slavers.

It began in a British colony. The inhabitants of a Sierra Leonean village lay deep in slumber until they were woken abruptly by the sound of an attack. Shocked and half-asleep, they were unprepared to put up much of a fight.

Torn from her mother's arms and forced to watch the kidnappers execute her father right in front of her, the little five-year-old princess was bundled off in an instant from her home and village.

Hands sore from the ropes binding them together and scalp bleeding from where they had shaved her jaggedly, her chest was now in agony from where they had branded her with an S to show which country she was from.

A few days later, she found herself being herded like an animal towards a ship. She shivered with cold and embarrassment as they stripped her naked and examined her from head to toe. At a nod, she was accepted on board. How she shook with terror and confusion as they shoved her into the women and children's compartment of the hull. Here they were not shackled at least, unlike the men, but more at risk of abuse from the crew.

She was squeezed up next to a young woman, whose lips began to move. The princess gestured back, pointing at her ears but making not a sound.

"I think she's mumu. She's deaf," a teenage girl suggested, which our little girl couldn't hear, of course.

The first woman, Hassana, nodded, shutting her eyes and swallowing hard against the empathy she felt. The poor child would be suffering all the more for not being able to hear what was going on. More importantly, what life could a deaf girl expect to live on a plantation? The White ones would have no patience with her. Hassana planted a kiss on the girl's head.

"Mumu," Hassana agreed. "But a princess too. Look at those scar markings on her forehead. She must be from the coast. She must be from my country, Sierra Leone. And now she will join us in becoming the lowest of the low in a foreign land."

"Shut up," an older woman said. "We have to stay alert. We could still escape before we leave the port."

"No," Hassana whispered sadly. "Only Allah can help us now. Only Allah."

*

Who could say how many days had passed since they had set sail? Who wanted to know? Every moment was hell and all hope had long since been lost.

The older woman vomited. It seemed she would not last much longer, but Mumu, as she was now called, kept offering her water all the same.

A toddler urinated, some of which splattered onto Mumu.

The crew dragged another child up out of the hull. A dull splash was heard as the lifeless body was thrown overboard.

Mumu struggled to breathe in the hot, airless hull. On account of the pelting rain, they had not been up to the deck for several days now.

The teenage girl, who was refusing to eat, was force-fed rice and beans when their second daily meal arrived. Mumu turned her head away and was glad she couldn't hear the muffled groans.

Hassana rubbed her expanding stomach in pain. Mumu had seen the crew do strange but clearly unpleasant things to her and now it seemed she would have a baby soon.

Out of nowhere, the crew started shouting animatedly at each other. Mumu watched their mouths open and move at ferocious speed. The ship lurched and picked up speed.

Hassana started to pray.

Again without warning, the ship jolted and shook. It slowed down, had possibly even stopped. Lips were moving all around her. If only she could hear their words!

A few hours later, unknown men were descending into the hull, shock written all over their faces. A few of them were Africans wearing clean clothes and with no chains around them. They began to shake hands with the women, one by one.

Tears glistened in Hassana's eyes, but she smiled also.

Everyone began scrambling towards the hull's entrance, desperate for air. Mumu's hand began to throb from being stood on, while her jaw complained from being bashed into.

But somehow, she too made it up into the dazzling sunlight, where she saw that the enslaved men were no longer chained up and that the slave ship had holes in its masts. Was something good about to happen?

Turning, she understood that another ship's crew had thrown over their anchor next to the slave ship and shot at the slave ship. The other ship had a flag with a red cross on it and a more complex red, white and blue design in one corner.

Once everybody who could still walk had emerged from the ship's belly, those who couldn't were being carried up. Some had died in the scramble or earlier during the day. Prayers were said and the bodies were respectfully carried to the ship's edge and cast into the choppy waters below. The older woman was among them. Mumu stifled a sob.

*

To reflect back on it was to enter a dreamlike state. It felt as if she had imagined it all or that it had happened to someone else. Did she really enter a slave ship and begin a journey out to a foreign plantation for a life of torture and inhumanity? Was she really rescued by crewmen from the West Africa Squadron, made up of Kru African men and British men? Did they really sail back to Sierra Leone to await legal proceedings? Were they really stuck there on the anchored and squalid ship for weeks on end watching co-survivors die of disease?

Did they really disembark and pass through the Gateway to the King's Yard in Freetown and into freedom? Were they really housed in the yard in order to be counted and have their names recorded, hers as Mumu since she could not speak and tell anyone her real name? Did they really have their wounds attended to and receive cotton clothing and rice to eat before having their fates decided for them? Did she really watch her fellow Liberated Africans be forced to become soldiers for the British Empire, wives for Liberated men and child apprentices that were sure to be abused and kept as virtual slaves in the city? Did she sigh with relief to discover she was one of the lucky ones who would be taken to a settlement instead?

It must all be true because if not, she would still be in her coastal village with her parents. She would not instead be at the Church Missionary Society's school for liberated girls in Charlotte, a mountainous village near Freetown. Mumu applied herself to the task of learning to read and write like a person wandering through the Sahara desperate for water. This was her passport out of her isolated life and into a world of communication. It was because of writing that she finally understood exactly why she couldn't leave the school. Her teacher wrote:

It is too dangerous for you to return to your village. Because your father, the chief, is dead, there is nobody to protect you there. You could be recaptured by the traffickers.

And so Mumu tried to make the best of the situation, putting up with wearing long-sleeved white dresses each day, no matter the heat, and studying hard each day as the years passed by and she reached her teenage years. Learning was not easy when she couldn't hear or speak and nobody around her could teach her to sign properly, yet she did well due to her natural intelligence.

One day, one of the White teachers approached her with a smile and wrote down:

There is a school for deaf children in England. You are going to study there.

Mumu made a sign for a boat with shaking hands and pleading eyes.

Yes. A safe boat. Good people. They will not send you into slavery, I promise.

Mumu nodded and made a sign for money.

They will not ask you for money. They will pay for your studies and give you food and a place to sleep.

Her teacher placed a reassuring hand on Mumu's shoulder.

Could this be another dream?

*

Weeks of seasickness. Weeks of remembering past trauma. Weeks of trepidation mixed with hopefulness.

Then, land. Cold land and pale faces.

Train journeys and carriages. A large town with flappy seagulls, pigeons, horse manure, crowds, bustle, traders, top hats and canes, cold air, children staring and pointing... There were men who barged past her looking cross, presumably as she hadn't heard them say, "Excuse me."

A tall terrace of sand-coloured houses. She counted 1, 2, 3, 4 storeys stretching up, plus one storey underground for each house.

Numbers 8 and 9 Walcot Parade. Arrival at last.

She curtsied before an array of people, whose names she would later learn to be Reverend Fountain Elwin and his daughter Jane, founders of the Bath Institution for the Blind and Deaf, as well as Sarah Butterbury, the matron, who was blind and profoundly deaf, Elizabeth Buck, a family friend and maid who was also deaf, along with a whole host of other teachers and students. All had turned out to see this brave girl who had survived so much and travelled from so far away to learn with them. What tragedies and difficulties she had faced! And yet here she was, ready to start afresh on a new adventure.

More weeks passed, weeks in which a new world was opened up to Mumu. With her natural intelligence, she swiftly learnt to sign more and more, giving her confidence and joy. The other children and teachers soon felt like family to her. Of course, life wasn't perfect and Mumu had to deal with people touching her curly hair without permission and without warning as well as sign language comments right in front of her such as:

<< I had no idea Africans could be so clever. >>

<< Deaf and a darkie but bright as a button. >>

<< Thank goodness we rescued her from a non-signing education. She must be *ever* so grateful every single day! >>

Mumu *was* grateful but it was hard to be seen as a charity case all the time. There was a sense of self-congratulation amongst the British for their West Africa Squadron and its role in combatting the trade in enslaved Africans without the accompanying shame for centuries of engagement in that trade.

More than anything, Mumu felt a whole range of emotions during her time there, plenty of positive ones but some negative ones too. And she yearned for her family in Sierra Leone. She still had memories of her mother dressed in bright colours and oiled hair, dancing in front of their home, smiling and lifting Mumu into the air. Mumu prayed for this woman every night before lights out. The school in Charlotte Village had introduced Mumu to Christianity; the teachers at the Institution in Bath had deepened her knowledge of it. Now, she hoped that her mother would one day convert, wherever she was. It was out of her hands, of course, and so all Mumu could do was pray for her.

The little princess became a girl of two cultures. She missed the chimpanzees and colobus monkeys whose energetic calls could be heard in Charlotte Village but grew to love Bath's urban foxes, magpies and waddling mallard ducks along the River Avon. Her schooling in Charlotte meant she was used to wearing long-sleeved English-style dresses and so she didn't pine for the traditional clothing that she barely remembered wearing. Yet she longed to once more taste tropical fruit, plantain bananas, jollof rice and manioc. At the same time, she was now rather partial to roast dinners, porridge and cheddar cheese (not in the same meal!). She missed the bright blue ocean and landscapes of endless green, which Bath's impressive architecture couldn't make up for. At times she sighed with loneliness for having nobody around her who could reminisce with her, who understood what she had been through and where she'd come from. Strangely, Sierra Leone's rain, which could stream down from the heavens in dramatic torrents, was something Mumu missed except for the flash floods that came charging down from the mountains and devastated the crops. Bath lacked those downpours and yet the delight of seeing Bath's streets blanketed in soft snow for the first time was indescribable.

On one such morning, four years after arriving, Mumu received baptism. On Tuesday 29th December, she had stepped out of the school building into the crisp winter weather in her best gown and over to the chapel at the back of the Institution, her friends trailing behind her. The Reverend Fountain Elwin baptised her and she was given the name Annie Jane Elwin, the middle name and last name in honour of his daughter, a woman Mumu deeply admired. The same woman interpreted the ceremony for Mumu and the rest of the deaf community, just as she did every Sunday service when her father led worship.

Mumu lost count of these services as time raced forward. Five years after arriving, she completed her education. It had been a whirlwind of chalk and blackboards, bonnets and long dresses, detentions and hard desks. The year was 1858 and it was time to start yet another chapter of her eventful life, perhaps in another town.

*

A steam train and hugs goodbye. A horse-drawn carriage jolting down the road. A large town with noisy seagulls, pigeons, horse manure, crowds, bustle, traders, familiar smells, familiar sights…

A tall terrace of sand-coloured houses. Numbers 8 and 9 Walcot Parade. Arrival at last.

Home. Yes, it felt like coming home.

After several years away working with the Church Missionary College in Islington, London, and as a servant in Suffolk, she had returned to her deaf community in Bath, ready to teach the young ones just as she herself had once been taught. Mumu had fought to make this happen, to hang up her maid's uniform for the last time and put to use her sharp intellect, signing ability and first-hand knowledge of deafness. She didn't know of any other Black person teaching deaf children in the country. Perhaps she was the first.

Day after day, she introduced the deaf children to new signs so that they could communicate better. She taught them the written word, which many children had been unable to learn at previous schools, where teachers had no training or patience for those with hearing impairments. Sewing was another useful skill she could pass on to them.

In 1866, it was nearly time for the annual fundraising bazaar. The staff were busier than ever preparing for it, during which time Mumu fell ill.

<< You must take to your bed, dear. You're burning up. >> Jane Elwin told her.

<< No, no. I must continue with preparations. >>

<< Let us take care of you. You are no good to anybody like this. >>

Mumu reluctantly retired to her room. She never complained as the days wore on and the sickness grew worse and worse. She'd already survived several tropical diseases in Sierra Leone and this new illness would be no different. Wouldn't it?

<< I'm afraid you won't be able to attend the bazaar this year. >> Jane wiped a tear from her eye.

<< I understand. My sickness could be contagious, after all. >>

<< We are all praying for you. >>

<< Thank you. May the Lord's will be done. >>

<< Amen. >>

'Thank goodness her faith is so strong, as I cannot see her lasting much longer,' Jane thought, taking in Mumu's sunken eyes with their faraway look and her bony body that was losing all appetite.

Sure enough, the following day her body was found cold and stiff in the bed with a peaceful expression on it.

Jane's chest tightened to see it, her knees buckled when she reached the bed and clasped her dear friend's hand. To think that she would never see Mumu's vibrant gaze again, see her smile or watch her sign.

'So young and full of potential but far be it from me to question Your will, God,' Jane thought.

A lump caught in her throat, making speech impossible so it was just as well she had to announce the news to the others using her hands, trembling hands though they were. Somebody else would pass on the news to the blind community who were taught in the house next door.

Jane gathered the children and teachers together and signed << I'm sorry to tell you all this, but Mumu is dead. >>

The little children's faces fell in horror; their bottom lips wobbled. Unable to stay a moment longer, Jane took herself off to her room to sob her heart out.

Though it was a Wednesday, Jane was sure her ageing father would lead them all in prayer on such a heart-breaking day.

Later on, Jane reflected on all the twists and turns Mumu's life had taken. She could've lived her whole life in the village with her parents in Sierra Leone. Or, after she got captured, she might have ended up living in enslavement in North America.

Or, after she got rescued, she might have stayed at the school in Charlotte Village and lived out her life in that part of Sierra Leone. Or, after finishing her education in Bath, she might have stayed in London at the missionary school or returned to Sierra Leone to teach deaf children there.

What a remarkable young woman to have navigated all those changes in her life with such grace, to have carved out a life for herself despite all the odds and to have even excelled in her education in spite of all the trauma. How she would be missed.

Notes

There's a lot to unpackage for Mumu so if I don't go into enough detail, apologies! You may want to do extra research or contact me for more information. The British colonisation of Sierra Leone and the abolition of slavery have a very complex history that I invite you to investigate in more detail. Also, I confess I have never been to West Africa. I've done extensive research for this chapter, far more than any other chapter, but I apologise for any mistakes made and would be grateful for any corrections.

Let's start at the beginning with Mumu's birth, the date of which is debatable. Accounts state that she was 5 when she was rescued from the slave ship in 1846, therefore she was born in 1841. But other accounts state was she 15 when she arrived in

Bath in 1853, therefore she was born in 1838. The 7th April 1861 census lists her as aged 21, meaning she was born in 1840, while her gravestone states that she died aged 25 in May 1866, therefore was born in 1841, making her 13 in 1853. Historical records are so fun sometimes! The Institution's policy was to admit girls aged between 6 and 13 so unless they made an exception, I think her most likely year of birth was 1840 or 1841 but I'd like to think she was born in 1838 because 3 extra years of life is always good. Moreover, the traffickers who raided villages often killed those very old and very young so was Mumu's father very old but Mumu old enough to be worth keeping?

Moving on to 1846, I ask myself why her father was killed by the abductors. It may have been his age, as captors were known to kill the very old and very young. It might be that he was trying to defend his family from capture or perhaps he was too disobedient. I guess we will never know. Her mother somehow escaped the kidnapping and Mumu believed (or hoped) that she was still alive when Mumu lived in Bath. I wonder how much she remembered of her early childhood. Her prayers for her mother show that she didn't forget her. I ask myself, though, if she knew her original name. If she had been born deaf, she wouldn't have heard her family use it. Aspects like this will likely never be known, nor will we know the precise cause of her deafness.

The scars on her forehead showed that she was from coastal Sierra Leone and that she was a princess. Online, I found mention of 6 different ethnic groups living there today so I suppose she belonged to one of those.

Mumu was very fortunate to survive the slave ship. We don't know how long she was at sea for, but a little girl could easily have died aboard. We know that in the 1800s 1 in 18 Africans died aboard slave ships.

The character of Hassana is fictional but the name is taken from a real-life woman. Born a Muslim, Hassana was rescued from a slave ship by the West Africa Squadron (much earlier than Mumu) and taken to Sierra Leone. She converted to Christianity, married the first Black bishop and was then known as Susan Asano Crowther.

The boat that rescued Mumu and the other enslaved people was part of the Royal Navy's West Africa Squadron. Ironically, the navy had been assigned the task of protecting British slave ships from other foreigners until the slave trade was abolished in 1807. From 1808 onwards, the navy's Squadron actually intercepted slave ships and freed those aboard. The squadron was made up of African and British Royal Navy crewmen. Sadly, the British looked down on the Africans, unable to accept the different traditions and beliefs of these people who were mainly Kru from Liberia and the Ivory Coast.

The Squadron was shoddily resourced and riddled with corruption, harsh working conditions and tropical diseases. Although it only managed to intercept 6% of all transatlantic slave ships, it patrolled the waters for over 50 years (1808–1860) and freed a total of 150,000 Africans from 1,600 ships. Of those, some were recaptured and enslaved. Again, Mumu was lucky to be freed and never captured again.

So Britain had this moral mission to end the slave trade, but they didn't go beyond that to tackle inequality, discrimination and so on for Black people. And a few years after slavery itself was outlawed in the British Empire, a new act came in to compensate slave owners for 'loss of human property'.

The rescuing of slaves was also linked to Victorian imperialism, the desire to expand the empire. In fact, Sierra Leone became a crown colony in 1808. By rescuing enslaved Africans, who had originated in Sierra Leone and often elsewhere, the British might have thought of it as preventing the "labour force" from entering the USA, which wasn't a British colony anymore, and bringing them to Sierra Leone, which was a British colony. There were certainly ulterior motives to the squadron.

Speaking of an African who became Queen Victoria's goddaughter, David Olusoga writes: "While Sarah was in many ways very fortunate and lucky, her story is also a tale of a rather patronising social experiment. She was used to demonstrate that under British guidance an African could become educated, Christianised, and – a keyword for the 19th century – 'civilised'." Perhaps the same could be said for Mumu. She was portrayed as a willing convert, a "teachable" person who "adapted well" to England, presumably taking on board English manners and beliefs as well as education.

On the other hand, it's true that Mumu's deafness meant that she was in need of a school that could cater to her; it's a shame nobody established one in Sierra Leone, one that respected local culture. It must have been a relief to be in a deaf community, like entering a new land where you can finally start to communicate with more depth and subtlety. I imagine those she lived with at Walcot Parade would have felt united by language on a certain level, regardless of any racial, cultural or social differences.

The history of the Institution is fascinating. It starts with Reverend Fountain Elwin (c.1775–1869) living in Bristol with his family and finding a profoundly deaf girl in his parish and taking her in. He then moved with his family to Bath around 1832, where his 18-year-old daughter, Jane (1814–1904), walked the city with her friend Miss White to find profoundly deaf children to help. They started to teach their new students in a room they rented in Orange Grove, right by the abbey.

In 1840, 9 Walcot Parade became the Bath Institution for the Deaf and Dumb. (I apologise for writing the pejorative term "dumb"; I've kept it only for clarity if people want to research the school further.) The incredible Sarah Butterbury (c.1801-1864) was the first matron. 8 Walcot Parade was later taken for educating blind children and the name became The Bath Institution for the Blind and Deaf and Dumb. It was pioneering for the time: Brian Nordstrom points out that it was the first school where somebody with multiple disabilities could learn since a child who had both a visual and hearing impairment could attend.

I wonder what journey exactly Mumu took. I imagine the ship landed in Bristol and she was taken by railway to Bath city centre and carriage or foot to the Institution. Did someone from the Institution meet her in Bristol? There are so many questions I'll probably never know the answer to.

In 1854, when Mumu was in her second year of attendance, there were 69 students in total, made up of 54 boarders (32 profoundly deaf, 18 blind and 4 partially sighted and profoundly deaf pupils), plus 3 day students (all profoundly deaf) and 12 Sunday students (10 profoundly deaf and 2 blind). Mumu must have been one of the 32 profoundly deaf boarders and I imagine she participated as a student and later a staff member in the annual bazaar, which was held in April or May, depending on the year, to raise funds.

(NB: I've used the term profoundly deaf throughout as documents referred to them as 'deaf-mutes', which is now considered an offensive term. It would appear that they did not take in partially deaf students. On the subject of offensive terms, the word 'darkie' is used in the story to exemplify old-fashioned language and racialised beliefs; I would never use it outside that context.)

The school closed in 1895 and nowadays there's not even a plaque on the building to make people aware of its remarkable history.

The Church Missionary College in Islington was set up in 1824 to train missionaries. We don't know what Mumu's role was there when she arrived around 1858. My guesses are training deaf missionaries or the deaf children of missionaries or teaching sign language to trainee missionaries and/or informing them about Sierra Leone culture via an interpreter. The college was permanently closed during the First World War.

The college's principal was Charles Childe from 1839 to 1858. Mumu appears in the 1861 census as Annie J Elwin, born in Africa and living at his rectory in Holbrook, Suffolk, as a servant. It seems she had followed Charles there after his tenure finished, before returning to the Bath Institution.

As stated in the story, Mumu may have been the first Black person to teach deaf children in the country. I certainly couldn't find any other earlier examples. Becoming a missionary teacher was the most common teaching role for a Black person at that time. She may have been invited back to teach or may have had to fight to do so, purely because of the colour of her skin.

As Sierra Leone was rife with tropical diseases, Mumu was fortunate to not have succumbed to any of them. Or perhaps she had recurring malaria and this is what killed her.

Here are the words on Mumu's gravestone at Locksbrook Cemetery (with apologies for printing the word "dumb"):

It is not the will of your Father which is in heaven
that one of these little ones should perish. Matthew 18:14 [quote around the edge]

In Memory of MUMU, a deaf and dumb African girl.
She was rescued in child-hood from a slave vessel and taken
to the Church Missionary School at Charlotte, Sierra Leone, from
whence she was sent to England for
education and remained 11 years
in the Bath Institution for the Blind and Deaf and Dumb.
She was baptized Dec 28 1857 and received the Christian names of
Annie Jane Elwin. After a short illness, she fell
asleep in Jesus. May 16 1866 aged 25 years.

Surrounded by crumbling neighbours, this headstone is in amazing condition with the words very easy to read still. It makes me think it was an expensive one, showing how highly Mumu was regarded by her friends at the Institution.

It's interesting that they maintained her African nickname on the stone. It even takes precedence over her baptismal name. In light of that, I used Mumu throughout my story. Perhaps she preferred it or everyone was used to it or there were too many other Annie's. Did she like being called Mumu? Or did she dislike being referred to as simply 'deaf one'? The nickname's meaning results in her very identity being solely related to her deafness. Yet it was African, at least, rather than the English Annie, a renaming in keeping with British colonialism. That makes me ask whether she was given the surname Elwin because she had no surname of her own. And/or was it a sign that she was becoming part of the Elwin family? There was no official adoption, of course. How did she feel about it?

African names or nicknames weren't used in documentation for the other African children who studied there. For example, on the same gravestone, we find:

> Also in memory of George Spear a blind boy, a native of
> Cape Palmas, W. Africa. He was educated in the above institution
> and died in peace, Septr 26th 1866, aged 11 years.
> He led them forth by the right way, that they might go to a city of
> habitation.

Like Mumu, the passive voice is used more than the active voice, highlighting their status as 'charity cases', provided for by 'magnanimous' White people.

Cape Palmas is in Liberia. From 1838 onwards, some freed African Americans, who were sponsored by the Maryland Colonization Society, began to journey eastwards across the ocean to settle in Cape Palmas. Therefore, George was likely the son of freed African Americans. That could mean that George was his original name rather than a name imposed on him by missionaries. George died just months after Mumu and so was likely her student at the centre. As boys weren't allowed to enrol and start their education at the school once they were past the age of 10, it's likely that George was sent there aged 9 or under. As he died aged 11, he had probably been there for at least 2 years or more. Three other girls share the headstone:

> also in memory of Anne Toone a deaf and dumb pupil in the same institution,
> she died Decr 10th 1866, aged 13 years
> also in memory of Eliza Feldwick who died January 22nd 1872, aged 13.
> and Mary Emma Pearce died February 18th 1872

Anne Toone was from Leicestershire, Mary Pearce (b. 1858) from Cornwall and Eliza Feldwick from Berkshire. It looks like we have a mixture of White and Black children sharing a gravestone; there's certainly no segregation going on here, rather they are all united for having attended the same school and being part of the deaf/blind community. Mumu is even given precedence over the White children, which I think was because she lived longer, therefore people had grown to love her more, had known her as a teacher as well as a student, and perhaps because she was royal and so had a class distinction. She was seen as special.

Two more African children who attended the Institution can be found, both of them boys. The 1861 census mentions William Henry Parks from West Africa of 9 years of age as a student at the Institution. He was profoundly deaf from birth and may have crossed paths with Mumu before the 1861 census, by which point she was in Suffolk.

Deaf People Living and Communicating in African Histories mentions a vicar visiting London in October 1859 with a deaf boy named Harvey Peets, who was the son of a Liberian chief and lived at the Bath Institution. Mumu was probably in London at that time so may have met him. By 1863, Harvey was very skilled at basket making and the vicar planned to take him back to Liberia to teach disabled people out there to weave baskets, but the vicar died before he could carry out his plan.

We'll never really know how happy or unhappy these African children were at the Institution, how much control they had over their lives or other details such as the precise sight-loss conditions that the visually impaired students had. I only hope that they did feel at home within the deaf community at Walcot Parade.

Chapter Bibliography

The history of British Sign Language on the BBC website

The Key Role of African Seamen in the Royal Navy's Anti-

Slavery Campaign by Dr Mary Wills

Life Aboard a Slave Ship (History Channel documentary)

www.blackhistorymonth.org.uk

Black and British: A Forgotten History by David Olusoga

Bath Abolition Movement Map

Mumu, aka Annie Jane, a deaf slave from Sierra Leone (ca. 1838-66) by H Dominic W Stiles

Mumu: Freed African Slave Grave at Locksbrook Cemetery, Bath. Some Notes by P J Bendall

Mumu, the deaf Sierra Leonean girl who became a missionary in the 1800s after her rescue from a slave ship by Elizabeth Ofosuah Johnson

remikapo.org

A urine soaked record – the Bath Home and a homeopathic hospital by H Dominic W Stiles

1861 Census

A Brief History of The Work in Bath connected with the Deaf and Dumb

QUICK TRIBUTE

Elizabeth Ann Savage née Palmer (c. 1801-1887)

Born and raised in Timsbury, Elizabeth married Thomas Savage in 1822 and moved to Norton House in Midsomer Norton. Their only child was a son, Frederick Stukeley Savage, who was educated at Eton and later went to fight in the Crimean War (1853-1856). Whilst out there, he wrote various letters to his mother in which he mentioned the lack of clean drinking water for the soldiers. Frederick survived the war but was left with injuries that caused his health began to decline until he died on 31st March 1866 aged 39. (Elizabeth's much older husband had already died in 1859 aged 73.)

In the same year, the lonely Mrs Savage had a memorial built for Frederick- an obelisk with two marble plaques beside St Chad's Well, which was on her land. She also had the well improved, having remembered his dismay about the drinking water in Crimea and therefore wanting to help the poor people in her local area. This seemingly small act is actually courageous and generous. In the midst of her terrible suffering, as a parent should never outlive a child, she was able to create something to benefit others, something beautiful and practical to honour her son.

Even well into her old age, Elizabeth visited the memorial every day, being pushed to the site in her wheelchair by a loyal servant, until she passed away in 1887 aged 86 and was buried with her husband and son at Bath Abbey Cemetery.

In 1939, Norton House was demolished; only the entrance gate posts survive. Nowadays, the well is part of Somervale School but with public access.

(St Chad's Well, Midsomer Norton)

Sources: St Chad's Well Memorial Garden– a brief history, Who was Major Frederick Stukeley Savage? by Aaron Kendall, Bath Abbey Cemetery – Memorial Inscriptions, historicengland.org.uk, The Life and Times of Major Frederick Stukeley Savage from Midsomer Norton Life Autumn 2017, myheritage.com, Midsomer Norton Audio Trail.

Chapter 19: Catherine vs Caste (late 19th century)

If I were a fly on the wall in Portway House, Street, 1848, I could've witnessed the birth of an inspirational woman, a woman ahead of her time.

Catherine Impey first opened her eyes to the loving gazes of her parents, Mary Hannah and Robert. As Quakers, they noted her birth date as 13th day of 8th month, rejecting the pagan names for the months (and days of the week for that matter).

There Catherine grew up, in the home built for the family according to Robert's instructions. On Sundays, they would gather in silence at the Friends Meeting House in Street to listen for God's voice. Once in a while, a Friend would stand and voice a message to the whole room in the form of a testimony, song, dance or somesuch. Most of the time, though, they sat in silence in a bare-walled room without distractions in order to have a direct connection with God.

"What does that connection mean, mummy?" Catherine's older sister, Ellen, asked one day.

"The connection, possible for all human beings, is rooted in our belief that everyone contains an inner light," Catherine's mother replied. "We must be aware of our own inner light and everyone else's light. If we do that, universal brotherhood can be achieved."

"Uni…?"

"Universal brotherhood. Friendship, kindness and respect for everyone around the world."

Although Street was known as the cradle of Quakerism, a place in which many had joined the Society of Friends, not everybody had respect for the Quakers. Their unique way of worshipping along with allowing women to preach and their refusal to take oaths, participate in wars or pay tithes to the Church of England made them often unpopular with the outside world but they grew used to it and developed resilience as a community.

Aged 3, "Katie" saw the building of a new Friends Meeting House in Street to replace the first one, which had been constructed in the 1680s. She squealed in delight and hugged 6-year-old Ellen.

Years later, the day came for Katie and Ellen to attend a boarding school at Southside House in Weston-super-Mare, a school for Quaker girls (and those from other denominations). With great enthusiasm, she delved into the worlds of Literacy, French, Geography, History, Maths, drawing and, in the afternoons, needlework. Her love of social justice grew too. Each student had to pick a form of humanitarian work to focus on when they left the Institution. Katie and Ellen chose anti-racism work, inspired partly by their family's connections to anti-slavery networks. Slavery had been abolished in the 1830s in the British Empire and 1865 in the USA, but brutal working conditions and human rights violations on non-White people were just some of the terrible legacies that slavery had left behind. This was what the Impey sisters wanted to fight against.

*

In 1878, the 30-year-old Catherine set out from her home in Street on an epic voyage to the United States of America. Courageous Catherine was heading out there to work with the Temperance movement, promoting teetotalism or at least responsible drinking. However, a very negative factor came to light: other Temperance activists wanted to segregate the organisation to reflect the laws at that time so that White and Black people wouldn't mix, Catherine felt utter frustration. She was appalled and would later part ways with both the US and UK Temperance societies.

On the other hand, a positive aspect of her trip was meeting African-American activists, such as Frederick Douglass, a man who had escaped slavery in his youth with the help of his future wife, Anna Murray. Frederick was now campaigning against the lynching of Black people.

10 years on, back at home in Street, would find her reading hand-written accounts of injustice, making notes, organising, planning... She was carefully assembling the very first issue of the journal she had started up, to be published in March of that

year, 1888. She was breaking the mould for sure: a woman setting herself up as a managing editor in order to combat racism throughout the British Empire and the United States. With the new journal, she aimed to provide a voice to people fighting prejudice and injustice, to opinions that were being suppressed elsewhere, mainly voices belonging to Black people, many of whom appreciated the fact that Catherine published their writings verbatim rather than editing their words. The voices would be heard by other campaigners but also by a wider audience than usual, so that White people could also gain insight into a concept many rarely – if ever – thought of: racism.

For years, she had thought of increasing her support for anti-racist activists. She even posted a letter addressed to Frederick Douglass in the US, saying:

I want to be doing more. I believe we want a great union or anti-caste society – to take up the work where the anti-slavery society dropped it.

Frederick sent a letter of encouragement back, which said:

The work you have undertaken must ultimately succeed.

Catherine told herself, "I hope I can make this work. Anti-Caste shall be its name. Some have suggested Anti-Race, yet I dislike the word 'race', for are we not all one human race the world over, though of different varieties? I disagree with certain

Abolitionists who see darker-skinned people as needing 'protection' from our supposedly 'stronger race'. Indeed, all arbitrary distinctions based on differences of physical characteristics or social rank are contrary to the mind of Christ. I shall write that last part down and include it in the first issue. Now, a price... 1/2d should cover postage costs." She sought no financial gain for herself.

From that point on, each month, she would send out the journal to the printers, John Whitby & Son in Bridgwater, and then distribution would begin. People subscribed to Anti-Caste from around the world, including her dear friends Frederick Douglass and Celestine Edwards. The latter was born in Dominica and had stowed away on a French ship aged 12 and had been living in London since the 1870s.

The journal contained many articles regarding campaigners fighting segregation, prejudice and lynching in the southern US, as well as social oppression in the US and the British Empire, for instance the abuse experienced by tea workers in India. The idea was to circulate "the current writings of prominent and thoughtful" non-White people with the "hope to give them fresh opportunities of presenting their case before White readers" as the opening words of the first issue stated. Katie didn't want to speak on others' behalf but to amplify their voices. One key aim was to show White people that the systems they had built sustained racial oppression and White supremacy. White people needed to step up and help to dismantle these systems. Catherine didn't shy away from other issues, either. Gender, disability and religion were also addressed.

It was clear that there was a great deal of interest in these important stories: around 1,800 copies of the journal were soon being circulated across the globe. And some of those copies would be read many times over, as they would be placed in clubs, school staffrooms and libraries.

The following year, her journal dared to condemn one of the most powerful men in Britain: the Prime Minister. He had attacked Dadabhai Naoroji, an Indian man who was running for office. The PM's exact words were: "I doubt if we have yet got to the point of view where an English constituency would elect a Blackman" and that Naoroji "was not only of a different race – widely separated from us – but that it was marked by his complexion ... and that, in the existing state of English opinion, was a very strong factor." Catherine pointed out that it was erroneous to refer to Naoroji as Black and that the PM had shown great prejudice in his remarks.

Disappointingly, this was a rare occasion on which Catherine touched on racism in her own country. The plight of Asian, Black and Irish people living and being oppressed in Britain was almost entirely omitted.

Despite the PM's scathing remarks, Naoroji became the first Asian MP in 1892. Votes for women, pensions for the elderly, and abolishing the House of Lords were among the issues he supported. In the same year, Catherine made her third visit to the States to visit subscribers, find new ones and learn more about discrimination happening out there.

In Philadelphia, she had a momentous encounter with the remarkable Ida B Wells, a journalist, public speaker and civil rights leader. Born into slavery, Ida's aunt had bought her freedom when she was 12. She had known slavery first-hand in her early life and had known prejudice, discrimination and racialised violence throughout her whole life. Ida had edited a newspaper for several years before a racist mob burnt her office down in 1892 after she had written an article to counter the common justification for lynching, which was that Black men raped White women. In reality, when relationships did occur they were very often consensual. In spite of their very different backgrounds, Katie and Ida were definitely on the same page as each other. "I am in no doubt, Miss Impey. We are agreed that there seems to be nothing to do but to keep plugging away at the evils both of us are fighting."

1893 was a whirlwind year for our Katie. Catherine invited Ida on a speaking tour of Great Britain.

Ida's voyage across the ocean left her feeling terribly seasick when she arrived in Liverpool on Wednesday 13th April. Her first stop was Catherine's house in Street, where she recuperated. At the end of an enjoyable 5 days, Ida signed the guest book: "A quiet beautiful Sabbath, my first in England and a typical English house. This experience more than ever convinces me that:

> *For whatever men say in blindness*
> *and in spite of the fancies of youth*
> *there's nothing so kingly as kindness,*
> *there's nothing so royal as truth."*

The tour was to begin in Aberdeen so there they went on a journey that lasted several days, to the home of Isabella Mayo, a Scottish author who was Catherine's great friend and a fellow activist. The home had been turned into a boarding house for South Asians. One of the boarders was Dr George Ferdinands, a young Sri Lankan of dual heritage: Indian and White British. George had graduated from the University of Aberdeen and begun his career as a dentist. When Ida and Catherine arrived, Geroge and the two other current boarders enthusiastically got involved with helping the three women prepare for Ida's lecture tour. Together over the course of two weeks, they wrote letters, arranged meetings, mailed 10,000 copies of Anti-Caste and met with the press.

Slowly but surely, Catherine's heart filled with love for George despite the age gap that Catherine estimated was around 20 years.

The tour got underway, with Ida accompanied by Isabella to Huntly, Glasgow and Edinburgh, while Catherine returned to England to arrange more appearances. Everything was going well until an incident took place, an incident nobody would wish to witness! Isabella and Ida were in Edinburgh when a letter arrived. The contents of it enraged Isabella, who ordered Catherine to come immediately back to Scotland.

"How could you write such an indiscreet letter, Miss Impey? Declaring to poor George! " Isabella demanded as soon as Catherine set foot in the room. She waved the letter in front of herself as if the very paper were disgusting. Then she smoothed the letter out and began to read snippets of it. "'I return the affection I am sure you have for me. I am taking this advanced step because I know you hesitate to do so because of your Indian origin.' Do you think it proper for a lady to speak so to a man? To be so *forward?*"

"Please, Mrs Mayo–"

"I am not finished!" Isabella thundered. Catherine flinched.

"Another section, hark: 'I have written to my family' – imagine, Ida, she was so sure of herself that she spoke to her family of this sordid obsession with poor George! – 'I have written to my family acquainting them with the state of affairs, to tell them to prepare to receive you as my husband. I rejoice to give this proof to the world of the theories I approve of: the equality of the brotherhood of man!' Do you know how this letter came into my possession, Miss Impey?"

"No, Mrs Mayo."

"George himself sent it to me," Isabella spat. Catherine gasped. "The poor man looks up to you. He sees you as a mother figure. And you write a letter declaring love for him, you horrid nymphomaniac! He had never dreamed of any such connection with you as your letter indicates. He does not deserve to be harassed by you in this manner."

"That is why–"

"I see clearly now, Miss Impey. You are the type of maiden lady who uses such work, which should be philanthropic, as an opportunity to meet and make advances to men that you would not otherwise meet. Who else have you written such letters to? Who else might you write such letters to in the future? You will throw suspicion and ridicule on our cause with your fancies! You will jeopardise all our work. You can no longer work for the protection of those we serve. You must withdraw at once. Do you not see? By behaving in such a manner, you make all of us look bad. I need hardly remind you how difficult it is for ladies to be taken seriously. Any threat to our cause *cannot* be tolerated."

"If I may speak, Mrs Mayo," said Catherine ever so softly, "I realised as soon as the letter had left my hands that I had made a mistake. That is why there was a second letter penned to Dr Ferdinands in which I apologised for the first and begged him to tear up the first. As humans, we are all bound to err at some moment in our lives. I cannot abandon the work that I have dedicated my whole life to."

"Cannot or will not?"

"Both." Catherine's eyes shone with tears.

"Then I shall distance myself from you. I will not accompany you anywhere and I strongly advise you, Mrs Wells, to do likewise. Miss Impey has brought disgrace upon herself."

Shakily, Catherine left the room. Ida's heart lay shattered in pieces after witnessing such cruelty and scorn. That night, Ida slept very little and prayed instead for guidance. In the morning, she told Isabella:

"I cannot do as you wish and quit Miss Impey. I am willing to concede that Miss Impey has made a mistake in yielding to her feelings and writing such a letter, but I cannot see that she has committed a crime by falling in love and confessing it and I do not believe she would do it again. Miss Impey is not the type of woman you accuse her of being. She is my friend and a friend to my race, who has sacrificed time and money fighting for us."

"Well then," replied Isabella. "In that case, you are no longer welcome in my home either."

Catherine and Ida fled the house and never saw Isabella again nor George, though he did write to Ida condemning her for staying with Catherine.

Ida gave only the lectures that had already been arranged, missing out on scheduling more events because of Isabella's abandonment. Then, Ida and Catherine visited William Wilberforce's son in Liverpool before heading to Southampton, where Ida boarded a ship for the journey back to the United States in March 1894.

"You should not have stayed with me, dear Mrs Wells," Katie said ruefully. "You have missed out on lecturing opportunities because of it. And look, it is affecting you even today, when Mrs Mayo would have paid for your fare home."

"Nonsense, Miss Impey! I made the correct choice when I stood by you. And we have achieved a great deal here. I am grateful for the time spent after the *incident* in Edinburgh. I have now toured England as well with Mr Celestine Edwards joining me on the stage for many engagements. The tour has sparked a fire in the people here and the Society for the Recognition of the Brotherhood of Man has been born because of it. Never mind the boat fare. You are a great friend of mine and a true crusader for justice. Let's put that episode behind us and continue the battle that God has put before us."

Isabella, however, was not ready to put it behind her. She attempted to turn Frederick Douglass against Catherine and Ida by association. But, once she got back to the States, Ida managed to convince him to remain friends with them.

Catherine was ostracised from her friends and fellow campaigners because of Isabella. Catherine was pressurised into delivering a humiliating public apology in front of the Quaker community for the letter she'd written to George. Anti-Caste ceased publication.

Another reason for Anti-Caste's discontinuation was more positive.

"Ellen, as you may know, the Society for the Recognition of the Brotherhood of Man, established when Ida did her speaking tour, is now producing a journal, named Fraternity. I feel, therefore, that my journal is no longer needed, especially since the new journal's editor is Celestine Edwards."

"The man from Dominica who accompanied Ida on stage many times?"

"Precisely. And this makes him Britain's first Black editor. Britain now has an anti-prejudice journal headed by a person of African descent. Celestine and other prominent Black people are better qualified than I am to be the editors for such stories of injustice. Anti-Caste will be put to rest and we can wait with enthusiasm for what the journal Fraternity will achieve."

The very first issue of Fraternity honoured what Katie had achieved with Anti-Caste with the words: "For more than six years Anti-Caste has been doing a quiet work in England, slowly but surely permeating society, and winning the hearts of good men and true women." The text left Katie speechless as she sat at her kitchen table, pouring over the journal. This was a new era of learning and spreading ideas of justice. She was glad to have partly inspired it.

But life is always in motion. Devastatingly, Celestine passed away only a year later, in 1894. Fraternity couldn't go on without its wonderful editor. That spurred Catherine to produce two final runs of Anti-Caste in 1895.

"Ellen, I will create an April–May edition and a July edition. The first will be a special memorial edition, dedicated to the memory of Frederick Douglass."

"That's a wonderful idea, sister. I know how much Frederick meant to you and his death this February has been a great shock to us all."

"We will miss Celestine and Frederick forever. And I shall miss Anti-Caste yet, our work will continue in other forms."

Though the end of Anti-Caste had come, Catherine continued to make a difference in her local community and the wider world. Despite all the personal mortification, pain and perhaps loneliness caused by never marrying but apparently wanting to, she did not falter or waver in her fight against racism and other social injustices.

Notes

Catherine Impey (13th August 1848-14th December 1923) was noted as being kind, intelligent, candid and extremely frugal but generous to others. Her parents were Robert (6th February 1820-30th January 1886) and Mary Hannah Impey née Clothier (10th May 1823-15th September 1895), born at Leigh Holt in Street. Her sisters were Ellen Impey (7th June 1844-January 1921) and Marian Levitt Impey (17th Dec 1854-1st May 1860). It must have devastated the family when Marian died aged just 6; Catherine and Ellen were teenagers at the time.

The family home was built in 1845 and Catherine lived there most of her life. Nowadays, it is part of Millfield School and has been renamed The Grange. The home was visited by a whole host of incredible people throughout Catherine's life, invited by her parents and then by Catherine and Ellen. For instance, other African Americans aside from Ida B Wells included the feminist teacher Fanny Jackson Coppin in 1888, the writer Paul Laurence Dunbar in 1897 and the linguist Georgiana Simpson also in 1897. In fact, "Impey was the main conduit for a stream of African Americans visiting Britain" according to Jonathan

Schneer. There were guests from elsewhere too: Sweden, Pakistan, South Africa...

Catherine's other campaign issues were animal rights, women's right to vote and pacifism. She was also a member of the Long Sutton school committee. As a tireless fighter for justice, there wouldn't be space here to mention everything she did. Do have a look at the chapter bibliography if you'd like to delve further into her life.

Not marrying or having children would've given her a lot of free time to pursue these interests. At one time, she was engaged to T. Beavan Clark of Clark's shoes in Street, but this came to nothing and of course her proposal to Dr George Ferdinands was utterly rejected. Likewise, she didn't have many family duties. Once her father died in 1886, Ellen took over his agricultural business, leaving Catherine time to travel, edit her journal and so on.

The rift between Catherine and Isabella was dramatic. I've used some of the phrases Ida noted down in her memoir *Crusade for Justice*. Although Isabella cited protectiveness of young George as her motive, it could be that Isabella was not as progressive as she thought she was. An interracial marriage itself might have been partly what she objected to. Ida, on the other hand, had seen Black men lynched for having relationships with White women on the assumption that it must have been rape.

This may have influenced Ida in sticking by Catherine.

(Carrubers Close Mission in Edinburgh, where Ida gave a speech around the time that Isabella attacked Catherine.)

Regarding Catherine's later life, she and her sister moved in 1900 to Old Tanyard House, another family property, having lost their mother 5 years previously. Their final address was a recently constructed chalet on Ivythorn Hill. They lived there from 1914 until their deaths.

This Swiss-style building was left to the Society of Friends in Catherine's will and has been leased to the Youth Hostel Association ever since her death in 1923.

Catherine was buried at the Friends' Burial Ground, beside the

Meeting House in Street, pictured below. The Library of the Society of Friends in London holds the only complete set of Anti-Cast journals known to have survived.

Chapter Bibliography

Silences in the archive: Anti-Caste and fighting White supremacy in Victorian Britain by Caroline Bressey

Empire, Race and the Politics of Anti-Caste by Caroline Bressey

UK Research and Innovation website

www.quakersintheworld.org

Descendants of Clothier by Charles E. G. Pease

Catherine Impey – Coda by Liam Drew

The Journal of Negro History by G R Simpson

Catherine Impey and The Black Atlantic by Thomas Quirk

Crusade for Justice by Ida B Wells

The forgotten woman who took on White supremacy by Liam

Drew

'Narrow-majority' and 'Bow-and-agree': Public Attitudes Towards the Elections of the First Asian MPs in Britain, Dadabhai Naoroji and Mancherjee Merwanjee Bhownaggree, 1885–1906 by Sumita Mukherjee

Black Women and the World: African American Women's Transnational Activism, 1896–1930 By Laura Renée Chandler

quakerstrongrooms.org

quakersatstreet.org.uk

QUICK TRIBUTES

Emma Sophia Sturge, née Mundy (1825–1895)

Like Catherine, Emma was involved in the anti-slavery movement. Born in Bath to a butcher's family, she became engaged to Thomas Sturge (1820–1852), a Quaker. Emma had to become a Quaker in order to be accepted by his community. But then she fell pregnant before their marriage, which meant she wasn't allowed to become a Friend. Thomas had to choose his community or his betrothed. Thankfully, he chose Emma. Together they had 4 children– Ellen, Hannah, Thomas and Rebecca, all of whom attended Sidcot boarding school for Quaker children in Winscombe. In 1850, the family moved to America, but Thomas was killed by a falling tree in 1852. As such, Emma and the four children returned to Bath. A year later, she opened an anti-slavery depot selling 'free labour' cotton and linen products. The cotton came from Egypt, South Africa, the British West Indies and the United States, and came with a certificate from Philadelphia to prove it wasn't a product of slavery. For the next six years, her business thrived, first at 2 Pulteney Bridge then 5 Terrace Walk, just behind Bath Abbey. By 1881, she was living in Melksham in Wiltshire. In 1887, she became a Quaker. Emma died aged around 70 and was buried in Melksham's Quaker burial ground.

Sources: Bath Abolition Movement Map, Bath's Extraordinary Women by Jane Sparrow-Niang, The Anti Slavery Movement in Bath by Roger Holly.

Adela Catherine Breton (31st December 1849–13th June 1923)

Adela lived almost exactly the same time as Catherine Impey (1848–1923). She was born in London but moved soon after to Bath: to 1 Bathwick Hill Villas then soon after 15 Camden Crescent, where she lived for the rest of her life, whenever she wasn't travelling. She came from a long line of globetrotters, for instance her parents had met and married in Tasmania.

Adela's own journeys began as a young child. As to be expected, they visited relatives in England, such as members of her mother's family in Bishop's Hull near Taunton, but they also regularly visited mainland Europe together.

Aged 37, Adela found herself alone as her parents were dead and buried in Lansdown Cemetery; her brother was married yet she remained single. Breaking with gender conventions, the intrepid solo explorer soon began to travel- to the USA, Canada and then Mexico.

In 1894, she was asked by a renowned archaeologist to use her incredible talent for art to copy wall paintings and reliefs. Adela was putting to use the skills she had learnt throughout her life, including at the Bath School of Science and Art and winning prizes at the Bath and West Show many years previously. It's hard to believe that some of her paintings aren't actually photographs, they're that precise.

Six years later, aged 50, would find her camping at Chich'en Itzá, a complex of Maya ruins in Mexico. Her meticulous copies of the wall paintings there as well as in Teōtīhuacān, also in Mexico, are the only full record of what was there at the time. Some of the walls have lost their colour since then, so Adela's images remain a major contribution to Maya studies and a vital reference for historians, as do her letter relating to her travels. In fact, Adela had a talent for languages: she copied documents, maps and codices, published her work and wrote letters with leading historians. For instance, using the pen name 'Your Mexican Correspondent', she sent accounts of her adventures in that country to The Bath Chronicle newspaper.

Although afterwards she went on expeditions throughout the world, e.g. the USA, Canada, Egypt, New Zealand, Peru and Brazil, but her main interest was Mexico. Adela made detailed drawings and paintings of archaeological sites, ceramics and frescos despite suffering from ill health as she got older, which was made worse but the conditions she had to endure like heat, humidity and insect bites. Having to wear impractical long skirts and ride side-saddle wouldn't have helped either.

Adela had taken thirteen trips out there by 1908, travelling with Pablo Solorio (1859-1903), who came from the Mexican state of Michoacán. Pablo acted as her guide, cook, general helper and fellow archaeologist, finding and labelling hundreds of artefacts and rock samples. Pablo even voyaged across the Atlantic with her and visited Bath in 1895.

Many of the artefacts found by Pablo and Adela were smuggled out of Mexico illegally for Adela to donate to museums. Although very modern in certain outlooks, such as her deep respect for Pablo and other Indigenous people, she followed the imperialist trend of the time in her view of where artefacts should be housed.

The Mexican objects she brought back to England went mainly to the Bristol Museum and the Bath Royal Literary and Scientific Institution (BRLSI).

The archaeological artist died in Barbados and in her will,

Adela left pretty much everything to her brother, Harry (whose son Hubert worked at the Lodway Brewery in Pill for a while). He gave 100 of her watercolours to the Victoria Art Gallery in Bath and over 1000 items to Bristol Museum, which included artefacts, notes and paintings.

Like Sarah Biffin, Adela was famed during her life for her talent but not celebrated when she was no longer useful, i.e. dead. Nonetheless, there have been a few exhibitions of her artwork, though, that were organised by the Bristol Museum and the Victoria Art Gallery. Plus, the BRLSI has a room at 16–18 Queen Square, Bath, named after Adela Breton.

(Camden Crescent with no. 15 marked with an arrow)

Sources: *The Remarkable Miss Breton: Artist, archaeologist, traveller* by Bath Royal Literary and Scientific Institution, *Adela Breton: A Victorian Artist Amid Mexico's Ruins* by Mary McVicker, *Adela Catherine Breton (1849-1923): A Career in Ruins* by Kate Devlin, oxforddnb.com.

Alice Seeley Harris (24th May 1870–24th November 1970)

Alice was born in Malmsbury but aged 12, she and her family moved to Frome, where they lived until she was 18. Her father ran a silk mill there and they lived close by with Alice learning to paint with watercolours with a local art master.

She then trained as a missionary in London and met John Hobbs Harris (29th July 1874–30th April 1940), who she married in 1989. Their honeymoon was spent journeying to Congo Free State, as they'd been posted there as missionaries. At that time, the country was privately owned by Leopold II of Belgium.

Upon arrival, they set to work learning the local language and customs, and teaching skills like housebuilding. But they were soon made aware of how the Congolese people were kept in slavery due to the king's greed for rubber and ivory. If they didn't produce enough, they were beaten, tortured and whipped. The children's limbs got amputated, the women got raped, entire villages got burnt down and mass murders took place.

Alice knew that the world needed to know about this. Using her box camera, she took hundreds of photos of these crimes against humanity. This was probably the first photograph campaign in support of human rights.

The couple's first child, Alfred, was born in the Congo but their second, Margaret, was born in Frome in 1901 and two more children, Katharine and Noel, were later also born in England. After a sabbatical year in Frome, the couple returned to the Congo without their children (all of whom were raised in a home for missionary children in London) until their missionary posting ended in 1905. Back in England, they got the photos circulated through the press and gave hundreds of speeches across Britain, the USA and mainland Europe. It was a punishing campaign trail. Pressure mounted on Leopold II, including a condemning report by Roger Casement. When Casement formed the Congo Reform Association, the Harrises became joint secretaries and kept fighting. Finally, in 1908, the king couldn't hold out anymore. The country became the Belgian Congo, ruled by Belgium rather than by one person. When Alice and John visited the Congo once more in 1911, they found that conditions for the Congolese people had improved. By 1930, Margaret had died and John and Alice had moved back to Frome, where Alice became a member of the Frome Society for Local Study and became a Quaker in 1931. (John had joined Quakerism in 1916.) Although she missed out on a title for her own work, Alice's husband was knighted in 1933, becoming Sir John and she became Lady Alice. Yet she often told people, "Don't call me Lady!"

Seven years later, John died in Frome. His funeral was at Sheppards Barton Church and he was buried in Frome's Dissenters Cemetery. The following year, 1941, Alice left Somerset to live in Surrey near her daughter Katharine.

Alice died in Guildford after thirty years of widowhood, at the age of 100. Her grave was extremely modest; it didn't even have a headstone for decades until two grandsons erected one. When Alice's daughter Katharine died in 1974, her body was taken to Frome and buried in the same cemetery as John. Katharine left her house to the Frome Society in her will in exchange for somebody putting a red rose on her grave at midsummer each year.

The following page shows the Frome plaque honouring Alice Seeley Harris. It reads: Anti-slavery campaigner, photographer, missionary to Congo, artist, scourge of King Leopold II of the Belgians, lived at 3 Merchants Barton 1882–1888. Born Malmesbury 24 May 1870. Died Guilford 24 November 1970.

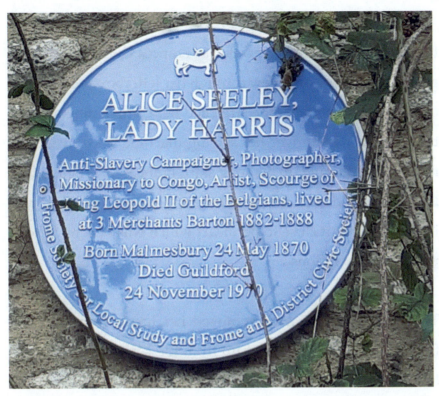

Sources: www.frometowncouncil.gov.uk, acelebrationofwomen.org, oxforddnb.com, rarehistoricalphotos.com, Plaques of Frome Trail by Discover Frome, myheritage.com, autograph.co.uk.

Chapter 20: Talk of the Town Hall (19th–20th century)

It was a mere slip of paper. But to Frances Connelly, it was a golden ticket. The card flew through her letterbox and fluttered onto the hallway floor. She stretched her complaining muscles that had been bent over her sewing machine since five in the morning. Gathering up her long skirt, Frances rose, entered the hallway, bent down and picked the paper up. Once she'd read it, she clutched it close to her heart which was beating fiercely underneath her blouse.

*

The day arrived. Frances removed her hands from the half-finished leather glove, leapt up from the sewing machine and left her home on Salisbury Terrace, Reckleford Road. William Tucker, who had invested in the local glove manufacturing, had financed the construction of the terraced building in the 1890s to provide housing for glove makers like Frances and her family.

It took 7 minutes, if that, for Frances to walk to Yeovil Town Hall, but she still managed to glimpse the suffragist car that was driving around the town with the slogan: "Mothers want votes".

'Quite right,' Frances thought to herself.

At Yeovil Town Hall, the first obstacle was the policeman standing firm outside the entrance, his moustache twitching as he saw Frances approaching the door.

"Excuse me, madam." His voice had an edge to it. "Can I help you?"

"I am here to cast my vote."

His face was a picture of shock that turned into a sneer. "You most certainly are not! I suggest you return at once to your household washing and cleaning."

Meeting his gaze, she said clearly and firmly, "My name is on the electoral register and I have been issued with a polling card for today's byelection. Look, it's dated 21st November 1911. I am here to vote."

"Let me see that."

As she held out the card to him, he snatched it, skimmed it, then sighed.

"The only reason you have a polling card is because somebody has made an error. They have spelt your name as Francis with an "i" and therefore have taken you for a man."

"All the same, I am eligible to vote and so I am here to vote. The rules for the by-election make no mention of gender."

"Oh, I'll let them deal with you inside. You won't be given a ballot paper, mark my words. More likely I'll be taking you to the station later."

"Thank you, sir." Frances tried to keep the sarcasm from her voice. Having passed the first barrier, she clutched her long skirt and made her way inside.

A sea of suits and canes turned to stare at her, the only woman in the building. Time seemed to stop until a voting official marched over to her, his shoes clicking on the polished floor.

"What on earth are you doing here?"

"I have come to vote. I have a polling card."

Grabbing it, he scanned it, then laughed. "Because there is a spelling mistake." His voice was deliberately slow and clear as if Frances were a child.

Frances wanted to reply with: "Yes, funny that. Men say that women aren't competent enough to vote and yet a *man* has made a silly spelling mistake and allowed an 'incompetent' woman to vote in the by-election!"

Instead she said, "I am eligible to vote. I pay rates and I haven't already voted. Those are the only two requirements."

"Now, see here. The card was issued in error. I shan't be giving you a ballot paper."

"Look at your electoral register. You will find my name there."

With a scowl, he did so and found:

Number 514 — Connelly, Francis — 25 Reckleford — Dwelling house

"Precisely. Fran*cis* Connelly, not Fran*ces* Connelly."

Just then, the chief unionist agent, Mr Johnson, came over. "What's all this about? Who allowed a woman inside?"

"The policeman outside, I imagine."

"He had no grounds to stop me from entering," Frances stated firmly. "I am on the electoral list."

Once My Johnson had examined her card and the list, he began to question Frances over and over.

"Don't you have a husband to vote on your behalf?"

"No, sir. He is dead."

"Or a brother? Or sons?"

"I have three grown sons and yet I should like to vote myself and as head of my household, I can do so."

"Surely as a woman, you'd prefer to leave this sort of *political* thinking to the men? I'd be concerned for your health, filling your head with all this *difficult* thinking. The female brain isn't equipped for this sort of thing but rather for washing and mending clothes, that sort of thing. You should go home and attend to domestic matters."

"My health is perfectly fine, thank you, sir."

"Goodness. You are stirring things up, aren't you? I don't know what we should do with you. What a to-do! Somebody fetch Mr King."

The local barrister, whose role was to advise on legal issues that arose relating to elections, made his way over. But, in typical lawyer fashion, Mr King was unable to resolve the situation. In the end, the presiding officer, Mr Hughes, had to be called over. The three men put their heads together.

"She has a polling card, yes, but her actual name is Frances with an "e". Does that not invalidate the card?" asked Mr Johnson.

"Not in legal terms," Mr King replied. "There have been cases of men's names being misspelt and they have been permitted to vote."

"She should be at home mending her stockings, not out here causing mischief. Ever since that 1894 Act gave female ratepayers the ability to vote in county council elections, they think they can vote any time they wish, even in a by-election for a Member of Parliament! Give an inch, take a mile, as always. Do we even know who she wishes to vote for?" Mr Hughes queried.

"No, but–" Mr Johnson began but was cut off by Mr King, who said:

"I don't think it wise to ask her. We don't want to make it look as though we are rigging the election."

Mr Hughes removed his glasses and massaged his head. "Good grief. I blame those suffragettes in London for whipping up a female frenzy right across the country. I suppose we should be thankful the women of Yeovil aren't out smashing windows like they are in the capital."

"Indeed. At least she is not being hysterical," Mr King replied. "Prime Minister Asquith keeps stringing the women along by allowing debates in parliament only to do an about-face. Now he claims he wants to focus on getting working men the vote. It would be easier for us all if the government could be clear on what they want to achieve."

"Quite. We wouldn't be in this pickle if there weren't loopholes in the law and so on." Mr Hughes sighed. "Well, given there is no ruling that states the voter must be male, I think we have no choice but to permit her to exercise her vote. We should try and make it happen as quietly as possible. Those darned suffragists outside don't need encouragement! It would cost a fortune to replace these windows if they got really stirred up."

"If you quietly give her a ballot paper and allow her to vote without making a fuss, then the law will have been upheld and the council can avoid embarrassment," the barrister suggested. And so a ballot paper was presented to Frances Connelly. How she struggled to keep herself from beaming.

As instructed by the envelope, she opened it at once in front of the election assistants and found two small sheets of paper inside. She signed the DECLARATION OF IDENTITY card, then passed it to the witness for a counter signature. Then she took her ballot paper to the booth and put her X next to Aubrey Herbert, leaving the box next to Henry Vivian blank.

Now alone in the booth, Frances couldn't help but smile. There was her X on the ballot paper for a Member of Parliament for South Somerset. She hoped her Conservative candidate would win against his Liberal opponent, mainly because of the National Insurance Act that the Liberals were proposing. It seemed a reasonable idea in theory: introducing sick pay and national insurance for the working population. However, poor people saw it as a way of reducing their wages. Frances feared coughing up the 4 shillings a week into the fund, even though her employer was expected to pay 3 shillings and taxation to contribute 2 shillings each week. Plus, like many, she feared that her boss would simply reduce his number of workers and make those left work longer hours. She was already labouring from 5am to 8pm with only an hour's break for lunch, yet she desperately needed the work to survive. Being laid off or having her hours increased were not pleasant prospects. This vote was about something very personal to her. Frances' aim was to help protect her livelihood.

'So, sorry Mr Vivian but my X is not for you!' Frances thought. She folded the paper ever so neatly and placed it slowly in the box provided. She took a deep breath in and out, engraving every detail of the moment onto her memory.

Despite the loud tuts directed at her from men who'd heard the gossip and despite their muttered comments like, "They'll all be storming the place in a minute now that one's been allowed to vote," Frances held her head high as she left the town hall.

*

"Cor, blimey, you kept that quiet, mum." William's eyes bored into his mum.

"Kept what quiet, Will?" Frances answered, genuinely confused.

"The fact that you voted!"

"Oh, that."

"Yes, that. I suppose the years we lived in London made you a modern woman, eh?" he teased.

"I never thought you'd find out about the voting, bab, truth be told."

"Not find out! It's in the Western Gazette. Page 5. Says you voted for Lord Carnarvon's brother, who won of course."

"What? I mean, I know he won. It was announced yesterday at the town hall, but the paper mentions *me?*"

"See for yourself. By the way, I reckon Dad would've been proud of you if he was still alive."

After giving him a loving gaze, she let her eyes fall on the paper before her, which read:

24th November 1911 Western Gazette

The election will be remembered for the first time in the history of the constituency a woman claimed and was allowed to exercise the Parliamentary franchise. At the very moment a Suffragist's car was touring Yeovil displaying to an amused crowd the legend "Mothers want votes", a lady was putting her cross against the name of Mr

Aubrey Herbert.

Notes

Frances Connelly née Parker (c.1866/1869-23rd March 1917) was the first woman to vote in Somerset but wasn't the first in Britain, though some reports have erroneously said so. The first was Scottish-born Lily Maxwell (c.1800–October 1876), who had worked for years as a servant in Manchester to save up enough to open her own shop. As a shopkeeper, she had to pay rates to the city council. In 1867, there was a by-election in Manchester and Lily's name appeared on the list of registered voters. That was because the rules stated that all ratepayers could vote; as with Yeovil, nobody thought to add "male" as an additional requirement. Don't you love it when the patriarchy shoots itself in the foot? So, Lily turned up to her polling station. Before the Ballot Act of 1872, you had to say out loud who you would vote for, with Lily choosing her local Liberal MP, a man who supported peace and women's suffrage. Lily's voice caused quite a stir. But, as with Frances, her ballot paper had to be accepted. A thunderous cheer rose up in the room as people acknowledged history being made with the country's first female voter.

After that, over 5,000 more female heads of households applied to get their names onto electoral rolls. These applications were put before Britain's court of law in 1868 but almost all their names were struck off the lists on the basis that women were simply not allowed to vote. Only a few slipped through the net and managed to vote, especially female heads of households and women whose names were similar to male names, like with Frances. The regulations were then tightened to prevent women from making use of any loopholes in the law.

Despite making history, Lily ended up in abject poverty: she died in a local workhouse in 1876.

As for Frances, not much is known about her life. The 1891 census states that 25-year-old Yeovil-born Frances was living in southeast London with her 27-year-old husband, Edward, who was a canteen manager. Their sons were: William, 2, and Walter, not yet 1.

Unlike many other women who were pro female enfranchisement, Frances cooperated with the 1911 census rather than spoiling the paper. An example of someone in Somerset who rebelled in the census was Charlotte Sophie Horwood née Potter (1856–?) in Shepton Mallet. She scribbled on her census paper: "The whole of the thinking women of Shepton Mallet send this message to government, praying that the women's suffrage bill may be passed in May next. SC Horwood, a moderate-minded liberal suffragette." Emmeline Pankhurst (see Quick Tribute) wrote a letter soon after the census to explain the general message they wanted to get across: "The Census is a numbering of the people. Until women count as people for the purpose of representation in the councils of the nation, we shall refuse to be numbered."

Back to Frances. The 1911 census has her living at Salisbury Terrace, Reckleford, in Yeovil and aged 42, meaning she was born c.1869 but the 1891 census would have her born c.1866. Did another male clerk make an error on a document related to her?! Her sons' ages match the 1891 census. William was then 22, Walter 20 and a third son Edward was 13. There is no mention of her husband and she is listed as the head of the household, therefore he must have died at some point between Edward's conception and the 1911 census, causing Frances to move back to her hometown. There is a 20-year-old boarder mentioned, showing that Frances was struggling for money as a widow.

The next mention of Frances is of course in the newspapers of late 1911, where many of the officials she talked to are named. But I changed their names to reflect the fictional personalities I created due to the lack of details surrounding these conversations. The papers also state who she voted for, which I find curious. Did she tell them this or did they find out some other way? Most newspapers didn't actually run her story, probably so as not to encourage the suffragists and suffragettes.

The difference between suffragists and suffragettes is as follows. In England, societies that lobbied for women's enfranchisement began to appear in the mid-1800s. Those involved were called suffragists. They believed in non-violent, diplomatic campaigning, including petitions, posters, leaflets and public meetings. By the early 1900s, their aims had not been achieved, which disillusioned many women and fired them up to take a more militant approach, such as chaining themselves to railings, smashing windows and destroying public property. In 1903, Emmeline Pankhurst founded the Women's Social and Political Union (WSPU), giving birth to the suffragettes, first dubbed by The Daily Mail as an insult but later adopted by the movement. We could therefore class Frances as a suffragist as she challenged the system by using a loophole in the law to cast a vote in 1911. (As a side note, we don't know the details of all the conversations that took place inside the town hall, so I have changed the names of the officials and used my imagination to create their characters to display common beliefs at the time.) Just six years later, in 1917, Frances Connelly died aged between 48 and 51. She succumbed to TB at her home in Yeovil (which was knocked down in the early 1960s along with the rest of the terrace). Although Frances voted, she didn't live to see women given the vote. Her 1911 vote was the only one in her life. The men made sure they didn't make the same mistake again with her name! A year after her death, wealthy, landowning women aged over 30 were allowed to vote through the Representation of the People Act 1918, which meant those women could vote in the December 1918 general election. The Act also stated that all men over 21 could now vote, irrespective of property ownership; working-class men could now vote. That meant Frances' sons (still very much alive) were able to vote. Frances' mother, who probably didn't own land anyway, died in 1918 so also missed out on witnessing the landmark moment.

The 1918 Act would therefore have included our working-class heroine's sons but possibly excluded her. During Frances' life, some renters had to pay rates; thus being a ratepayer did not necessarily mean she was a property owner. Frances would've perhaps had to wait until the Representation of the People Act in 1928 to see all women aged 21 and over given the vote. This would've enabled her to vote in the May 1929 general election at the age of 60, had she lived. The polling stations had a 76% turnout overall, of which 52% were women.

Frances Connelly's story lay forgotten in dusty archives until a journalist named Laura Linham found the original 1911 newspaper article. In 2017, a hundred years after Frances' death, Laura wrote an article about Frances. Without Laura, Frances' story would probably be lost to history.

The painter Sally A. Barr was inspired to paint Frances' portrait based on a photograph of her. She turned her painting into a banner and took it through the streets of London on the 2018 march that marked 100 years of (some) women's suffrage.

It's crucial for us to remember Frances' story and others like her. A lot of working-class women's contributions to the Suffragette Movement were hushed up due to classism. Yet these working-class women made huge impacts. For instance, Frances' simple act of defiance, as Sheena MacLeod puts it, made people think: "If one woman can vote, why not all?"

(Frances may have feared ending up here, Yeovil Police Station, for her bold action.)

Chapter Bibliography

So You Say I Can't Vote by Sheena MacLeod and Laura Linham

Secret Yeovil by Bob Osborn

Yeovil's Virtual Museum, the A-to-Z of Yeovil's History by Bob Osborn

Frances Connelly: The British woman who quietly made history voting seven years before it was legal by Rachael Pells

myheritage.com

familysearch.org

2018 Reflections of Women's Suffrage in the UK by Sheena MacLeod

Frances Connelly: The Yeovil woman who made history voting seven years before it was legal by Laura Linham

www.thehistorypress.co.uk

QUICK TRIBUTES

Suffragists and Suffragettes

There were so many incredible women in Somerset who fought for women's right to vote that I couldn't include them all. Here is a quick list for those who might want to do research of their own. Please contact me if you'd like to know more of what I found about each of them.

Suffragists

Helen Clark née Bright (1840–1927) in Street. A Quaker and

suffragist, she was a member of the Bristol and West of England NSWS (National Society for Women's Suffrage) and spoke on their behalf in Taunton in 1872. She married William Clark of the Clarks shoe company.

Helen's daughter Alice Clark (1874-1934) served on the executive committee for the National Union of Women's Suffrage Societies (NUWSS), which grew from the NSWS. Helen's other three daughters (Hilda, Esther and Margaret) and her son Roger were all keen to support women's rights. Hilda also supported an organisation focused on gay rights and acceptance, ran a maternity hospital in France during the First World War and ran the Quaker relief programme in Vienna after the war.

Suffragettes

Mother and daughter Emily (1852-1940) and Mary Blathwayt (1879-1962), cousins of the Blathwayts of Dyrham Park, lived in Batheaston, where they opened their home to suffragettes who needed to recuperate after being tortured in prison and as a meeting place for the movement, with Emmeline Pankhurst being a regular visitor. In the diary she kept from 1908 to 1913, Mary documented how some of the women were intimate with each other, including herself. On top of their courage and insight as suffragettes, these gay women also knew their true identity and weren't afraid to express it together in the safe house.

Ivy Millicent James (1879-1965) and Maud James (1877-1930) were suffragettes in Weston-super-Mare. Ivy was also an artist. Two more suffragettes in Weston-super-Mare were the sisters Emmeline Pethick-Lawrence (1867-1954) and Dorothy Pethick (1881-1970). Emmeline, a close friend of the more famous Emmeline Pankhurst, created a double-barrelled surname with her husband when she married. This was evidence of their shared belief in gender equality, which they put into action when they co-founded the publication *Votes for Women*. Emmeline also became treasurer of the Women's Social and Political Union, a suffragette group, and offered money and a headquarters to the organisation. She was arrested and imprisoned six times. Dorothy was arrested and imprisoned several times too during the early 1900s and was active in the women's suffrage movement across the country. Both sisters visited the Blathwayts' house.

Ellen Crocker (1873-1962) was born in Stogumber. Emmeline and Dorothy's cousin, Ellen was the honorary secretary of the Women's Liberal Association in Wellington but resigned because the Liberal government wouldn't support women's suffrage. Ellen protested as a suffragette and was arrested several times at the turn of the century.

Joan Beauchamp (1890-1964) was born and grew up in

Midsomer Norton. She became a leading suffragette and was one of the first women to graduate from the University of London. Joan and her younger sister Kay (1899-1992) were also founding members of the Communist Party of Great Britain.

Other

Margaret Bondfield (1873-1953) in Chard was chair of the Adult Suffrage Society, believing that the vote should be given to all adults regardless of their gender or property ownership, hence was not a suffragist or suffragette per se but campaigned for wider voting rights. She was also the first female cabinet minister in British parliament.

Sources: Weston Museum, A-Z of the Women who built Bristol by Jane Duffus, online Working Class Movement Library, Shepton Mallet Heritage Trails, freereg.org.uk, www.suffrageresources .org.uk, Alice Clark – a suffragist from LSE by Gillian Murphy, menwhosaidno.org, quakersatstreet.org.uk, Weston-super-Mare and the Suffragettes by Lucienne Boyce.

Hedwig Green (February 1869-1935)

In 1900, Hedwig Green née Deislinger, originally from southern Germany, had lived in Oakhill with her husband Richard for eight years of their 11-year marriage. They had had 4 children together but only three boys were still alive. Richard was an alcoholic and a violent abuser. Hedwig's brother was visiting from Germany and he stood up for his sister. Annoyed at this affront, Richard spread a lie through the village that this man was not his wife's relative but her lover.

The community came together to expose the woman's "immorality". They decided to perform a skimmerty or skimmerton riding, the name coming from skimming ladles used to make cheddar and other cheese since these were used to attack the "guilty party".

One night, Hedwig was at home with her brother and children while Richard was out drinking. An angry influx of over fifty men descended on their house, banging pots and pans while hurling abuse at her. Locking her brother and children in the bathroom, she tore downstairs to secure the front door, while the swarm of men yelled at her to come outside with her lover. Bravely, Hedwig refused and denied their accusations, so the mob broke down her door and dragged her out to throw stones and dirt at her. Richard was part of the crowd but stayed hidden. Hedwig withstood the attack with courage until the men left.

Later, she took seven of the rioters to court, where they admitted to being present but denied assaulting her. Their justification for the shouting was that skimmerty was a longstanding tradition. Despite a doctor providing evidence of Hedwig's bruises, the judge charged only one man and his punishment was a two-shilling fine.

Understandably, Hedwig, whose name means battle, had had enough of Oakhill. Not long afterwards, the Green family upped sticks and settled in Bath, where she had a 4th son and then finally a daughter, who she named Hedwig. Nonetheless, after she died aged 66, she was buried in Oakhill.

(Hedwig and her husband's headstone at All Saints Church graveyard, Oakhill)

Sources: Mysterious Somerset by AM Gould, 5th November 1884. 'Riding the Skimmerty' by Colin Dunkerley, Somerset, England, Church of England Baptisms, 1813–1914, 1911 England Census, England & Wales, Civil Registration Death Index, 1916–2007.

Chapter 21: Women in War (early 20th century, a Quick Tributes chapter)

Nurses

Alice Batstone (1878–11th March 1969) was born into a large family who lived in the St Nicholas parish of Weston-super-Mare and moved to nearby Uphill village before the First World War broke out.

Her brother Percy went missing in action on the Somme in 1916 and was assumed dead 5 months later. Meanwhile, Alice was serving as a nurse for wounded soldiers based at Weston's Ashcombe House Auxiliary Red Cross Hospital.

On 8th November 1917, she was presented with the Order of the Royal Red Cross by George V. Other Uphill women were given this award on the same day: Edith Mary Graves-Knyfton for organising the Weston branch of the Red Cross (she also later received an OBE), Alice Byrnes for serving as the hospital's treasurer and May Lilley Whitting for fundraising for the hospital.

Alice died in 1969 aged 91 and is buried in Uphill Old Churchyard.

The next page shows a photo of Weston-super-Mare taken around 1901 when Alice was in her 20s.

Sources: *warandpeaceinsomerset.wordpress.com, Uphill Remembers The War Years 1914 – 1918.*

The First Female Tram Driver

Beatrice Page (1882–1976), the first female tram driver in England, worked in Weston-super-Mare. The town's tram system was fairly new at the time, having opened in 1902. She was one of several women recruited to drive the trams in either 1914 or 1916 to replace the men who had gone to war.

The tram companies were unenthusiastic about hiring, as evidenced by a photograph of Beatrice driving a tram that was taken in January 1916. It shows her wearing a woollen coat, rather than the tram company's uniform, because their reluctance to employ women meant that she probably wasn't issued a uniform until she had proven her ability. This is one of the ways in which these pioneering women were discriminated against. Despite that, Motorwoman Page, aged around 34 at the time, meets our gaze with a proud and determined expression. Although Beatrice had to give up this employment when the fighting men returned from mainland Europe in 1918, she was invited back to drive the last tram before the tramlines were pulled up in 1942.

The documents refer to her as Mrs Beatrice Page, but I couldn't discover her maiden name, full date of birth or death or any details about her family.

Sources: Weston Museum, tramwaybadgesandbuttons.com, thewestonmercury.co.uk.

A Doctor in Both Wars

Annie Wainwright Hyatt (12th April 1879-1965) was brought up at 1 and 2 Waterloo Road in Shepton Mallet (now the YMCA) with her two brothers and four sisters. Her father, who had a medical practice and served the prison too, inspired young Annie: from an early age, she was determined to qualify as a doctor.

After studying via a correspondence course and taking extra lessons from the grammar school headteacher, she took a science exam at University College, Bristol (the precursor to Bristol University), which was the first higher education institute in England to admit women on equal footing to men... except in medicine. For that reason, Annie's next stop was the London Royal Free Hospital School for Medicine, the only medical school that took women. The 2-year course finished in 1906 with the 27-year-old Annie passing all her exams.

Dr Hyatt returned to Shepton to work with her father, among the whisperings of neighbours commenting on the rarity of a female doctor. Many preferred to call her a nurse, even though she was better qualified than most local male doctors. Her first job was at the town's workhouse and infirmary. Then she was also appointed as medical officer to Shepton District Hospital, which was a voluntary role.

When World War I struck, lots of male doctors were called up to fight. Alongside running a ward at the hospital for injured soldiers, Annie and just one other doctor took on extra patients in Evercreech, stretching themselves thinly.

After the war, Annie strove to improve healthcare for women and children, setting up a health insurance club aimed at them. Medical treatment for men was paid out of taxes, but healthcare for anybody else was not funded. The best Annie could offer was that they paid money each month to avoid a hefty fee later on.

By the outbreak of World War II, her address was Merrymead, Charlton Road, still in Shepton Mallet. During this war, Dr Hyatt became a medical officer at a maternity hospital at the nearby Cranmore Hall for pregnant London women who'd been billeted with families nearby. The only lighting in the facility was a spotlight run on batteries in the delivery room and instruments had to be sterilised using a stove. The hall has come on a fair amount since then: it's now part of All Hallows School in East Cranmore.

In the same year this war ended, Annie hung up her stethoscope for good. She bought a property in Evercreech, where she lived out the remainder of her life. She died in Wells in early 1965, having chosen to stay single throughout her life.

There is a road in Shepton Mallet named in honour of her family's contribution to the town: Hyatt Place.

(1 and 2 Waterloo Road, now the YMCA)

Sources: Shepton Mallet Heritage Trails (audio), ancestry.co.uk, Darshill & Bowlish Conservation Society Heritage Project website, myheritage.com, www.hyattfamily.co.uk, www.bbc.co.uk/history/ww2peopleswar, www.allhallowsschool.co.uk, www.bristol.ac.uk.

A Factory Girl

Sheila May Fraser (c. 1922–6th September 1940) grew up in Wincanton with her parents and two brothers, Alex and Tony. Once she left school, she worked at the newly built Cow & Gate factory alongside Tony and her father.

When World War II began, the family moved to Woking, Surrey, while Tony joined the army. Sheila found employment at the nearby Vickers-Armstrong factory assembling military aeroplanes.

Sadly, on 4th September 1940, the German Air Force bombed the Vickers-Armstrong factory, leaving 83 dead and 419 wounded. Sheila was among those badly injured and was transferred to Walton Hospital, where she died two days later, aged only 18.

Tony didn't survive the war either, passing away in May 1944. Both of them are included in the memorial in St Peter and St Paul church, Wincanton.

Sources: www.brooklandsmuseum.com, www.myheritage.com, roll-of-honour.com.

Air Force Women from Wells

Corporal (CPL) Esma Beatrice Singleton (22nd August 1919-3rd March 1943) was born in Australia but the family moved to Wells soon after and she grew up there. Her parents ran a bakery/grocer's on Wookey Hole Road.

In July 1940, Esma began volunteering for the Women's Auxiliary Air Force (WAAF) and signed up officially in Mary 1941.

While posted in Hampshire in 1943, she grew ill with leukaemia. Her Fight Officer noted that she never complained and was cheerful and reliable. Although she was transferred to an RAF hospital in London on 1st March 1943, the illness killed her two days later at the age of 23. She was her parents' only child.

Esma is buried in Wells Cemetery and listed in the rolls of honour at the cemetery and in the Town Hall.

Sybil Antoinette Mullins (18th November 1924-31st July 1944) was born in Wells. She joined the WAAF in early 1943 and trained as an aircraft mechanic. Becoming a leading aircraftswoman (LACW), she was posted to northern Cornwall. Aged 19, on 31st July 1944, she was on a test flight with three male crew members. Straight after take-off, one of the engines caught ablaze in a fire that quickly spread to the wing. They tried to land the plane in a nearby field but hit a hedge, cutting the aircraft in half and causing the cabin to crash land and break out in fire. All four were killed and all were under the age of 30. Sybil's funeral service was held in St Thomas' Church, Wells, on 11th August 1944, and she was buried in Wells Cemetery. Her gravestone includes the inscription: "There is a land of pure delight!" Like Esma, Sybil is also remem-bered on the rolls of honour at that cemetery and at the Town Hall.

(The rolls of honour at Wells Cemetery)

L.A.C.W	S.A.Mullins	W.A.A.F.
L/SGT	F.W.Pople	Coldstream Guards
SGT	J.C.Samuel	R.A.F.
CPL	E.B.Singleton	W.A.A.F

(Previous page: close-ups of Esma and Sybil from the rolls of honour)

Sources for Esma: www.wellsmuseum.org.uk, www.rafcommands.com, , www.rafdavidstowmoor.com, Commonwealth war graves website, roll-of-honour.com. / Sources for Sybil: Wells Journal: Friday 12 March 1943, www.wellsmuseum.org.uk, www.rafcommands.com.

French Resistance Agent

Born in Brittany, Andrée Marthe Peel née Virot (3rd February 1905–5th March 2010) joined the French Resistance during World War II and was known as Agent X alias Rose. She distributed newspapers, gave intelligence reports about the German armed forces and saved the lives of 102 allied pilots by guiding them to make-shift landing areas lit up with flaming torches. After their bumpy landings, she found civilian clothes for the pilots to wear and families for them to stay with. The final step was to organise the pilots' repatriation, often to Britain for which she'd take them to the town's port on a moonless night to get a secret submarine.

In May 1944, the agent was arrested, interrogated and tortured, then taken to Ravensbrück concentration camp. One day, her prisoner number was written on a list of people to be sent to the gas chamber. But a fellow friend and prisoner, a Polish aristocrat, sneakily grabbed the piece of paper and ate it without getting caught, thus saving Andrée's life. Andrée's time at Buchenwald was also dramatic. There, in early April 1945, the Nazis knew the Allies were on their way so they forced all those able to walk to line up and begin a death march. Andrée hid in a block with those too ill to line up. They'd begged her to stay with them as she had a gift for speaking words of encouragement. But the Nazis had a plan for the sick as well. Just when the firing squad was approaching her block to murder them all, the phone rang in the camp's office. The call said that the Americans were at the town gates and that the Nazis had been seen entering the camp to kill the prisoners. "If you want to live, spare their lives." The Nazis fled, the camp was liberated and Andrée returned home.

With the war over, Andrée moved to Paris and opened a restaurant. One of her customers was John Peel (21st March 1926–5th December 2003) who asked her to help him with his French. They fell in love, married and came to live in England. After a few years in Nottingham and Cambridge for John's studies, they settled in the North Somerset village of Long Ashton, just outside Bristol, where they lived there for the rest of their lives. John worked as a neuropsychologist at Barrow Gurney Hospital for his entire career and Andrée as a healer. Using the power of touch, she was able to locate and cure others' pain by pushing a tendon back into place, for instance.

She cared for a total of 24,600 patients, as stated on her gravestone, which she shares with her husband, in All Saint's Churchyard, Long Ashton.

For her bravery, Andrée was decorated by the French, British and American governments. She published her fascinating memoirs, Miracles Do Happen, in 1999. She died in 2010 aged 105.

Sources: Miracles Do Happen by Andrée Peel, news.bbc.co.uk, womenshistornetwork.org, Heroine of the French resistance who rescued 102 shot-down aircrew by Dan van der Vat, Women Heroes of World War II: 26 Stories of Espionage, Sabotage, Resistance, and Rescue by Kathryn J. Atwood.

Chapter 22: Disarmament and Dance (early to mid-20th century)

As the long-nosed car bumped along the potholed road, the village came into view, little by little. Kathleen Tacchi saw once more the meadow, green hedges, quaint-looking pubs and houses that were white-washed or red-brick. Nothing had changed or lost its charm: the Chard Canal remained – never commercially viable, disused now but pretty nonetheless – the memorial to Queen Victoria, known as the Pepper Pot to the locals, the parish church with its striking octagonal tower, the general store with its Post Office…

A far cry from the glitz and glamour of her hometown, London, and yet quaint old North Curry felt like home. It felt exquisite. It made Kathleen's eyes dance with excitement.

The circumstances that had brought Kathleen, or Tacchi as she was known, back to rural Somerset were dramatic. In December 1936, the 37-year-old Kathleen married Flight Lieutenant Walter Allan Stagg. They rented a house in North Curry aptly called The Warren for its labyrinthian layout made it resemble a rabbit's warren. Allan was then posted to Malta. His wife went too.

Kathleen's strong background in dance, having run her own dance school and theatrical business in London as well as starred in some silent films, meant that she wanted to establish a children's dance school on the island. She was forbidden. Air Force families weren't meant to "fraternise" with the locals. Kathleen grew resentful, eventually telling her husband, "Leave the forces or I will leave you– your choice." He chose his job so Kathleen divorced him and returned to North Curry in 1939. She bought a house and set up the school she'd dreamed of.

When the war hit, Kathleen's focus was to care for children of all nationalities who needed a home. The 30 children included German Jewish refugees and mixed-race children with White British mothers and fathers from British colonies, such as Africa and India. Shock waves went around the entire village that not only dark-skinned children but also youngsters from an "enemy country" were invading their village.

"I refuse to pay any attention to these nasty comments," Kathleen decided.

Soon after the war, she married Richard Rodham "Rod" Morris, who she'd met in North Curry. Native to the village, Rod was an auctioneer and surveyor. Our dancer became Kathleen Tacchi-Morris.

"I know it goes against tradition to create a double-barrelled surname," she told Rod. "I know it's unusual but I've established myself as a dancer and actor using my maiden name. I hope you understand."

Her husband nodded and supported her decision, making her love him all the more.

Together they lived at Long's House, a 17th-century farmhouse made of limestone and Ham stone with various wings, a house that inhaled and exhaled the love she had for it, seeming to have its own personality.

After dismissing all the servants, she got to work converting the now-empty rooms over to projects that were dear to her heart. Rod watched with amazement and said, "You know, I'm filled with admiration for you, Tacchi. You have so much energy for all these projects. You'll have this barn converted in no time."

Once the barn had been converted into a theatre, a London-based ballerina came down and taught ballet while Kathleen taught Kallirhythm, an original form of dance she had invented.

In 1949, Kathleen took on Somerset County Council.

Her request was reasonable enough. In fact, it was generous. She wanted to educate twelve of the children born in Somerset to African American soldiers and White British mothers.

She told Rod, "It's a disgrace that these soldiers are forbidden to marry the mothers of their children. Segregation has a lot to answer for. American racism, in fact. Their commanding officers will not permit the marriages. That means the babies are either raised solely by their mothers or by extended family or are put into care. In Somerset, many of them live at Holnicote House in Holnicote near Minehead. Now, I propose to have twelve of them live here."

"Sounds like a good plan. You already have a school set up."

"Precisely. I'd be happy to house, feed and teach the children only in exchange for the cost of keeping them. The lessons would be free. And we can include subjects that they might not otherwise receive: horse riding, music, piano playing, dance and languages. Not religion, of course. Children should be kept free of the fear of punishment that religion brings. And I can give them the chance to stay in Italy and France during the summers at no extra cost to the council. In fact, the council would save money by sending them to me as they wouldn't have to pay for so many staff at Holnicote. That settles it, I shall write a letter right away."

Months went by. Kathleen heard no response back from Somerset County Council. So she spoke to the press. At that, the council could no longer ignore her. The county clerk penned her a letter stating that they had received no such application. They were stalling for time. Meanwhile, abusive letters began to arrive at Long's House: 'So you want to keep in this country the n***** bastards of near-prostitutes? You are the kind of woman who is making England unfit for white people!'

"The comments are disgusting but they do not scare me. The

council's lies are hurtful though. And meanwhile, those children are missing out on a great opportunity."

Picking up her trampled heart from the floor, Kathleen continued to be an ally to Black people in Britain. She arranged for her Trinidadian friend Malcolm Joseph-Mitchell, secretary of the League of Coloured People (LCP) to come and lecture and various organisations and clubs in Somerset. In May 1949, Malcolm spoke at Taunton on the subject of world unity and in October 1949 at her school on the topic of young Black people. She was very keen to be involved in anti-racism education.

Malcolm agreed to support her application with the county by writing a letter of recommendation.

Once they could no longer fob her off, the council gave her application a thumbs down without giving any explanation and rejected Malcolm's letter.

Meanwhile, the Taccomo International School received other non-white children through referrals from the LCP and from women who wrote to Kathleen directly. In June of the same year, a half-Jamaican boy aged 4 1/2 joined her school. Little Tony Blackwell, whose mother was housed at a refugee camp in Dorset, was a delight. In November, three more Black children arrived. Kathleen very happily announced in a letter to Malcolm: "In the kindergarten house, the colour will be fifty-fifty- enough to frighten everybody in Taunton."

The county council in Taunton had dashed her dreams. Nevertheless, she persisted! In 1950, Kathleen offered to foster one of the Holnicote children. The council once again rejected her proposal.

Kathleen sank to her knees when she found out.

"Tacchi, my dear, we almost knew that this would happen," said Rod.

"You're right," Kathleen admitted. "And I suspect my atheism and decision to not teach children religion may have been part of the reason. I will be alright. I will find other ways to help children. Just sadly not those children."

She later discovered the main reason behind the council's rejection was that they viewed the youngsters as "problematic" based solely on their racial heritage. They had a plan to tear these children from everything they'd ever known and ship them out to the USA. Thankfully, this cruel plan never came to fruition.

1950 was also the year in which her long-time friendship with Picasso would take her life in a new direction.

It all began when she found herself in Bradford staring at a newspaper article reporting on the World Peace Conference in Sheffield. She made up her mind to go.

With no entrance pass, she wasn't allowed in but waited outside. A door opened. She peeked in and saw Picasso on the platform. It turned out that she had a friend on the inside! Grabbing an old envelope, she scribbled a note: 'Tacchi's outside – please can she come in?' She charmed a police officer into passing on the note to Picasso, who exclaimed to the officer, "Of course, bring her in!"

Kathleen strode passed the hundreds of guests and up to the platform. It soon dawned on her that not a single delegate was female, a concern she expressed to Picasso.

"I've an idea," he said. "I'm sure you heard how England almost banned this conference but thought its reputation would suffer if they did. Instead, they denied hundreds of visas. I only got in after intense questioning. It's now been decided that after today, we will relocate to Warsaw so that far more people can attend. Only, I can't go. Why don't you go to Poland to represent me? Take my place."

Fired up, Tacchi replied, "I've hardly any money on me but yes. I'll telegram my husband, who won't be best pleased but I shall go nonetheless."

"That settles it! And when you get to Poland, do something about the lack of women. Get out there and get more women interested in peace!"

"Alright."

"Promise you will?"

"I promise."

Consequently, Kathleen found herself on Day 1 of the World Peace Council in Warsaw on 16th November. She had no idea that her visit would alter her life forever.

Fascism and the war had taken a heavy toll on the Polish capital. Kathleen's heart broke for the survivors, who were caught in the crossfire of war and of history and had to pick their way through the rubble each day with unimaginable horrors ingrained in their memories. Even five years after the war had ended, the inhabitants were breathing clouds of dust on a daily basis and corpses were still emerging from the debris. Yet, to see such destruction made her long to *build* something new. Her heart was full of hope for the future. Upon arrival back in Somerset, Kathleen forged ahead with a project that would place women at the forefront: she founded Women for World Disarmament (WFWD). She knew that she must devote the rest of her life to the struggle for peace.

"You know, Tacchi," Rod commented. "This reminds me of that story you told me about your boarding school days. You didn't like violence back then either and knew that the way to try and stop it was to unite people together to protest. Rallying your fellow students together to lead a campaign against caning at school when you were... what was it? 11?"

"Ha! I was 10 actually." Kathleen laughed. "Yes, I suppose you could say that my anti-violence stance began a long time ago. I hope the outcome of the WFWD is better than my childhood campaign. I got expelled for that, you know. But it didn't dampen my spirit. I only lasted a month at the next boarding school I was sent to. Well, what was I supposed to do when they'd made a girl stand in a corner and had left her there all night long? Of course I defended her. And they expelled me too!"

"But your parents forgave you and decided to homeschool instead. Which did you the world of good. You got to meet HG Wells, George Bernard Shaw…"

"And I got good at mingling and interacting with people, which should come in handy with this new endeavour."

WFWD started as a tiny organisation run just by Kathleen at Long's House but soon turned into an international peace organisation linked with the United Nations. Tirelessly, she built up contacts between women in the UK and abroad, raised awareness about the dangers of nuclear weapons, wrote to and visited peace campaigners across the globe and so on.

Seeking peace and compassion also kept the doors of her home wide open to all in need. In September 1959, Typhoon Vera devastated parts of Japan, orphaning many children. Kathleen made plans to take in 10 of these orphans, which shocked North Curry to the core. The outrage was most keenly felt by the ex-military men in the village, who felt racial hatred towards an entire nation for the actions of the Japanese government.

Rather than voice their opinions to Kathleen, they went straight to the press. One was quoted as saying, "Anything Japanese appals me after what I saw happen to my comrades."

As various newspapers began to publish the story, Kathleen held her hands up in exasperation. "If this is true, it's a dreadful attitude. I never imagined my offer would be misconstrued as something political."

It was time to defend herself. She wrote a letter to the Somerset County Herald, which was printed on 5th December and included the words:

There was no motive behind my offer. Nationality, creed, or colour does not make any difference to me. If I saw a child running in front of a bus I would not wait to see what nationality or colour the child was: I would run and try to save that child and this was exactly my approach in offering to help.

She also offered to meet anybody who wanted to talk to her about the matter at any time and to anybody who wanted to help. She would talk to those who opposed her, yes, but she wouldn't be bullied by them. "I shall carry on. I'm not going to ask anyone whether I should or not."

In the end, North Curry residents were spared the *terrible fate* of having these innocent children arrive in their village. When Kathleen visited the Japanese Embassy in London, she heard the happy news that homes had already been found for the children in Japan. However, they did need clothes and so Kathleen set to work organising clothing donations.

Three years later saw her attending the Moscow Peace Conference to deliver a message from the Taunton Group of the Campaign for Nuclear Disarmament: "We believe that food for the whole world is more important than arms production. People in Asia are starving – Russia spends millions on arms. People in the Americas are starving – the United States spends millions on arms. Even in Europe, people are starving – our own country spends millions on arms."

The WFWD kept her busy for the next 45 years until 1987. Well, 88-year-olds are allowed to retire, eh? Mind you, she remained active in other ways. Even on her 90th birthday in 1989, she set up a Trust to establish creative exchanges between British students and students across the world. She declared, "Future generations will need lots of help to deal with environmental problems and world peace. I just want to spread peace after I peg it."

Notes

Kathleen Tacchi-Morris (24th January 1899–12th May 1993) was born as Ellen Kathleen Tacchi (pronounced 'tackie') in Johannesburg, the eldest of Percy and Rebecca Tacchi's five children. Although both Londoners, Percy and Rebecca met in South Africa, where Percy was working in the gold mines and Rebecca was training to be a doctor, as she had little chance of becoming one in England at the time. (Another trailblazer!) Percy hated the appalling working conditions in the mines, which is why he began a business to make bicycles for Black Africans, who otherwise had to walk for miles on end.

Soon after Kathleen's birth, the family returned to London, specifically Acton, due to the tough life in the goldfields and the Second Boer War. Kathleen's parents remained in London until they came to live with her in the 1950s. Both parents died in North Curry, her father in 1970, aged 95 and her mother in 1975 aged nearly 100. Her second husband also died in the village: Rod Morris (1903–1988) is buried in St Peter and St Paul's Church in North Curry. Likewise, Kathleen passed away in the village in 1993, aged 94.

Kathleen's unpublished autobiography titled *I Promised Picasso* was written down by Gordon Schaffer journalist based on interviews with her. While we're on the topic of Picasso, one of the parts of Kathleen's story that I find most moving centres around the peace conference in Sheffield. The British government pulled out all the stops to try and prevent it due to their fear that it would threaten national security due to tensions with Communist countries. But the conference still went ahead: they simply relocated to Warsaw. The international community was persistent. And that relocation took Kathleen to Warsaw, where Nazi destruction broke her heart. More than 85% of the city had been destroyed, yet it would later be rebuilt little by little through remarkable determination from authority figures and the general public. It is so much easier to destroy than it is to build and yet the reconstruction was achieved; the destroyers did not win. And Kathleen's heart-wrenching glimpse of the city in ruins prompted her to set up WFWD. The Nazi government and then the British government had carried out anti-peace actions yet these led to one woman setting up a peace organisation that spread across the globe.

The Trust Kathleen set up became the Tacchi-Morris Arts Centre, which opened in Taunton in January 2000, nearly seven years after Kathleen's death, and is still going strong today. Kathleen would've been over the moon to see her last wish fulfilled, namely to establish an arts centre to "promote, maintain and advance education by encouraging the use of exchange and understanding of artistic skills and talents in a spirit of peace and mutual understanding amongst all peoples". Unlike this citation, none of the conversations between Rod and Kathleen in my story are direct quotations but other spoken words are paraphrased or verbatim.

(The Tacchi-Morris Arts Centre in Taunton; photo used with kind permission from the centre)

Chapter Bibliography

www.keverelchess.com

Women Remember: An Oral History by Anne Smith

tacchi-morris.com

www.greatbritishlife.co.uk

warandpeacesomerset.wordpress.com

www.fosterhillroadcemetery.co.uk

somerset-cat.swheritage.org.uk

Brown Babies: The stories of children born to black GIs and white women in the Second World War by Lucy Bland

Intimate Legacies by Hazel V Carby

Lamp Magazine, August/September 2013

Peace Child 2020– Introduction by Julian Breeze

The Tampa Tribune, 1st December 1959, page 11.

Somerset County Herald, 5th Dec 1959

A landmark in the struggle for peace by Liz Paine

QUICK TRIBUTE

Blanche Robbins (1880–1950)

An intrepid teacher named Miss Robbins worked at the Infant School in Chilcompton (built in 1864 and closed in 1993 to create St Vigor and St John School). It appears this is Blanche Robbins, listed as being 10 months old in the April 1881 census and who in the 1901 census was listed as a teacher in Chilcompton.

Miss Robbins asked for a pay rise in 1904. Not only was her request refused but she was fired on the spot. Today we salute you, Miss Robbins, for knowing your worth!

Another interesting fact is that in 1923, the infant school was overstaffed. They chose to ask for Mrs Bevan's resignation because she was the only married teacher and women were expected to resign from teaching posts once they took husbands.

But, back to Miss Robbins. It appears that she was undaunted by this dismissal and found employment elsewhere: at Downside C of E School on Stockhill Road (later called Chilcompton Junior School), where she worked for over 40 years until retiring a few years before her death in 1950. Her funeral was held at Christ Church in the village, just next to the school.

(Christ Church with its graveyard on Stockhill Road, Chilcompton. We searched to see if Blanche was buried there. My son found the graves of other people with the surname Robbins but no trace of Blanche herself.)

Sources: Meandering through Chilcompton by David Strawbridge, ukcensusonline.com, freecen.org.uk, Somerset Guardian and Radstock Observer – Friday 18 August 1950.

Chapter 23: Margery's Memories (early to mid-20th century)

Initially, Margery had tried to wake Doris, lying next to her in bed. She shook Doris. No response. She whispered. No response. She shouted. No response. The body was cold. With great affection, Margery kissed the cold hand, wearing the signet ring that bore the Communist symbol of the hammer and sickle.

Margery walked mechanically downstairs in a state of total shock. She reached for the receiver and dialled, one number at a time. With a shaking voice, she broke the news to her friend on the other side of the line.

But even before the kind friend arrived at the house, having offered to do so, Margery knew. She'd taken in the unseeing eyes. Her partner was gone, died in her sleep.

Margery began to sob. More than forty years of love. Gone. Well, not gone but with no outlet for the love now. Only memories. The spacious, white house echoed with emptiness. The paintbrushes lay gathering dust in the studio; Doris would never touch them again. The rounded entranceway looked forlorn; Doris would never walk through it again. The whole house breathed Doris' name. It was uniquely hers, designed by her in the Art Deco style she so loved.

Their other house, Greenfields in Watchet, which Margery had inherited from her sister in 1953, was dear to them too, as was

Watchet itself. The plan had been to minimise their possessions and move there the following month. But it wasn't meant to be.

*

As time wore on, the initial sting of grief wore off and her steady mourning began. Margery reflected back on her love story with a fragile tear falling down her lined face.

Doris and Margery first met at an Independent Labour Party summer camp in the 1920s.

"I was born and raised in Bath," Doris told her. "My family ran a perfume, hairdressing and wig-making company. My mother was a concert pianist and music teacher, so I'm used to being around teachers like yourself! After attending Bath High School, I went to finishing school at the age of 16. I was sent to Germany, where I was enthralled by the art galleries. That settled it in my mind. I wanted to be an artist. My next step was the Bath School of Art, which I enrolled in shortly after my dear sister, Rayonette, passed away. In 1914, I started another course, this time in London. One of my first commissions was in 1915. The government contracted me to create a soldier recruitment poster, which I based on St George slaying the dragon in some sort of glorification of warfare. Yet, when news came of the horrific injuries and deaths happening on the battlefields, I was shocked to the core. In 1916, two of my cousins were slain in battle. That was it. I came to hate the war and disowned my poster. It was a sad sight to see poor soldiers returning to London and to see the city's poverty. That's why I joined the Independent Labour Party in 1917. Two years later, our family business was sold, my father having passed away a few years previously. That's when Mother and I moved to Bristol. I've had some of my work exhibited there. But listen to me prattling on. Tell me about you."

"Well, I've an older sister, Dorothy, and younger brother, Wilfred. We were born and raised in Barton Regis, just the other side of Bristol. My primary school teaching career began many years ago in the midst of the Great War. In Bristol, I trained in art and was hired by Mortimer House School in Clifton. I've worked at various other institutions in the city ever since. I'm also a textile artist, with weaving being my particular forte and… obsession, really."

Teaching. Painting. Weaving. Social justice. Those passions had united the two women right from the start.

A delicate smile lit up Margery's face, as she remembered feeling overcome with love and pride to see Doris' paintings exhibited for the first time, a woman, an openly gay woman, entering a predominately male domain. Standing in the gallery in London, they had squeezed each other's hands and soaked in the atmosphere. They were both twenty-eight at the time and the war had ended. It was 1918, a happy time for them.

In 1924, Doris moved to Clevedon with her mother, renting a smart townhouse: Corsica Villa on Marine Parade. It was supposed to be a temporary move, but fate had other ideas. Doris never moved out of Clevedon. How could someone who loved colour and liveliness not fall in love with the seaside town? Her regular walks showed her lush, green coastal paths juxtaposed with the grey seas, pearly white clouds and sapphire blue skies. A hazy peach sunset reflected on the glassy waters delighted her one evening. The town centre was always bursting with activity: fish being brought in, neighbours chattering, horse hooves clip-clopping and children giggling.

There was nothing for it: a plot of land had to be bought! In a remote part of town, they found land and had a wooden ex-army building moved there and made into a bungalow. Two years after Doris relocated to Clevedon, Margery followed suit to be nearer her.

Sadly, Doris' mother passed away in 1929 and was buried in St Mary's churchyard in Bathwick. The silver lining was that Margery could now live with Doris and as such, an extension was added to the bungalow three years later that included a studio, bedroom and bathroom for Margery. This allowed them to work without disturbing the other but still spend plenty of time together.

But Doris was gone now. Gazing at the 1925 painting of Richard

Hatt, Margery heaved a sigh that echoed through the lonely house. Doris' brother would die just 8 years later, aged 40, leaving behind a wife and a baby boy. This nephew, little Robin, became a regular visit to their home so that Doris and Margery could support Richard's widow.

When in 1938 Doris inherited money, Robin watched with wide eyes as a new home was built. Doris had enough to design her own home that would sit in the same location as the first. The bungalow was demolished and Littlemead was born. It was this Art Deco house that Margery was now shuffling around in, her voice bouncing off every Doris-designed corner, every modern kitchen surface, every flat roof, every unique bathroom, each of its kitchens– one for each woman. Doris felt the house was her greatest achievement, paying no attention to the comments of certain Clevedon residents who felt it very odd indeed that a *woman* should go about designing her own home! The construction manager from Weston-super-Mare had no such qualms, of course. Doris and Margery had kept in touch with dear Rex and his wife, Valery, over the years.

Yes, Littlemead was a work of genius. It showed Doris' individuality and courage. It was fitting, perhaps, that she had died inside its walls, having lived there ever since the building was finished in 1939.

While she had lived, Doris had breathed so much life into the big white house that radiated spaciousness and light. Margery passed through the living room, gently stroking the curtains she herself had made. She went on into the main reception room and drew back the curtain that separated this area from Doris' studio, where Doris liked to work each and every day, the house's biggest room with plenty of natural light and space. It was not always a solitary room, though. Children and teenagers from Clevedon used to benefit from the couple's free weekly painting, drawing and weaving classes. Margery now passed into her own studio in the annexe, where many a child had sat at her loom to discover the magic of textiles. When they first arrived, the children were always astounded that Margery made her own natural dyes and used them to colour her fabrics. They were also shocked that Margery had made many of the soft furnishings around the house as well as lots of her own suits and Doris' too. Margery hoped this knowledge would spark the youngsters' creativity. The potential of the next generation was extremely dear to the women.

Adults had come to Littlemead too. A steady stream of visitors, in fact. Neighbours and the local vicar came over for chats, while artists, writers and political activists – in the form of progressives, socialists and feminists – came for larger meet-ups to discuss ideas. Margery and Doris encouraged open conversations with the belief that ordinary people should work together in their community to create a better and more equal society.

These meetings reflected Doris' and Margery's changing politics. While Littlemead was being built, fascism was tearing lives apart in mainland Europe. Astute to these horrors, Doris and Margery left the Independent Labour Party behind and joined the Communist Party in 1935, with Doris labelling herself a Christian Communist. Two years afterwards, they journeyed to the Soviet Union for the anniversary celebration of the poet Alexander Pushkin.

The gatherings were often joyous occasions. Sunday parties at Littlemead became the stuff of legends. Littlemead's living room held endless memories for Margery. She smiled to think of how the descent of Communists into Clevedon had been quite a shock to the town's more conservative residents, even though the women's kind of communism was gentle and compassionate.

When Margery reached the dining area with its curved window, she opened the French doors and stepped onto the patio. In this large garden with its lily pond, she remembered their summer garden parties that were held to raise money for the Communist Party. The garden was also where Margery grew all kinds of fruit and vegetables. They were largely self-sufficient and sometimes had a surplice that they provided to the local school, neighbours and friends. People thought it odd that they were vegetarians, as it was rare, but the meals they created from home-grown food were divine.

As part of her commitment of sharing her knowledge and ideas with the wider community, Doris used to regularly give public lectures on art. "I don't want to live in a vacuum," she'd say. "I don't want to feel isolated from the world." These talks were interrupted by the Second World War. The women found other ways to serve their community then: they became fire wardens and Margery's garden was part of the Dig For Victory campaign.

One of the war's personal tragedies for Doris and Margery was the fate of Jadwiga Zak, known as Madame Zak, one of the few art dealers whom Doris trusted. On her frequent trips to Paris, she often met and did deals with Jadwiga, a Jewish lady who ran Galerie Zak in Paris. The Nazis sent Jadwiga to Auschwitz with her son. Both were killed there in 1944.

The end of the war saw Doris resuming her public speaking and stepping her politics up a notch. She stood as the Communist Party candidate for Clevedon Urban District Council in 1946. How heartbreaking when she lost. Even so, she gave it a second go in 1947. And lost again. Margery was sure her gender and "scandalous" sexuality, as well as her Communist beliefs, had played a role in her failure. Most voters had therefore overlooked the many sensible and wholesome ideas Doris had for the town, such as social justice, universal housing, equal educational opportunities for all children, regardless of how much money they had, and plans to enhance Clevedon as a seaside resort.

All the same, Margery was proud and had kept copies of Doris' election poster with its photo of Doris in a Communist beret, as well as her leaflet, which opened with the lines:

I believe that Clevedon Council cannot be representative of the majority of the Clevedon people unless there is an increase of Councillors with working-class sympathies.

I think also that Women should be represented on the Council. At present, there are no Women Councillors.

Margery reflected on their commitments to feminism – involvement in the New Woman and Women's Suffrage movements – as she fingered these leaflets, which were fading with age. She also found piles of old Daily Worker newspapers beside a desk. Doris was known in Clevedon for going out every Saturday evening to hand out Communist literature and try and flog copies of this newspaper to the locals, regularly going from pub to pub, such as the Old Inn. 'These days, it's known as the Morning Star paper,' Margery thought to herself. 'But Doris was there when it was a new creation, playing her part for decades. And she never complained that some of her customers only bought the paper for the horse racing tips!'

Throughout the house, there were paintings that reminded Margery of all the exhibitions, though most were packaged up ready for the move or had been given away to friends.

Margery had supported Doris with her success every step of the way. There were 40 exhibitions in total over the decades. Margery admired Doris' painting style with its meticulous attention to detail and vivid colours in rural and urban locations, and the world grew to love it too. Doris' motto was that she aimed "to simplify and at the same time intensify". And she was always trying out new methods to update her own style. Early on, she had included portraits but then focussed on landscapes, still lifes and tableaux of working people. For all her paintings, she'd been inspired by landscape painters to begin with, then by more modern approaches like cubism, abstraction and purism. Doris was a pioneer, heading out in bold new directions with her work that was always full of life and movement. Somerset itself breathed in her paintings, as well as other far-flung settings. Then there was the variety of materials she used: watercolours, pencils, oil on canvas and woodcuts.

Doris was loath to sell her work, as she felt art was for everyone, to be displayed publicly, not bought and kept by the privileged few. This hindered Doris' career somewhat, as did staying In the West Country rather than relocating to London. She was suspicious of the commercialisation of art, suspicious of art dealers.

It wasn't until the 1950s, when the couple were in their 60s, that Doris had her first solo art exhibition. By then, Margery had retired as a school teacher and so it was lovely to have something fresh to focus on. When time brought more exhibitions, they'd travel to the Minerva Gallery in Bath and further afield throughout the country to open the art shows.

Gazing out of an upstairs window, she reminisced on their travels together, especially to southern France, stopping off at Paris on the way to remember Madame Zak, to learn the latest goings on in the art world, to seek inspiration and to see Doris' work, which was often exhibited there. Doris had continued to see her work exhibited into her old age, despite the heart condition she'd developed that had worsened over time. Only last year she had shown more than 40 pieces of work at exhibitions in Clevedon and Clifton.

Another favoured holiday destination was Spain. One of their Spanish holidays was funded in an unusual way. Being very pragmatic, the couple had decided to sell their bodies to university science labs once they'd died and they got the money upfront. With the same pragmatism, Doris had one day invited her friends into her studio to choose one of her paintings as a gift. Knowing she was ageing, she wanted to have things all arranged before she went. The dreadful angina had been plaguing Doris for many years before she... died. Another tear slid down Margery's cheek.

The van would be coming later on to take Doris' body away to be studied by scientists. There would be no grave to visit or scattering of ashes, but Margery knew her partner would live on through her paintings.

"Well, my love," she whispered to the face lined by thousands of smiles, "It's time to say goodbye to your body. But you will be with me in spirit always. And I promise to keep your legacy alive so long as I have blood in my veins."

Notes

Doris Brabham Hatt (1890-27th August 1969) was born at 30 Milsom Street, Bath and raised in the city by her parents William Hatt (1861-1916) and Mary Hatt (1862-1929). Her older sister, Rayonette (1889-1911), died in her early twenties. The family's perfume, hairdressing and wig-making business was located at 10 The Corridor and with continued success, they later bought another spot. All of Doris' family members are buried at St Mary's Church in Bathwick (now part of Bath), except for Doris, whose body was taken to a medical science lab.

We would have lost all the records relating to Doris had it not been for her loving partner, Margery Mack Smith (8th July 1890–February 1975). When Doris died, a family member burnt all her letters and personal records to try and hide the fact that she was gay and a feminist. However, Margery managed to save just two crates of Doris' sketchbooks, portfolios, drawings, letters and writings. She took these to the house in Watchet, which she moved into on the same day she and Doris had planned to. Faithful Margery spent the last 6 years of her life making sure Doris' life and body of work were not lost.

To mark fifty years since Doris' death, the Museum of Somerset put on an exhibition of her work in 2019. It included Hatt-inspired artwork created by local students, very much in keeping with Doris' guiding principle that art is for everyone. Still a relatively unknown artist, the exhibition helped to boost knowledge about her. She has also recently been spoken about by various LGBT+ charities and public speakers. In a time when few people were "out" as non-hetero, Doris and Margery were incredibly brave in not just living openly together but inviting countless people into their home for the art classes and meetings. This openness would certainly have affected sales of her artwork, so they were lucky to have other means of supporting themselves.

On the next page is Clevedon with its pier, built in the 1860s.

Chapter Bibliography

swheritage.org.uk

LGBT+ History Month – Meet Doris Brabham Hatt, modernist painter & feminist activist by Open Table

Doris Hatt: Revolutionary Artist by Adrian Webb, Christopher Stone, Denys J Wilcox and Stephen Lisney

The Art of Doris Hatt by Denys J Wilcox

www.courtgallery.com

myheritage.com

Doris Hatt: Local Artist by Jane Lilly in Clevedon Civic Society Issue 5, Spring 2012

A Life in Colour – The Art of Doris Hatt by Drive Creative Studio (documentary)

Doris Hatt 1890 – 1969, A reflection by Liz Payne in Red Lives

Communists and the Struggle for Socialism

Artist Doris Hatt on BBC Front Row (audio episode)

findagrave.com

blogs.canterbury.ac.uk

http://deborahharvey.blogspot.com/

QUICK TRIBUTES

Joan Tuckett (1895–31st August 1957) and Doris Flinn (15th October 1892–1977)

This couple were firm friends with Margery Mack Smith and Doris Hatt, becoming regular visitors to Littlemead due to a shared love of communism and art.

Born and raised in Bristol, Joan was a women's rights and political activist, qualified pilot, international hockey player, playwright AND theatre producer. She was also one of Bristol's earliest female lawyers.

Doris Flinn was also a pilot and hockey player as well as a successful sculptor.

By 1920, Doris had moved from northern England to Bristol and the two were soon living together. In 1930, they bought a house in East Dundry, close to Somerset's border with Bristol. Five years later, Doris made a sculpture that she called "Lawyer, Athlete, Aviator, Woman." The sculpture was dedicated to Joan. Doris and Joan lived in their East Dundry home until each of them passed away in turn.

Sources: Encyclopedia of Communist Biographies by Graham Stevenson, arnosvale.org.uk, The Art of Doris Hatt by Denys J Wilcox, archives.bristol.gov.uk, sculpture.gla.ac.uk

Eunice Overend (1919-2016)

Nicknamed the Badger Lady and the Badger Mother, Eunice was born in Yorkshire and grew up in Frome. After a biology degree at Exeter University, she worked at Slimbridge but after a few years had to return to Frome to care for her sick mother. From then on, she worked as a supply science teacher in the Somerset town, sometimes wowing the kids by arriving with a grass snake draped around her neck. In her spare time, she studied nature and local history, becoming a founding member of the Frome Society for Local Study and carrying out digs at Whatley Roman Villa and Egford Medieval Village.

Eunice developed a keen interest in badgers and wrote several monographs and articles about their conservation. A talented illustrator, her badger artwork is still used by the Somerset Badger Group and in some RSPCA publications. She was strongly against badger culling, arguing that badgers were more likely to catch TB from cattle rather than vice versa. She advocated for vaccinating badgers and cows instead.

In 1987, she left Frome to live in a caravan in a Cotswolds

village in Wiltshire with 4 dogs... and about a dozen or so young orphaned badgers at any one time! Eunice raised them, bottle-feeding the unweaned ones, caring for the ill ones etc. She released the female badgers after a year and the male ones after a year and a half. She also spent time dismantling badger traps, sometimes in the middle of the night.

When Eunice died, she was buried in St John's churchyard in Frome.

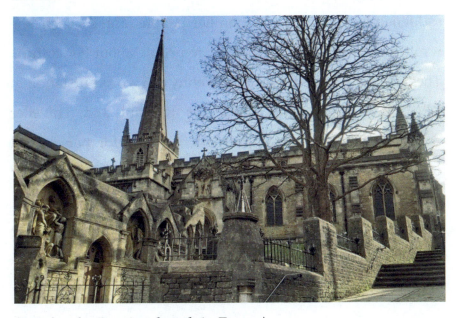

(St John the Baptist church in Frome)

Sources: stjohnfrome.com, thebadgercrowd.org, In bed with a badger that bites in the night by Peter Dunn, "Badger Woman" Survival episode (1995 documentary), A–Z of Frome: Places-People-History by Mick Davis, David Lassman.

Maggie Smith-Bendell (1941–present)

A member of the Romani community, Maggie was born on the edge of a pea field near Bridgwater as the second of eight children. Growing up, she and her family moved around the country, earning what they could by working for farmers as well as selling wildflowers, catching animals and collecting scrap metal and rags.

Her upbringing made her incredibly proud of her heritage and saddened by the discrimination her people face. As such, she wrote a number of books to educate people about her culture. The one I read, Rabbit Stew and a Penny or Two, is outstanding. When laws make life harder for Romani and Traveller communities, Maggie campaigned tirelessly for herself and others. She went on to receive a British Empire Medal for her work in 2012.

Sources: Maggie, the Gypsy queen by Veronique Mistiaen, Rabbit Stew and a Penny or Two by Maggie Smith-Bendell.

APPENDICES

Named After Her

Below is a list of places in Somerset that are thought to be derived from a woman's name or influence.

Aquae Sulis (now Bath): 'Waters of Sulis' for the pre-Roman goddess Sulis. Much more interesting than the name Bath. I vote we change it back! (See Chapter 2.)

Abbas Combe: 'Valley of the abbess', because the village was part of the vast estates of Shaftesbury Abbey in northern Dorset. The abbey was founded by Alfred in the 800s and Ealswitha and Alfred's daughter Ethelgeofu was the first abbess. (See Chapter 6 for more on Ealswitha and Ethelgeofu.)

Alford: 'Ford of a woman called Ealdgyth'. Ealdgyth became Edith in modern English.

Avon River: The river and gorge take their name from the Celtic word for river (abona) BUT a more romantic story developed in the Middle Ages is that a woman named Avona asked two giants, Goram and Vincent, to drain a huge lake that covered what is now the Avon Valley. Goram got drunk and fell asleep, whilst Vincent worked hard, digging a long gorge and draining the lake. Avona wisely chose to give her heart to Vincent.

Binegar: 'Wooded slope belonging to a woman called Beage' or 'Wooded slope with berries'.

Bride's Mound: Also known as Beckery, this hill is named after

St Bridget (also known as Bride, Brigid or Brigit). (See Chapter 4 for more about Beckery.)

Buckland St Mary: This village's name means 'land granted by a charter' with its church's dedication tacked on.

Butcombe: This is possibly 'Beadu's valley', where Beadu is a female name meaning war.

Chewton Keynsham: Is this village named after St Kew and St Keyne? Or would that be too good to be true?! (See Chapter 3 for more about these saints.)

Chew Valley and related villages: These are possibly named after St Kew. (See Chapter 3: Quick Tribute.)

Coxley: 'Wood or clearing belonging to the cook'. This could be a reference to Manasseh the cook's wife. (See Interlude.)

Donyatt: 'Dunna's gate', first recorded as such in the 8th century. Dunna was a female Anglo-Saxon name. For instance, a 7th-century abbess of Withington in Gloucestershire was named Dunna.

Ebbor Gorge: Ebbor means 'homestead belonging to Aebbe' (also spelt Aebba). There were a few Anglo-Saxon saints named Aebbe, some of whom were abbesses. I couldn't find a link between any of them and Somerset so this could be a different Aebbe or there's a link that has been lost through the passage of time.

Edington: 'Farmstead of a man called Eadwine or a woman

called Eadwynn'. (NB: The Edington in Ealswitha's story is widely believed to be Edington in Wiltshire rather than this one in Somerset.)

Edithmead: 'Edith's meadow'. This is said to be in reference to Queen Edith, wife of Edward the Confessor. She certainly held lands in Somerset. (See Interlude for more on Queen Edith.)

Godney: 'Goda's island'. Some list Goda as a male name but it was certainly used for women, as with Goda (or Godgifu), daughter of Ethelred Unraed. (See Chapter 8 for more on Ethelred.)

Keynsham: 'Keyne's settlement' or 'Ceagin's settlement'. (See Chapter 3.)

Kewstoke: possibly 'Kew's hamlet'. (See Chapter 3: Quick Tribute.)

Kingston St Mary: The parish once belonged to the Saxon kings, hence the first part of its name means 'the King's settlement'. The village was sometimes referred to in documents as Kingston-juxta-Taunton and it's only since the 1950s that it became officially known as Kingston St Mary after the parish church dedicated to the Mother of God.

Lantokay: an early name for Street, thought to mean 'Thecla's settlement'. (See Chapter 5: Quick Tributes.)

Little Solsbury Hill: possibly means 'Sulis' little hillfort'. (See Chapter 1: notes.)

Queen Camel: 'Hill on the River Cam belonging to the queen'. (See Chapter 9: Quick Tribute.)

Queen Charlton: Originally just called Charlton, it was an estate of Keynsham Abbey until the Dissolution. The 'queen' part was added when the estate was given to Queen Catherine Parr by her husband Henry VIII. (See Chapter 16: Quick Tributes.)

St Audries Bay: Within the parish of West Quantoxhead, this bay is named after the church's dedication since St Etheldreda is also known as St Audrey.

St Catherine is a village in the Batheaston parish named after its church.

Seavington St Mary: Seavington means seven settlements and St Mary comes from the church's dedication to the Mother of God. A previous name for this village was also female in origin! Alice Vaux was the tenant of the manor in the late 1100s and/or early 1200s and the village was therefore known as Seavington Vaux. By 1212, her son Robert was the tenant and by 1698, there were 2 names for the village: Seavington Mary or Seavington Vaux.

Stoke St Mary: This is another village named after its church's dedication and 'stoke' means farm.

Temple Cloud: The 'temple' part refers to the village's link to the Knights Templar and 'cloud' could be 'clud' meaning rocky outcrop or the female Celtic name Cloda.

Thorne St Margaret: This tiny village near Wellington is named after its parish church, dedicated to St Margaret of Antioch.

(a view of Ebbor Gorge, named after Aebbe, an unknown woman)

Sources: A Dictionary of British Place-Names by AD Mills, kepn.nottingham.ac.uk, The Place-Names of Somerset by James S. Hill, The Somerset Villages Book by Somerset Federation of Women's Institutes, www.nationaltrust.org.uk, A–Z of the Women Who Built Bristol by Jane Duffus, A Selection of North Somerset Place-Names by AGC Turner, www.achurchnearyou.com/church/11404, www.british-history.ac.uk, www.quantockonline.co.uk, pase.ac.uk, wessexarch.co.uk.

Recommended Reading

I had to be selective about which women I focused on, especially from 1500 onwards, as otherwise the book would never end!

I didn't want to step on anyone else's toes and try to tell stories that have already been told so excellently by others. With that in mind, here are some recommendations for further reading about historical women in Somerset (and don't forget to check the chapter bibliographies too for more on each woman).

For more on the fascinating history and archaeology of the marshlands, The Lost Islands of Somerset and Avalon Marshes Archaeology, both by Richard Brunning, are a good read.

For a look at more of the women who lived at Dunster, I recommend The Ladies of Dunster Castle by Jim Lee.

For a great read about Margaret Pole, who was born at Farleigh Castle in Farleigh Hungerford, I enjoyed Faithful Traitor: The Story of Margaret Pole by Samantha Wilcoxson.

Mysterious Somerset by A M Gould explores local legends of landmarks, properties and people in the county.

For medieval women across Europe (including Aethelflaed), there's the brilliant Femina by Janina Ramirez.

Brown Babies by Lucy Bland and Imperial Legacies by Hazel V Carby are both incredible books that include sections on Black and mixed-race people's experiences in 20th-century Somerset.

Working Women of Somerset by James Crowden outlines the working lives of 30 Somerset women, as told in their own words.

Maggie Smith-Bendell (from Chapter 23: Quick Tributes) writes about her childhood as a Romani girl in Somerset and neighbouring counties in her book Rabbit Stew and a Penny or Two.

Acknowledgements

With thanks to family first of all: Margaret, Tom, Dianne, Mindal, Yutsu and Jake for all your help with my research trips and research baking!

I'm also grateful to Ian Penrose, the Mouth and Foot Painting Artists charity and staff at Sally Lunn's Eating House as well as at Shepton Mallet Library and Wells Library for help with research. Likewise, I'd like to thank AM Gould for introducing me to Hedwig Green.

I'm also so appreciative of all the women in this book (almost all of whom are dead). Somerset would be nothing without its women and that's no exaggeration. We stand on their shoulders, buoyed up by their contributions, kindness and courage.

A Note on Inclusivity

One of my aims for this project was to make it as inclusive as possible and include as diverse a range of women as possible. It's been wonderful to find Somerset's diversity in terms of things like ethnicity, disability, culture, religion and sexuality. Gender identity is a category that I've sadly failed in.

I wasn't able to find historical examples of trans women in Somerset. (I did come across a trans man, born c. 1725, who chose the name Charles Hamilton. He married Mary Price at St Cuthbert's Church in Wells in 1746. Soon after, she outed him and he was prosecuted for vagrancy and having intercourse with Mary.)

Similarly, I couldn't find any examples of non-binary or intersex people, though as they were often not able to be open about their identities, some of the "women" in this book might well have identified as non-binary and/or intersex (or indeed as men) had they been alive today.

If you have any information you'd like to share, I'd love to do a second edition to include more LGBTQIA+ people in my book.

About the Author

A first-generation 'Somersetonian', Helen grew up in Chilcompton. She went to secondary school in Bath, then attended the University of Bristol (only just over the border!). After more than 8 years living abroad (a short spell in Italy and 7+ years in Ecuador), she returned to Somerset in 2018 and lived in Shepton Mallet with her husband, kids and step-kids for 4 years before moving to Midsomer Norton.

Helen is currently working on a Junior Edition of this book and has already published books about South America, including Jungle-tastic Tales and Inca-tastic Tales, having previously lived in Ecuador for many years. She also works as a proofreader and Spanish–English translator.

If you have enjoyed this book, please leave a review on the retailer website you bought it from.